S0-BBG-073

Caught in the dungeon of torture . . .

Selissa's hands were bound over her head and shackled to the wall. Her wrists bled where the rings of iron gouged her skin, her shoulders ached, and her entire body stung from sweat that irritated the countless scratches inflicted by the coarse jute fabric of her prisoner's tunic.

Her hair stuck to her temples and she felt a crusty layer of dirt on her forehead. Chained near the fire pit, Selissa was blasted with heat on her left side while a cold draft blew across her moist thighs from the right. When she tensed her arms it felt as if a knife were cutting into her shoulder, but when she let her leaden arms relax, the iron shackles bit deeper into her raw wrists.

IGI Senior Officer Baroness Ada of Westinger ordered the guard to stoke the fire with some more wood. "It has gotten very cool these last days, don't you agree, guardswoman? And the moon of Travia has not even waned yet."

Selissa did not reply.

REALMS OF ARKANIA

The Charlatan

A Novel

ULRICH KIESOW

Translated by Amy Katherine Kile

PRIMA PUBLISHING

Proteus™ is a trademark of Prima Publishing, a division of Prima Communications, Inc.

P™ is a trademark of Prima Publishing, a division of Prima Communications, Inc.

Prima Publishing™ is a trademark of Prima Communications, Inc.

Der Scharlatan copyright © 1995 by Wilhelm Heyne Verlag GmbH & Co. KG, München und Schmidt Spiele + Freizeit GmbH, Eching.

Translation copyright © 1996 by Prima Publishing. All rights reserved.

Realms of Arkania is a registered trademark of Sir-Tech Software, Inc.

No part of this book may be reproduced or transmitted in any form or by any means, electronic or mechanical, including photocopying, recording, or by any information storage or retrieval system without written permission from Prima Publishing, except for the inclusion of quotations in a review. All products and characters mentioned in this book are trademarks of their respective companies.

Cover Art by Oliver Frey

ISBN: 0-7615-0233-5
Library of Congress Catalog Card Number: 95-72001
Printed in the United States of America
96 97 98 EE 10 9 8 7 6 5 4 3 2 1

Welcome to the Realms of Arkania

THE CONTINENT OF Arkania is a land mass on Ethra, a primitive world that most Arkanians staunchly maintain is flat. Although some unorthodox Arkanian scholars have advanced the view that Ethra is a sphere, no one has managed to escape the geographical confines of the continent to prove that hypothesis. The Arkanian continent is enclosed to the east by the Iron Sword, a formidable mountain range more than 10,000 strides (30,000 feet) high. To the west lies the Sea of Seven Winds, a treacherous ocean unnavigable by Arkania's meager flotilla. In ancient lore, however, stories unfold of lands beyond.

The far north of Arkania is characterized by vast plains, forests, and treeless tundra. These few northern settlements were established by the Nivese, a race of steppe nomads who follow the trail of the huge herds of grazing karen. In the northwest lies the Orc Skull Steppes, a highland surrounded by the Olochtai mountain ranges and the Stony Oak Forest. The countless Orc tribes that

inhabit this region often feud over hunting grounds, pasture lands, and serfs. Occasionally the tribes band together to raid the lands to their south, especially the northern regions of the Cental Empire ruled by Prince Brin I, son of his divine magnificence, Emperor Hal I, whose recent disappearance was surrounded by mysterious circumstances.

To the far west of the Orc Skull Steppes lies Thorwal, the empire of a race of pugnacious and rapacious, hulking seafarers. Their light, single-masted dragon ships, locally known as ottas, probe the coasts of Arkania in search of trade and small, unfortified harbors that can be easily raided and plundered.

To the northeast is densely forested Borland, known for its harsh winters and poor but hard-working peasants that make life for their numerous barons, counts, and princes quite enjoyable. Festum, the region's capital and residence of the nobles' marshal, is regarded as one of Arkania's most spectacular port towns. Its citizens are known to enjoy the pleasures of the flesh.

Spanning the midsection of the continent is the Central Empire, a well-populated region known for its mild climate and its well-developed infrastructure of roads that makes travel between cities convenient. Gareth, the capital of the Central Empire, has approximately 120,000 inhabitants and is the largest city in Arkania. Despite the expansive growth the region has experienced over the long period of its settlement, extensive virgin forests remain. These woods, especially those of the Red and Black Sickle Mountains and the Mountains of Kosch, are impenetrable, dark places and home to the dwarves.

South of the Central Empire begins the Khom Desert, home to the Novadis, a proud tribe of desert nomads. The region between the Khoram Mountains and the Unauer Mountains is guarded to the west by the Etern and High Etern Mountains, whose slopes shield the Khom from the rain clouds that drift in from the west.

The Lovely Field, by contrast, is a region of high precipitation. Located in the southwestern part of Arkania with the city of Vinsalt as its capital, the Lovely Field is said to have been settled by the first immigrants from the legendary Golden Coast beyond the Sea of Seven Winds. The area around the cities of Grangor, Kuslik, Belhanka, Vinsalt, and Silas provides the most fertile soil on the entire continent. Naturally most of the residents are prosperous farmers who fortify their settlements to protect themselves and their riches from the constant raids of Thorwalian pirates and Novadi tribespeople.

To the southwest of the Etern Mountains extends Arkania's tropical region. Inhabited by aborigines and settlers from the north, the landscape is marked by dense rain forests and high peaks of the Rain Mountains. While the settlers live in trading posts along the coast, the aborigines, known as Mohas, live in small villages secured on stilts deep in the damp woods. The Mohas are expert shaman; alchemists throughout Arkania are willing to pay good money for the herbs, poisons, tinctures, and animal preparations of these small, copper-colored tribespeople. Even the Mohas themselves are valuable trading commodities in some regions.

Indeed, slavery is widespread in the southern regions of the continent, and in many wealthy homes it is considered fashionable to have an aboriginal servant. Al'Anfa, a city state on the southern end of the east coast, is the main center of the slave trade and has long borne the moniker "City of Red Gold." Those opposed to slavery have another name for the city; they call it the "Festering Boil of the South." The staunchest adversaries to Al'Anfa and its policies can be found in the small kingdom of Trahelia. Located on the south coast of Arkania, Trahelia recently gained its independence from the Central Empire.

The far southwestern point of the Arkanian continent leads to an archipelago whose largest islands—Token, Iltoken, and Benbukkula—are famous for their exotic spices.

Arkania itself measures approximately 3,000 miles from the most northern to the most southern coastline and about 1,900 miles across at its widest point—not much of a distance it seems, but it would take an Arkanian more than three months to cross the continent from the icy lands in the north to the steamy jungles in the south. Only those who know how to wield a sword would dare to travel through the vast territories and hostile lands overrun by Orcs, ravenous Ogres, and wild beasts. It is this world that you are about to enter, a world ruled by powerful gods, populated by faithful worshippers, and governed by corrupt and greedy feudal lords. May Praios be with you on your travels . . .

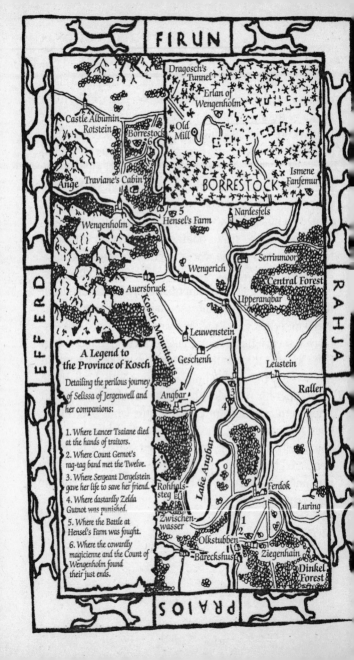

FIRUN

Dragosch's
Tunnel

Erlan of
Wengenholm

Castle Albumin
Rotstein

Borrestock

Old
Mill

Ange   Traviane's Cabin

BORRESTOCK

Ismene
Fanfemur

Wengenholm

5
Hensel's Farm

Nardesfels

Wengerich

Serrinmoor

Auersbruck

Central Forest

Upperangbar

Leuwenstein

Geschenh

Leustein

A Legend to
the Province of Kosch

Detailing the perilous journey
of Selissa of Jergenwell and
her companions:

1. Where Lancer Tsaiane died
at the hands of traitors.

2. Where Count Gernot's
rag-tag band met the Twelve.

3. Where Sergeant Dergelstein
gave her life to save her friend.

4. Where dastardly Zelda
Gutnot was punished.

5. Where the Battle at
Hensel's Farm was fought.

6. Where the cowardly
magicienne and the Count of
Wengenholm found
their just ends.

Angbar

Raller

Lake Angbar

Rohfals-
steg

Zwischen-
wasser

Ferdok

Luring

1
2

Olkstubben

Bareckshus

Ziegenhain

Dinkel
Forest

EFFERD

RAHJA

PRAIOS

Chapter 1

A S THE GONG in the Temple of Praios struck twelve noon, what should have been the brightest hour of the day in the city of Ferdok was unnaturally dark. The winding alleyways were dusky, and heavy gray clouds dripped like great skeins of wet wool over the spires and gables. Large drops of rain fell from the sky and ended their plummet in splashes on the shiny cobblestones. Rivulets of muddy water ran together and formed puddles that in turn became shallow lakes with concentric waves quartering each other and churning up a foam. An old Kosch saying attributed days like these to Efferd, the god of water and provider of rain: "In the foam you can plainly see, this shall be Lord Efferd's fee."

Even the pigeons on the cornice of the Temple of Praios had given up all hope that the rain would stop. Perched on the edge of the carved stone with feathers ruffled and heads pulled in, they stood still enough to pass for part of the chiseled frieze. There were many days

1

when street urchins skilled with slingshots brought pigeons down from this lofty roost. The temple pigeons were infamous for their tough, grisly meat, but if stewed long enough they made a hearty soup. Today, however, was not a day for the hunt, and there was not a slingshot in sight.

On a day such as this the people of Ferdok stayed home if they could possibly manage, and thanked the Twelve for the sound roof over their heads. The market peddlers on Praios Square realized this a bit late. None too happy, they sought protection while waiting for the rain to end, and for customers to come. They resembled the pigeons with their heads drawn into their shoulders, trying not to move so their clammy wet clothes would not touch their skin any more than necessary. The merchants stood as still as statues and watched the rain seep through the baldachins, run off their hat brims, and ruin their wares. It pelted the delicate flowers, bruised the freshly picked berries, soaked the rolls of precious fabric, and dripped on the children's toys and leather goods, so carefully arranged earlier that morning.

The rain drummed against the fishmonger's barrels and filled the potter's bowls. It soaked through the coats of the draft animals as they waited on the edge of the square nibbling with disinterest at wet hay. The marketplace was crisscrossed with tiny streams carrying straw, flower petals, and manure to the wide, gurgling gutter in front of the Golden Lance Tavern at the far side of the square.

"Shut that trap, old man. I'm freezing my ass off over here," a harsh female voice rang out. Gerion shrugged his shoulders, took his eyes off the rain and market stalls, and carefully closed the small wooden door beneath the bull's-eye panes. The dull, hand-blown glass washed the tavern scene with an amber light and obscured the view out onto the damp street. Gerion turned around to see who had made such a rude request. A stocky, red-haired woman looked over at him from a table of three lancers. She had probably seen at least forty harvests. A broad scar streaked across her forehead and slashed past her hairline. "Go out in the street if you want to see what is going on out there, but don't let the cold air in. I don't take kindly to the heathen fresh air, especially not in this hallowed sanctuary." She smiled and raised her beer to him.

Gerion nodded curtly and thought to himself that it was a sad day indeed when a forty-year-old called someone his age an old man. He deliberately ran his left hand through his mop of gray hair. "What do they teach you at the famous Ferdok Lancers besides boozing, brawling, and how to muck out stables?" he asked gruffly, "Good manners perhaps?" He bit his lip. How many years would it take him to learn to think before he opened his mouth?

The guardswoman slammed her tankard on the table so hard that the stout flew a good stride into the air. "You're lucky I don't hit cripples and old men, you disheveled heap, or I would have to learn you some good manners!"

A wise voice in Gerion's head said 'hold your tongue,' but he continued, his right index finger raised in an arrogant gesture, "One says 'teach you' not 'learn you'."

A chair flew back and skid noisily across the wooden

floor boards. The guardswoman jumped up and cleared a path, tossing aside tables and chairs as she barged through the tavern. The other guests cleared a path for her, carefully cradling their beer and backing against the wall. When the guardswoman reached Gerion's seat at the window, a mottled gray and black creature with gnarled claws crawled out from under the table and blocked her next step. She grabbed a chair with both hands and raised it over her head.

"Call your mongrel off, or I'll pulverize him."

"Beat it, Gurvan," Gerion ordered his dog as he rose to his feet.

The dog returned to his spot under the table, still growling and snarling, while the guardswoman's two companions smoothly strode forward until the three formed a semicircle facing Gerion. The youngest among them—Gerion had noticed her long black curls and her dark, fiery eyes earlier when she entered the tavern—screwed up her nose. "What is that awful stench?" she asked mockingly. "Is that your mongrel or did you relieve yourself in your breeches for fear of us, you wizened smart ass?"

Gerion feigned a bow. "Gerion Eboreus Eberhelm Rothnagel is my name," he said. "With whom do I have the pleasure?"

"Selissa of Jergenwell," replied the pretty woman with jet-black hair. "Fiona Dergelstein," said the stocky guardswoman, still holding the chair in front of her ample bosom. "Tsaiane of Willowbruch," added the third one who was about thirty years old and bore a slight resemblance to her younger companion. All three wore the short, quilted leather skirts and high boots of the Ferdok Lancers. But because they were off duty, they were without helmets or cuirasses; instead they sported small, blue wide-rimmed hats, each with a jay feather, and dark blue velvet jerkins that bore the crest of their regiment on the back—a red, lion-headed steed.

"How are we going to do this?" asked Gerion as he stepped to one side, gaining some room to maneuver. "Is this going to be a *ménage à trois*, or should we proceed one by one?"

"By Rondra! This fellow thinks that I would need help to crush him!" The redhead set the chair down, threw off her hat, and assumed a fighting stance.

"Hit him, fatso!" shouted a voice from the tavern door.

Fiona cast an angry glance toward the source of the insult and Gerion took the opportunity to punch her chin with all his might. The pain in his right hand told him that he had solidly struck the guardswoman. So rather than hit again he rubbed his right fist and waited for Fiona to slump to the ground. But the guardswoman did not fall. She shook her head, red locks flying, and repositioned herself for the match.

"Give 'em all you've got, my chunky lady!" came another holler from the door. This time Fiona did not waver. She faked a left—once, twice—and then threw a hook with her right. At the last moment, Gerion ducked to the side and Fiona's knuckles only grazed his cheek. He tried to kick her, but the guardswoman blocked his foot with lightening speed. As his foot bounced off the reinforced knee of her boot, Gerion felt as if a massive stone had been catapulted into his solar plexus.

"Did you see that? That's what I call a ram's head!"

The expert commentary came from the youngest guards-woman on the effect of the two-fisted maul.

Gerion gasped for air, just barely evading a fierce right jab as he stepped back. He had to stall.

Gurvan barked from under the table, and the high pitch from his muzzle gave away the mutt's anxiety. "You're right, old comrade, we're in a bit of a tight spot," wheezed Gerion.

"What is it going to be," jeered Fiona as she advanced, "a fist fight or a foot race?"

Gerion stumbled back. He tried to stay on his toes and keep his fists up even though his arms were burning with all of hell's fire. A break was all he needed, a chance to catch his breath. None of his magic spells would work on this gorilla of a woman if he didn't succeed in evad-ing her blows. Even the trick with the voice from the door had failed to distract her. Gerion shifted his weight to his back foot and, just as Fiona was raising her fist ready to strike with a wicked hook, the gray-haired man leapt for-ward and bashed his forehead against her nose.

"That's what I call a Honing headbutt," he explained with a glance to the pretty dark-haired guardswoman. He released his opponent, stepped back to arm's length, and offered her his right hand, "Truce?"

Fiona tossed his arm aside. Two streams of blood ran from her nose and flowed over her lips. "Shut up and fight!" she said advancing.

Backpedaling, Gerion's foot tangled on the legs of a toppled chair. Caught like a rabbit in a snare, he shook his leg and tried to free himself. Fiona seized the mo-ment to club him on the head and heave him across the room like a sack of potatoes. For a moment, it looked as if Gerion was down for the count.

Shaking his head and squinting his eyes, Gerion saw the toes of two shiny boots. A strong hand grabbed him by the nape of the neck and picked him up off the floor. There he stood, with Fiona's unsympathetic aid, in the midst of a group of gawkers, at pains to recognize what he could of the tavern scene through his blurred vision, while trying to ignore the high-pitched ringing in his left ear.

"You'll want to apologize to me now, you old fart," he heard the redhead say. She seemed somehow familiar to him, and for some reason he knew he didn't fancy her at all. He willed his tired arms to fight although they were as heavy as lead. "A Rothnagel never apologizes, and certainly never to an ogress," he said, flailing weakly with his fists.

When Gerion awoke he found himself on a bed of fresh straw. Someone was energetically washing his face with a damp cloth while administering some terribly foul-smelling salts under his nose. "Gurvan, you really do smell like a foul Duglum," croaked the magician as he opened his eyes. He looked into the dog's dark face. Warm breath rushed past two shiny canine teeth and dried the moisture that the rosy tongue had drooled onto Gerion's cheeks. He sighed, then carefully lifted an arm to push back the dog's head. His shoulder hurt, his biceps burnt, and his raw knuckles stung. As he wiped his brow with his jacket sleeve, he realized that his jaw and his right eyebrow weren't much better off.

Gerion covered his eyes with his arm and lay back in

the straw. "Gurvan, you filthy creature, the way it looks isn't at all the way I'd like it to." The dog whimpered in reply and tried to nuzzle his cold nose between Gerion's arm and face. "Settle down, will you? It could have been much worse. I could be dead and that would leave you in quite a predicament, old friend. You're too stupid to even ask a butcher for scraps. Isn't that so?" Gurvan let out an almost human sigh. "You know that you aren't handsome enough to find another owner. Or do you think you could find yourself a princess who would serve you the finest delicacies on a silver platter every day? Not a chance, foul friend. Some people have all the luck, and others spend their lives in the Muhrsape swamp near Havena. Look at me. I've been waiting almost sixty years for the Twelve to give me the time of day, but you are one lucky dog. Why? Because you've got me, you dumb cur, that's why."

With his eyes still closed Gerion touched the point of his chin. "Well, it doesn't seem to be broken. Hmm, by Holy Ingerimm, that wench packs the punch of a blacksmith."

"Fiona is the best fighter to ride under our banner," said a loud voice from the side.

Gerion shot up, but then returned to his bed of straw, sighing, "Oh, it's you . . . uh . . . Tsaiane."

"I'm Selissa, Tsaiane's friend. We kind of look alike, don't we? Sometimes we pretend to be sisters."

"You don't say," mumbled Gerion, his voice dull and his eyes closed. "Rest assured I won't confuse you again. You are certainly the lovelier one. Please excuse my . . . uh . . . rash remark."

"Oh, you needn't excuse yourself. It's an honor to be confused with Tsaiane. She is an exceptional guardswoman. On the field I am always at ease with her at my side."

Gerion sighed again. "That may well be the case, and you're at liberty to have your personal opinion." He twisted his face into a grimace. "But tell me, what do you want from me? Have you been waiting for me to wake so you could knock me out again?" Suspiciously Gerion lifted his head to survey his surroundings. "Where am I anyway? And how did I get here? Am I a prisoner of the guardswomen?"

Selissa shook her head laughing, her black ringlets bouncing. "The guardswomen take no prisoners. Didn't you know that? Our battle cry is 'For Rondra, for Kosch, no prisoners!'"

Gerion took a deep breath and looked up at the rafters. There was a wall of straw next to him and the soft evening light came through an open barn door. Outside it was still raining. "Where am I?"

Selissa, who sat in the middle of the barn on a barrel of grain, tapped the floor with her boot. "Where else? In Ferdok, of course. This barn belongs to Fobol, son of Farnim, who also runs the Hammer and Anvil Inn. Remember?" She stood up and approached Gerion to investigate the extent of the injuries on his face. As she ran her cool finger tips down the bridge of his bent, yet refined nose, she continued, "You have a lovely nose. Luckily, it's not broken. All in all you seem to have gotten off rather lightly. You should have seen how bad you looked lying on the floorboards back at the Golden Lance.

I thought you were dead." As she bent down to get a closer look at his forehead, her hair brushed his face.

"You smell like a rose," said Gerion.

"The innkeeper thought so, too," Selissa continued unwavering, "that you were fatally injured, if not dead. In any case, he begged us to get you off his premises. 'If the scoundrel dies here in the Lance,' he said 'I'll have a lot of explaining to do. Take him back to his quarters at the Hammer and Anvil!' Then we loaded you onto a cart and brought you here with the intent of taking you to your room. But your innkeeper—"

"That Angroschim is as cheap as he is short," interjected Gerion.

"—insisted that your bill had to be paid first or else he'd have no place for you to stay."

"Like I said, he's tight."

"There was nothing we could do. He did let us bring you out here, though, to the 'royal suite' as he called it."

"How long have I been here?" asked Gerion.

"I'd say for about five hours."

"And you have been holding watch all this time? What an honor!"

"Don't flatter yourself," Selissa stood up. "I just got here. I wanted to see if you were among the living again." She picked up an earthenware water bowl, carried it over to Gerion, and dabbed at the dry blood on his cheek and chin with a soft cloth. The magician winced. Selissa lowered the cloth and sighed, "If you don't care for my nursing, I'll leave it to your dog. I'm sure he'd be more gentle."

Gerion attempted a friendly smile, but it pained him.

"I once read in a wise book that the saliva of a dog can heal wounds, and that a puppy's lick can even heal internal damage."

Selissa continued to look after his wounds. "I find that hard to believe. And even if it's true, is that so for all dogs? Even for the ones that reek as much as your cur?"

"As with all medicines," Gerion explained, "the worse they smell the better they work." He moved Selissa's hand aside and sat up. "Why are you so kind to me?"

Selissa made one more pass over his face with the cloth. "Not leaving you to die has nothing to do with kindness," she said, "it's a commandment from our Goddess Peraine."

As soon as Gerion stood up and brushed the straw from his jacket, Gurvan leapt up and ran out the barn door and back in again, wagging his tail and barking with excitement.

"Knock it off!" warned the wizard. "Why would you want to go out in that barbaric rain? But wait, maybe you're right."

He turned to Selissa, "May I invite you out for a drink? Please do not deny me the honor."

She laughed. "How do you want to pay for that? We spent your last silver crown to pay off the innkeeper at the Lance. There's not a copper bit left in your pockets."

"You went through my pockets? Fine manners you have!"

A hint of red overcame Selissa's cheeks. She defiantly threw the cloth into the bowl and water splashed out on all sides. "What else were we to do? We wanted to pay for the bill you'd run up at the Hammer and Anvil!"

Gerion raised an open hand. "Calm down, don't get

worked up over it. I'm sure you did the right thing. But I'm not without means, thank Phex. Not yet." As he spoke, he unrolled the cuff on his left boot allowing two gold ducats and a handful of silver crowns to roll across the barn floor.

"Look at that," said Selissa. "You have plenty of money! And old Fobol is worried about you being a swindler . . . But why should I have a drink with you? You insulted my sergeant and took your lumps for it. I just came by to see how you were doing and to make sure you weren't dead. That's all. I owe you nothing. Please allow me to leave."

"No."

"Excuse me?"

"I won't allow it."

Selissa hesitated for a moment. "Well, then I will have to go without your permission. It's only an expression, anyway."

"Philandering Phex, how serious you have suddenly become! Did my invitation affect your humor? I think it would be a pleasant undertaking. You're a very beautiful woman in a smart uniform. If you were to join me at my table, we'd certainly give the other guests something to talk about."

Selissa smiled. "Very charming words indeed, but they only talk of the advantages to you. Give me one reason why I should go out with a poor barn dweller who looks the worse for wear."

Gerion stepped closer to the guardswoman, staring deeply into her shining black eyes. "A reason, you say? Well, let me convince you with the following . . ." As he spoke his voice got fainter and fainter and faded off.

"What did you just mumble?" Selissa asked softly as if lost in thought. "I didn't understand the last bit of what you said."

"I'll never set foot in the Lance again," declared Gerion as he walked along behind Selissa under the protection of the house eves. Although the rain was heavy they managed to stay relatively dry. "I bet your good friend Fiona is expecting me to show up there."

"I doubt it," replied Selissa over her shoulder. "Sergeant Dergelstein is on guard duty tonight. But if it makes you feel better we can go to a different tavern. How about the Bard's Tankard? It's right around the corner."

"When your mongrel is wet he smells even worse than the rank city of Selem," said Selissa pinching her nose shut. A prolonged yawn came from under the table, and Gurvan curled himself up, finishing his practiced motion by placing his chin on his front paws. "You should sell him to the Goblins. People say they prize old dogs for stew. Probably because of their aroma."

"Oh, well," Gerion raised his glass of red Yaquir Valley wine, "dogs stink and birds sing. It wouldn't be right any other way. Enjoy the wine's bouquet and drink! Once you've had a few glasses you won't even notice good old Gurvan anymore. Tell me a little bit about yourself. Where are you from, and what brought you to the Ferdok Lancers of all things?"

Gerion had to prod her and almost beg for an answer before she told freely of her childhood and youth at Castle Albumin. The castle was a few days' ride away and had been the seat of the Jergenwell family for almost one hundred and thirty years, ever since the Princess Lorinai of Eberstamm appointed Jandelinde, Selissa's great-great-great-grandmother to be, Baroness of Albumin. The Jergenwell family enjoyed good luck with their holdings, not the least because of one particular passage in the charter that stated "with all that is in or on the soil"—a true blessing as it turned out in later years. For some seventy years, ore had been mined on the estate, and for more than forty years the furnace had been stoked at the Albumin iron works, a dwarf-run foundry that had brought significant wealth to the family.

Selissa was the second of three children born to Baron Lechdan and his wife Elvine. Selissa said she liked her younger brother, Ulfing, very much, but that her elder sibling, Reto, was a real twit—at least he tried his best to be one. But then she admitted that she didn't know him well enough to say for certain. He was more than ten years her senior, while she was just two years ahead of Ulfing. This small difference in their ages had led the family to compare her constantly with her younger brother. Everyone always said "the two little ones" cannot do this, cannot do that, or have to go to bed now. As far as Selissa was concerned, there was only one "little one" at Castle Albumin, namely her annoying, whining little brother, Ulfing.

"As we grew older," she continued, "I began to like him more and more. We learned to ride and fence together, tamed our first falcons together, and shared our first love. He was a fencing instructor from Almadan, a handsome young man—strong, cheerful, with a dazzling smile. Unfortunately, father shamed him terribly and ran him off after he caught the three of us in the wine cellar." She laughed, lifted her glass, and took a big swallow. "My loves seldom find favor with my father. He didn't like the coach driver, upon whose mule I rode all the way to Elenvina either. He didn't even approve of young Erlan of Wengenholm who is, after all, the son of our count. But why am I telling you all of this? I think I'm getting a little tipsy. I'm not accustomed to drinking wine. We guardswomen prefer good old Ferdoker ale."

"You've got to be kidding me," Gerion waved his hand, "A true guardswoman should be at home in every saddle." And he began singing, "*Pour the spirits, decant the wine, tap the Ferdoker ale.*"

"You know our song?" Selissa was surprised.

"Certainly, it's a beautiful song, even though it's a bit sad. But please continue with your story. You were just talking about a very interesting subject—love. Happy or unhappy, I always like to hear somebody talking about love. You were speaking of young Wengenholm. What did your father have against him? A familial bond with a count, what more could a baron wish for his daughter?"

"You see, the young count is a bit strange. It is hard to get to know him. But he is very smart and very well-mannered, a born courtesan, and thus not the man for me. Well, I know that now. Still, Erlan is terribly good-looking, and he can be very charming. Back then I was very flattered that he courted me. We always had to meet secretly, because my father has no kind words for the Wengenholms. You see, our families have feuded for a long time over the ore mines. The Wengenholms claim the mines are theirs. We've already gone through two hearings, even one at the high court of Gareth. And although the Wengenholms lost both times, they are still our lords. They know ways to make my father's life difficult. But hopefully, things will improve. Count Hakan, Erlan's father, died last winter and Erlan and his young stepmother Ilma are now quarreling over their inheritance. That leaves them no time to dispute with us. My father wants to use this chance to approach the prince to see if our lands could be combined with those of another count. Perhaps then we could finally live in peace. The question remains, however, if it would be better to seek protection from Count Falkenhag or if we should align ourselves with Count Schaetzneck. There are advantages to going with Falkenhag, assuming Prince Blasius agrees. Say, you don't seem to be paying much attention anymore."

Gerion, touching his painful chin, looked up. "You think so? I was just wondering if all the Jergenwells are as good-looking as you are. Save that, I've been following your story attentively, even though you have digressed from the fascinating subject of love. What led to your breakup with Count Erlan? You didn't submit to your father's will, did you? That doesn't seem like your style."

"Oh really, you think you know me that well already, do you? But you're right. True love, I believe, can never be suppressed by parental decree."

"By Rahja, that's the way it should be!" added Gerion with a grin and raised his glass. "Let's drink to that!"

Selissa raised her glass to her lips. Her cheeks were

blushed, and her dark eyes shone contentedly. "No, no, another love got between Erlan and me, as usual."

"Oh, now it's getting interesting." Gerion leaned forward, resting his left forearm on the table.

Selissa laughed and brushed her dark hair from her face. "You are an odd fellow, and curious as a gossiping housewife. But I'm starting to think that you're making fun of me."

"Why in the name of the Twelve do you think that? Did you not call me an old codger this afternoon? Therefore, you must have noticed that I don't have that many years before me. I want to use my remaining time the best I can, and to talk with a beautiful woman about love is, I believe, a fine choice. I find so-called conversation an absolute waste of time. What good would it do for us to talk about Vinsalt minstrels, the politics of Gareth, chicken or horse breeds, or the ironwork of Tulamid? That truly would be a waste of time. What matters is not how you spend your time, but how you enjoy it. But, perhaps, you are too young to understand what I mean."

Gerion motioned to the innkeeper and ordered another carafe of wine. There were only a few guests at the Bard's Tankard at that early hour of the evening. A few regulars stood at the bar and ate soft white cheese with dark, crusty bread. A giggling couple, caught up in each other's eyes, sat at a window table. Nearby two musicians were exchanging chords and melodies on the lute. Hesitant tunes and single lost notes—hinting at desire, adventure, and faraway places—hung in the tavern, creating a stark contrast to the confident laughter of the innkeeper, the crackling of the fire, the homey feel of the massive ceiling beams, the earthenware pitchers on the fireplace mantle, and the dark, smoke-stained walls.

Gerion and Selissa sat at a table near the small raised stage upon which, as Selissa remarked, bards and jesters would soon appear.

The innkeeper brought over the wine and engaged Gerion in small talk about the recent change in weather. He commiserated that the weather used to be significantly better at the time of Emperor Reto; even under Emperor Hal, the weather was bearable, he continued, but now under the young Prince Brin's aegis, it had gotten noticeably worse. Days like these, he concluded, could be expected in far-off Havena, perhaps, but never here in sun-graced Kosch. Gerion agreed, and added a comment about the infamous bad weather in Tobrien. When the innkeeper asked him about the scratches on his face, Gerion went off on a bitter tirade about an unscrupulous coach driver.

While Gerion spoke, Selissa was deep in thought observing the magician from across the table. She decided to ask about his age at the next opportunity. His curly, icy gray hair, which was as thick like a sheep's coat, reached his shoulders. It made him seem relatively old. The deep crow's feet at the corners of his eyes and the wrinkles on his forehead above his bushy eyebrows also indicated that he had reached a ripe age. His mouth, however, was well-formed, and his were not the pale lips of an old man. His sparking and attentive blue eyes, which were set off by long lashes, shone like those of a young man. She could not tell much about his figure. His heavy, hip-length jacket was of the sort worn by the river men in the winter, and it disguised his true form well. The wrinkled collar of what had once been a white shirt poked out from beneath his jacket. The resulting fashion resembled that of a pauper, or perhaps a court jester.

It was a bit of a comfort that her companion had chosen the Bard's Tankard and not the Marshall or the Golden Lance. It was unlikely that a guardswoman would see them together here. If any of her comrades saw her with this strange old bird, she would have to endure at least a week of teasing. Why did she go out with him anyway? Try as she may, she could not recall the exact wording Gerion used to convince her. The entire event was shrouded in mystery. Only when they entered the Tankard did she completely regain her senses. Probably the result of too much wine, she thought. I really should stop drinking so much, she resolved as she lifted her glass again to take a small sip.

Gerion brushed his finger against the palm of her right hand. "What beautiful, small, strong hands," he commented, "and what delightful calluses, so small and round."

Selissa pulled back her hand. "Too much riding," she replied, "When you spend a few hours every day—"

Gerion raised his left hand, as if to protect himself from a blow. "Fine, fine. I like them already. They give your small hands something, what shall I say, something serious, energetic. Now, please continue your story. We had just gotten to the exciting part where you broke off a love affair because true love entered the picture."

Selissa asked herself again if she should take Gerion's smile as friendly or if he was poking fun at her. But his eyes glowed with youthful curiosity, and she could not withhold her story from him. "Actually, that was because of the Ferdok Lancers," she explained. "If I hadn't bumped into the Lancers . . . that is, if Count Growin, son of Gorbosch, had not visited us at Albumin, and my father had not asked my little brother and me to perform a jousting demonstration for our guest, who knows, I might still be sitting at home in our castle. But I still would never have married young Wengenholm." She added, "That much I know. Anyway, Count Growin was very impressed with my equestrian skills. At least that's what he said. He promised to approach the guardswomen as soon as he returned to Ferdok to make sure that I would be admitted. I can still hear the count's words, 'Prince Blasius looks all over the world for talent to grace his guard, but he overlooked some of the best little riders here at home.' Little rider, my eye," Selissa screwed up her nose. "Less than fourteen days later I got a letter from Ferdok, signed by Govena Glaidis of Hirschingen-Berg, our Lady Colonel. I was to report immediately to Ferdok to introduce myself. That was three years ago.

"Two years ago, around the winter solstice, I traveled with my comrade Yasinde to her native Borland where I met her brother, Count Arvid." Selissa looked up and leaned back in her chair.

Gerion watched her with anticipation and nodded. "Now I understand. That is the man who changed the world, Count Arvid of Borland . . ."

"Count Arvid of Geestwindsberth," Selissa corrected, "that's where his family resides."

"Tall, blond, generous, and well-traveled, I take it."

"That's the case. How did you know?" Selissa laughed

dreamily. "How tall are you?"

"I'm a good stride and forty fingers tall. I suppose he's twice my height."

"Not quite, but he is almost two strides tall. And he has a beautiful voice. When he sings the songs of Borland his servants can't help but start to cry. Once I've resigned my commission, we'll be married and live in Geestwindsberth. He is coming to visit soon, probably within the month. Then I will introduce him at Albumin."

"What does your father think of your current choice? Is he happy at last?"

Selissa furrowed her brow angrily, "What do you think? He called him a dowry hunting ne'er-do-well and a bridge count. Father is under the impression that all Borish noblemen are so poor that they have to sleep under bridges. . . . Granted, Geestwindsberth is not Albumin, but I certainly will not starve to death in Borland. Wealth isn't all that matters!"

"Indeed, he is a man to be envied, your man from Borland. Oh, to be blond and two strides tall. I have wished for that all my life. I never knew why I carried that strange wish around with me, but now that I've met you, I know why," Gerion sighed a deep sigh, which woke Gurvan. The dog crawled out from under the table and put his paw on his master's lap. "I know you love me as I am, old friend, but it's just not the same . . ."

Selissa waved her hand under her nose and mumbled, "On second thought, maybe he does smell worse when he's dry."

Gurvan cast her a lasting gaze, then returned to his spot

under the table. It took him a while to arrange his limbs and find a new, comfortable sleeping position. Gerion flagged down the innkeeper and ordered a small pitcher of Borish meskinnes. Selissa was touched.

"That is very kind of you. You must want me to remember Borland. At Geestwindsberth we always drank meskinnes." She emptied the small, hand-blown glass and ran her tongue along the rim to enjoy the last drop of this potent honey liqueur.

"Gerion, you are a remarkable person. You have listened to me for such a long time, but you have not said a word about yourself, even though I am sure that you, too, are full of stories. Don't try to pretend that you are shy. Or are you hiding something?"

"I could never hide anything from you, most beautiful of the guardswomen. Ask me whatever you like. You can read me like an open book."

"Well then, how old are you?"

"Fifty-nine years, and next Hesinde I will be sixty."

"Well, well. And where are you from?"

"From Tobrien, from the island of Tisal."

Selissa paused. "Does the island belong to your family?"

"Not as far as I know. My father was a miller's assistant. Some years later, though, he inherited a mill near Ilsur. I think we would have been better off had he been lord of the island."

Selissa threw back her head and laughed. "You really are a strange, old bird. And you would sleep in a barn even though you've got money to spare. Is that an example of the frugality for which the Tobrien people are famous?"

"I don't know how much that has to do with being

from Tobrien. You see, I came to Ferdok to ply my art at the annual fair. But the fair doesn't begin for another two weeks, and I have to make sure that I have enough money until then. Besides, I also have to make some significant purchases."

"Significant purchases? That sounds intriguing. What might they be?"

Gerion shrugged, "Things I need for my art. It would only bore you if I went into detail."

"What kind of artist are you? Are you an entertainer?"

"You could call me that."

"Then you will need to buy new props and things."

Gerion shrugged again.

"Will I be able to find you at the fair?"

"Oh, I think so. I have a small wagon. Right now, it's over at the Hammer and Anvil. You can't miss it." Gerion reached for Selissa's hand again. This time she did not pull away. Instead, she picked up her meskinnes glass with her left hand and emptied it.

"That's a beautiful ring you are wearing," remarked Gerion. "I noticed it right away. Can I take a closer look at it?"

Selissa raised her hand for him. "Why certainly. Look, this is our family's crest: the woll and the swerd." She laughed, "I mean, the well and the sword. I wear it all the time, because it's so hard to get it off my finger. Well, that way it's also very difficult to steal."

"Don't be so sure," replied Gerion. "A skilled thief, yes, even I, could steal it from you very easily."

Selissa raised her eyebrows and looked at Gerion questioningly. "You wouldn't do that. You couldn't. I mean, you wouldn't be so cruel as to cut off my finger, would you?"

Gerion reached for her hand again. "What are you thinking? I would never do anything so terrible. Anyway, that would be maiming and not theft!"

"Well, then you will never get it. It's impossible." Selissa shook her black curls. "You would never be able to steal it without force."

"Do you wish to wager? Five ducats say I can."

"That's a safe bet. I raise you to one hundred, old friend. Shake on it, or forget it. That's the way guardswomen bet." Selissa slammed her left fist on the table. Gurvan shot out of his hiding place and surveyed the events. He turned and growled at the bar, where he noticed a one-legged dwarf, who seemed suspicious to him.

"I don't have one hundred ducats, and I don't think I could go and find them either."

Selissa held the meskinnes pitcher over her glass and carefully watched the last drops fall from the spout.

"So he doesn't want to bet," she mumbled. "Perhaps he's afraid. He's a chicken. Fine, then I will make you another shruggestion." She laughed so hard that tears came to her eyes. "I mean, another suggestion. If you win, you get one hundred ducats. But if you lose, I get to cut off your terrible head and sell your remains to the Goblins. Well, what do you think?"

Gurvan sat down next to the guardswoman and put his muzzle on her knee. She pushed the dog's head away and made a face. "Didn't I already tell you that you have terrible breath?" Turning to Gerion, she continued, "So, have you made a decision?"

The magician took a long look at his gray dog and

finally extended his right hand to the guardswoman, "You're on."

Selissa shook hands.

Soon, just as Selissa had said, the first jester appeared on the stage at the Bard's Tankard. The guardswoman, however, was no longer in any shape to concentrate on the act, and Gerion suggested to Selissa that they leave.

"Where do you want to go? To your place, or mine?" Gerion asked when they were outside. He had his arm around the guardswoman's waist, even though he was almost half again as tall as she. Selissa leaned her head against his shoulder. The rain had let up a bit, but there was a cold wind sweeping the empty alley.

"We can't go to my place. No men allowed in the barracks after 2000 hours, says Lady Colonel Praioshin-gen-Berg. And you, you live in a barn!" Selissa began to giggle. "Well, why not? I haven't had a roll in the hay in a long time." She took a step forward and pulled the magician along with her.

On the way through the dark, quiet alley in the lower part of Ferdok, Selissa sang the song of the Ferdok Lancers, "*Ride, Rondra, ride on. Ride Boron, ride at our side. Pour the spirits, decant the wine, tap the Ferdoker ale.*"

The further she marched into the night with Gerion, the slower and softer her song grew. As they reached the barn door, she fell quiet. Once inside, Selissa threw herself down on the straw and fell fast asleep. Gerion pulled off her long boots and covered her with a thick blanket from his wagon.

Chapter 2

"SECOND SQUADRON, mount up!"

For a moment the long row of guardswomen erupted into a colorful flurry of activity—blue capes fluttered, lance points with blue pennants dipped, horses danced in place, and brass helmets and cuirasses shone in the pale, watery light of dawn. Then thirty mounted guardswomen directed their steeds with gentle squeezes of their thighs until they formed a solid front. Here and there an excited horse pulled down its mighty head and bucked in protest. Finally, pats and reassuring words saw to it that the beasts stood as close to perfectly still as possible.

Thirty riders with serious faces looked straight ahead into the distance, their slender lances pointed to the sky. A strong southerly wind blew across the barracks, tumbling a few pieces of wet straw across the square and fluttering the pennants hanging from the shiny points of the lances. The wind ruffled the horses' tails and manes, as well as the thick, black horse hair cascading from the guardswomen's helmet decorations and down their backs.

"Eyes left!"

The riders' heads snapped to the side. Two women mounted on muscular, perfectly groomed white horses trotted down the alley between the stable and the mess hall. One wore the helmet of an officer with a tall red plume made of ostrich feathers and a piece of leopard fur at its crown. The gray head of the other rider was not covered. They paused for a moment at the group of wagons, beasts of burden, and pages that had gathered next to the stable, then they continued on their way.

Sergeant Fiona Dergelstein, who lead the guardswomen from the back of her stout, gray gelding, raised her right hand in greeting and announced in a powerful voice, "First guard pennant, front and ready!"

The woman in the officer's helmet returned the greeting smartly, while the gray-haired rider gave a restrained nod and turned her mount's white breast to the line of riders. "Good morning, guardswomen!"

"Good morning, Lady Colonel!" echoed throughout the square. Then came a shrill, lone whinny, followed by a wave of low laughter.

Lady Colonel Govena of Hirschingen-Berg smiled, "Guardswoman Hornshoe, when will your horse ever learn to speak only when it is spoken to?"

"I don't know, ma'am."

"Didn't you bring him from Gareth?"

"I did, ma'am . . . um . . . yes, ma'am."

"Well, then that explains it. Every Garethian talks too much."

"Yes, ma'am."

"Guardswoman Jergenwell!"

"Colonel?"

"You look terrible this morning . . . as pale as an ice worm. And your horse looks like a molting turkey. Haven't you ever heard of a handy little tool called a curry comb?"

"Yes, ma'am!"

"Oh, before I forget, was that you I saw creep past my window fifteen minutes before wake-up call, Jergenwell?"

"That is possible, ma'am."

"Well, we will have to discuss that. Right now there are more important things at hand. Lieutenant Singer, present the order of the day."

A broad-shouldered, blond, thirty-something guardswoman with a red plume on her helmet advanced her white mount a few paces. "Rondra be praised, guardswomen!"

"Rondra be praised, Lieutenant!"

"Let me keep it brief. Yesterday we received news that a group of supporters of Count Answin of Ravenmund is on the loose in a forest some twenty miles southwest of here. According to the reports the group consists of a Darpatian count, a baroness, a few knights, and a number of armed pages. The rogues have split up and have already raided and plundered several farm houses in the area. We have reason to believe that they will try to regroup down at the Great River, attempt to escape through the Kosch Mountains, and then continue on to Albernia. As you know, Albernia is still considered a troubled province and a favorite hideout for villains and troublemakers of all kinds. The peasants around Dinkel Forest estimate the number of intruders at about fifty. Most of them are neither mounted nor well-armed."

At that moment, Lady Colonel Hirschingen-Berg stepped forward. "Your orders are to capture the leaders of the rebellion and to bring them to Ferdok so they can stand trial here or in Gareth. Take as many prisoners as you can. The royal mines can always use a few more strong backs. But remember that the life of a guardswoman is far more important to me than a villain's hide. So don't take any unnecessary risks. If you encounter resistance, skip the formalities and use your swords."

The gray-haired colonel nodded her head in the direction of Lieutenant Singer who revealed the details of the colonel's plan. "Our mission shouldn't last more than two or three days. We will move out in fifteen minutes. Twenty riders will come with me and advance along the river to the southeast. Sergeant Dergelstein will take ten lancers and the supplies directly southwest to Dinkel Forest. They will scout out the region and wait for us or further orders in the village of Ziegenhain. Both groups should reach Ziegenhain by the fourth hour of this afternoon at the latest. In case only one group is there we will use the standard code and message protocol. Today's code phrase is 'raven's blood.' Any questions?"

The guardswomen stood silent.

"Let's go. Rondra be with you!"

"In twos! At ease!" Sergeant Dergelstein commanded. Selissa spurred on her chestnut mare, Phexchild, down a tree-lined alley to catch up with her fair-haired comrade Zelda. Then she turned in her saddle to take one last good look at the walled city of Ferdok with its steep, slate roofs.

Still wet from the previous night's rain, the walls and slate tiles glistened in the bright morning light, giving the city on the Great River the appearance of a carefully arranged toy village. The ships in the harbor on the far side of the city looked very small. Selissa's gaze followed the skyline until she identified the gable of the Temple of Praios, the dome of the Temple of Rondra, and the tall, red tile roof of the Guard's barracks. "Beautiful," she said, raising her hand to her helmet to shade her eyes. She briefly looked to the east where the sun shone brightly over the wide plains, then turned west to look at the distant blue mountains of Kosch. The jagged, bare peaks on the far side of the river and the dark tree line on the slopes were remarkably clear to the eye this morning. It almost looked as if one could reach out and touch them. "I don't think it is going to rain today."

Zelda was preoccupied with tying her helmet straps to the saddle horn. She had put her arm through the loop of the handle on the lance in order to free both hands; but the pole had slid out of the bracket on the right stirrup, and she was having a difficult time keeping hold of her helmet, lance, and reins while the wind tousled her blond hair. She responded with an unfriendly grunt.

"Oh, I see, the guardswoman is having a bad day today," commented Selissa sarcastically. She decided to skip the small talk and enjoy the view instead.

Selissa reached out and picked a large yellow "royal" pear from a tree along the road. "All fruit borne by the trees along the streets of Kosch belongs to the crown of Kosch. However, the citizens may take of this fruit if they are hungry," Selissa repeated to herself. The pear was exceptionally sweet and so juicy that she had to lean from her saddle while she took a bite to keep the juice from dripping on her uniform. These pears can only be picked from horseback, she thought with content. All the fruit in arm's reach of a pedestrian was long gone before it could even ripen. After Selissa had eaten the pear, she picked a second, less perfect one. I'm as hungry as a wolf, she thought. No wonder. My host forgot to serve me a decent breakfast.

In the early hours she had awakened with a start. After shaking her head, she had realized she was on a bed of straw in a dark barn. There was a leaden, painful dullness in her head, no matter how much she shook her head and squeezed her eyes shut. Only after the old sorcerer laid his hand on her forehead and told her to think of something beautiful and cool like a dew-covered meadow had she felt any better. Gerion Eboreus Eberhelm Rothnagel—what a name. How he had cursed Fiona. Selissa looked ahead at the broad shoulders of her sergeant and smiled. Yesterday certainly was a strange day. First, the brawl at the Golden Lance, then the trip through the city pushing the half-dead showman in a wheelbarrow lined with straw, then the strange evening at the Bard's Tankard. She had never told a stranger that much about herself. But she had enjoyed Gerion's attention and his teasing, clever remarks. An odd bird, but a man of honor. He could have done anything to her last night. . . . She couldn't have stopped him.

Selissa furrowed her brow. She recalled how she had nervously felt for her ring after she awoke, remembering her stupid bet.

"It's still there. Who do you think I am?" Gerion had asked. "Do you think I would steal from a drunk woman?

Apparently you are of the opinion that only people who wear helmets live by a code of honor, hmm?"

Selissa had searched her dizzy head for a reply, but couldn't find one. Just thinking about it made her blush. She had put on her boots and found her way out without saying good-bye, as if she were a foolish kitchen servant.

"Of course, I recognize that you live by your own code of honor," she should have said. "As far as the wager goes, you could have taken advantage of my state. One has to know how to take advantage of an opponent's weaknesses. But now it is too late. And you will never get a second chance. Farewell, my good man." Yes, that would have been the right thing to say.

Oh well, what's done is done. Besides, why should she care what that migrant fool thought of her anyway? The only reason he didn't do anything to her was probably because he was too old for that sort of thing. Selissa angrily hurled the core of her pear onto the street where it splattered into bits.

The mid-day sun beat down on Selissa's bare shoulders and legs. She stretched and unbuckled the straps of her heavy brass helmet, placing it on the saddle horn between her thighs. White foam covered the mare's rump and flanks.

The group of riders had since left the cobbled street and was now trotting southwest along a sandy country road toward distant, forested hills. Selissa looked over her shoulder toward the river valley and saw that the wagons and pack animals had fallen far behind. Fiona had them trot several times, so they had outpaced the other group by more than two miles.

Selissa smiled at a peasant who had steered his ox-drawn cart off the street in order to allow the guardswomen to pass. He stood next to his long-horned, brown animals and doffed his straw hat.

Tsaiane reined her gray gelding to Selissa's side and pointed to the sun. "Master Praios is certainly shining on us today. I'm cooking alive and sweating in places that a respectable woman shouldn't even call by name." She delivered her wry comments without even cracking a smile.

Selissa looked over at her intensely. "What is with you, dear sister? You look unhappy. It's a beautiful day, isn't it? A little bit of sunshine shouldn't slow down a guardswoman from Ferdok." She patted Tsaiane on the shoulder. "If I didn't know you as well as I do, I would say that you were worried about our mission. By Rondra, we will hunt down these treacherous Answinites like rabbits. Just wait and see."

Selissa's friend remained serious as she looked out across the country side. "You are so young and naive. And you place such trust in our goddess. Does it ever occur to you that she might be busy when you need her most?" Tsaiane shivered. "What am I saying? Don't listen to me. No one wants to hear that kind of thing. It's just . . ." She placed her hand on Selissa's padded shoulder. "Please be careful, sister. Life would be empty without you. I just want . . ." Tsaiane trailed off and looked at the far off hills.

At the head of the group Fiona raised her right fist and drew a circle in the air—the signal to come together. Selissa pressed her heels in the flanks of her chestnut mount.

Phexchild shot forward, as if she had just been let out of the gate. The animal was not at all tired from the long ride. Selissa had to yank her head strongly to the right so that she would come alongside the sergeant.

After the guardswomen formed a semicircle around Fiona, the sergeant pointed at the dark hills in front of them. "Do you see the distinctive pair of hills to the south-southeast? The ones that look like someone's backside?"

The guardswomen laughed and nodded.

"A hair to the left is a bare spot, a clearing. See it?"

"Yes, ma'am."

"That is the godforsaken village of Ziegenhain. We are supposed to be there in two hours. Since we made such good time, go ahead and dismount and stretch your legs for awhile."

"Sergeant, I see a plume of smoke just to the right and a bit closer to us than Ziegenhain," said the Nivesian guardswoman, Juahan, who had the best eye in the entire squad.

"Yes, I see it now too," Fiona confirmed. "It could be a cooking fire."

"The smoke is awfully dark for a cooking fire," added Juahan. "It has only been burning for a short time. And what peasant starts his cooking fire after noon?"

Sergeant Dergelstein looked at the distant smoke, then at her riders, thoughtfully biting her lip. She sat up straight in her saddle. "Put on your helmets! In twos! Follow me!"

The guardswomen fastened their chin straps, led their horses from the road into the dry, autumn field, and cantered toward the distant forest.

Before the group reached the first tree, Fiona gave the signal to stop. The smoke had grown denser. It was clear that it was coming from a large fire no more than a mile off. A wagon path led into the forest and went straight toward the wafting smoke. "There's no time for inquiries," said the sergeant more to herself than to her riders. "Tsaiane, Selissa, come with me. The others will follow. Ready your lances. Move out!"

With their lances drawn, the guardswomen followed the threesome up the forest path. Heavy, muffled hoof falls broke the silence of the forest. Divots of grass and earth flew into the air as the women spurred their beasts to ever faster speeds. The guardswomen trilled a high call of "heyheyheyhey" as they raced along a narrow break in the trees, dappled sunlight rushing over their gleaming helmets. Small branches whipped against their mail and lances. Only the rider at the front of the group could see where they were going; those following behind had to trust blindly that no one in front of them would stumble or lose her way.

Suddenly, the forest ended and the lancers shot across a clearing flooded with light. Fiona waved her hand to the right and left, ordering the guardswomen to fan out. At the same time, she reined in her foaming mount so that the last rider could catch up.

The guardswomen formed a broad front as they thundered over the field. Their lances were lowered and held firmly with the shaft under arm. Red and blue pennants sailed through the wind.

Beyond the field, flames leapt into the sky from the thatched roof of a farm house. A dozen armed men and women had stormed the structure and were in the midst of looting its contents. A man carrying out a battered trunk caught sight of the guardswomen and let out a yell, causing his companions to scatter in every direction. A few rushed to their horses while others formed a ragged attack with raised spears and swords. A dark-haired woman nocked an arrow to her bow.

Selissa targeted a bearded young man with a helmet and mail, who held a long sword with both hands. Looking at the tip of her lance and then at her opponent, she quickly sized him up. His right hand was above his left on the sword's grip. He was right handed, so he would jump to the right, she thought. I will aim to my left. The thoughts came to her without any hesitation as she spurred Phexchild toward the swordsman.

Never, never lose your composure, thought the man from Darpatia as he saw the black-haired warrior on her red mount bearing down on him. He gripped his sword tighter. Move at the last possible moment. Feign briefly, then dart to the other side and bring the sword around completely so that the blade just hits her back. If you do it right you will cut her in half.

The bearded man with the sword stood motionless. His broad chest was Selissa's target. Now a mobile target! That's why you aim at the last moment. Not yet. Now! Oh, Rondra, he is going the wrong way! No, he isn't!

A heavy blow knocked the lance from her hand. It rang through her shoulder and numbed her arm so that it fell limply to her side. She threw herself to the left and pulled on the reins just barely steering the racing Phexchild past the burning house. "Whoa," called Selissa as she pressed herself into the saddle. The mare came to a stop and tossed her head wildly.

Selissa massaged her right arm with her left hand. Finally, life came back to it. She took up the reins again and drew her saber from its sheath and looked all around.

Nearby, Tsaiane held a woman in a leather jerkin at bay against the barn wall. The stranger tossed her saber aside. Fiona and Tirelle were facing off against a well-armed rider. Out on the field Yasinde and six or seven lancers were chasing a handful of deserters. In the middle of the yard, next to the well, the bearded man knelt on the ground and stared at Selissa. His hands held the shaft of the lance. Its point extended more than the width of a hand out of his back. Blood gushed out of his mouth and ran over his beard.

The tavern in Ziegenhain was packed. There were thirty seats in the house, just enough for the thirsty men who were discussing the weather and harvest over tankards of good home brew after the Peraine prayer on Praiosday. Almost half of the village had gathered in the tavern that evening. The country folk stood shoulder to shoulder along the bar and walls. The lancers from Ferdok sat at the tables and sent their servants to the bar again and again, where the owner and his wife could barely keep up with demand. There must have been about one hundred and fifty people packed together under the inn's low ceiling. The heat inside rivaled a humid night in Rondra. The lancers smoked the finest tobacco in their short clay pipes, its sweet, heavy scent mixing with the cheap weed the peasants puffed.

Helmets, armor, tankards, and empty wooden plates piled up on the tables to form a colorful still life of disarray. More tankards rolled on the floor among cast-off boots and dozing dogs. It was unearthly loud.

The group from Ferdok had shrunk to two dozen riders, the sergeant, and Lieutenant Singer. Yasinde and two other lancers had sustained serious injuries in the fight at the farm house. Fedora had been badly burned while putting out the fire. Two guardswomen accompanied the party of wounded and their four prisoners back to Ferdok.

"Well done, guardswomen," said Lieutenant Singer, for the second or third time that evening. "Our Lady Colonel will be impressed." The officer sat with Fiona, Selissa, and Juahan at a table near the open door that allowed a bit of fresh air to enter. Nonetheless, the lancers were drenched with sweat. Selissa felt the perspiration trickle down between her breasts and soak the padded vest under her cuirass. She pressed the cool tankard to her forehead.

Suddenly she felt a small, warm hand on her shoulder. The guardswoman looked up and saw the round face of a blonde girl, about seven or eight years old. She was beaming as she ran her fingers along Selissa's cuirass. "You are so beautiful," the girl said with enchantment, "When I grow up, I want to be a lancer too."

The image of the Darpatian appeared before Selissa's eyes. The iron helmet, the chain mail that hung over the rusty torn edge of a yellow tunic, the shiny, silver glint of his sword, his face with close-set eyes and the short, dark beard. She remembered that his white teeth flashed against the dark stubble as if he had opened his mouth to smile. Yes, he did smile, a victorious smile, even as he took his last breath. Selissa thought it must have been Lord Boron himself who looked at her from the eyes of the stranger. A chill ran down her sweaty back.

"Stay on the farm and marry the neighbor's son," she snapped at the girl, who was shocked by the tone of her voice.

"Sometimes these little beggars can really get on your nerves," called Lieutenant Singer, who had watched the entire scene without hearing what had been said.

"Please excuse me, Lieutenant," said Selissa. She squeezed past the crowd and stepped out into the cool of the night.

The next day, the guardswomen rode along a country road that led directly to the west down to the valley of the Great River. The sun hung low and red in a bank of rosy clouds before them. To their left stretched the dark Dinkel Forest where the Darpatian rebels were hiding, probably in bands of two or three. The rebels planned to regroup in Bareckshusen, a hamlet on the banks of the Great River. From there they would cross the river and continue toward the Kosch Mountains. It had not been particularly difficult for Lieutenant Singer to get this information out of one of the pages taken prisoner. Baroness Gwynna of Newborn, by contrast, who had also fallen into the hands of Fiona's group, was less cooperative. The royal rebel would not say a word, not even under Juahan's intense interrogation. But the mercenary, a hireling from Kuslik, only had to be promised free passage by Lieutenant Singer before he sang like a wine dealer from Almadan at market. The rebel leader was Count Gernot of Streitzig, former governor of Mark Rommilys and heir to a house that had long been closely allied with Count Answin of Ravenmund.

After the rebellion was overthrown, the Imperial Headquarters sent two battalions to Castle Streitzig to take the count prisoner. The count, however, had been forewarned and thus was able to assemble his troops and escape, leaving his castle in flames. The count's family and the mercenaries had joined Baroness Gwynna, along with a few loyal noblemen and peasants. Originally, Count Gernot had planned to make his way across the country by way of friendly territory. But all throughout the land there was unrest and sympathizers were being chased from their fiefs, leaving Count Gernot's group alone and surrounded by enemies. For the fugitives that meant sleeping during the day and marching through the night over rough fields and rutted forest paths. The peasants in Count Gernot's entourage were forced to abandon their wagons and leave their few possessions behind. Most of his mercenaries had deserted him. And now, with Baroness Gwynna and her following in the hands of the enemy, the group numbered no more than three dozen men who, according to the mercenary, were extremely loyal to the count.

Lieutenant Singer gave the order to ride as quickly as possible around Dinkel Forest to reach the meeting place before the rebels. "To give them the reception they deserve," as she put it. The guardswomen spent almost the entire day in the saddle. The provisions and servants followed as fast as they could, but they were soon out of sight.

Now that evening was approaching, the guardswomen were as exhausted as their horses, whose heads hung as they dragged their hooves over the dusty road. Many of the women had made additional reconnaissance rides. There had been no break since morning, because Lieutenant Singer wanted to keep her squad combat-ready. Their heads buzzed under the heavy helmets, which had baked under the hot autumn sun all day. All conversation was long over. The line of riders traveled along the street in silence. Even the pennants hanging from the lances seemed to flap listlessly. Selissa's pennant was still. It was stiff with dried blood.

Selissa lay on her back and looked up at the faraway stars. She saw bright Ucuri and the numerous points of light that together formed the wild horse in the sky. She thought it curious that the people in faraway Borland saw the same stars. If Arvid were to look at Geestwindsberth's starry sky right now and if the stars were mirrors, I could see him. Oh, Arvid, you are probably asleep in bed like a sensible person at this hour. Selissa forced herself to get up. Don't rest too long, she told herself. Sleep was a cunning fellow, he takes advantage of you whenever he can.

She strode over to Phexchild who seemed to mumble a greeting and placed her hand on the mare's velvety muzzle. "You're not asleep yet? Why not? It has been a long day."

A low owl hoot pierced the night air. Selissa cupped her hands in front of her mouth and returned the call. She squinted as she tried to see across the moonlit meadow to a group of trees about two hundred strides away from

Serindai's post. But she could see neither the guardswoman nor her horse. Cautiously, Selissa led her mare a few paces back into the undergrowth that she had chosen for cover. Then she turned toward the dark wall of Dinkel Forest.

All was quiet.

Selissa repeatedly checked the sky above the trees for any sign of light announcing the approach of morning and the end of her watch. She closed her eyes for a moment and thought of Arvid, but the smiling face of the Darpatian once again came between her and her memories. Selissa opened her eyes quickly and angrily stomped her right foot. Would she always have to think of this moment when she lost her trust in Rondra and was scared to death? Even though she had been afraid, she had done the right thing. She did not give in to her fear. Shouldn't this be worth something?

The Darpatian, she suddenly asked herself, what had he seen in the yard? Did he notice my fear? Or did he, too, notice Lord Boron looking at him through my eyes? Did he know that I was going to be his doom? That I would take everything from him? Why was Rondra at my side and not his as he collapsed, still smiling? Was she really at my side, or is she truly only with those who call upon her? No, she told herself, when the colonel calls 'Rondra be with you!' or when I say, 'Rondra be with you!' to Tsaiane, then it is certainly not a death wish. So the goddess is with me, even though I may not be a superior warrior. Maybe she favors me because I'm . . . I'm . . . a decent person . . . kind of pretty and honest. Perhaps it is for the better that I will be resigning in two years. Five years of service will be long enough. I am sure I can serve the goddess in other ways. No longer haunted by the smiling face of the Darpatian rebel, Selissa returned with her thoughts to Geestwindsberth. She envisioned the dark beams of the main hall and a warm fire with Arvid at her side, singing a sad Borish song. The door opened and snowflakes swirled in along with her three daughters, each as blond as Arvid . . .

Selissa waited until the gray streaks in the sky over Dinkel Forest were bright enough that she could clearly make out the tree tops. Then she mounted Phexchild and guided the mare in a steady trot to the camp. At the same time she met the last guardswomen of the long night's watch. They had patrolled a two-mile-long path between the riverbank and the forest. No one had seen anything out of the ordinary. Only Tsaiane, who had the furthest post, was not yet back.

Selissa noticed that Lieutenant Singer was ready to send a guardswoman out for Tsaiane, so she quickly volunteered to do so. She knew that Tsaiane had a hard time staying awake during watch, and she wanted to spare her friend any embarrassment. The lieutenant briefly described Tsaiane's hiding spot and Selissa rode off.

She soon reached the small barn that had been described to her. Then she rode up the small hill, behind which her friend had taken up watch.

Thirty strides from the hill, Selissa dismounted. She decided to sneak up the rest of the way in order to startle Tsaiane. It was easy to sneak up across the soft grass. Not even a Darpatian bull would have made a noise on this footing. There was not a sound to be heard from the far side of the hill. Even Tsaiane's stout gelding was silent. It was eerily quiet. Selissa ran the last few steps around the hill. There was not a trace of horse or guardswoman to be seen. A few strides to the left lay a figure in the grass without a helmet, boots, or saber, hair wet with dew and her chin in a large dark pool.

Selissa threw herself at her friend and then shrank back as she touched the ice-cold skin on her shoulders. It was easy to roll the limp body onto its back. There was a wide gash all the way across her throat, and her two eyes stared into the heavens.

"Tsaiane . . . why? Dearest sister . . ." Selissa choked on a heavy lump in her throat that made it difficult for her to breathe. "Your helmet, your beautiful helmet, they stole your helmet." She reached for Tsaiane's cold, limp hand and raised it to her cheek as if she wanted to warm it. "Dear sister, how could they do this to you?"

Almost fifteen minutes later three guardswomen approached Selissa from behind. They had been sent by Lieutenant Singer. Selissa did not hear them coming and first noticed them as a hand touched her shoulder. Then she shook her head and looked up. "They stole her helmet and boots, Serindai," she said quietly. "They shouldn't have done that."

Juahan was a member of the trio sent out to look for Selissa and Tsaiane. As soon as she saw what had happened she ran up the hill to survey the river valley. She then returned silently and examined the ground nearby. She took her horse by the reins and walked toward the river, stooping now and again to feel the ground.

In Juahan's absence, her three fellow warriors wrapped

Tsaiane's body in a blanket and carried her back to the camp. Lieutenant Singer said a few words about loss, mourning, revenge, and the halls of Rondra. Before she could finish, Juahan returned in a full gallop and reported that she had found the trail of the rebels. The entire group had rounded the guardswomen to the south, she explained breathlessly. Right now they were in the forest, approximately two miles from the Great River. Apparently, they were going to try to ferry over to the tiny village of Olkstuben.

"Most likely," Sergeant Dergelstein agreed. "There is a small ferry and a few river fishermen over there. There would be enough boats."

"How much of a lead do the bastards have on us?" asked Lieutenant Singer.

"About four miles," replied Juahan. "They aren't moving very fast. The three who killed Guardswoman Willowbruch were on horseback, however. They must have been securing their flank when they discovered Tsaiane."

"Couldn't you have stayed awake this once, big sister?" Selissa thought as she looked at the figure wrapped in blankets. Only two bare feet protruded. "Just this one, cursed time?"

"The three have caught up with the others by now. There are no more than ten riders in total."

Without waiting for the end of Juahan's report, Lieutenant Singer gave Fiona a signal. As the sergeant ordered her troop to mount up, Lieutenant Singer walked over to the dead guardswoman. She pulled the blankets off Tsaiane's ashen face and tenderly arranged the dark curls. Singer and Tsaiane had ridden together for twelve years. Tsaiane had always been one of Ferdok's top riders. The lieutenant looked up at the lancers assembled around her, who were impatiently awaiting the order to move out.

"Do you remember our Lady Colonel's orders? She told us to capture the fugitive rebel leaders and to take their followers to the royal mines, didn't she?"

The lancers nodded their helmeted heads.

"I, however, ask you," continued Lieutenant Singer in a hoarse voice, "what is our battle cry?"

"For Rondra, for Kosch," a few voices yelled, then more chimed in, "no prisoners."

"Lancers, I can't hear you!"

"For Rondra, for Kosch, NO PRISONERS," echoed through the morning.

Sergeant Dergelstein issued a few commands to call the group of warriors to order. The guardswomen immediately secured their lances in the fittings on their stirrups, points to the sky, and waited for Lieutenant Singer to spearhead their troop before trotting off.

Their ride continued to the west, over the flat grasslands along the river. They passed herds of dozing cattle and sheep, but exchanged no greetings with the shepherd children. Soon they came to a small cluster of alders in the middle of a meadow. There were glints of silvery water among the trees and in the misty distance beyond a curve the Great River shimmered. There were a few dozen houses nestled on a low hill near the river's bank. The green-gray slate roofs were just barely discernible as they emerged from the morning fog that hugged the river valley. Ancient chestnut trees of gigantic proportions shaded the snug cottages. Narrow piers with small boats attached jutted into the river at irregular intervals. A small group of dark figures moved along a sandy path that cut between the meadow and freshly tilled fields, about half-way between the lancers and the village. Even more noticeable were the few riders to the front and rear of the group.

"Lances ready!" came a call from the front.

Lieutenant Singer's saber shot into the air and cut to the right and left, ordering the lancers to form a line. Two by two they lined up behind Sergeant Dergelstein. Only Lieutenant Singer was out in front, but she closed in more and more to the right flank. When all the horses were in place, they continued on in a fast trot. The lancers posted with ease, as if they were riding in a Tulamidian tournament. They took turns riding ahead and to the center of the line where their pennants with the red and blue lion-headed steed and Garethian griffin flew. Each was careful neither to fall behind nor to ride in front of the pennant. They waited eagerly for Lieutenant Singer to give the order to attack.

The lancers began to make out more details about the group of rebels. The small dark shapes had almost reached the last farm before the village. They were bunched tightly together and a few sword blades, spears, and scythes could be seen. Nine riders had formed a line between the rebels and the lancers.

"For Rondra!" Lieutenant Singer stabbed her saber into the sky.

"For Kosch!" replied the guardswomen, adding, "NO PRISONERS!"

Selissa rode close to the pennant, almost in the middle of the line. She would be among the first to meet the enemy. The small band of riders left their comrades and rode toward the guardswomen at a slow, reluctant pace. Far to the right and beyond Selissa's range rode a large man with a full helmet and plate armor on his arms and chest. Perhaps the count, she thought. At that moment, however, it didn't really matter to her. Her eyes went to her three opponents, two women in leather jerkins, one of whom gripped a shield and a saber in her hands, and a young man in a bright blue tunic with some type of hunting spear.

Three strides closer.

Fine, my blond boy. You're the one.

Closer yet.

The blond youth held his spear like a knight would a lance. He hid his upper body behind the horse's raised head.

Selissa took aim quickly and drove the tip of her lance through his throat. She let go of the weapon and drew her saber without looking back. A good one hundred paces in front of her, the rag-tag bunch of fighters was waiting.

"Phexchild, run!"

The faceless crowd resolved into individual forms. Selissa chose her target. Fiona had taught her never to ride blindly into a row infantry. "Pick one. Look into his eyes. Let him know he is the one. If you're lucky he'll run scared. Then you can get him from behind and can take advantage of a weak spot in the line while you are at it."

Selissa saw a woman with a flat helmet and sword. "Heyheyheyhey," she cried as she bent from the waist to jab the tip of her saber at the unlucky wench. The guardswoman leaned so far forward that she was almost eye-to-eye with Phexchild.

The woman raised her sword, looked anxiously to the left and right, then turned to run. Phexchild's broad chest crashed into her back, sending her flying.

Selissa sat up in the saddle and used all her strength to pull the reins to her stomach. Phexchild stopped as if she had run into a brick wall, dropping her hindquarters and sliding her belly across the ground. Selissa didn't give her mount, who was whinnying in protest, much time to get back on her feet. The guardswoman caught sight of her victim twenty strides behind her. She was lying on the ground and had just pulled in her right leg to stand up. By the time she was back on her feet, Selissa was on top of her, driving her saber into the woman's unprotected neck.

Through the chaos, Selissa quickly perceived that no guardswoman was in eminent danger. She exchanged a glance with Zelda who also was not engaged in battle. She pointed with her saber at two fleeing figures, Zelda nodded, and the two of them set off.

A few moments later they were galloping between the low fruit trees, a row of trees between them. At the end of the meadow they slowed down and saw the two rebels disappear near the farm house. An old man with a gray beard stood next to the corner of the building and furtively waved his hand. Selissa and Zelda approached him. "They ran into the barn," whispered the old man.

"How many are there?" Zelda asked in a low voice.

"Three or four."

"Let's go back for reinforcements," suggested Zelda, but

Selissa had already jumped out of the saddle and ran around the building. Zelda ran after her, cursing.

Selissa threw the large barn doors open. "Let there be light," she yelled.

Zelda and Selissa advanced side by side with sabers drawn. After a few steps they stopped. Zelda froze.

They could hear heavy breathing in the half-dark barn behind a broken-down wagon. Selissa nodded in the direction of the noise. They stormed past the wagon, one from the left and one from the right.

A woman was standing against the mud wall of the barn. She was of medium height and had narrow shoulders. She held a pitch fork across her chest that heaved with her breath. Hiding behind the woman were a boy and a girl, thirteen or fourteen years old, who looked at their assailants through dark, wide-open eyes. They stood still, frozen in fear.

The woman gripped the handle tightly. Her slender fingers were white. "Kill me, if you must," she said, "but spare my children."

Selissa looked at her, the pitch fork, and the children, as she tried to think of dead Tsaiane. A sob escaped her throat and she drove the point of her saber into the barn's dirt floor. "Get out of here, you despicable rebels," she said, "Go, go, didn't you hear me? Run!"

Chapter 3

COUNT ERLAN OF Wengenholm flew up the last flight of stairs and hurried across the old armory in the castle's south tower to a narrow window. The tower provided the best possible view of the village of Wengenholm, the bridge over the Ange River, and the winding road that led up to the castle. It was an ideal vantage point from which to spot approaching travelers. This was not the first time the young count had raced up the winding stairs to the tower this morning. During the past hour, he had come to this lookout several times to see if the guests he anxiously awaited were approaching. Finally, he caught sight of a group of four riders, two of whom rode on black horses. They were just crossing the village's main square, waving to passing peasants. No doubt, it was them.

Count Erlan turned and hurried to the great hall to give his servants some final instructions for greeting the guests. It was important that the visitors felt welcome and comfortable. He entertained the notion of having someone call Ismene, but then he decided to sprint to the sorceress's chamber himself. Without waiting for her to answer his knock he entered her room and announced, "They're here."

The woman of magic was reading a book. She slowly raised her head and ran her hands along her thin, gray and black braids that went down her back. With an amused laugh she welcomed the count, "By good Hesinde, you're awfully excited. You look like a groom on his wedding night—not exactly the mood that matches your intentions, though. Well, some people get just as excited about gold ducats, as others do about—"

"First of all, I am not concerned with the gold, as you know. And second, I am not in the mood for your mocking remarks," the count replied curtly. "Actually, I just came to make sure that you are ready."

Ismene raised her eyebrows. "Don't worry about my business, dear count. When the time comes, I will act. Just be careful that you don't get too excited and foul up your plan."

"Fine," Count Erlan calmly replied, "I just want to be sure we can rely on each other. I will call you when the time has come."

He closed the door behind him and paused to regain his composure before proceeding down to the hall to greet his guests.

Baron Lechdan of Jergenwell pulled a large white napkin from his sleeve and carefully dabbed at his lips and well-trimmed beard. "In truth, Your Honor, that is what I call roasted wild boar." The baron gestured at the long table with its white table cloth, silver bowls, candelabras, and the crispy, brown remains of the roast and piles of Kosch dumplings. "Please be so kind as to tell your cook that she is welcome at Albumin, should she ever want to leave Wengenholm."

"Thank you for the compliment," Count Erlan nodded. "I have heard that the food is exceptional at Albumin, better than at many a baron's table in the land. But even though your words were intended in jest, I can tell there is some seriousness in your request. Therefore, I am willing to let you have my good Vermilla. Since I do not place great value in the pleasures of the palate, Vermilla's art is wasted on me."

The baron raised his hand in protest. "No, Your Honor, that would be too great a gift. A count's cook in a baron's household. No, no, each man should till the field he inherits, as my father used to say. But my dear Reto is cast in a different mold. He is a true gourmet, always bringing recipes back from his travels. What do you think, Reto, should we accept the count's gracious offer?"

Reto forced a smile, "You know, dear Father, how much I enjoy your speaking of my eating habits, but I fear that you will bore our host if we continue."

The gray-haired baron grinned, "He doesn't see the humor in this. He is constantly afraid that I will embarrass him. How typical of someone his age." He turned to the count, "I am impressed by how much you know about the cuisine at Albumin. Your comments reveal the true interest of a feudal lord."

For a moment it was quiet at the table. The count and countess exchanged a glance, then Countess Ilma rose.

"Come children!" She said to Jallik and Nadyana, Count Erlan's younger half-brother and sister. "Let's retire to our chambers. The gentlemen want to discuss politics and that is of no interest to us. Jallik, please!" she warned her son as he began to protest. "We don't want to bore our guests with a lecture on good manners and obedience, do we?"

The boy said some unintelligible words and then took a quick bow before rushing to join his mother and sister as they walked with dignity from the hall.

"Your stepmother is a very attractive woman, Your Honor," said the baron.

Count Erlan nodded. "You may be right. One never has enough perspective to judge one's own relatives. I see a trusted member of the household in the countess, but not a woman, whose feminine attributes might inspire my imagination . . ." Erlan's voice trailed off. He turned the heavy crystal goblet in his hand before continuing. "To return to the topic you brought up earlier, Baron. Do you not think it important that a count is informed about what happens among his subjects? My father placed great value in being informed about the state of affairs in our baronial holdings. And I intend to carry on the tradition."

"I am sure that my father did not mean to criticize you for your principles, Your Honor," added Reto and, looking to his father, he continued, "We did not come together to criticize each other, but to bury that which divides our houses."

"Hear, hear, my boy! Let's drink to that," Count Erlan raised his glass and his guests returned the gesture.

After the goblets were set upon the table, the count turned to the elder Jergenwell. "That which divides us, as your son put it, has truly been a problem in the past. There must be a certain displeasure afoot, a displeasure large enough to have you go to Ferdok and ask to be released from your feudal duties. That is regretful, my dear Baron, and it pains me to know that these disputes began before I was born."

Lechdan of Jergenwell had nodded in agreement with the first part of the count's remarks, but as he continued, the baron found it difficult to maintain his composure.

"You . . . know . . . ?" he stuttered, "Your Honor has been . . ."

Count Erlan played with his blond curls and laughed. "Oh, yes, I know. I already told you that I like to keep up with all important happenings—as well as moods—in our lands. Imagine how much more important it is for me to maintain good contacts with the royal palace where decisions are made that affect all of us. I take my oath very seriously. That is how I feel about feudal duties as well. But, dear Baron, this insignificant affair should not cause you uneasy feelings. I am sympathetic to your concerns, and I am sure that your comments were not directed at me personally. Anyway, perhaps you've decided to refrain from your initial intent, especially since you have not yet spoken to our prince, as we both know."

Baron Lechdan remained quiet, but Reto responded, "Certainly, that is possible. We will discuss this matter when we are back in Albumin. The entire issue started because your father pressed too hard on my family during his final days. In the meantime, however, many things have changed. We could—"

"Could do what?" thundered the elder Jergenwell. "Do you realize what you are saying, Son? Didn't we agree to turn our backs on the Wengenholms? I am sure that when the prince returns he will take our side. No insult intended, Your Honor, but I have never favored your secret dealings."

Reto looked at the ceiling and sighed as he shook his head.

The count addressed the elder Jergenwell, "I am in favor of clarity, old friend. Your words are to my liking. You speak like a true man from Kosch. I wish all of our barons were as honest as you. I take it that in regards to the question of the ore mines your opinions are set in stone?"

Baron Lechdan forcefully nodded his gray head. "You can say that, Your Honor. In all honesty, I am of the opinion that there is no 'question' surrounding the ore mines. The ore in our mountains belongs to us. And that's the end of that."

"Valiantly spoken, Baron, and just as I expected from you." Count Erlan slowly ran his hand through his silken hair again. Then he threw back his head and laughed. "I just imagined how this evening would have progressed if my father were still alive. I am certain that some harsh words would have been exchanged and the Jergenwells would have left in a hurry before the Wengenholms could have them thrown out . . ."

Lechdan began to stand up, but his son placed a hand on his arm. "We do hope the times have changed, Your Honor."

Count Erlan nodded. "I just was about to say that things

used to happen very differently, but today . . . Today I am simply glad that I know better than to argue with my guests. Let us enjoy some more wine and change the topic as a sign of the new era?"

Reto nodded in clear agreement, while his father muttered, "As you wish. That's what we should do, and confidentially, I don't like to travel at night any more."

"Well, then," Count Erlan signaled to a servant. "With your permission, I would like to invite another guest to join us. She specifically asked to be called only when the discussion of politics was over, which, I assume, is now the case."

The Jergenwells nodded and the count whispered to his servant.

As soon as the servant rushed off, a conciliatory smile grew on Lechdan of Jergenwell's face. "There was always one good thing about the feud between our houses, my dear Count. We always fought face to face. Credit for that goes to your father. I always knew where I stood with him. Almadan, by contrast, with its passion for intrigue and its magicians and elves, is another story. There it would be unwise for a nobleman to ride unprotected through the lands of a neighbor with whom he is feuding—too much bad blood and Almadanian treachery, if you know what I mean. No, I much prefer the way we do things here in Kosch. I recently heard a story about a place called Cress—the Twelve know where it lies—where the baron—" but he was cut off, because the servant had just returned and proclaimed with a loud voice, "Lady Master Ismene Fanfemur!"

A woman dressed in a floor-length dress of burgundy

silk with delicate fur trim at its hem and cuffs entered the room. A high collar with black lace framed her face. An elegant sweep of her matching lace fan accompanied her entrance.

"How lovely, the Barons of Albumin. Please remain seated, my dear gentlemen." Ismene took her seat and smiled at her companions. By the torch light her braids sparkled as if they were made of silver. "You must be Reto," she said to the younger Jergenwell, then she turned to Count Erlan, "Did you not speak of three guests, Count?"

"You must be thinking of my youngest, Ulfing," added Baron Lechdan. "He is an adventurous one. He had not yet returned from the hunt when we were ready to depart, so we had to leave without him. After all, we did not want to be late. If we didn't know that Ulfing is often tardy, we might have had reason to worry. Instead, we left him a message where he can find us, if necessary. Let him stew back at Albumin. It will be a good lesson for him. His punishment has already been administered: He missed the chance to meet you, Your Honor, and your charming guest."

Ismene nodded, "In Perricum, my home town, one sometimes says in jest, 'as charming as a baron from Kosch' when criticizing a fool. I have now seen how distances can make prejudices out of manners. I will have to tell everyone back home about the true charm of the barons of Kosch. I thank you for the lesson, noblemen."

"I thank you for your friendly words," Baron Lechdan slightly bowed his head. "By the way, I have one more child, a daughter. She is the apple of my eye. If you would like to see a portrait of her, I have one right here."

"Father, I don't think . . ." interjected Reto, but Ismene did not let him finish his sentence. "Of course I am interested. Please show me, if it is no trouble."

The baron took a slim, black wooden box out of his pocket and opened it. Inside was the tiny painting of a child with black curls.

"Selissa is much older now, but she is still as pretty." He passed the miniature across the table to Ismene. "She is serving in the Royal Guard of Ferdok," he added in a proud voice.

"She's very pretty," said Ismene after she had carefully examined the picture. "She has the same beautiful curls as your son Reto."

"It is seen as an achievement for the entire family when a daughter is accepted into the Guard," explained Count Erlan. "My father always regretted that my mother never bore him a daughter, and my stepsister is still too young. I would have liked to please him by joining the Guard, but there was one problem, of course."

Baron Lechdan laughed heartily. "Yes, there is a problem, indeed. Quite so! You see honored Lady Master—"

Ismene raised her hand, "You are underestimating the reputation of the Ferdok Lancers, Baron, if you think that you have to explain the count's joke. Even in far away Perricum everyone knows that only women are accepted into the royal guard. Where this tradition comes from or why it is so, however, I do not know."

"It would be my pleasure to tell you," assured the old baron. "I know all about the Lancers. The Guard was founded many years ago, long before the Dark Years, they say, but no one can say for sure if women warriors were the only ones ever allowed to join. The Guard was first mentioned in the year 641 before the rule of his divine magnificence, Hal I—not a particularly glorious account, if I may say so. At that time the Guard was driven to the mountains by the ruling priests. Rondra be praised that they survived and were able to make up for their earlier mistakes in the year 393. I'm sure you've heard of the Orc Battle at Ferdok?" The Baron took Ismene's interested expression for an affirmative reply and continued, "That day, the guardswomen of Ferdok made history and brought eternal honor to their pennant. Considering that Countess Niam V of Ferdok and her mother were glowing worshippers of the goddess Rondra and believers in the mythos of Amazone, I would say that most of the Guard's warriors must have been women. Both are said to have spent their childhood years at Amazone castles where they were instructed in the Amazone art of warfare.

"In any case, Countess Niam made the Ferdok Guard what it is today and it remains much the same today as it was then. The Guard has one commander, who reports directly to the emperor. She traditionally has had the rank of a Lady Colonel. In earlier times the Guard was led by the Countess or Count of Ferdok. Thank Rondra that Emperor Reto changed all that. Imagine if Count Growin, son of Gorbosch, were to lead the proud lancers into battle. Any Orc worth his salt would start laughing so hard that he would wet his britches. No, the count may support the Guard financially, and he may call them 'his girls,' but they are truly an imperial guard, and it is better that way.

"Blasius of Eberstamm, Prince of Kosch, also has his own private bodyguards, but none of them are lancers. Instead, his Highness employs dwarves, in order to improve relations with the clans in the Kosch Mountains . . ." The baron stopped and looked at the rest of the guests. "I hope I'm not boring you with my account. Once I get to talking about the military history of our province and its Guards, I could go on all night."

"No, no, this is all very interesting," reassured Ismene. "Please continue. What rank is your daughter at the Guard?"

"Oh, she is only a guardswoman, but then she has only been a member for three years. The last time I was in Ferdok, I spoke to Commander Hirschingen-Berg and she said that Selissa had all the prerequisites for sergeant, and perhaps even lieutenant. I tell you, in ten or fifteen years, my little girl will make it big. If she can stop thinking of men, that is; but I'm sure she'll get over that nonsense. It's just a matter of time, even her colonel agrees." Oblivious of everybody around him, he turned to his son, "By the way, Aunt Govena has gotten damn old. I thought when I saw her that I should tell you how gray she has gotten. Everyone thinks she is on her way out."

"When I was very young, I once called Lady Colonel of Hirschingen-Berg 'Aunt Govena,'" explained Reto, slightly blushing. "Since then my father counts her among the family. He has known her for a long time. They fought together in the Orc Battle."

"Oh, you were there too, dear Baron?" asked Ismene.

Lechdan smiled in embarrassment. "Well, yes, but I didn't do much damage. I was almost sixty years old back then. But I did see the light cavalry attacks of the Guard.

And let me tell you, seldom have I seen such courage and daring. Almost half a squadron had been carried off, but nonetheless the lancers gained half a mile on the ogres, bah, what am I saying, more than half a mile!" The baron slid his chair back and forcefully put his hands on the table to stand up. As he stood up straight, he put his right hand behind his back and began to sing in a pleasant voice:

Ride, Rondra, ride on. Ride Boron, ride at our side!
The Ferdok Lancers are blessed protectors and our pride.
Pour the spirits, decant the wine, tap the Ferdoker ale.
Come and listen to the Lancer's tale.

"Father, please," Reto tugged on his father's jacket.

Baron Lechdan pushed his hand away. "Leave me alone. Do you think I don't know what I'm doing? I am sure that our hosts enjoyed this beautiful song."

"How true, dear Baron," confirmed Count Erlan, and Ismene added, "I beg you, please continue. You have such a beautiful voice."

Baron Lechdan continued to sing all sixteen verses of the song of the Ferdok Lancers. Not once did he stumble over the lyrics. When he was finished, the count and the sorceress smiled and cheered. But the baron raised his hands in protest and took his seat, "I have been the focus of attention long enough," he said. "Your turn, noble Lady Master. Please tell us a bit about Perricum and your doings there."

Her silver braids whipped like snakes when she shook her head. "No, that is a topic that would make us all yawn.

My most recent interests are very theoretical and dry, and not particularly suitable for enjoyable conversation. But as far as the city of Perricum is concerned, I am sorry to say that I do not miss it too much. It was by bad fortune that I ended up there at all. One sailor's ball after another can certainly wear your nerves thin. Recently, we have been graced with a series of new celebrations in which the people of Perricum commend themselves for their lack of courage to join Count Answin of Ravenmund in his futile rebellion and so by coincidence they ended up on the side of the victor, after all."

"How bitter, dear Ismene," said Count Erlan. "One would almost believe that you are upset with your countrymen that they did not side with the usurper. Watch your tongue! The rebels are not viewed kindly here in Kosch, isn't that true, honored Baron?"

"That is indeed the case," replied the elder Jergenwell. "I wouldn't believe for a blink of the eye that the delightful Lady Ismene would side with those villains. No, no, she was just criticizing the fickleness of the city folk, and I couldn't agree with her more. As Emperor Reto used to say, 'The Empire's pulse beats strongest in the country.'" He raised his glass and the others followed.

Then he turned to Ismene, "You very cleverly answered only one part of my question. Perhaps we shall later have the opportunity to speak of your recent interests. Be assured that you will have my undivided attention. But at least tell us what brought you to Wengenholm."

Ismene peered over her fan at the baron. "To answer that question, I would have to tell you all about my scholarly pursuits, and that is what I wanted to avoid. But, if you insist. I am particularly interested in ecstasy and other extreme conditions of the human soul. Most recently I have examined the differences between the state of mind in humans, animals, and other creatures which fit neither category and which are known to the layman as hybrids. Humans are generally considered to have a soul, a pattern of thinking that is reinforced by the Praios clergy. The soul is believed to give humans a certain divine quality. Animals, on the other hand, are said not to have this trait. But what about the hybrids? Recall that most accounts say that the Twelve have chosen to appear as animals when they have shown themselves on Ethra. Does that mean that a person in the form of an animal is more godlike than a nonhybird? Or is there something in the souls and astral patterns of these creatures that limits the expansion of their souls? As you can see, I am exploring a branch of science that has been hereto ignored."

Ismene folded her fan and placed it on the table. "These hybrid creatures are incredibly rare, as you can imagine. Personally, I have only been able to attain a limited number of so-called Borbarad Mosquitoes. Research on this species, however, does not yield useful results. And although I could conclusively prove that these mosquitoes are indeed a human-animal hybrid—which in itself is a breakthrough—I must admit that my findings are still controversial among my conservative peers. For my part, I am convinced that my theory is rock solid. Let the honorable Ikanio rant and rave as much as he wants in his writings."

Suddenly, the sorceress underwent a strange transformation. Her friendly smile disappeared, her eyes filled with anger, and her small fists bent the fan almost to the point of breaking as she continued with a dramatic toss of the head. "Calling these mosquitoes animal-demon hybrids just because we have no past record of fertility in hybrids is, in my opinion, Selmitian drivel. I ask you, what do we know about the fertility of the demonic?"

Baron Jergenwell opened his mouth as he sought an answer, but Ismene did not give him the opportunity to reply.

"Nothing, if we are honest!" She banged her fan against the table. "How can a scientist who proposes such a ludicrous theory call my theories 'unreliable suppositions'?"

"That is terribly rude indeed," assured the baron.

Ismene nodded to him, lost in her thoughts. "There is no other way to describe this behavior. The evidence is overwhelming. The deformations of the mandibles and the eating habits of the Borbarad Mosquitoes do not allow for any other conclusion—the part of the creatures which is not animal, is human. And that is final." Ismene cast an inquisitive look around the table. "It seems that I got off track. It is an absolute outrage, you know. Let's see . . . oh . . . now I remember where I was. Due to the constant reproduction and the related generational mutations, the original human aspect of the Borbarad Mosquito hybrid is now so small that it is almost impossible to trace. In addition, the original animal creation part in these creatures is of such a simple type that the combination of the two—the lowest animal and the smallest human components—makes them practically unsuitable for my research into the measurement and inquiry of the soul and its extreme conditions. And now," Ismene's familiar smile returned, "I will finally answer your question of what brought me to Castle Wengenholm, my dear Baron. Because of the lack of live specimens, I rely on literature for a large part of my research. The eminent authority on the subject of hybrid creations is a certain Master Zurbaran. In an amateurish transcription of one of his late works I found a reference that the Master spent time in Wengenholm while he was writing his manuscript. Call it destiny at work, but I was an old friend of the late Count Hakan of Wengenholm. So the choice was obvious. I took the next express coach here. I had to know if the original manuscripts were in the count's library. So, now you know why I am here at Castle Wengenholm."

"And did you find what you were looking for, Lady Master?" asked Reto.

Ismene shrugged her shoulders. "So far the search has not yielded much information, I must admit. But the library is very large and yesterday I found several folios that look like they could have been written in the hand of the Master. I remain optimistic."

Baron Lechdan shook his head in dismay, "I must say you had me fooled. When I first saw you enter the hall I thought to myself, that is certainly a beautiful, wealthy woman from Gareth who is traveling the world to pass the time. And now, I hear that you are a very serious and ambitious scientist. My greatest respect. I have always been very impressed by scientists, but I never knew that they could be so lovely."

Ismene lowered her head. "You are a very gallant man, dear Baron."

The elder Jergenwell reached across the table and touched the magicienne's hand. "How would you like to visit us at Albumin? There are lots of old papers in our library that no one has looked at in years. You could research to your heart's content with the best accommodations provided. None of our guests have ever complained about a stay at Albumin. Well, what do you think?"

Ismene stroked the baron's hand. "Your offer is most tempting. I will certainly consider it. I can imagine that I would feel quite at home at Albumin." She cast her eyes downward and smiled, and a grin crossed Count Erlan's lips.

"You will, most honored one, you will." The elder Jergenwell stood up with a groan. "We will have a wonderful time together, I am sure. But please excuse me for a moment, and you as well, Your Honor. I have to go check on the horses, as the saying goes."

As the baron left the hall, Ismene and Count Erlan exchanged a glance. The sorceress slid over to an empty chair so that she sat directly across the table from young Jergenwell. "Dear Reto," she said, "you have to tell me a bit about yourself. You have hardly spoken a word all evening."

An uneasy smile came to Reto's lips. He shrugged and said, "Oh, there is not much to tell, but I do thank you for asking. Oh yes, I do recall an anecdote that my brother Ulfing told me while we were out riding last week. We had left early in the morning and had not paid much attention to where we were going. Actually, we hadn't paid any attention at all to our whereabouts. In any case, suddenly it dawned on us that we were completely lost. Right there in the middle of our own forest! It was indeed an embarrassing situation . . ."

Ismene leaned towards him. As if spellbound she watched the young baron's lips. Then she turned her attention to his eyes. Twisting her eyebrows, she concentrated and then softly mumbled a few set phrases without emphasis.

Reto cut himself off in mid-sentence and raised his hand to his forehead. Then he stood up quickly and shook his head. He took a step back. "What was that?" he asked in a daze. "What are you doing? Say, I do believe that you are using magic on me. Father, Father, they are—"

Before he could finish his warning, Count Erlan, who had stealthily approached Reto from behind, landed a solid blow to the young baron's head with an earthenware pitcher. Reto crumbled to the ground as if he had been hit by lightening. "Move, move! Why are you standing there?" Erlan yelled at his servant who was staring at the events with an open mouth. "Quick, take him up to the tower. Bind and gag him and remember the seven-horned bears will get you if you don't tie the boy up right." He turned to Ismene. "What is the problem? You are ruining everything. I thought I could count on you. If you keep—"

Ismene protested, "Now don't get worked up over nothing. It will work. The old man is much more susceptible to—"

"Quiet, here he comes," hissed Count Erlan.

The servants dragged Reto over the tile floor and up a few wide steps. Then they disappeared through a small door at the head of the hall. They had just closed the door behind themselves as the old baron entered the hall.

"Oh, there you are again, dear Baron," greeted Count

Erlan. "You must have just passed your son. He wanted to . . . um . . . get something from his luggage to show Lady Master Ismene. I sent along a servant to escort him to your chamber. He should be back shortly."

"Something from his luggage?" Baron Lechdan furrowed his brow. "What would that be? I don't think the boy brought anything special . . ."

"I think it is so amusing," said Ismene, after the baron had sat down, "that you still call Sir Reto a boy. Your son must be at least thirty."

Baron Lechdan smiled. "Well, old habits die hard. And he is still very boyish. Now and then he blushes right in the middle of a conversation. Haven't you noticed?"

Ismene had moved so that she was now sitting directly across from the elder Jergenwell. She motioned to a servant who was approaching to let her refill the baron's glass. "Drink, dear Baron, and tell me a little about Castle Albumin. I find your home most interesting."

He made himself comfortable and began his story. "Well, in order for you to know what makes Albumin such a special place, I should start at the very beginning." Then he related the details of the Tax Treaty of the fourth year of Ugdalf, which was recorded in the Emperor's archives and contained the first mention of the "stout Albumin, a defensive, well-constructed estate" as a fortress against the "Goblin forces." Then he continued and discussed the blueprints by Master Antogosch, son of Armark, which were drawn up two hundred years later and which were the foundation for the castle today and how it was "designed with all sorts of defenses against the catapult, which was, at that time, responsible for the demise of many fortresses."

Ismene looked deep into his eyes and, as if in a trance, recited a sentence in an odd tongue.

Baron Lechdan hesitated and looked questioningly at the sorceress.

Ismene stroked his hand gently, "Are you feeling well, dear Baron?"

The elder Jergenwell grew very serious. In a solemn tone he continued, "Do you know that you are very, very important to me, dear Lady? I do not know you well, yet I treasure you more than a blood relative. I have never experienced such feelings, I swear on the Twelve."

Ismene exchanged a glance with the count and then turned to the baron. "Oh, I am so happy to have made a friend in you."

"The best of friends."

"Well, it is as you say. So please do me a favor. Please imitate the crow of a cock. I like that sound very much."

The baron looked confused. "A cock's crow? Should I really?"

"Oh, please."

The old Jergenwell stood up with difficulty, leaned his head back and, cupping his hand in front of his mouth, let out a loud crow. Then he looked inquisitively at Ismene. "Did you like it? I have never done that before."

"Yes, that was very good. And now I have another favor to ask. Could you tell me, to the crown, how much silver is in your coffers at Albumin?"

The baron glanced at the count.

"Please, Baron!"

Jergenwell looked at Count Erlan again, wrinkled his brow and mumbled, "12,890 gold ducats and about 200 silver crowns, I believe. Why do you want to know?"

"Twelve thousand!" the count stared at the baron with wide eyes. "That is more than—"

Ismene warned him with her hand and nodded to the count. "Everything is going fine, there will not be any problems. We just have no time to waste. We should get started right away."

Count Erlan took a few sheets of parchment out of the small chest at one end of the table. Some of them had writing on them, others were blank. He also produced a quill and several bottles of ink. He passed Ismene a document and she placed it on the table in front of the baron. After she dipped the quill in ink, she passed the writing instrument to the elder Jergenwell. "If you would please sign here, dear Baron?"

Baron Lechdan skimmed the document. "But that is an evil scheme. Rebel rubbish! Why?"

Ismene put her hand on his shoulder. "Because I want you to. It is all part of a joke. Now sign."

Shaking his head the baron scrawled his name beneath the text.

"Once more. Please copy this text as if it were a letter you were writing."

The baron studied the note that Ismene had written. "I would never write such a thing. That is a call for conspiracy. That is the worst crime a house of Gareth can commit."

"A joke, a joke. Now start writing if you don't want to anger me."

With deep concentration the elder Jergenwell copied

the text word by word onto the blank parchment.

"And now, the date: 5th day of Rahja, in this year 19 in the rule of his divine magnificence, Emperor Hal I of Gareth."

"That is more than two years ago."

"What difference does that make? Write what I tell you to write!"

Baron Lechdan dated the letter as she wished and signed it. Then he followed Ismene's wishes and wrote several more documents. As soon as each page was finished, Count Erlan grabbed it and put sand on it and dried each carefully. Finally, he put them back into the chest.

"That was very good, dear Baron," said Ismene finally. "Now be so good as to follow me up to the tower room. I want to show you something there."

"Well, you have certainly piqued my curiosity," the baron smiled, pleased by the thought of a surprise. "But you will have to have patience with me. My old legs don't like stairs as much as they used to. Where is that boy? He's always been a bit of a dreamer. I bet he lost his way."

Ismene took the baron by the arm as Count Erlan led the way. "Come along now. We will find your son. I want to see you reunited."

Chapter 4

ALGUNDA SWEPT STRAW, horse dung, and spilled oats down the middle of the large stable with powerful strokes of her birch broom. As she worked, her eyes traveled between the brick floor and the long row of low stall doors above which the strong, graceful curves of horses' flanks of every conceivable color could be seen. Occasionally, her eyes drifted up the ochre columns to the broad white arches of the vaulted ceiling that sheltered the endless line of stalls. The sound of her sweeping was nearly drowned out by the horses' snorting, stomping, and munching.

Algunda wiped her hand across her skirt and pushed a thick brown strand of hair back into place under her scarf. "You horses live like royalty. Just look at your stable. It's much nicer than our cottage!" she said to a black gelding, who had turned its head and attentively watched the maid's movements with pricked ears. Algunda looked past the horse through one of the many arched windows, and her thoughts drifted to her home and family.

She recalled the harsh northern winds that would force the smoke back down the chimney each time her family lit a fire, filling the small, dark room with biting clouds of smoke. Just the thought of it made her eyes burn. Even during the day, it was much darker in their cottage than it was in the stables of the Royal Guard of Ferdok. One small window covered with stretched hide let in a shaft of light. There was a small, wobbly table under the window where her mother did needlework. And right next to the table was the cradle with her newborn son, Erborn.

"I miss him so! Good Mother Peraine, how I miss him," she whispered to herself with tears in her eyes, recalling the injustices of peasant life. "He's still so tiny. What does the Uhlengorm family have that we don't have? They're starving to death, and their house is even smaller than ours; but since they call themselves 'free peasants,' the Royal Marshal does not meddle with them. But he harasses us whenever he wants. Even though he has father and brother plow the royal fields for him, he sent me back to the stable as soon as little Erborn was born."

Blinded by tears, she looked down at the broom as it brushed over the same spot again and again, as if guided by an invisible hand. "Ela Uhlengorm takes her little Haldana with her into the fields in a basket," she continued to herself. "No one stops her. And at night she has her fat and stupid Bosper to keep her warm in bed. Who do I have to keep me warm at night? The Marshall ran off my Jangu, because he spoke rebelliously. Rebelliously, my eye. He only spoke the truth. And now that he's gone, my bed is cold and little Erborn has to grow up without a father. But that doesn't concern the important lords and ladies. I wonder what will happen to me? To us all? Why all this toil? What did we do to make the gods hate us? Don't we take everything we can spare to the Temple?"

As Algunda closed her brown eyes she returned to the familiar scene of the little window and the dark cradle in front of it, and the tiny hand stretching toward the light, its fingers reaching for the dust hanging in the air and the golden rays of sunlight. Algunda ached so much she could barely breathe. She stomped her foot angrily on the floor and began to sing a song that Jangu had taught her. Jangu always smiled when he sang the forbidden song, but Algunda couldn't help but cry.

Close your eyes, little baby, fall asleep!
When the morn' comes it's yours to keep.
All the pretty little colts and fillies,
Brown and white, roan and chestnut,
All the pretty little colts and fillies.

Dream of silver, gold, and precious stone,
The sun smiles and they are all yours to own.
All the pretty little colts and fillies,
Gray and palomino, foal and stallion,
All the pretty little colts and fillies.

The sun doesn't shine on the rulers alone,
Some day you too will be free to roam.
You and all your pretty little colts and fillies
Better fed than Cella, lovelier than Hal,
All the pretty little colts and fillies.

Soon the sun will smile on peasant and knave . . .

"What is that awful noise?" yelled a shrill voice behind Algunda. The stable maid turned around. A blonde guardswoman in full regalia stood before her. While reprimanding her, the guardswoman reached for a halter that hung next to a stall door. Algunda shrank slowly back. "But I didn't even . . . ," she stuttered.

"Oh yes you did!" hissed the voice. The heavy halter whipped through the air faster than Algunda could raise her broom in defense. The leather straps and iron buckles struck her across the shoulders and forehead, knocking her to the ground. In desperation she tried to scoot away on her buttocks, but the guardswoman caught her in two strides. A small smile curled her lips as she reached for a long riding whip hanging on a nail.

"Please, don't!" sobbed Algunda, as she threw her arms over her face.

A soft hiss accompanied the whip's lash, followed by a loud slap. Algunda's thin blouse split open across her back and a thin red line opened on her pale skin.

"I'll teach you to sing, you annoying bitch!"

Algunda's whimpering stopped for a moment as the whip cut into her back again.

"When I'm finished with you, you will wish you had never been born. By Praios and Rondra, you'd better believe it!"

The whip hissed through the air again. Algunda curled into a ball and tensed all her muscles, but the blow never came. Instead she heard a malicious laugh. "I've waited for this a long time, you slut. You'll never sing your annoying rebel songs again, and you'll never get another chance to tell the sergeant that I ripped my horse's belly with my spurs."

The next lash struck without warning. Algunda screamed and tried to press her head against the boots of her tormentor. An angry kick pushed her away.

"Mercy!" she cried. "Please have pity!" She crawled toward the guardswoman's boot again. Another fiery lash on her back drove the air from her lungs. "You're killing me," she mumbled with anger in her weak voice.

"So what? Who would miss you anyway?"

Algunda tried to crawl away, but all her strength was gone. She sighed like a wounded animal and waited for the next blow. Then she heard an odd noise behind her: scraping and rustling, followed by heavy gasping. She cautiously turned her head.

The blonde guardswoman had dropped the whip. She cowered on the floor, forced to her knees by a black-haired woman, who had her in a wrist lock. "Zelda, you're behaving like a pig!" bellowed the black-haired woman. "I wouldn't be at all opposed to the idea of tanning your hide." She looked to the side where the whip lay on the floor next to an open stall door. Just then a loud whinny was repeated by numerous horses as if there were an echo under the stable's high ceilings.

The blonde lancer exploited the moment of confusion to free herself with a powerful thrust. Her saber flew from the sheath and came around to point at the face of her opponent. "Go ahead and try it, Corporal Selissa of Jergenwell. I'm ready!"

Selissa raised her left hand in a casual gesture of protest. "No, Zelda, I don't think so. You are not worth the trouble, or the time it would take to clean my saber." She turned as if to leave and then pivoted on her left heel, driving her fist into the blonde woman's face.

Zelda's shoulder mail clattered noisily as she crashed to the brick floor. Spooked by the noise, the horses stomped their hoofs and tossed their heads, their whinnies resounding through the long hall. Then it grew quiet. Selissa placed her foot firmly on top of Zelda's saber and looked down at her. "Be good, you ogress! And don't even think of laying a hand on her again."

Zelda wiped the blood from her lips with the back of her hand "A fine corporal you are. Goddess Rondra's champion for the poor and weak." Her lips curled into a grimace as if to suppress a feeling of disgust. "You'll have to reckon with me again."

Selissa shrugged. "There are a thousand other things I could reckon with if I wanted to ruin my day, and nine hundred and ninety-nine would be more worthwhile than you." She kicked Zelda's saber across the brick floor, then strode away down the long row of stalls.

"There was not just one original message sent. There was also a duplicate," insisted the man from Gareth to the chief scribe of the Royal Guard of Ferdok. Trying to remain patient he adjusted the silver glasses that framed his intense blue eyes, which, though he appeared to be a busy and serious man, sparkled with a mischievous glint. "Both times they were dispatched by the couriers of the Imperial Army, if that means anything to you, my dear. The documents were duplicates sent from the Office for Military Affairs. Their contents stated that I, Secretary Frenulfius Grottencloth, am traveling to Efferd, Travia, and Boron on assignment from the Office to introduce the Imperial and Royal Troops to my new apparatus that will significantly improve their efficacy and mobility on the battle field. The communiqué also stated that, baring any complications in his travel plans, Secretary Grottencloth would arrive in Ferdok on Windsday in the third week of Travia and that he would be at the Guard's barracks on the tenth hour, in time for the regular lesson on strategy and strategic thinking during which he would give a lecture-demonstration of his technological marvel. This way, he would not interfere with the guardswomen's valuable riding and fighting exercises. Well, in fifteen minutes it will be ten o'clock. I am here as announced, and must note much to my dismay that the scriptorium has made no preparations."

The first scribe had barely been able to follow the secretary's remarks, but she determined that this strange man with his black, outdated frock-coat, dull, black curly wig, and wire spectacles must indeed be a well-traveled and highly educated scholar, someone who best not be turned away. She decided to call in the sergeant and have her decide what to do about this disheveled character whose intense sapphire eyes did not at all match his darker Tulamidian skin and jet-black beard.

Sergeant Fiona Dergelstein also had difficulties following the strange scientist's explanations, but when he was done she nodded energetically and took a careful look into the red wooden box where the secretary's shiny, golden device was cradled on a blue velvet pillow.

"Well then," she concluded in a firm voice. "Everything seems to be in order. Since the commander and lieutenant are usually at the market at this hour, I will have to take you under my wing. It would be best if you followed me to the instruction room immediately. The bells have already struck ten."

Grottencloth gestured toward the wooden box and shrugged with a smile. "Could you perhaps . . . ? The apparatus is fairly heavy and my doctor has warned me more than once not to submit my back to any extra strain."

Fiona closed the wooden lid and clamped the box under her arm. Grottencloth groaned and pranced around the sergeant waving his hands. "Please be careful! If you could please hold the box horizontally . . . um, straight?"

On their way to the guardswomen's lecture hall, Fiona pointed out the various buildings around the square and explained their functions. "The tall building without windows to your left is the straw and hay barn. Do you have any idea how many cartloads of hay we have delivered here every year so that the horses make it through the winter?" Grottencloth wrinkled his forehead as he contemplated the answer and then decided to treat the question as a rhetorical one. He pointed out the roof of the horse stable and indicated that he found its form most unusual. "You have a well-trained eye," praised Sergeant Dergelstein. "Princess Lorinai had a Tulamidian stable copied. She had seen one on a trip to Fasar. You know how much those desert dwellers spoil their horses. Our stable looks like a palace, doesn't it? But it is terribly impractical because there is no room to store hay above the stalls. But the horses do seem to like the high ceilings. We have not had any trouble with the animals balking at the stalls. The magnificent stable in Fasar allegedly burned down years ago, but ours still stands proud. We know how to build here in Kosch."

The pair reached an impressive whitewashed building with a bright red tile roof. Three doors and a long row of windows stretched toward a courtyard. "With your leave, I will go ahead," said the sergeant as she entered. Grottencloth had difficulty keeping pace with her up the wide, well-lit staircase and down a long hall with mirror-like stone floors to the instruction room where about three dozen guardswomen were waiting at their desks, chatting among themselves. The women quickly rose to their feet as Sergeant Dergelstein and her companion entered the room.

"Morning lancers," replied the sergeant to the guardswomen's greeting. She placed the wooden box on the table and introduced Grottencloth, who was staring shyly at his shoes. "Today we have a guest speaker from faraway Gareth, Secretary Grottencloth." An icy look accompanied her introduction. "He will show you a new, most promising device. I ask for silence and your complete attention. At ease!" Fiona waited for the lancers to take their seats and then extended her hand in a gesture of introduction, "Secretary Grottencloth."

The secretary took a deep bow, looked around the room and began his lecture. "Honored guardswomen, what you see in front of me is a pioneering piece of equipment in many ways. I've called it the Omnidetector. It is—"

Grottencloth stopped and looked at Sergeant Dergelstein with a hint of confusion. "Honored Sergeant, may I have a word with you?"

"Well, what is it, my good man?"

"In the message that announced my arrival, which seems

to have never arrived, it also stated that the guardswomen should only wear cloth doublets, but no helmets, armor, or weapons, because metal can affect the operation of the Omnidetector."

The sergeant looked at her guardswomen in their shiny coats of mail, and the tall helmets placed on their knees. "Hm," she mused, then turned to explain to Grottencloth, "We always hold class in full dress because afterwards we go straight to prayer in the Temple of Rondra. That spares us a change of uniform." Then she turned back to the class. "Well, lancers, you heard the man: Take off your cuirasses and weapon belts and take them, together with your helmets, to the hall."

The sergeant's words set the guardswomen in motion and for a short period the classroom was filled with confusion as several guardswomen tried to squeeze themselves through the door at the same time with their bulky helmets and armor. After the guardswomen had returned to their desks, Grottencloth smiled a friendly grin, folded his hands behind his back, tapped his toes, and looked at his students. Then he took off his glasses and polished them with his head bowed deeply forward.

Sergeant Dergelstein also cast her eyes over the guardswomen. A playful smile came to her face. "Guardswoman Kufmann, Guardswoman Haslinger, Guardswoman Orneck, Corporal Jergenwell: How often have you been told that a lancer wears a doublet underneath a cuirass even if the armor is only going to be worn for a short time and not for battle? Well, Guardswoman Haslinger, how often? I can't hear you!"

"Very often, Sergeant, ma'am!"

"Stand up when you are spoken to!"

The red-haired guardswoman with very pale and freckled skin and blue eyes jumped up and crossed her arms in front of her ample bosom.

"It's a bit cool, isn't it?" Sergeant Dergelstein was looking for an affirmative answer.

"Yes ma'am, fairly cool."

Although the Sergeant's face was very serious, it took quite a while for the laughter to quiet down.

"Kufmann, Haslinger, Orneck, Jergenwell, at attention!"

The other three women quickly rose from their stools. All four stood with their hands at their sides and their chins forward.

Grottencloth had put his glasses back on. He looked out the window and then at the floor, but he couldn't help but steal a glance at the guardswomen now and again.

Sergeant Dergelstein crossed the area in front of the desks with slow paces. "Cool, perhaps," she said, "but not so cold that you couldn't follow orders, no?"

"No, Sergeant!" resounded four times.

"All right, take your seats again!" The sergeant looked at Grottencloth. It took him a moment to notice she was looking at him. "I trust you will not be distracted by their appearance, my good man."

"Um, I beg your pardon? No, um, yes. With your permission I think it would be best if the women . . . um . . . guardswomen would cover themselves. Yes, with your permission, it seems appropriate to me."

"Well, fine. Go get something to wear. Guardswoman Rotbach, count to one hundred. Anyone who isn't back by then will be assigned one week of mucking out stables."

As all four guardswomen rushed back to the instruction room gasping for air, Grottencloth lifted his device from its case, and set it up on the table. The Omnidetector was cylindrical and about ten fingers tall with a diameter of twenty fingers. It seemed to be made of polished brass or perhaps even a light-colored gold. A few thin, shiny gold wires coiled around the exterior. There were all sorts of gears and knobs attached to the wires which appeared to be used for calibrating the instrument. On top there perched a domed glass about four fingers in diameter with a rotating needle underneath.

Grottencloth observed the motions of the needle with concentration and then began to explain the function of the Omnidetector. "We are all familiar with the shortcomings of the conventional South Detector. During certain constellations of the heavens it is so inaccurate that every navigator aware of his responsibilities, and every responsible sergeant, prefers to rely on the stars or the Praiosdisc, rather than place his or her trust in that particular instrument. And when it's cloudy, you may as well run to the next enemy post and ask for directions." The class responded with polite laughter. "With the Omnidetector, however, loss of orientation is a thing of the past!"

The guardswomen looked on in rapt attention as Grottencloth explained in detail how to use the Omnidetector to line up one's point of origin with one's bearing. He pointed out the small openings on the edge of the cylinder's lid where a bead could be placed to indicate the direction of the destination. Even the intermediary targets that did not line up with one's point of origin and one's final destination could be marked and located easily in the field. The more detailed Grottencloth's explanations became, the more hands shot up among his increasingly skeptical audience. He asked the guardswomen to be content and wait for the second part of his presentation, during which he would invite individual guardswomen to test for themselves the fantastic possibilities the Omnidetector offered. In the meantime, he awed his listeners with calculations of travel times, precise within fifteen minutes to all destinations, and how long it would take to traverse the same distance at various paces. He explained that these times could be read on the small, built-in scale that even a child could learn to use in minutes.

Then Grottencloth called on a chubby-cheeked blonde junior guardswoman and asked her to set the indicator in the direction of the Praios Temple. She could easily see its tall roof through the window. With a gasp of amazement the lancer saw how the delicate pointer in the center circle of the indicator as well as the bead on the rotating bezel always swung back to point at the temple, no matter how she turned the instrument. Grottencloth called on another guardswoman and removed the bead. Then he took a bearing on the Temple of Rondra, which lay significantly to the west of the Temple of Praios and replaced the bead at the new mark.

Again, the instrument performed its uncanny work.

A murmur went through the ranks. The secretary lovingly patted the Omnidetector. "Impressive, isn't it, honored guardswomen? But there's more! I treasure this golden box, but it still has two disadvantages. It is heavy and it is not very convenient to use on horseback. The

Office for Military Affairs, of course, lost a lot of sleep over this. We tested and researched, not for days, not for weeks, but for years, and came up with the following solution to our problem." Noticeable excitement had taken hold of the secretary as he fumbled with jittery fingers in the pockets of his frock-coat and finally produced a golden disk that was barely a finger thick and no larger than the palm of his hand. "The field Omnidetector!" Without looking where he pointed, he asked a second guardswoman to join him down front.

Selissa of Jergenwell stood up. "Do you mean me?" The secretary looked in her direction and distractedly answered. "Oh, yes, please join me."

When Selissa reached his side he carefully placed the golden disk in her hand and gave her instructions on how to place the smaller markings on the field model. Selissa did as she was told but the small marked bezel did not move while the pointer wildly bounced back and forth.

Grottencloth wrinkled his brow and tapped his finger on the domed lens over the pointer. "By the fundamental goodness of Master Zampanilo, I don't understand what is going on. Give me the instrument again, please."

Selissa handed him the disk. The instrument functioned perfectly for the secretary. Grottencloth shook his head in dismay. "Inconceivable, that simply does not make sense." Suddenly he reached for Selissa's right hand, and she flinched involuntarily. "That's the reason! Your ring! As lovely as it is, please take it off. I told you there can be no metal near the Omnidetector, otherwise it won't work properly."

Selissa turned the ring on her finger and pulled on it

as hard as she could. "I fear you will have to call on an-other volunteer, dear sir. I cannot take this ring off. I've been wearing it for years." She paused. "Why does my ring affect the Omnidetector, anyway? Since its housing is made of gold, I would assume that the Omnidetector should interfere with itself."

"What?" Grottencloth was obviously caught off guard by the guardswoman's observant remark. "Oh, I see what you mean. The Omnidetector is made of the most precious herald gold. It is the only metal from which the instrument can be made." He fished around in his pocket and pulled out a small wooden container. "And as far as your ring is concerned, I have just the answer right here. Let me dust your finger with this powder and you will see that it will come off as if you had just put it on for the first time." The secretary took a pinch of the white powder and sprinkled it carefully onto Selissa's index finger. "Now try it again!"

The guardswoman grasped the ring with her left hand and with one good pull she held the ring in her hand.

This time the Omnidetector worked perfectly for Selis-sa. Grottencloth praised the careful way Selissa used the instrument. "I know my precious invention is in good hands with you," he jested. "That is why I think that you should be the one to conduct the next experiment. Please set the sight to the dome of the Temple of Rondra. Yes, that's it. Now go outside and cross over behind the sta-ble. There is an ancient elm tree there, as you know. With your back to the elm, determine the direction of the Tem-ple of Rondra, which you cannot see from your vantage point behind the stable. Then go in the direction of the

Temple of Rondra until you are at the stable wall. On the ground you will find a small present hidden under a leaf. Please bring it back with you. Now go."

Selissa turned to Sergeant Dergelstein. "Corporal Jergenwell requests permission to be dismissed for . . . umm . . ."

"Omnidetector survey?" Grottencloth suggested.

"Omnidetector survey!"

The sergeant nodded.

Looking at the disk in concentration, Selissa left the room.

Grottencloth crossed his arms behind his back and tapped his toes again. "Now let me tell you about everything else the Omnidetector can do for you—" He suddenly stopped and looked anxiously at the door. "Holy Rasparatox! I totally forgot to give the guardswoman the most important piece of information!"

Sergeant Dergelstein nodded to the junior guardswoman. "You there, go catch up with Jergenwell and bring her back!"

But the secretary had already darted to the door with surprising agility. "No, no," he protested. "I'll take care of it myself. It would ruin the entire experiment if Selissa had to turn back half way. I'll go catch up with her myself." The door closed behind him.

"Strange," determined Sergeant Dergelstein after a few moments. "The secretary used her first name. Who would have thought that they knew each other, and that they were on a first name basis? Would Jergenwell know a Secretary at the Office of Military Affairs and never have mentioned it? Where is Secretary Grottencloth? Maybe someone should check . . ."

"Ma'am?" asked a guardswoman, who sat in the second row.

"Lancer?"

"The instrument on the table, the large Omnidetector, I think . . ."

"What do you want to say? Spit it out!"

"I can't help but think that it looks like an old hat box."

"What?" Sergeant Dergelstein looked over to the table and recoiled. "By the Twelve, I think you're right! What in the world happened? It must have transformed itself."

The guardswomen, who could not be kept in their seats, crowded around the table. "Yep, it's an old hat box, all right. I can't believe it!" they confirmed among themselves. "Fraud!"—"Magic!"—"Sleight of hand!" they exclaimed furiously. It took a while until the first woman dared to touch the box and take off its lid. Inside they found a few cobblestones and old horseshoes. "That's why the damn thing was so heavy!" sighed the sergeant.

Just at that moment the door flew open and Guardswoman Jergenwell burst in. Out of breath and her curls in disarray, she glanced at the corner of the table, where she had put her ring, but it was gone. "What a despicable villain!" she cursed. The field Omnidetector fell from Selissa's hand and shattered on the wooden floor. If anyone had bothered to go to the trouble of reassembling the transformed shards they would have recreated a cheap, earthenware pill box with the words "I won" etched on the bottom.

Chapter 5

SUDDENLY, THE FEATHER- and bone-covered bodies of the two colorfully painted Moha tribespeople turned pale, just like the bushes, blossoms, and leaves of their jungle environment that had grown noticeably lighter in color, too. Even the well-fed, shiny green snake that had slithered closer to the pair of natives and was ready to lash its murderous coils against its oblivious victims became a faint, misty shape in the grass.

Gerion took a deep breath and focused all his energies on the scene before him. An odd wave rolled through the Alanfahian jungle and the lianas, Mohas, and snake suddenly regained their form and bright color. The Mohas continued braiding the long strands of hair on shrunken heads, and the snake slowly began to move again. An attentive observer might have noticed that the Mohas and the snake never were in motion at the same time. At that particular moment, it was the snake that was creeping closer to the jungle dwellers.

"Mohas, look out! A snake!" squealed little Ludilla.

Her brother Golambes reached for Gerion's index finger and squeezed it in his warm fist. Only their older brother Fuldik, a chubby thirteen-year-old who was scratching his substantial belly with one hand while turning his cap with the other, was not impressed. "It's just an illusion. In reality there's nothing in this box."

Gerion sighed. The snake tensed for a moment and then continued through the grass. A lone sun beam cut through the canopy of leaves and glinted on the powerful snake's body. The snake's wide head advanced further and further along the ground. A bright red forked tongue appeared between its fangs and sensed the air. There was barely half a stride between the serpent and its prey. Soon it would be over!

Then a bright yellow streak dove down onto the green, deadly snake with lightening speed. A lioness's golden, muscular body and the green coils of the snake tumbled and rolled in inextricable chaos.

"Yeeyeeyeeyee!" said Ludilla and Golambes squeezed Gerion's finger harder still as if he wanted to strangle it. Even pudgy Fuldik grew quiet. In the small box before them, which measured no more than twenty by forty fingers, raged a battle between life and death. First, the mighty lioness had the snake in its jaws, then the slippery monster freed itself from the big cat's snowy white teeth and wound its thick body around its attacker. The Mohas had jumped up and were watching the tumult with wide-open eyes. Apparently the idea of fleeing did not occur to them. The grass was flattened and sprinkled with large round pools of blood.

Finally, the lioness seized the snake in her powerful

jaws. She tossed the snake's body through the air like a coachman's whip, bringing large tree boughs crashing to the jungle floor. The snake made one last desperate attempt to coil around the cat, then its green length grew limp. The cat opened her bloodied mouth and let the snake fall to the ground. She threw back her head to let out a thundering roar, but there was not a sound to be heard. The entire drama had unfolded in ghostly silence.

Gerion closed the blue gathered curtain in front of the box.

"That was stupid," criticized Fuldik, gesturing to the small stage with his chin. "A lioness in the jungle . . ."

"What's wrong with that, my little angel?" grumbled Gerion.

"Lions live on the steppe," corrected Fuldik. "Tigers and leopards dwell in the jungle."

"Careful, careful, the snake may not be dead yet!" exclaimed Gerion. Ludilla, who was about to move the curtain aside with one finger, jerked her hand back as if a snarling animal had snapped at it. Gerion opened the wagon door and looked at Fuldik with a serious face. "The lioness is the queen of animals. Who would dare tell her not to live in the jungle, hm?"

Fuldik shoved his pudgy hand under his cap and scratched his head. "I don't care anyway," he finally replied "Will you show us more?"

"Do you have any more money?"

"Let me see here," he fished around in his purse and produced a few coins. "Here, five copper bits. Now show us more!"

"That's not enough."

"What do you mean?" The boy screwed up his eyes in anger. "Just now we only paid five copper bits . . ."

"All the other shows cost more."

"How much more?"

"The second cheapest one is called, 'A Demon Raids the Gastetood Bakery.' It costs one silver crown. I'm sorry. Now get a move on, if you will."

"One silver crown," mumbled Fuldik to himself. "You've got to be kidding."

"Oh, no. That's the sad truth, my little jack of hearts," reassured Gerion as he gently guided the boy to the door of the wagon. "But don't take it too hard. Some day you will inherit the earth. Save your copper bits until then, so that you always have one more bit in your purse than you need." He lifted the two little ones down the wagon stairs and then climbed back in and locked the door behind him.

Through the thin walls he heard Ludilla's tiny voice, "The queen of the animals can live anywhere she wants. No one can tell her what to do."

The magician opened the lid to his magical box and pulled out a thin piece of wood that had served as the jungle backdrop. The paint was gray and the brush strokes were crude. He held it up and took a closer look at it by candlelight. Neither the snake nor the Mohas were there to be seen, only a few vertical lines and a variety of curves and shapes. If one squinted at it, one could barely recognize a tangle of branches, twigs, and leaves. But when Gerion looked at the ash-colored lines they began to glow in bright colors, clear forms emerged, and light was differentiated from shadow. A forest clearing appeared with

a small well and a fairy ring of large red-topped mush-
rooms nearby. And there, next to an ancient, regal pine
tree, stood a teeny tiny, black-haired, bare-breasted guardswoman at attention.

The magician smiled to himself and the scene melted away. Gerion replaced the piece in a rack labeled
"forest scenes" in cramped writing. Other labels bore
the inscriptions "Tulamidian Interior," "Battle at Sea,"
"Land of the Yeti," "Witches' Night," "Old Bosparan,"
and "Dragon's Lair."

The magician aimlessly puttered about his wagon, which
was barely three strides long and one stride wide. He
trimmed the wicks of the wall candles and drank a sip of
water from the jug on the wardrobe in the front of the
wagon. Then he reached for a broom to sweep out a bit
of dirt in front of the bench at the wagon's rear. He looked
up at the new patch on his canvas roof that was painted
with stars, and then over at the pile of clothes that had
accumulated on a stool.

"Gurvan, you old stinker, what do you think? Should
we pack it up, or wait a bit?" As Gerion mumbled these
words he walked over to a small trap door on the side
wall of his wagon and looked out at the fairgrounds. There
were only a few people moving among the torches and
lanterns that lit the aisles between the wagons and tents,
and some of the entertainers and peddlers had already
packed up and left. The fair had been a success this year,
he thought, better than in previous years. But tonight
was the last night and people were holding on to their
money a bit tighter than they had a few days earlier. Lost
in thought, Gerion picked up the three pillows from the

bench and shook them out in front of the tiny stage. "Can you believe that woman didn't keep her bet? No, you thought she would pay up, too. She's sure hidden herself well. She's probably locked herself up in the barracks and doesn't dare go outside. She preferred to skip the fair, just to get out of paying me what I rightfully deserve. Selissa of Jergenwell, a baroness no less! I bet their holdings are truly Kosch's pride. Their pantries are empty, their children are starving, but they call themselves baron and baroness nonetheless. Gurvan, I bet they roast dogs like you and talk about it for years to come as the finest feast. I am happier to be a rich magician and show people the wonders of the world. Even little chubby cheeks like Fuldik! What do you think, Gurvan, should we lock up and go get a drink?" Gurvan lifted his sleepy head, gave a hearty yawn, and opened his dark eyes. "You're always right. I have to grant you that. Give me a second to get ready."

There was a timid knock at the door.

"We are cloooooosed," called Gerion in a falsetto voice. "The wonders of the world are thirsty. Come back next year!"

There was another knock.

Gerion slid the bolt to one side and looked through the crack of the door. "Oh, you are such a darling child. How I would love to make an exception, but I have important appointments to keep." He started to close the door again.

"Please listen to me, dear Master," said the peasant woman as she stood at the foot of the wagon stairs.

Gerion opened the door again. He cocked his head and

looked down, "What, you haven't come to see the wonders of the world?"

The woman shook her head in silence.

"Well then, what do you want?"

The woman cleared her throat. "You know the Guardswoman Selissa of Jergenwell, don't you?"

"Oh, that's what this is all about. You are a courier. Please do come in! What a strange coincidence, I was just speaking of the baroness and made a point of mentioning the generosity of said lady. Won't you please take a seat?"

The woman carefully sat down on the very edge of the bench and surveyed her surroundings. Gurvan walked over to her and put his gray muzzle on her knee. She turned up her nose, but said nothing. "I . . . um . . . didn't bring you anything," she mumbled. "I swear that I don't even know what you're talking about, honored Master."

Gerion sat down next to the woman, who immediately scooted to her right. "You don't know what I am talking about? And you didn't come to ask for a forbearance?"

"No, I don't know about any of that." The woman's eyes were wide open with fear. "But I can give you a little money. I thought you might want some. Here, please, this is all I have."

She pulled a gold ducat and three copper bits from her skirt pocket and carefully laid the coins on the pillow. "Lady of Jergenwell gave me the gold ducat when my little Erborn was born," she said.

Gerion cocked his head and looked at the woman. "I fear that you will have to be a bit more specific. I am confused. Perhaps we should introduce ourselves, as parties usually do." He jumped up and took a bow. "Gerion

Eboreus Eberhelm Rothnagel."

The woman also got up and curtsied hastily, "My name is Algunda and I am a stable maid with the Royal Guard of Ferdok."

They sat down again and Algunda continued, "I thought that since you know the young Lady of Jergenwell that you would perhaps have some advice—"

"What makes you think I know her?" Gerion interrupted.

"You told me just a minute ago, at the door . . ."

"So, I did?"

"And, um . . ." Algunda blushed. "I also saw you with the guardswoman last week at the Bard's Tankard."

"Yes, I can't deny having made Lady of Jergenwell's acquaintance. However, my memories of that evening are, shall we say, not so fond and the later events also give me little in which to rejoice."

"Does that mean that you can't stand the young baroness?" Algunda interjected as she raised her eyebrows in fear. "Then there's no reason for me to finish my story." She started to get up, but Gerion gently put his hand on her shoulder. "By Mother Peraine's poundcake! Tell me what is going on and why you are here!"

"They have thrown the young lady into the dungeon! But they are wrong! She has never done anything bad. She is not an Answinite. Not at all. They just promoted her to corporal, because she fought so well against the rebels, so how could she be a supporter of the superer or whatever you call it?"

"You mean *usurper*," corrected Gerion.

"It doesn't matter," Now she talked without stopping

to take a breath. "She is the best guardswoman of all, and the prettiest. She rides like a goddess, and she's always nice to the stable help. She gives us money on our birthdays, and when my little Erborn came she also gave me something. Just recently she saved my life. That horrible woman Zelda Gutnot tried to kill me. How can they do this to her? On top of it all, her father and brother just died. They jumped off a tower at Castle Wengenholm . . ."

"Whoa, whoa," said Gerion. "You have listed too many terrible things at once. I think you should tell me the whole story again slowly."

It was not easy for Gerion to make sense of the stable maid's fragmented story and to tell truth from fiction. Algunda mixed her personal observations with rumors and wild speculation. The horrors facing Selissa of Jergenwell were mixed in together with the torture the "horrible Zelda" had inflicted on poor Algunda. The whole story was a sad picture of desperation and hopelessness. Large tears landed on the stable maid's lap. The magician handed her a plaid handkerchief, while Gurvan gently nuzzled against her knees.

Gerion patiently asked numerous questions to sort out the facts. It turned out that Algunda knew an amazing amount about what had happened to Selissa. She was very observant, had good ears, and was always alert. She had also gained some insight from the cook, armorer, and a guardswoman named Juahan, all of whom were very fond of her Selissa. After a while Gerion summarized the following: A guardswoman, probably Zelda Gutnot, had denounced Selissa for refusing to obey orders. During their last battle against the rebels, Selissa had ignored the colonel's orders and allowed several rebels to escape. Because Selissa had an advocate in the commander, the affair didn't end up as bad as it could have. Instead, the newly promoted corporal got off with a serious lecture and two days of arrest. Everything seemed to be fine, but then a terrible message arrived from Count Erlan of Wengenholm. The Jergenwell's feudal lord reported that several incriminating documents—personal letters, written commitments and the like—had fallen into his hands. The entire Jergenwell family had sided in the worst possible way with the Arkanian Count Ravenmund and his rebels. They had entered into a pact and devised plans to take over Kosch and restructure the state after the revolt. They even had plans to eliminate the prince, who was loyal to the emperor.

After Count Erlan received the documents, he had immediately invited Baron Jergenwell and his two sons to Castle Wengenholm to show them the evidence. Ulfing, the youngest son, must have known the count's plans and did not arrive at Wengenholm. Instead, he had disappeared without a trace. The count gave the Barons Lechdan and Reto one night to consider their reply to the horrible events described in the documents. Baron Lechdan and his son had chosen instead to leap to their death from a room in the castle's highest tower that night. This was generally accepted as an admission of their guilt. Two letters from Baron Lechdan also incriminated Selissa. The letters said that his daughter knew of the treacherous plans and supported them. In one passage the baron tried to convince his daughter not to have Prince Eberstamm killed by a hired assassin. He insisted that such important details "not be left to strangers." In another letter, the baron thanked Selissa for an exact copy of the duty schedule for the prince's royal bodyguards.

"Yes, and then a woman from Gareth came and had Selissa locked up," said Algunda, concluding her report. "They threw her in the dungeon of Ferdok because they were concerned that one of her comrades might try to free her if they locked her up in the barracks."

"Who was this woman?" asked Gerion "Was she from the IGI—the Imperial Garethian Intelligence?"

Algunda shrugged. "Could be. Her name was Westinger and she was accompanied by four armed riders. Dear Master, believe me, it's all lies! There's no way that the young lady is a traitor, I would have known. I can always tell if someone is bad."

"She may well be innocent, but it may just as well be that you are wrong . . ."

Algunda shook her head energetically. "No, no, I'm not wrong! I even went to the Temple of Rondra where I'd never been before in my life. I was very scared to go, but I thought that if anyone knew if the young lady were a traitor, it would be the Goddess Rondra. And I prayed to the goddess for a sign if I were wrong. But there has been no sign, so I must be right. Master, please do me a favor."

"Don't tell me you came to ask me to rescue her from the dungeon?"

"Yes, that's why I came. I wanted to ask you to get her out of the dungeon."

Gerion scratched Gurvan's head. "I was afraid that

was what she was going to say, old friend. I was worried that she would ask me to, and that I would, of course, have to refuse, and that more tears would be shed . . ."

Algunda sighed and wiped her cheeks with the back of her hand.

"Tell me, my little soldier," he put his right arm around Algunda's shoulders, "Why do you think I could do something like that? Do you think that because I am old I have nothing to lose? And why should I care about your lady? I hardly even know her . . ."

"You left with her on your arm. I thought you liked her."

"Yes, yes, I admit it, I do find her very likable—and she doesn't seem to be a sore loser."

Tears flew through the air like bright pearls as Algunda shook her head again. "No, she's not! And I'm sure she isn't a traitor either!"

Gerion leapt up and was pacing back and forth in the wagon. Now and again he stopped to lean on the wall and think. Gurvan got up and was at his heels, loyally following his every turn. "I'm sorry, Algunda. No one can help her. It may be that this is unjust, but . . ." The magician swept his hand through the air. "But this kind of thing happens to some people. That is just part of life when you own castles, lands, and serfs. That's part of the price you pay for being a member of the privileged class. Don't you understand?"

Algunda raised her head and looked at the magician with her big, brown eyes. Tears had collected on her lower lids and were beading on her eye lashes.

"Well, fine. You don't understand." Gerion opened the wagon door.

"I will give you money," Algunda pointed at the coins that were still on the cushion. "Maybe I can get a little bit more together. Not a lot more, but at least some."

Gerion got down on one knee and pulled a small chest out from under the bench. He opened the lid and held the chest so Algunda could see its contents. It was full of sparkling silver coins. "I don't need your money. Here, look. I have plenty."

Algunda swallowed and tugged at the neckline of her shirtwaist. She was looking at the floor and spoke so softly that Gerion could barely understand her. "You can have me, if you want, dear Master. I am not an ugly girl—that's what my Jangu always said . . ."

"By all Twelve! What have I done to deserve this?" The magician ran his hands through his gray mop.

Algunda sighed loudly. "You don't want me. I'm not pretty enough."

"No, I mean, yes! Yes, you are pretty, very pretty indeed. But I cannot take anything from you because I cannot do anything for you. Do you understand?"

Algunda stood up. She left the wagon and went down the steps without saying a word.

Gerion closed the door behind her. He looked out the trap door again and saw that the crowd had thinned even more and that it was almost dark. He replaced a few painted backdrops in their rack and bent down to put the chest back under the bench. When he stood up again he saw the coins that Algunda had forgotten. He gathered them up and hurried down the stairs with Gurvan on his heels. Perhaps he would be able to catch up with the stable maid somewhere. If he could not help her, he didn't want to keep her money.

Algunda was sitting on the sandy ground only a few steps from the wagon. Her head was between her knees. Her round shoulders heaved.

Gerion stepped up behind her. She didn't see him. He looked down at her and extended his arm toward her and then pulled it back. "Oh, holy demon's ass!" he groaned so loud that the girl jumped in surprise. "Child, run over to the Red Fox! Get a pitcher of beer for the master of the wonders of the world. They owe me a pitcher, and then come back to the wagon. Let's think about how we can help your guardswoman."

When one-armed Tilda came to take up her post next to the city gates early that afternoon, she was a few hours later than usual and a strange beggar had beaten her to it. A good, well-practiced beggar, Tilda had to admit after watching him for a while. The man was probably in his fifties, but he looked to be well over eighty and standing with one foot inside Lord Boron's door. His face was as white as a corpse and covered with deep, gray wrinkles. He was wearing a gray coat of rags with one arm longer than the other. He was barefoot and gray with road dust. When he moved his arm his hand began to tremble so fiercely that his entire gaunt body shook.

His face drew the most sympathy. The countless years had transformed it into a true ruin. A large, black eye patch covered his right eye socket, but not the blood red scar that started at the edge of his dirty, gray hair and continued down his cheek. The upper lid of his left eye was turned inside out and the lower lid was pushed up. Between the two there was a swollen white eyeball with red veins and no pupil or iris.

Whenever someone walked by he would raise a wooden box with a few measly copper bits in it. The exertion of lifting the box made his hand shake so violently that the coins rattled loudly. This made the blind man think that the passerby had tossed a coin into the box. He called in a shrill old voice, "Thank you, noble citizen, thank you! I will pray to the Goddess Travia and Peraine as fervently as I can! I will testify that you are a good person. You are truly worthy of the Twelves' blessings!"

A few people continued on their way shaking their heads, but many stopped, turned around, and decided to put a coin in his box. It was seldom a crown that they gave, as Tilda bitterly observed, but there were lots of copper bits and silver coins.

"Be thanked," croaked the beggar, "be thanked again. Oh, the people of Ferdok are so kind!"

From time to time, Tilda observed how his left hand shot out at lightening speed and without shaking to fish the silver coins out of the box and hide them in his jacket. At the same time the iris of his left eye became apparent and he glanced at his money box and the passersby on the square in front of the city gate.

One-armed Tilda had seen enough. She forgot all about the frailty that she usually exhibited and stomped across the square and tapped the stranger with her foot. "Get out of here, you smelly lump! You stole my spot! Take your pathetic show elsewhere!"

"Noble citizen, I'm a blind man and ask only for alms!"

Tilda grabbed the beggar with her left hand. She took hold of his hair and threw his head back. "Now take off, you cesspool cleaner! Or I'll kick your jaw in two—or rather, what's left of it!"

Two dwarf warriors who had each just given the blind man a copper bit hurried over. "Leave the old man in peace this instant!" commanded the dwarf with a long beard. "Or will I have to tan your filthy hide, you slovenly strumpet?"

"Thank you kindly," said the old man in a shaky voice, "thank you for your help, but please be kind to this friendly woman. She means no harm, she is just joking with me. She wanted to sit down next to me so that we could discuss something, didn't you dearest Tilda?"

The two dwarves looked Tilda over from head to toe and then went on their way. The beggar then sat down next to the "blind man." "How do you know my name, you wily devil?" she asked.

"Oh, I know a lot about you," he whispered. "I know, for example, that all I have to do is cut the string that runs from you right hand that you carry under your breasts, and that ridiculous-looking infected stump of yours would fall to the ground."

Tilda shrugged. "Yeah, well so what, *blind* man? Everyone has their own method."

"It is said that you are rather good looking underneath all the dirt you smear on yourself. And younger looking than you are. No one can tell that you are forty-five. They say you have accumulated a fair amount of wealth and even own a house on the Peraine Dam. It seems that you no longer need to beg, because you are involved in shady dealings here in Ferdok." The beggar extended his box to a passerby. "Please, kind sir, alms for the poor . . ."

"Are you a man of the cloth? Are you going to give me a sermon?" demanded Tilda. "I have heard better than that. By the way, you're still sitting on my spot. May I ask when you are finally going to cut to the quick?"

The beggar cocked his white eye at Tilda. "I am supposed to say hello to you from your son. I met him on the road, two days' ride from here."

"There's no way you've met Terek, you crazy loon! He's far away and he won't be back for quite sometime."

"Thanks be with you, thank you, noble sir," the beggar said to another passerby. Then he turned back to Tilda, "That's what you think, but you don't know the whole truth. Terek is on his way to Ferdok, believe me. He looks a lot like you. He has the same eyes, the same hair . . ."

"That proves it, you're crazy. Terek's hair is much lighter than mine."

"True, it's a bit lighter, almost this color, don't you think?" The beggar reached with his shaking hand under his jacket, pulled out a lock of blond hair and tossed it on Tilda's lap.

"That is Terek's hair, by all the Twelve!" She angrily got up on one knee. "Why doesn't he ever listen to me? He's supposed to stay in Angbar, damn it! How did you get his hair? And what do you want from me?" Tilda slid a few fingers away from the beggar.

Instead of giving her an answer, the old man asked, "You watched me for almost fifteen minutes, didn't you?"

"Yeah, maybe. So?"

"You saw how much I made in that short period of time. I've been sitting here since seven this morning. Do you want to earn all the money that I have collected since seven?" A coin rattled in the box and he turned to call, "The gods will thank you, dear lady! Look at that, sometimes they even give to the poor out of their own free will without me having to ask for it. Interesting!"

Tilda scooted closer to him again. "Cut the bullshit, and tell me what my son said. We can talk about the money later."

"You're impatient, Tilda. I'll tell you the whole story, just be patient. Patience is a virtue that you do not seem to have. Do you know that you're not very well liked in your circles?"

Tilda sighed. "Here we go again, talking about other things. Will it never end? Okay, fine, maybe people don't like me. Maybe they begrudge me my fortune. So what? Now tell me about Terek!"

"They also say that you always get out of the clink fast. Apparently, you have good connections . . ."

"No better than others. What are you getting at?"

She jumped back. The old man was facing her again, but this time he was staring at her through one bright blue eye. "When your sweet Terek was thrown in the dungeon last year for killing a city guard, he was out in three days—'escaped,' they say. It seems to me that you must know someone down there . . . oh, what am I saying . . . that you have something on someone down there. Something so big that that someone is willing to risk his ass for you. I want to know who it is, and what makes him get out his keys."

"You're not well in the head, old man," Tilda raised her hand. "First, I don't know anyone who has anything to say at the dungeon. Second, even if there was some-one—I'm not saying there is—what makes you think I would deliver him to his death for a few meager silver coins, you repulsive fool? You must be out of your mind!"

The beggar rocked his head and shook his box again. "That's a shame, I was hoping that we could agree to financial terms. Well, perhaps we'll be able to agree to other terms. It would be a shame for Terek if we couldn't. He may be a little mucker, but he's good with a dagger. He could have been one of the greatest—"

At that moment, Tilda reached for the knife she carried on her thigh, but before she could get to it, she felt a sharp point in her side. A slender blade had cut through the beggar's tattered jacket and was poking into her rib cage. The old man draped a fold of the jacket over the glistening knife with his shaking hand. Then he lifted up his box again.

"—a true great," the beggar continued. "Too bad that he's about to die before he can kill again."

"Where is Terek? What have you done to him?" asked Tilda, who was careful not to make any sudden movements.

"He's sitting in a goat stall, about two days' ride from here. A friend is looking after him. If you tell me what I want to know, I will send a messenger to my friend and Terek will be free by the day after tomorrow. If you decide to keep your little secret to yourself, I won't send a messenger, and Terek will die the day after tomorrow. It's as simple as that."

Tilda tried to make her voice sound casual, but she couldn't suppress her hesitation. "How can I know that you really have Terek? He could have given you that hair. Or perhaps that isn't his hair at all!"

"Believe whatever you want! But if you don't believe me, I will have to go see Terek myself. It will take me two days to get there and two days to get back. So I could bring you proof in four days—the rest of the hair of your promising offspring, complete with the head attached. As you make up your mind, just keep one thing in mind: I am deadly serious."

While the old man spoke, he stared at Tilda through his one eye. An unearthly chill ran through her bones when he looked at her. "It's the vice captain of the City Guards," she mumbled "His name is Rudon Mirdok. He had his sister Esmelda murdered so he could inherit it all."

"How do you know that, and how can you prove it?"

"There's a genuine contract, signed by Mirdok."

"By smiling Phex! Why would anyone put something like that in writing? You people of Ferdok are certainly strange!"

Tilda looked at the beggar in surprise. "I don't think you're as experienced as I thought. If you're going to get involved with the City Guard's leadership, you need some security. Otherwise, you might not live as long as you planned to!"

The beggar nodded. "That's true. And how do you know about the contract?"

"How do I know?" Tilda smirked. "I stabbed the wench."

The beggar whistled through his teeth. Then he started to get up. He inched himself up the wall. "Won't you please help a blind man?" he asked.

Tilda waved her hand. "What about my money?" she asked. The old man dropped a purse of coins to the ground. "And nothing will happen to Terek? Swear on it, by Phex!"

The beggar raised his right hand and swore, without shaking and in a normal voice, then he slowly limped off.

After he was a few blocks away, he looked around carefully before he disappeared into a dark doorway. He pulled down his eyelid and wiped the makeup from his face. Then he took off his jacket, turned it inside out, and slipped it back on. In his pocket he found a few locks of hair of various colors that he had collected from laughing children for a few shiny coins at Rahja's Chalice. "I can't believe that none of the other beggars could tell me what color rotten Terek's hair is!" Gerion mumbled as he threw the locks in the air and watched the wind blow them down the cobblestone alley.

Chapter 6

SELISSA'S HANDS WERE bound over her head and shackled to the wall. Her wrists bled where the rings of iron gouged her skin, her shoulders ached, and her entire body stung from sweat that irritated the countless scratches inflicted by the coarse jute fabric of her prisoner's tunic.

Her hair stuck to her temples and she felt a crusty layer of dirt on her forehead. Chained near the fire pit, Selissa was blasted with heat on her left side while a cold draft blew across her moist thighs from the right. When she tensed her arms it felt as if a knife were cutting into her shoulder, but when she let her leaden arms relax, the iron shackles bit deeper into her raw wrists.

IGI Senior Officer Baroness Ada of Westinger ordered the guard to stoke the fire with some more wood. "It has gotten very cool these last days, don't you agree, guardswoman? And the moon of Travia has not even waned yet."

Selissa did not reply.

The thin-lipped officer from Gareth put her feet, which were clad in calf-length red boots, on the table. She took off her glasses, breathed on the gold-rimmed round lenses, and then proceeded to clean them with a green flannel cloth. With a few energetic motions of her hands she arranged her blonde curls with the help of a small mirror. After she picked at a stray loose thread on her black velvet pants, she turned back to her prisoner, "You're right. Why should we talk about the weather when there are so many more important issues to discuss? Let's get back to business. What were the names of the rebels that escaped thanks to you?"

"I do not know their names."

"Where did you meet them before?"

"I had never seen them before in my life."

"What kind of agreement did you make with these people?"

"There was no agreement. You have asked me all this a thousand times over the last few days and I've always given you the same answer. By Rondra, I see no sense in questioning me further."

The baroness raised her eyebrows. "If I were in your shoes, I would take care not to use the goddess's name so freely. The divine lioness does not look kindly on traitors. She will discipline you for your careless speech, and I'll be glad to give her a helping hand. Where did the rebels flee? Where are they hiding?"

"They were peasant folk. How should I know where they ran to? Maybe they went back to Darpatia?"

"Ah ha! Yesterday you said that they presumably made their way through to Albernia . . ."

Selissa groaned, "If you will pardon my saying so, I don't give a shit. Don't you feel ridiculous asking me the same questions and coming to the same foolish conclusions over and over again?"

The officer stood up, grabbed a slender walking stick, and confronted Selissa. "Why should I feel ridiculous? I'm just doing my job, that's all. Incidentally, I'm trying to make your life easier by giving you a chance to speak on your own free will. If you would only talk you could spare yourself a lot of pain. You should know that I sent a messenger to Gareth to present your case before Prince Blasius of Eberstamm. At my request, the prince will temporarily expel you from the Guard, divest you from your rank of baroness, and hand you over to me as an ordinary prisoner. And then, you treacherous wench, our conversations will take a different turn!" She struck Selissa's thighs with the walking stick—twice, three times. Then she tossed it aside. "Just a taste of things to come, my dear Baroness. For now I'm obliged to spare you our more intensive methods of interrogation. So just pretend this little incident never happened." She gently ran her finger along the narrow, red line on Selissa's thigh, turned and sat down on the chair behind her desk.

"Why won't you just talk? I admit, you've put up a good show so far, but don't start to think that you could stand up to a real, rigorous interrogation. Baron Nemrod himself was my teacher, and I can assure you anyone I want to make talk talks, sooner or later."

Selissa tried to rub the sweat and dirt from her forehead with her upper arm. "I've told you everything I have to say."

"I know, I know, you're innocent, your family is innocent, and you have all fallen victim to an evil plot devised
by the young Count of Wengenholm. I know your lies by
heart."

"What if they aren't lies? Did it ever occur to you that
I may be speaking the truth? And, if you're already absolutely sure about what has happened, why do you need
me to confirm it?"

The baroness impatiently tapped the tip of her boots.
"Whether you admit your guilt or not means nothing to
me. As an IGI officer, it is my duty to completely uncover
the conspiracy and that's why you are going to tell me the
names of your fellow conspirators and the full extent of
your plans. However, since you can't tell me your accomplices' names without admitting your own guilt, you might
as well start confessing to your crime. I trust you now
understand what this is all about."

"I told you already, the count must have forced my
father to sign those documents," said Selissa with conviction. "There is no other explanation."

"Really. We have page upon page of letters written entirely in your father's hand."

"He was forced to write those as well."

"Some of the letters are more than two years old."

"Letters can be backdated."

"One letter bears the signature of Baron of Horklach
along with your father's. Horklach died a year ago."

"My father must have added his signature later."

"Under coercion, of course?"

"Under coercion."

"The corpses of your father and brother exhibit injuries

typical of a fall from great heights, but there is not even the slightest mark that would suggest torture."

Selissa sighed. "There are other ways to make a person do something that is against one's nature. You know that."

"Are you speaking of magic? The count gave us his word of honor that he did not submit your relatives to any type of magic during their conversation."

"What is a villain's word worth?"

"It's a count's word against a baron's." The baroness bent a small, wood letter opener between her fingers. "The Wengenholms fought against Count Answin and his supporters in the front lines at the Battle of Silk Meadow. There was not a Jergenwell in sight."

"My father feared an attack from the Wengenholms if we left our lands."

The baroness raised her voice, "How could they have attacked you? The Wengenholms were carrying out their feudal duty on the Silk Meadow—a brave deed for which the elder count paid for with his life, as you know."

Selissa raised her shoulders and said nothing.

The officer signaled the guard who had stood the entire time in silence by the door. "Take her away. But don't take her back to her cell, throw her in the pit. Maybe she will be a bit more talkative after spending a night in the company of other riff-raff."

Up high, four or five strides over Selissa's head, a bright rectangle opened up. A heavy rope tumbled down, just missing her. She slipped the loop in the rope over her head and shoulders and gripped it under her arms. The clanking of a winch stop could be heard above. The rope grew taught. There was a jerk and Selissa's feet swung in the air. Inch by inch her body was lifted out of the darkness.

Once Selissa emerged from the hatch and was standing on her own feet, the guard drew a saber at her neck as another snapped iron rings around her wrists.

"One prisoner is dead," gasped Selissa. She grew sick to her stomach as she told of the last night's events. She didn't speak of the pitch-black darkness and the revolting stench of decay, sweat, and feces that was so heavy in the air that it seemed to force its way into her mouth and nose like a nauseating, viscous mass. She did not speak of the horror that overcame her when she heard the grunts and rustling, the panting and the smacking all around her and could not distinguish if people or animals were making the sounds. What could she tell the guards of the sweet-stale breath in her face, of the deranged, shrill laughter in the darkness, and the endless mumbling chorus of "soft, fresh womanly flesh." Selissa also avoided mentioning the withered, bony body that pressed against her and the skeletal hands that groped beneath her jute shirt, and the soft cracking sound that she heard as she blindly grabbed her attacker by the hair and threw him with all her strength. "A man forced himself on me," was all she said. "I defended myself and he died. It was not my fault."

"I've been told that you killed someone last night," said Baroness of Westinger when Selissa was again bound in the interrogation room. "I don't even want to know what you have to say about this matter. I also think if one were to ask the creatures in the pit what happened they would have a completely different story to tell. But I don't want to hear their version of the events either. You have nothing to worry about. After all, you are a baroness, for now. And the fellow you killed was only a peasant scoundrel and child molester besides. You might even get to spend tonight in your own private cell again. You probably would not survive the night back in the pit. After all, the folks down there have all day to come up with plans for your reception. Just think of the irony: Whatever the riff-raff did to you they would have nothing to fear. No one is ever called to trial from the pit. Down there it's anarchy in its truest form. Yes, perhaps you could be spared spending another night down there, but you would have to accommodate me first. Tell me the names of the rebels you helped to escape!"

Selissa did not answer. She looked out through the tall, curtainless window at the city wall. Two helmeted constables were conferring with a third person that Selissa could not see—the foot of the wall was hidden behind the low slate roof of a building. Along the coping of the wall was a covered walk that obscured her view of the far-off mountains of Kosch and the lands of the Jergenwells and Castle Albumin nestled somewhere at their base. If Selissa closed her eyes she could see the massive castle keep in her mind's eye: The palace with its windows of varying sizes—her mother had some of them enlarged, but she had died before the renovations were complete—and her father standing at the well arguing with the stable master. Selissa tried to imagine Albumin without her father or Reto, but it was impossible. She shook her head.

"No?" the baroness was seemingly surprised. "So you finally agree. One can only interpret their tower leap as an admission of guilt. An attempted escape can—"

"Oh, that's ridiculous—I did not agree to anything you said because there is nothing to agree to. I just wasn't listening to you."

The senior officer leapt to her feet, reached for the cane, and struck Selissa without mercy several times on the stomach, back, and thighs. "You weren't listening to me, you rebel slut? Dreaming of coups, murder, and plundering, I assume? I'll wake you up from your dreams. Take this, and this, and this!" Breathing heavily Baroness of Westinger threw the walking stick aside. "Now, that I have your attention again, dear Baroness, I would like to continue our conversation. I'm listening."

Selissa took the lashes without uttering a cry. She now forced her voice to remain calm before she answered. "Perhaps someone pushed my father and Reto from the tower, or maybe even magic was involved. There is no way they killed themselves. They would never have done that. Nor would they have had a reason to admit to any wrong doings."

"There is a testimony under oath from the count that he was the last person to see your relatives before he had them taken to the guest quarters . . ."

"The oath of a liar!"

"The testimony of the head servant to the Wengenholms and that of the stable master support Count Erlan's account."

"Liars that swear for a liar."

The baroness paced across the room with small energetic strides. "The world is full of inexplicable phenomena and liars. Only you, even though you were miles away, know what really happened and only you speak the truth."

"I'm telling you—"

"What are the names of the assassins you wanted to hire to murder the prince?"

"I don't know."

"Did you forget their names? What did the man look like? Or was it a woman or even an elf?"

"I don't know any assassins, nor have I ever spoken with one."

That night Selissa was surprised to be taken to a clean, private cell. She was given a large pitcher of water to wash with and a shirt of pale linen.

When she was taken to the interrogation room the next morning, there was a small chair in front of the desk. In front of the fireplace was a rack with numerous slender iron rods, each about an arm in length. Some of them were sharp, some of them were shaped like brands. All were in the fire and glowing red hot.

Near the fireplace stood a long table outfitted with shackles at either end.

"You look good, Baroness." The officer greeted Selissa with a nod from behind her desk. "Perhaps a bit pale...Won't you take a seat?" She gestured toward the chair in front of her desk.

Selissa had trouble collecting her thoughts. It was odd how intensely she felt the soft carpet on her bare feet as she stepped in front of the desk. She took a seat. The two guards who had led her from her cell were now standing behind her with their sabers drawn. She hadn't seen these men before, though she was certain they were Baroness of Westinger's hand-picked thugs.

"Did you have a pleasant night?" asked the senior officer.

Selissa was silent.

"You are so quiet this morning. Well, as you like. By the way, I received an interesting letter last night that I wouldn't want to keep from you. Please, read it."

The letter was sent from the capital city of Gareth and bore the seal of Prince Blasius of Eberstamm, Lord of Kosch. After a brief greeting and a few remarks about life in bustling Gareth and plans for his trip to Beilunk, Vallusa, and Festum, the prince addressed Baroness of Westinger's request. While he conceded that he was familiar with the House of Jergenwell and that in the past he had no reason to doubt the loyalty of the family, he did understand that the events presented by the baroness were outrageous. The fact that the accusation came from Count Wengenholm, whose family had an impeccable reputation, gave the prince cause for thought. Therefore, he agreed to temporarily suspend Guardswoman Jergenwell's rights as a noblewoman and soldier in the Royal Guard if that would expedite the IGI's inquiry. But he was clearly opposed to sending the accused to Gareth, since he hoped that the guardswoman would prove herself innocent under the baroness's rigorous interrogation. If she were found to be guilty after all, he would personally administer justice upon his return to Gareth. His sentence, he assured the baroness, would in no way be less severe than that of the

High Court of Gareth, since a guardswoman who had committed high treason could certainly never be pardoned.

The letter concluded with a greeting from his Highness to the baroness and a request to extend his best wishes to their common friend, Baron Dexter Nemrod.

The baroness took the letter from Selissa's hand. "As you can see, I now can perfom my duties as thoroughly as usual. But I'm still of the opinion that there is an easier way for us to come to an arrangement. Don't think that I prefer a rigorous interrogation to a friendly questioning. What civilized person likes pitiful cries, disgusting stench, tears of despair, and the like? That is why I'm asking you one more time, from noblewoman to noblewoman: What are the names of the rebels that you let escape at the river?"

"They were Darpatian peasants. I don't know their names."

"Undress the treacherous wench and strap her to the table."

Selissa jumped to her feet. She immediately felt the point of a saber in her back. One black-bearded, broad-shouldered guard in his mid-forties pulled her shirt over her head while the other guard kept the point of his saber in her back. The guards dragged her to the table, pushed her onto the wooden planks, and yanked her arms over her head. The iron cuffs snapped shut around her wrists and ankles.

The bearded man punched Selissa's stomach with all his might. She screamed and gasped for air with her mouth wide open. The second guard stuffed a wad of cotton in her mouth. With lightening speed a leather strap was wrapped around her head to secure the gag.

The baroness approached the torture table. She ran the silver grip of her walking stick along the body of the prisoner, from head to toe. "Nice and cool, isn't it? Cool silver on hot skin. . . . If you want to give me a response, you only need to nod or shake your head. I will keep my questions simple. Now, will you tell me the names that I so much want to hear?"

Selissa shook her head.

"The small iron," demanded the senior officer. The second guard, a dark blond man with close-set eyes, used tongs to pull the iron from the rack by the fire. He wrapped a thick cloth around one end before handing it to the baroness. She held the glowing point close to Selissa's face. "Do you feel the heat? You can feel it just fine, can't you? And the skin on your face is not even that sensitive to Ingerimm's art. There are other places . . ." There was a soft hiss as the dark red iron brushed across Selissa's tense stomach and paused there. Her naked body arched like a bow between the shackles not in pain but in indescribable terror. The pain came later, increasing and then staying with her like a stinging curse on her unprotected skin. Tears of despair and hate burned in Selissa's eyes She could barely recognize the glowing hot, silver crown-sized iron tip that hung over her face. From faraway she heard a woman's voice say, "Now that you know what the small iron feels like, imagine what this demonic brand will inflict! I will give you one day to decide if you want to cooperate. If you don't, your body will bare many more of my marks before the day is over. And I will not be as forgiving next time . . . take her back to her cell!"

Chapter 7

THOSE WHO SAW the giant blond man approaching instinctively stepped out of his way—something about his features and body language suggested it was a wise thing to do. The stranger kept his gloved left hand on his rapier's bell-shaped brass hand guard. His right hand held the brim of his large brown hat, which was adorned with a blue ostrich feather. His upper body leaned slightly forward and he stormed ahead with such great strides that his gait resembled a continuous forward fall. His hat shaded the angry furrows of his brow while his mouth, framed by a well-trimmed blond beard, emitted a steady stream of curses in the most provincial Borish dialect. There was no need for the people of Ferdok to understand a word he said—they simply knew it was best to get out of his path.

Count Arvid of Geestwindsberth had just completed a rough, albeit exceedingly accelerated, journey. In Vallusa, he had embarked on the Perricum-bound *Ismeralda II*. He had planned to get off in Mendena and from there take the country roads to Ferdok. But when a northerly storm blew the cog off course and past Medena's harbor, the captain had no choice but to steer his bedraggled ship toward its final destination. The count immediately hurried from Perricum via Darpat to Ferdok without stopping in Gareth. Despite the longer route, he reached the city ten days sooner than he had expected.

In high spirits when he arrived, the count rushed to the guardswomen's barracks to throw his arms around his fiancée. But his mood soon took a turn for the worse when Sergeant Dergelstein, after much hemming and hawing, finally told him of the accusations of treason leveled against Selissa. She hastily added that nothing had been proven yet and that many guardswomen believed Selissa to be innocent. In fact, they were hoping that the prince would quickly put an end to this degrading and horrific incident.

Count Arvid had hardly heard the entire story before he demanded to see his bride-to-be immediately. He was informed that Selissa was not confined in the barracks but that she had been taken to the dungeon of Ferdok. "A fine bunch of guardswomen you are to let your comrade be hauled off by the City Guards!" Count Arvid thundered, adding a few curses that could only be understood by ears from Borland.

He rushed to the dungeon, his face a mask of grim determination. Once there, a sullen guard told the count that Selissa was in satisfactory condition and that she was being detained in a cell. However, the guard continued, he was not authorized to allow even such a fine nobleman as the count to see the prisoner. All visitation rights first had to be cleared through Baroness of Westinger. "Then get Lady Westinger out here, or I'll have your hide!" bellowed the count. But instead of submitting to his request, the guard called out six of his comrades and proceeded to tell him that the baroness was staying at the Burgundy Arms Inn, and that she would not be back until the next day when she would continue the interrogation.

Too livid to reprimand the guard for his insolent behavior, Count Arvid stormed from the dungeon and stalked toward the Burgundy Arms Inn. Muttering a torrent of curses in his native tongue, he barreled down the bustling Angbar Street, pushing his way past chatting pedestrians. He kicked the hat a beggar extended toward him, pushed away the rump of a cart horse that backed into his way, and then strode into the hotel.

The middle-aged man behind the counter, wearing a blue jacket with gold trim draped over his slight frame, jumped up from his chair. "May Travia welcome you! How may I help you, sir?"

"Is a certain Westinger staying here?

"Um, yes . . . Baroness of Westinger is lodged here. What do—"

"Is she in?"

"Um, yes, I think so, my—"

"What room is she in?"

"Dear sir, I do not know if—"

Before the poor man could finish, Count Arvid drew his rapier. The blade crashed down on the large guest book with such force that the top pages split and an ink well, complete with quill, jumped off the desk. The count grabbed the concierge by the collar and pulled the terrified man toward him. The concierge was horrified when he realized his feet were off the ground.

"Twetwetwe . . . twenty-five," he gasped.

The giant raised his brows questioningly.

"Go up the stairs and then turn left. The numbers are on the doors."

Count Arvid threw the man back into his chair and stormed up the stairs three steps at a time. He quickly found room twenty-five, threw open the door, and strode in. A petite blonde woman jumped up from behind a writing desk. "What are you doing? Who are you?" she demanded.

The count doffed his hat and tossed it onto a chair. "Count Arvid of Geestwindsberth—Lady of Westinger, I presume?"

The blonde woman nodded curtly. She had overcome the initial shock and looked fearlessly at Arvid. "Tell me this instant why you are behaving so boorishly, Sir Count! What gave you the idea of barging into my room like this?"

"I want to see my fiancée but you are holding her prisoner, Baroness. "

"What are you talking about, Your Honor?" the baroness turned away and spread drying sand over the pages in the book in which she had just made some notes.

"I am speaking of Baroness Selissa of Jergenwell. You will now accompany me to the dungeon and let me see her."

The IGI officer calmly blew the sand from the page. "I'm afraid that is impossible, Your Honor. In this phase of my investigation I cannot permit any visitors to see her."

"I don't think I heard you right."

"What do you mean?"

"I mean that you are putting on your jacket, madam, and accompany me to her cell this instant."

"She will be able to have visitors next week at the earliest, Your Honor. You had best be happy with that."

Count Arvid's face grew red. "I've come from Geestwindsberth in Borland, the northernmost province of Arkania, to bring my fiancée back to my home. Do you think that I'm going to let a pint-sized baroness like yourself get in my way? Now make haste before I forget my manners."

Baroness of Westinger straightened her glasses with a casual motion. "You are truly a lout!"

"If you weren't so malnourished I would challenge you to a duel and slice you into dainty pieces." Count Arvid patted the guard on his rapier, menacingly.

"It would be a pleasure to teach you good manners," Baroness of Westinger's voice was now slightly shaky. "However, my office prohibits me from accepting such challenges."

"Enough talk, little lady. Now get your royal ass in gear." Count Arvid lunged for the agent with his right hand.

The baroness fell back. There was a red blush on her cheek.

"Let's go," ordered the count.

"I'm warning you," her voice quivering. "You'll get nowhere with force!"

"We'll see about that!" Count Arvid surged forward, grabbing the baroness's jacket with both hands. He lifted her off the ground. "Now what?"

"Guards!" screeched the baroness in a shrill, cracking

voice.

Arvid tossed her aside. She flew through the room and landed in a heap across the bed and floor. She slowly rose to face the count, her right arm hanging limp at her side. She felt it with her left hand and grimaced, "It's broken."

"Put it in a sling," suggested Count Arvid with a shrug. "After you've taken me to the dungeon you can look for a healer. Now get a move on!"

"You broke my arm!"

"And you have broken my patience, Baroness! We—"

In that moment, three armed guards—two helmeted men and a red-haired woman—burst into the room, sabers drawn. Arvid turned and jabbed his rapier into the first attacker's thigh before the man could gain his bearings. The guard stared at his leg in dismay and stepped back, stumbling into his two comrades.

"Get out of here, you bumbling fools!" Arvid yelled at the guards. "My next move won't be any fun at all. As for you, my red doll, I'm going to nail you to the wall!"

Intimidated by the count's threat and the sheer volume of his voice, the red-haired woman paused and looked over her shoulder at the door. The count's long blade cut a swath through the air, nicked the helmet of the second guard, and sliced his cheek and nose.

"Are you deaf? Out!" commanded the count, the blade of his weapon hissing menacingly near their faces. The three guards exchanged helpless glances. Nodding their heads they motioned to each other to attack the giant from the north, but instead each shrank away from the quick steel of the rapier.

Meanwhile, with Count Arvid so preoccupied with

the guards, the baroness had stealthily made her way around the back of the room, her face wracked with pain. Suppressing a scream of agony, she reached for the slim dagger she always carried under her jacket. The blade was no longer than her thumb, no bigger around than a knitting needle, and coated with a sticky, black potion that could knock out a bull. She silently came up behind Count Arvid and buried the three-sided blade deep into his upper thigh.

The count struck his left fist blindly backwards and hit the retreating baroness in the face, smashing her glasses and sending her sprawling to the ground. As the count turned to take on her three henchmen, his left leg buckled beneath him. With a deep, panicked yelp, he crashed to the floor. The count saw the approaching boots of his attackers and raised his rapier but even his hand and arm were numbing. The weapon fell from his limp fingers. "Holy demon's ass!" mumbled the count and then everything around him became dark.

The baroness squatted on the ground and held her broken arm tight. Her face was ashen and blood was dripping down over her lip. "Bind and gag him!" she hissed through closed teeth. "Throw him on a cart and smuggle him down to the dungeon. Give him another dose of sleeping potion, and early in the morning take him down to the harbor. But make sure no one sees you. Ask for Captain Fedora of the *Elenvina*. She knows all about these matters. Tell her to set sail as soon as possible and to keep the count detained below deck until the ship reaches Havena. Then she can kill him, for all I care." She looked over at Count Arvid's massive hulk. "You demon dog, you should be happy that you are a foreigner and that I have to avoid any political trouble. I wouldn't go to this much effort for a local." She turned to her guards, "Now, get to work! You, Elgor, go down to the concierge. Tell him to get a healer over here this instant!"

Chapter 8

ERION HUMMED THE Hetman Faenwulf song as
he rounded the corner and walked out onto
Angbar Street, barely avoiding a collision with
a reckless brute wearing a wide-brimmed hat. By smiling Phex, he thought, what a whopper of a man! And
what an expression on his face—as if he were passing
Praios's judgment. Gerion shook his head, repositioned
the roll of tent fabric on his shoulder, and resumed his
song, "*Only the Nivesian oarswoman in the boat of hide
will take you safely to the other side.*"

Although Gerion appeared to be happy, he would rather
have been hundreds of miles away from Ferdok and wished
he had never stumbled across this wretched place. Though
he kicked himself for getting caught up in this insane
plan to rescue Selissa, he had to admit that so far things
were running fairly smoothly. Spending half a day treat-
ing every stinking beggar in town to shots of expensive
liquor had finally paid off. It produced the lead to one-
armed Tilda and Rudon Mirdok, Tilda's special contact

in the dungeon of Ferdok who turned out to be just the right man for the job.

At first the fat guard had squirmed and writhed, trying to convince Gerion that it was impossible to spring someone out of the dungeon, that everyone involved would be caught, and that it would cost him his head. Just thinking about Mirdok's pathetic protests caused Gerion to chuckle. Who was he trying to fool, anyway? Who would care about what happened to a man who killed his own sister? Gerion kicked a small, green apple and watched it bounce down the cobblestone street. "*From the Amber Bay, where the whales sing, there'll be news of Faenwulf's destiny to bring.*" In the end, that fat pig Mirdok had caved in to Gerion's threats. He realized that he had only one choice if he wanted to continue to enjoy racks of mutton washed down with foaming Ferdoker ale: He would have to go along with Gerion's plan and make certain that it remained a secret. Everything should run smoothly tonight. Gerion had done what he could, the rest lay in Phex's hand.

"*I would gladly give ten thousand crowns to know if Faenwulf were still alive.*" The magician had reached the fairgrounds where only one wagon remained, hitched to a mule at the far edge of the grounds. On its side large, carefully scripted yellow letters announced: *From the Windhag Boulders to the Coast of Medena—From Ifirn's Icebergs to the Jungle of the Mohas—The Wonders of the World.*

"I've got to do something about that slogan, it's just too long," mumbled Gerion, resolving to come up with a catchier phrase if he survived the insane plot he had agreed to. When he was within ten strides of his wagon,

Gerion could hear Gurvan's excited barks. "You still have sharp ears, old buddy. I'll grant you that."

Suddenly, the piercing cry of a baby rose above the dog's yelps. Gerion dropped the roll of fabric, hurried up the wagon steps, and threw the door open. Gurvan rubbed his furry gray head against his master's leg, but the magician only had eyes for the woman in peasant's clothes sitting on the bench, swaying a large basket in her arms as if it were a cradle. Algunda cringed and pulled the basket to her chest. "This is Erborn," she said with a nervous giggle.

Gerion's brow furrowed. "I figured that much. What is he doing here . . . and what are you doing here?"

Algunda's lower lip began to tremble as Gerion caught sight of a second basket that was partially covered by a towel and a fat roll of clothes. He sighed loudly. "Don't tell me, let me guess. You moved in while I was away?"

Algunda nodded with her head lowered.

"I can't believe it. Good Phex, protector of the truly just, give me a sign. Don't tell me what I'm seeing here is the real truth!"

Erborn, who had turned his tiny bald head for a moment to peer curiously out of his basket, began to cry again. Algunda threw her body over the basket, shaking with an agonizing sob.

Gerion pressed his forehead against the door frame. "You can't live here," he said so quietly that Algunda couldn't hear him. "Gurvan and I live here. I've been living in this wagon for almost twenty years and Gurvan has been here for twelve now. We get along just fine, we're used to each other. In all these years we've had only one female

visitor. She stayed for three weeks. We had three wonderful days together, followed by eighteen horrible ones,
five of which were unbearable. Since then we've refrained
from expanding our household. We can—"

Algunda looked up with tears in her eyes. "What are
you saying, master?"

"Oh, skip the 'master.' My name is Gerion."

"Dear Gerion, mas . . . it's just . . . I don't know where
to go. I ran off from the barracks because I'm afraid of
that terrible Zelda, and I can't stay at home because they
will find me there and take me back to the barracks. But
since you're leaving town tomorrow morning anyway, I
thought I could spend the night here and you could take
me through the gate and when I'm outside the city walls,
I could continue on my own. I've an aunt in Elenvina.
I'm sure she'll take us in."

"I need the wagon tonight to hide your Baroness of
Jergenwell—if I succeed in freeing her, that is, and if they
don't throw me into the pit. There is no way I could hide
a crying maid and a whining baby in my wagon as well."

"And a stinking, barking dog!" added Algunda defiantly. "Erborn doesn't always cry and he sleeps at night
and is real quiet then. And if I'm in the wagon I can hold
your dog's muzzle shut so he doesn't bark."

Gerion looked up at the stars painted on the wagon's
ceiling. "By all Twelve, what should I do? My plan is so
crazy that a little detail like this probably doesn't even
matter. Cunning Phex surely knows why he is sending
me these companions." The magician walked to the door.
"Fine, you can stay."

Algunda leapt up and threw her arms around Gerion's

neck, pressing her hot, tear-drenched face against his chest. He freed himself with difficulty and said, "Come, now, my accomplice, you can make yourself useful. I have to throw a few tarps over the wagon so people won't recognize it."

Outside, Gerion unfolded the bundle of old fabric he had obtained from the cartwright down at the harbor and threw the tarps over the high roof of his wagon. With Algunda's help, he straightened the strips of fabric and pulled them tight by tying them with a rope underneath the wagon. Finally, he stepped back and took a look at the results.

"Looks kind of strange," determined Algunda.

Indeed, the tall, angular vehicle with its smooth sides of tent fabric did not at all look like the covered wagon of a coach driver as Gerion had hoped. "More like a covered wagon with a showman's cart underneath," he grumbled.

"You could use your magic!" There was confidence in Algunda's voice. "Perhaps you should make the cart invisible!"

"Perhaps I should lift up a corner of the prison so that Selissa can sneak out."

Algunda glanced quizzically at the magician. Gerion patted her on the shoulder. "Go on, climb in and hold on tight and make sure that your little one doesn't fall off the bench. I'm going to drive the wagon to the prison now. You know how the saying goes: 'If you want to dine with demons, you have to get there on time.'"

Gerion was hoping that if he parked the wagon on a side street near the dungeon at an early hour it wouldn't attract any undue attention at nightfall. He knew the trip from the dungeon to the city gates early the next morning with the freed baroness on board would cause him more than enough worries as it was.

Gerion wore a large hat and a heavy blue jacket as he pulled his vehicle to a stop. He put a feed bag on the mule, combed its neck, and patted its croup, and arranged the harness. Then, pulling his hat low over his eyes, he took a nap on the coach box. When he arose, he began to brush his mule again and repeated all the little motions that a coachman would make just before departing. In this way he hoped to distract a casual observer from the fact that his wagon remained at the same spot for hour upon hour, hitched to a mule. When night finally fell and the street grew still, Gerion ended his pretense. He climbed one last time up on the box, emptied a bottle of cheap hooch over the floorboards and street, wrapped himself in a blanket and crouched down to play the roll of a drunk coachman asleep on the job.

His plan worked. Twice two city guards passed by, and both times they paused briefly at the wagon and interrupted their favorite topic—women—to exchange comments about the drunk and his terrible punishment, but neither went to the trouble to arrest Gerion or even wake him up.

Every once in a while, Gerion agonized that little Erborn was about to raise his voice inside the wagon, but Algunda kept the baby quiet by slipping sweet oatmeal into his little whimpering mouth.

Four strikes of the gong at the Temple of Praios rang out through the night. The magician stretched his stiff limbs and climbed down from the box. He discreetly knocked at the wagon door, which opened immediately. "I'm going in now," he whispered. "Be ready! If everything goes as planned, Selissa and I will be strolling back in no time. But you never know . . . we might be in a big hurry. Over there, the prison door—keep an eye on it. If we come out slowly everything is fine. But if you see us running, lock up the wagon and be as quiet as a mouse. Wait awhile and then try to bring the wagon to the harbor. I will find you there, Phex willing . . ."

"Be careful!" said Algunda in a quiet but excited voice.

"If I were careful, I wouldn't be here," muttered the magician, trading his large hat for a felt cap before walking over to the prison gate. He glanced around then closed his eyes, concentrating on the image of a uniformed rider who once flew past him in full gallop on the road to Gareth. With the image firmly in his mind, he lifted and let drop the heavy iron door knocker. He waited awhile, then knocked again. Eventually he heard shuffling steps inside. A rusty lock squeaked and a pudgy forty-year-old woman's face appeared in the doorway. She blinked sleepily in the moonlight. "What, in the name of the many-horned beast are you doing here at this ungodly hour? Is the prince's palace on fire, or what?"

Gerion spoke with a serious voice. "I bring an important message from Angbar for the city guardswoman Elvine Hageldonf. Take me to her immediately."

The woman cringed. "I'm Elvine Hageldonf!" She nervously eyed the young blond courier in the uniform of the famous Riders of Beilunk standing on the steps before her. "By the Twelve, tell me what it is. Did my father or my brother send you?"

Gerion cast a glance to the side. "It involves a matter of the utmost importance. Should I really tell you here?"

"No, please come into the guardroom. Wait, I'll go ahead." The woman opened the door, let Gerion in, and locked the door behind him. She reached for a torch to light the way. There was a hall about ten strides long with faint light entering from a door at the far end.

"Now tell me!" demanded the woman, turning over her shoulder, "What brings you here?"

"The matter involves the freeing of a prisoner," said Gerion as he blackjacked the woman on the back of the head with a leather bag filled with sand and pebbles. She gasped in surprise and fell to her knees. Gerion grabbed her under the arms and helped her to the floor.

"What's going on, Elvine?" called a man's voice from the door at the end of the hall. Gerion looked up. With small, silent footsteps the magician quickly crept up to the door and pressed himself against the wall near the opening.

"Elvine?"

The creaking of wood announced that someone in the room had gotten out of bed and was crossing the floor. Gerion pulled the small dagger from his belt and banged his left hand on his chest while making choking sounds.

A dark figure appeared in the door and froze: The point of a dagger had just pierced the soft skin under the man's chin.

"That's a good fellow," hissed Gerion. "You're standing

as still as a temple column. Open your right hand!" A saber crashed to the floor. "Now turn a bit to your left. Good. Put your hands behind your head! Slowly, very slowly."

Without reducing the pressure of the dagger, Gerion looped a leather strap around the guard's hands and pulled it tight. Then he wound the loose end around the crossed wrists a few times. Finally, he put away the dagger and worked with both hands to make the bonds more secure.

"Feel free to scream if you like," murmured Gerion. "The question is will the Twelve grant you permission to enter Alveran if you're standing outside the gates all tied up and screaming."

The man, who was around thirty, dark blond, with round cheeks and a strong build, watched Gerion with wide eyes. "I'll be quiet," he reassured in a hoarse voice.

"That's very smart of you," replied Gerion. "Your comrade tried to warn you, so I had to send her to Boron! But you stand a good chance of surviving the night if you are clever. Where are the keys?"

The guard gestured toward a shallow cabinet with his chin. Gerion opened the doors. "The key to the cell hall is the big one at the top left," the guard whispered eagerly. "The others below it belong to the individual cell doors. Do you see the numbers?"

Gerion nodded. "In which cell will I find Lady Jergenwell?"

"Number six."

The hook for number six was empty.

"What?" Gerion pulled the dagger from his belt. "Where's the key?"

The guard made a noise that sounded like a soft whimper. "The woman from the IGI has it. By Phex, swear that you will let me live!"

"But there's a master key, isn't there? That's what you were going to say, right?" The tip of the dagger darted out and cut the man's cheek.

The guard suppressed a cry of horror. "Yes, yes, there's a master key—it's the one next to the big one, the one with the jagged teeth."

Gerion grabbed the key then saw another door on the far side of the room. Gerion unlocked the solid oak door and looked down the dark hallway lined with more heavy wooden doors.

"Number six is the second one on the right," said the guard.

Gerion took him by the arm and shoved him down the hall. He slipped the master key into the lock, then used both hands to turn it over. With a recalcitrant creak and moan, the door opened a crack. The magician grabbed the guard with both hands and pushed him into the pitch-dark cell—just in case a chair leg should come flying out of the darkness. But there was no motion in the impenetrable blackness.

"Selissa," whispered Gerion. "You still owe me for a bet. I've come to collect."

A figure in a light chemise glided out of the darkness. "Gerion . . . How? Why? What are you doing here?"

"I've come to rescue you, guardswoman. Your stable maid asked me to and I couldn't refuse. But get a move on! I don't want to stay here any longer than necessary. The atmosphere is quite depressing, don't you agree?"

"I can't believe it," stuttered Selissa and ran both hands

through her hair in astonishment. "When I'm free I can finally prove that . . . Oh, Gerion, dear Gerion, how can I thank you?"

The magician placed a handful of leather strips in her hand. "Here, take these. You can probably see better in the dark than I can. Is there anything in here we can tie this fool to?"

"The cot. It is fastened to the wall with iron hinges."

"Good, get to work!"

She efficiently tied the guard to the bed as Gerion ripped a strip of fabric from the guard's jacket, rolled it into a gag, and stuffed it into the bound man's mouth.

"Come on, let's go!"

On the way through the guardroom, Selissa excitedly grabbed at Gerion's arm while telling him bits of her story. "That Westinger is an Orc of a woman. What could I tell her? How could I tell her names that I don't know? Oh, Gerion, how can I ever repay you? These are terrible, terrible days. The count will pay, when I—"

They suddenly stopped before the body of the unconscious Hageldonf. Gerion bent down over the guard. "Now help me!" he ordered Selissa. "We have to lock her up with the other guard in the cell, but we will have to tie her up first!"

The woman came to as she was being dragged across the station, but Gerion made it clear to her with a few drastic words that her life was hanging on a silk thread. The woman showed her cooperation with a hearty nod. After the guard was tied up at the other end of the bed, Gerion locked the door again. Just to be sure, Gerion also locked the door between the guardroom and the hallway.

"Phew, we're done!" he sighed, as he rushed down the entryway to the prison gate with Selissa at his side. "It could have been much worse!"

Just at that moment there was a loud knock at the door. Selissa and the magician froze and exchanged baffled looks. Then Gerion gestured toward a niche next to the door where a broken chair, an open chest, and a few empty baskets were stored. "Crouch down over there!" hissed Gerion. "Make yourself small and don't move!"

The knock came again, more energetic than before.

Selissa hid in the corner among the rubbish. Gerion threw off his heavy jacket and draped it over the lancer so that she was completely hidden from sight while still being able to see through a gap in the fabric. Then he closed his eyes, forced his breathing to be calm, and concentrated on the image of Elvine Hageldonf.

More knocks and angry shouts interrupted his concentration, but he gathered all his powers and focused his thoughts. As he opened the door he was certain that his thin disguise would immediately be seen through, but the three figures in long dark coats barely looked at him as they pushed by the gate. "We're here to pick up our prisoner, guardswoman," snapped a red-haired woman. "What are you waiting for? Quick, come along, open the hall!"

Gerion looked out at the dark street. His eyes caught sight of Algunda's small body in a dark entryway across the street. The stable maid was looking anxiously up and down the street. Oh no, child, stay put! I have enough to worry about, he thought.

"Are you asleep?" the redhead snarled behind him. "Let's get a move on here!"

Gerion followed the trio into the guardroom. Who are these people? he wondered. They're obviously not City Guards. Why are they carrying a long wooden plank with them in the middle of the night? And what do they mean by "our prisoner"?

They reached the door to the hallway. Gerion produced the key from beneath his jacket and opened the door. The strangers hurried into the corridor and stood in front of the door across from Selissa's cell. In order to unlock the door, Gerion had to step into the hall, read the number on the door, and then hurry back to the key cabinet to get the corresponding key—a procedure to which his guests responded with moaning and grumbling. Finally, Gerion opened the locked door and the three shoved him aside and stormed into the cell.

Soon they reemerged breathing heavily and grunting. On the plank, which they had carried into the cell, lay a giant blond man tied up like a baby in swaddling clothes secured with heavy ropes. The man was either unconscious or asleep. Two of the strangers carried the head end of the board and one was struggling with the foot end. As they rounded the corner into the hallway, a loud groan issued from Selissa's cell. Gerion tensed. The long-coated visitors had also heard the noise. They set down their load in the hall.

"Did you hear that?" the red-haired woman asked her companions. "That came out of Jergenwell's cell. What's her problem?" She turned to the city guard. "Unlock it!"

Gerion took half a step back and felt for the master key under his jacket. Finally, he said in a high voice, "The woman from the IGI has the key."

"That's right," confirmed one of the men. "Lady Westinger always has the key with her. Oh well, if I were in Jergenwell's shoes I'd moan and groan, too! Come on, let's get going. We're already running late. It won't be long before daybreak!"

The three picked up the board again and carried it through the guardroom and foyer, cursing their heavy load in every possible way. Gerion mused over the uncertain but probably terrible destiny that awaited this blond man and briefly wondered if he even recognized the fellow. Never mind this bloke, he thought, I certainly have my own problems. Gerion feared that the mask of the City Guard could fail him and reveal his true identity at any minute. Phex, stand by me! Please! The illusion only had to last a few more moments and then they'd be safe.

The strangers had almost reached the prison gate when they were suddenly confronted by a woman in a short chemise. Unarmed but for her clenched fists, she stormed forward. "That is Arvid!" she yelled. "By the Twelve, they have Arvid!"

The plank with the sleeping giant crashed to the floor. The three thugs fumbled with their coats to get at their weapons.

Silence! Gerion thought in desperation. Above all this noise would have to be silenced. He pressed a finger to his lips and called upon the invisible powers and forces that penetrate all worlds, creatures, and objects to obey him—not all of the powers, not a chance, after all, he was not a god, but a relatively small area in the entryway of the Ferdok Dungeon that was emitting these telltale sounds into the night. With a thud it grew quiet. Totally silent.

The thugs exchanged shocked looks, unable to decide whether to attack or to flee. They glanced up the hall and saw the portly lady city guard approaching, then suddenly, as if he had passed through a thin curtain, a slender, gray-haired man appeared in her place.

"Watch out! It's black magic!" one of the thugs tried to cry out, but as his lips formed the words no sounds emerged. He grabbed at his throat as if he were choking.

Gerion approached him quickly and aimed a sharp kick at the man's groin. As the man buckled in pain, Gerion raised his fists and crashed them into the man's face. The man sank silently to the floor. Selissa quickly wrestled the saber from the other man and, holding the grip with both hands, drove the blade through his breast before he could even raise his hands to defend himself.

The red-haired woman turned and ran through the gate, her coat flying behind her as if she were being chased by demons. A petite figure in peasant's clothes emerged from the darkness and kicked her in the back of the knees as she ran by. The woman fell to the ground and slid across the cobblestones. Before she had shaken off the fall, she felt the blade of a saber against her neck. In the eerie zone of silence Selissa could not warn the woman that any careless movement would mean her death, but the redhead understood her anyway.

Together with Algunda, Selissa and Gerion hauled the thugs, including the dead one, into Count Arvid's cell. With no rope to bind them, Gerion instead ordered the man and the woman to stick out their tongues while Selissa held them at bay with her sword. He ran his right index finger and his thumb over their tongues, "Tungaradon,

Tanguradon, Tarangutat, Shumarhassav," he mumbled in a deep voice. Then he explained to the captured if they were to move within the next two hours or even make the slightest noise their tongues would swell up in their mouths and grow and grow until they finally split open their heads. But if they remained quiet the spell would leave them unharmed.

"Come on, come on! We have to get going!" Algunda said tugging on the magician's sleeve.

"Heed my warning!" Gerion threateningly called one more time into the cell. Then he locked the door and followed Algunda.

Selissa had already run ahead and was kneeling next to Arvid's unconscious body. She was patting him on the cheeks. "Arvid, dear Arvid, what have they done to you? Please wake up! Do you hear me? Wake up!"

Gerion tapped her shoulder. "That won't help. The drugs are still in effect. Help me move him back onto the board. Algunda, help us!"

They struggled to maneuver the count's considerable weight through the prison door, with Selissa at his head and the other two at his feet. At the threshold Gerion stopped and listened. "Not a sound to be heard!" he determined happily. "The best magic is the kind that isn't! Ha ha!"

In the eastern sky the first hints of morning light appeared as they unceremoniously shoved the sleeping count into the showman's wagon. The women climbed into the wagon and closed the door behind them with relief. Gerion took the mule by the halter and led it slowly down the street.

Chapter 9

ERION LOOKED OUT over the waters of Lake Angbar through a cold, gray drizzle that had arrived with the new moon of Boron. The magician thought longingly of the rare streak of warm, sunny days that had just passed. Indeed, benevolent Travia had graced the region with the most beautiful autumn since the time of Emperor Reto. Why do we old folks always say "since the time of Emperor Reto" whenever we want to label an experience exceptional? Gerion mused as he gazed at a dead oak along the shore. Why is it that the pages in Satinav's chronicle of bygone days glow ever more golden the further back one turns the page?

For young intellectuals, of course, that glow is nothing more than a figment of the imagination, the result of deceptive memories that spread sparkling dust over the past. This shiny veil of dust is often so thick that one can only see the gilded surface and no longer recognize what's truly beneath it. There can be nothing better about the past, those clever young minds maintain, because the world is constantly evolving. Just as a tiny acorn grows into a strong and mighty oak, claims youth, so does the world develop over time, ever increasing in complexity and value.

Gerion pulled his head down lower between his shoulders as he looked out again at the ancient oak. It would take three people to reach around the base of the trunk, but the wooden column had long been hollowed out by a weathered gray and mossy rot. One branch as big around as a man's arm remained on the trunk, boasting a handful of limp, brown leaves at its end that bore witness to the spark of life that still remained within this ruin of a tree. Gerion noted, a wary smile creeping across his face, that a web of vines had wrapped itself around the trunk and was slowly choking this last trickle of energy.

In Emperor Reto's day there was indeed the odd sunny month of Travia, thought Gerion as he scratched the wiry hair on Gurvan's hard skull. We old folks are right about that. Perhaps we're right, too, for dwelling on the past. What if everything inevitably becomes worse from the start and it's the youth who spread gold dust on the future and the present because otherwise they couldn't bear to face the true course of life? What if dying is our only purpose in life? What if we exist just to entertain the gods with our small and grandiose failures? Isn't it just as the young bard sings: There is no success that exceeds failure, but failure is never success?

Even if *something* is evolving, what is it leading to? Just because our lives are arduous doesn't mean that they're leading us to better things. Who knows what possibilities the heavenly lottery gives the seed that grows into a tree? Perhaps it could have become a golden dragon, maybe a god, a ruler of the world and time. Didn't the tree limit itself by taking the shape it did? Only the seed is timeless and without form. He who plants it kills it by subjecting it to Sumus's chains and Satinav's horns.

Gerion sighed. When will I have the chance to bud, to become the magician king of the world, or at least the equivalent of a splendid oak tree? When did I begin to tie myself down, so that nothing is left of me but a sharpening stone for Satinav's high spirits? We start dying the day we are born and everything that we receive in life is always taken away again. We learn to treasure whatever we have only after it is gone. Isn't that the golden dust of things gone by!

As Gerion continued his reverie, a bright alley in Mendena appeared in his mind. A small horse-drawn carriage clattered over the road, past the Cheery Cupbearer with its green shutters still closed tight and past the bakery, where the baker with his big belly waved his hat amidst the warm scent of baking bread. "Greetings! Praios be with you, Master Rothnagel! A wonderful morning, isn't it?"

"Good morning, Master Polk! It is indeed a lovely day!"

But Gerion's eyes were already focused on the white house at the end of the alley, searching for the two little redheads that always appeared at the door when the coach brought its tired passenger home after a hard night's work. But the twins were nowhere to be seen. Only good old Semjago stood by the gate to take the carriage horse by the halter and lead him through the narrow entrance. "Good Morning, Sir! Isn't it a spectacular day?"

"Morning, Sem. It couldn't be better!"

A woman in a simple gray dress stood near the kitchen door of the house. She was petite, boyish, but with delicate curves, as if she combined the beauty of both sexes. The morning breeze played in her red curls. Her face was serious, an expression that did not really suit her small nose and countless little freckles. "Good morning, my love," said the woman in a soft, hoarse voice as she wiped her tearful eyes with the back of her hand. "There were bad tidings from Festum last night. It seems my father Phexdan is dying. I want to go home. I've already arranged for a ship. It leaves at noon. I think I will take the twins along with me, you wouldn't know what to do with them here. . . . You look tired, love. You should rest."

Gerion gathered her in his arms. "Not now. Not if you're leaving . . ."

"Oh, nonsense, it will be hours before we go. I will wake you in time to accompany us to the harbor."

A whine from Gurvan brought Gerion back to the present. He felt for the purse around his neck and pulled out a well-worn slip of paper. He unfolded it carefully so that the almost transparent sheet would not be further damaged. Flattening the paper on his knee, he looked at the small round letters as if he were reading it for the first time. *I couldn't bring myself to wake you, Love. You were sleeping like a baby. Besides, what good is that superstitious waving of handkerchiefs on the pier? We will see each other very soon. Until then, keep me in your heart, my love. Your Winja.*

Gerion put the note away and gazed into the distance where the choppy waves, rain, and clouds blurred into an indistinguishable fog in which the hint of a dainty,

eternally young woman with wild red curls took form.
The magician closed his eyes and began to sing.

> Oh gray demon time—
> You accompany me past my prime.
> You're always at my side,
> Scornfully and stride by stride.
>
> Pale demon of fright,
> It's you in the dark night
> Reaching for my days
> With your cold gaze.
>
> Black demon of hate,
> Casting a bleak fate.
> Never at rest
> Evil boils in your breast.
>
> A new harsh wind blows
> Everywhere grass grows
> Dearest, fear not
> Each other we've got.
>
> Horned one, come on by!
> Now it is you and I.
> My love conquers you
> Tonight you are through!

"That's a sad song," mumbled Algunda, who was sitting quietly under the awning of the showman's wagon
and had just put another piece of wood on the small fire.

Gerion smiled at her. "Why is it sad? It has a happy ending, so it can't—"

"Not when you don't have a lover," interrupted Algunda. "If one doesn't have a lover, it's not happy. And you didn't sing it like a lighthearted song. I don't think that you are as happy as you always pretend to be. You jest and make jokes, but no one can be funny all the time."

Gerion patted the maid on the shoulder. "You worry too much, dear Algunda! Just because you are weepy doesn't mean everyone else is."

"If you don't have anyone to love, you can't be truly happy," insisted the maid. "We humans were not meant to be alone. Anyone who is alone too much gets dark thoughts, according to my mother." Algunda nodded her head in emphasis. "It's true."

"Dark thoughts . . . ," repeated Gerion as he smiled at the old oak. "I would know, wouldn't I? Besides, I haven't had as much company in years as I've had in the last two days. So much pleasant company . . ."

With these last words he turned to Selissa, who sauntered down the wagon steps and under the tarp. Arvid was right behind her.

Selissa wrinkled her brow. "With you one never knows if you're jesting or telling the truth . . ."

"He's a joker, isn't he?" Algunda nodded.

Gerion looked at Arvid to come to his aid. "Your Highness, I ask you, can you imagine anyone referring to the Lady Baroness as 'pleasant company' in jest?"

Arvid put his hand on Selissa's waist and drew her close. "No," he replied laughing. "Anyone who did would not be in his right mind." He let go of the baroness and stepped to the edge of the tent roof to look up at the bleak sky. "I realize that I've been asleep for a long time, but to fall asleep in the warm summer and to awake in the damp fall is quite depressing. Lake Angbar, hm? I've read about it. 'The sapphire of Kosch,' they call it. I must admit I imagined it a bit differently." He suddenly turned around and shook Gerion's right hand with both his hands. "I thank you for everything that you have done for Selissa and me. You are a good man. Excuse me for not thanking you earlier this morning when I first awoke . . . but I was disoriented and—"

Gerion pulled his hand free and waved him off. "Fine, fine, your Highness, your tongue was not yours to command this morning. You really just rolled your eyes around and fell back asleep . . ."

"I had many strange dreams . . . mostly I was at sea—"

"And you were snoring," Selissa jumped in, "like a gang saw! Loudest, of course, right in front of the city gate guard! If I hadn't pinched your mouth and nose shut . . ."

"That's true, I also dreamt of an octopus that tried to suffocate me with all its might. What a horrible dream!" The count crouched down next to Gerion and looked out over the lake. "Why did you put your life on the line for us, my good man? As much as I thank you for your courageous act, I cannot understand why you did it. How does your destiny relate to ours?"

"Oh, it wasn't that big of a risk, your Highness." Gerion glanced up from the lake and the oak tree and laughed. "I wanted to collect on my bet. Besides, I was being blackmailed."

Count Arvid was surprised, "Blackmailed? What do

you mean by that?"

"Look into Algunda's eyes when she wants something and you'll know what I mean."

"It's not my fault . . . I just wanted to . . ." Algunda leapt up and her lower lip began to quake.

Selissa cheerfully put her arm around the maid's waist. "Calm down, my dear. Master Gerion is only joking. You are a fine girl." She pulled the maid to her side and spun her in a circle so fast that Algunda's feet left the ground. Selissa put her on the ground laughing. "If you only had bigger feet and a second pair of shoes! It's too cold to go barefoot now." The lancer flexed her naked toes in the wet grass.

"It's a shame that you have to wear my clothes and go without shoes," said Algunda. "You're not a maid."

Selissa ran her hands over the leather girdle that was tightly laced around her torso and smoothed the black knee-length skirt of heavy winter wool. "Anything is better than that horrid prison shirt. I thank you kindly for your clothes and once we see better times I will buy them from you with good gold ducats so that I will always have them to remember you by."

"Better times," grumbled the count. "Do you mean when we have something to chew on again? I'm as hungry as an ogre! Master Gerion, didn't you remember to pack a basket of hearty provisions for our trip to the country?"

"I must admit I didn't think of it. I never buy provisions for my travels. If I need something on the road, I get it from the local peasants. It's fresher and cheaper and the folks always tell you the latest news. However, we're not yet far enough from Ferdok to knock at a farmhouse.

I'm sure they're already looking for us, and what peasant wouldn't like to earn a few extra ducats to help him make it through the winter?"

"A few ducats?" asked Selissa. "Do you really think that they put a price on our heads?"

Gerion nodded. "Don't forget that in their eyes you're a follower of Count Answin. Besides, you sent an IGI man to meet Boron."

The lancer looked at him seriously. "Are you reproaching me for killing that man?"

"No, why should I? Each person fights as he or she was taught. And to truly cherish life, life in and of itself, you are definitely not old enough."

"All life?" interjected Count Arvid. "Even that of a rat? Come on now, Master Gerion, you are talking like one of Tsa's sentimental sisters. Tell me, what is the worth of an IGI rat? He snoops around his entire life, threatening and torturing people, bringing misfortune—by Rondra, I truly prefer a river rat! My girl, you certainly did the right thing. If I hadn't slept through the best part I would have slit the other scoundrel's throat."

Gerion smiled thoughtfully. "Back home in Tobrien they say that everyone who has ever killed will be visited by their victims one night. They will ask you why you did it. And if you don't have a good answer, they'll nail your soul to the bedposts and you will never go to Alveran."

Count Arvid stood up and walked out into the rain from under the shelter of the tent and stretched. "What the people say . . . Even if it were so, I'm certain that I would have the right answer."

"I'm not so sure," Gerion mumbled quietly. Then he

raised his head. "I saw a small herd of half-wild goats by
the road this morning. If we could get one, your Highness, the table would be provided for. 'Land on the Bor,
land of the hunter,' isn't that the saying?"

"Give me a bow of Norburg ash and show me a well-built
buck, then, with Firun's help, I will triumph in the hunt,
but this here . . . This is utterly ridiculous. The beasts
will laugh at us, Master Gerion!"

"I admit it's easier said than done," Gerion pulled his
improvised hunting spear—a slender tree branch with
a dagger lashed to one end—from the grass and threw a
glance towards the herd of six large female goats that had
gathered about forty strides away. The goats flicked their
tails while skeptically watching the hunters.

"Come on, your Highness, let's try it again. Or do you
have a better suggestion?"

"How should I know what to do? This is my first goat
hunt, my dear sir. This time you go to the left and I will
go around to the right. Be careful not to throw too soon
again!"

"I didn't throw too soon," muttered Gerion. "The beasts
just knew what I was up to, right Gurvan?"

The old dog looked attentively at the magician. His
large ears were pricked, his fangs sparkled, and his wet
tail wagged happily, distributing a fine fog of water drops.

"You seem to find this all rather funny. I'll tell you one
thing, you lazy bum. When we roast the goat, you aren't
getting any of it! Look, they're up there. Go get the fat
one with the white spot on its forehead and herd it this
way. Get going, what are you waiting for?" Gurvan jumped

up in excitement and rubbed his damp head against Gerion's thigh. Then he sat back down and scratched himself in peace. Gerion shrugged. "Oh, well . . ."

The goats raised their heads now and again, chewing grass as they meandered along. Though they appeared nonchalant, the beasts maintained a safe distance from the men. If one of the hunters attempted to get closer, the goats leisurely trotted ahead. If the hunters stood still, then the goats froze, too. One animal always kept its eyes on the men while the others nibbled at the wet, yellow grass.

"By Firun! You are making this hard!" cried Count Arvid as he threw a fist-sized stone at the herd. The goats took a few casual steps to the side and then returned to their grazing.

The count took off his large hat with the limp feather dangling from it and slapped it on his thigh. "I haven't made this big of a fool out of myself in a long time," he called over to Gerion. "I suggest we give up before I explode with anger."

"One last try, your Highness!" replied Gerion. "This time I'll stay here and won't move. You go around the herd and drive them back towards me. Maybe we will be luckier this way."

Count Arvid did not answer as he marched ahead shaking his blond head. Once he had skirted around the herd, he turned and headed back toward the goats, swinging his broad-brimmed hat through the air. The animals watched him approach and hesitantly began to edge toward Gerion, who was standing as still as a statue with his spear poised to throw. When the goats were just thirty strides from Gerion, they turned to one side and in two quick leaps they reestablished the distance between themselves and the hunters.

Furious, Gerion thrust his spear. The weapon flew in a flat curve through the air and dug into the grass a few strides from the herd. One of the animals lifted its head and let out a long bleat.

"That's it!" Gerion yelled. "You stupid animal, I'm going to kill you! I will strangle you!" Without knowing what he was doing, he lunged through the grass after the goats, Gurvan hard on his heels. Suddenly the black dog shot forward, letting out a high-pitched hunting bark as he tore across the meadow. With one last energetic leap, Gurvan's sharp canines dug into the thigh of a goat, sending both animals rolling through the grass. The goat freed herself for a moment and struggled to her feet, but the dog soon wrestled his prey to the ground again.

Leaping wildly through knee-high grass with his heart hammering against his ribs, Gerion reached the scene of the drama and drove the spear into the goat's neck with all his weight. Blood bubbled onto the grass. Gurvan's jaws snapped at the goat's throat, took hold, and held tight. The goat's head tossed less and less violently until the brown body lay still.

"Let go, Gurvan!" yelled Gerion, but his voice sounded foreign to him. Black spots danced before his eyes and his heart drummed more painfully than ever against his ribs.

"You're still very fleet of foot when need be, Master Gerion. I'm impressed!" Count Arvid patted Gerion on the shoulder. Then he bent down and grabbed the dog by the nape of his neck and pulled him up. "Let go now!

That's a good dog."

Gerion looked down at Gurvan, who was panting as if in throws with Boron himself. "We haven't run like that in years," he puffed smiling. "Right, old buddy?"

Gurvan fell to one side with his rib cage heaving.

"Why didn't you set the dog after the goats sooner?" asked the count. "It would have saved us a lot of trouble."

"I tried to," Gerion explained with a wry smile, "but he had forgotten what a hunt is. Anyway, I'm glad he finally remembered."

"What's keeping them? It's almost dark," Selissa sat on the wagon steps watching the path that Gerion and Count Arvid had taken a few hours earlier.

"They'll be back soon," replied Algunda from inside the wagon. She was feeding Erborn a mush of stale bread mixed with a bit of milk and sugar water. Selissa turned around and watched how the tiny wooden spoon disappeared between the baby's lips and reappeared licked clean. She wrinkled her nose. "Your son seems to be a gourmet. I don't know how he can eat that gruel."

Algunda seemed not to hear Selissa's comment. "I will have to get some milk tomorrow," she said. "If I could only breast-feed! Imagine, Lady of Stubbo nursed her son until he moved out to attend the military academy. My cousin told me that. I've never been able to nurse. My mother said it's because I don't have a husband. But that can't be—many wet nurses don't have husbands, either." She wiped Erborn's lips and laid him back down in his basket. "You're laughing, aren't you? Now you're content, hm? If you only knew how hard it is not to eat your bread!

Oh . . . I'm so hungry!" Algunda crouched down by the wagon door and watched the path with Selissa. "I'm sure they will be back soon," she said once again and then continued without pausing, "Your Sir Highness is a very handsome man—big and strong, and when he laughs I always have to laugh, too. You must be very pleased to have such a fine fiancé."

"I am. Arvid is a good man."

"Are you going to move to Borland with him now?"

"Not immediately. I first have to make someone at Castle Wengenholm explain himself and take back what has been stolen from me." Selissa pressed her fist against her teeth. "No, I can't go to Borland like this."

"But aren't you afraid to go to Castle Wengenholm? I mean, Mr. Gerion told me that they're looking for you. They could easily set a trap for you. That evil Count of Wengenholm certainly is after your blood. He has to if—"

"Don't you think I know the danger that awaits me?" Selissa interrupted. "Certainly I'm afraid, but why should I give in to my fear? Should the cad who killed my father and my brother escape unpunished because I preferred to save my own skin?"

Algunda cringed against Selissa's torrent of bitter words and answered in a quaking voice, "But I just meant that . . . I mean, if you go to Wengenholm and you are killed there, it was all for naught. All the trouble that Mr. Gerion went through to free you from prison . . ."

Selissa laid her hand on the maid's shoulder to comfort her. "You are really a good soul. I'm sorry that I lashed out at you. But don't you think the magician freed me from the dungeon so I can do what I need to do rather than spend the rest of my life hiding? Go ahead, ask him why he helped me when he returns. You will see that I'm right."

Algunda said nothing for a moment and then she shook her head. "I'm not so sure. Mr. Gerion is not a soldier. I think he thinks more like I do. By that I mean that he got you out so you could live." She smiled. "Besides, didn't he say he freed you because you still owe him a hundred gold ducats?"

Selissa smiled in return. "He's a funny fellow. I like him very much. It's too bad we won't be able to be together much longer. I shall miss him. Have you thought about where you are going? Arvid and I can't really take you with us to Wengenholm. Perhaps you can accompany Gerion. Perhaps he needs a loyal maid . . ."

Algunda quickly rubbed her eyes. "No one needs me," she whispered, then continued louder, "Gerion doesn't like to have women in his wagon. He told me that himself. I also promised him that Erborn and I wouldn't be a burden for long. I told him that I would go to my aunt in Elenvina, but that isn't true. I mean, I do have an aunt there, but she is a wicked, miserly old woman. Perhaps I will go south. With a bit of luck I could find my Jangu and show him our Erborn. Then we could be married. Jangu could work in a sattlery, he knows a lot about awls and leather. I would stay home and keep the house and when little Erborn is a bit older, I could take care of the horses for our neighbors . . ." She suddenly fell silent. "I'll never find my Jangu again," she said quietly.

"Come on, now, didn't you promise me to stop crying so much?" admonished Selissa. "How can you give up before you've started? You have to—" She stopped short. "There, something is moving on the path. It's them! They're coming!" By the time Gerion and Arvid returned with their bounty darkness had fallen over the lake. It took a while for Arvid and Algunda to clean and skin the animal with a knife and a dagger, and then it took longer still until the roast had hung over the fire long enough for the outer layers to be edible. It was late at night before they were able to satisfy their hunger. When the others crawled inside the wagon to sleep, Gerion, who felt he wouldn't get any rest soon anyway, stayed by the fire to stand guard over the land and roast, as he put it. He fed the fire more wood so the goat would finish roasting by morning. As the fire died down he stared into the dark expanse of Lake Angbar, Gurvan snoring contentedly at his side.

"Should I wake you up if there is any excitement, old boy?" Gerion asked quietly. "It would be very embarrassing for you as a watch dog to miss any important event." Gurvan awoke and blinked sleepily at his master, then smacked his lips once, twice, and began to snore again.

It was then that Gerion noticed soft gurgling noises coming from the lake. While he was pondering if these sounds were any different from the other watery noises that emanated from the shore, he heard the soft sounds of footfalls. Without raising his head he opened his eyes and peeked out to see three figures, too few to be pursuers from Ferdok, more like . . .

"Uh-oh, visitors so late!" Gerion crowed in the shrill, shaky voice of an old man. "What brings you three wanderers here?"

The three figures stepped into the soft light of the dying fire. Gerion quickly assessed they were all female.

"Yes, it's late, and you should be asleep, old man." The woman in the middle of the trio spoke. She was the largest among them, a corpulent woman with a dark hood. In her hand she carried a long saber. The other two women were armed with rapiers. "You built your little fire so cleverly so no one could see you from the road, didn't you?" mocked the fat woman. "But you didn't think about the view from the lake. What should happen to you if you are seen by lake pirates? Did you consider that?"

Gurvan woke up, sniffed at the strangers, and growled. Gerion reached for his collar. "Quiet!" he warned softly, then he raised his voice, quaking with fear, "Lake pirates, by the Twelve! I didn't think of that."

The three moved closer and stood about three steps away from Gerion. The leader was wearing well-worn leather armor. The other two had scarves tied around their heads and wore wide, light-colored pants and dark jackets of the kind preferred by rivermen and fisherpeople.

"Oh yes, horrible, terrible pirates," explained the woman, her armor gleaming in the low light of the fire, "who will cut open an old fellow's neck and take away his money. That's why you should give it to us instead, old man. If you have nothing, the pirates won't do you any harm. See, we have come to save your life. That's why they call us the 'good fairies of the lake.'"

Gerion began to shake, "But, but I'm just an old charlatan!" he stuttered. "I don't have any money, not a crown, good fairies. Believe me!"

The fat woman stepped closer and raised her saber.

"Do you think we're idiots, you blabbermouth! You charlatan folks always put aside a few silver coins! Hand 'em over and make it fast, otherwise you will have peed in your pants for the last time tonight."

Gerion went to get up. "It's in the wagon," he said in a falsetto voice. "I'll go get it for you."

"You won't move your ass a finger!" barked the fat woman. "You are going to crawl into your wagon and come out holding a cross bow, huh? Do you think we were born yesterday? Hitta, go see what you can find!"

"Please, go ahead!" croaked Gerion. "I won't budge."

One of the pirates climbed up the wagon stairs and threw open the door. There was a dull thud and then the woman flew backwards through the air as if she had been kicked by a horse. "By Rondra!" thundered Arvid's powerful voice through the darkness. "These fools were sent to us personally by the goddess!"

The fat woman in front of Gerion cowered in fear, her eyes jumping nervously between the magician and the wagon. She lifted her saber and took half a step back. Gerion raised his right hand and made a delicate gesture with two fingers at the woman. "Lightening strikes you!" the magician hissed.

The robber was about to swing her saber when a burning white flame bit at the woman's eyes. She raised her left arm in defense and heard the same terrible voice say, "Gurvan, get her!" She then felt a dog's jagged teeth sink into her weapon hand. She spun around in wild fear and experienced a second charge that caused a terrible pain in her head. She saw a wall of red flames licking around her and heard a horrifying crackling that drove all other sounds from her ears, sending her falling into endless darkness . . .

"Let go, Gurvan! Let her go!" commanded Gerion as he tossed aside the thick piece of wood he had used to club the robber over the head and into the fire. He removed the weapon belt from her large midsection, found a dagger in her boot, and quickly used it to cut through the thong that held her purse to her chest. He investigated the contents. There were almost eight gold ducats in all sorts of coinage. What poor devils once owned these coins? Gerion counted three silver coins and put them back into the bag and tossed the lot back onto the unconscious robber's belly.

Selissa approached through the darkness. "The third one got away!" she announced angrily. "I think she ran straight into the lake. Anyway, the boat they came in is still there."

Arvid was holding the pirate he struck by the collar of her jacket and was dragging her limp body through the grass. "I broke your stool, Master Gerion," he explained, shrugging his shoulders, "By the Twelve, this wench has a thick skull." The woman had a large gash above her cheekbone and her right eye was already almost swollen shut. Arvid took a careful look at her face and mumbled something like, "She'll be alright; she wasn't a beauty to start with." He reached for her rapier and made a few energetic motions with it in the air. "Oh, it feels good to finally have a decent piece of iron in hand," he determined. He tossed Selissa the leader's saber. "Here, catch! Now you won't have to travel naked."

"The shoes, Lady Baroness," said Algunda, who had

just climbed out of the wagon with the whimpering baby on her arm, "take her shoes! They aren't badly made and I will clean them for you."

Selissa pulled the mud-crusted buckled shoes from the pirate's feet and slipped into them. "Indeed, they fit!" she rubbed the shoes on the grass to get some of the dirt off them. "I'll clean them myself," she said smiling to Algunda, "you are no longer my maid, you are my friend."

"Your friend? But . . ." Algunda couldn't find the words. If it weren't dark one would have seen the blush come to her cheeks. "But that's impossible, Lady Baroness . . ."

"Stop calling me Lady Baroness, if you will!" Selissa's face was ironically serious. "You don't want to get in a fight with your friend, do you?"

"I can't stand aside now, either," said the count with a broad smile. He extended his right hand to Gerion. "Call me Arvid, my friend!" Over the bodies of the unconscious robbers the four shook hands. Just as Selissa was about to extend her index finger to little Erborn, the leader of the pirates awoke. She reached for the back of her head and carefully looked around the group assembled around her. "Mercy," she stuttered. "I have three small children at home and an old blind father—"

Gurvan growled and the robber stopped short. Gerion looked thoughtfully down at her and then he turned to Arvid. "I think we should kill her right now, Captain! She'll hang anyway and we could spare her the horrible interrogation in Ferdok. That would be the merciful thing to do."

The robber suppressed a cry of fear.

"Where do you live? Where is your hideout?" Arvid

barked at the woman.

"Not far from here, your Honors! In a house on the edge of the lake, over that way." Without getting up she pointed at the lake.

"Oh, Sir Inquisitor," said Arvid to Gerion. "I'm in such a benevolent mood today. Perhaps that is because I have sent too many people to the gallows over the last few days. Let's interrupt the blood letting. Why don't we just let this rogue go? She has taken her lumps."

Gerion swayed his head in thought. "I don't know if I can approve of that, Captain. Our mission to rid Angbar of thieves is scheduled to last a week. This fat fool will never be able to stay in her house for that long. What will happen then? Our simpleton will run into other patrols and then it will come out that you were too lenient. When our hefty woman here is caught, you'll be in trouble back in Gareth. No, Captain, it's not worth it."

"I won't . . . ," wailed the robber. "I won't go a step from the house. By Phex, by the Twelve, I swear no one will see me!"

"Now look, your honored Inquisitor," Arvid bowed at Gerion. "She understands how important this is. One could grant her mercy."

The magician wrinkled his forehead. "If you assume full responsibility, Captain . . ."

"I will gladly do so," Arvid bent over the robber. "Fine, I know I'll regret it, but I will give into Phex this time, although I don't know if he will grace your kind. Take your sleeping companion and beat it. What are you waiting for? Go home to your children. And say hello to your blind father from Captain Bardo Bloodfist!"

As fast as a weasel the well-rounded robber stood up. She pulled her unconscious companion up with one arm, threw her over her shoulder, and rushed panting toward the lakeside.

"There are no rewards for robbery if you're not clever," called Gerion. "Never forget that, my stout daughter!"

Chapter 10

OUNT ERLAN STRAIGHTENED the short black cape on his shoulders, placed his left hand on the grip of his sword, and crossed the great hall with a bounce in his step. On the right side near the tall, narrow windows, the count noticed an assembly of men and women garbed in exquisite garments trimmed with fur and white lace fraise collars. He quickly determined that they were only merchants and guildspeople. He touched the brim of his hat with his thumb and forefinger to suggest the curtest of greetings, and responded to their murmur with an ironic smile in passing. The count strode towards the double door at the head of the hall that was flanked by armed guards. A liveried servant, dressed in dark green with his back to the door, looked at him with a mixture of snobbery and insecurity.

"New to this post?" Count Erlan asked the young man. "Well, then we will attribute the fact that you are not greeting the Count of Wengenholm to your naiveté." He waited until the lackey raised up from a hasty low bow. "Hurry! I must see the prince, the matter is most urgent."

The servant opened the door. Count Wengenholm walked half a stride behind him into the chamber and then pushed him aside before the lackey announced his presence. When he reached the center of the study, he doffed his hat and waved it in a gracious gesture. "Praios be with Your Serene Highness! As I can tell, Your Highness has returned from his travels in good health. This news is most welcome and comforting to me in these troubled times."

Indeed, Prince Blasius's plump face was healthy and ruddy as if he had recently spent extended time outdoors. His broad forehead was crowned with short gray hair and involuntarily wrinkled at the sudden interruption. It took a few moments until the prince's expression changed to a smile of acknowledgment. "Praios be with you and Ingrimm's grace!"

The prince was seated on a burgundy wing chair behind an enormous desk of dark brown, highly polished wood. In front of the desk a well-fed woman in the clothes of a merchant was seated on a delicate, high-backed chair. The woman stood up as soon as the count entered the room. She was holding a very large hat like a shield in front of her breast and lowered her head to greet the newcomer. At the left end of the table sat a slight man with blond silken curls dressed in a finely woven gray frock coat and breeches. The chancellor of Kosch, the Imperial Knight Duridan of Sighelms-Halm, determined Count Erlan in dissatisfaction. He would have preferred a private audience with the prince.

The chancellor stood up and made a hasty bow. "Praios be with you, Your Highness!" He sank back down in his chair and invited the merchant to continue. The woman cast a shy glance at the prince and then at the count standing next to him and said hesitantly, "Your Highness will understand that if the shipping tariffs are affected by a prohibited arrangement between the rivermen—"

Count Erlan interrupted her with a clearly audible sigh. "Good woman, can you not see that this is not the time for your complaints? I rushed here from Castle Wengenholm to have His Highness tell me all about his travels and the latest political developments in the world. Why don't you proceed out to the hall where you can discuss your concerns among yourselves?" He winked at the prince conspiratorially. "Well, what are you waiting for?"

The woman looked at the prince and chancellor in dismay, but there was no opposition to be heard. She mumbled a barely intelligible, "Yes, but—", and backed toward the door with repeated curtsies.

Count Erlan sat down on the chair in front of the desk. "Your Highness, do tell! You must have experienced and seen an amazing number of interesting things. I am terribly excited when I think of it." Before the friendly, smiling prince could open his mouth to respond, the count turned to the chancellor and said in a casual tone, "You will want to retire, dear Duridan. We won't be talking about politics. I am sure that His Highness would be willing to excuse you for a moment."

"True," nodded the prince. "Duridan, please leave, if you will. You have more important deeds to attend to."

The young chancellor smiled politely as he turned to

the count. "As you know, Your Honor, His Highness just returned from his voyage the day before yesterday, so that I have not had a chance to hear the tales of his travels, about which I, too, am terribly excited. So I would like to stay and listen, so that His Highness will not have to tell the same story twice. And if the topic changes, albeit unexpectedly, to politics, I will be at hand."

"He is right, Count Erlan," said the prince. "Please stay, Duridan, but spare us your humor—you certainly know what we mean. So, now let us think so that we start at the beginning and omit nothing important."

Prince Blasius began with a description of how a sloppily secured lead horse came untied the moment he had left the court and how it could only be lured back with a bushel of carrots, which took a terribly long time to obtain although there is no dearth of roots of all types under the moon of Efferd. Count Erlan shifted on the hard chair. As the story continued, the count's fidgeting movements became more frequent until finally the count rose to his feet to pace up and down in front of the desk. In the meantime, the chancellor stretched in his upholstered chair, making certain that the prince continued his story in the proper order. Whenever His Highness threatened to lose his place by asking the count how things were back at Wengenholm, the chancellor knew the right question to ask to bring the prince back on track—much to the dismay of Count Erlan who grew increasingly annoyed with the chancellor's presence.

In Kosch it was an open secret known to everyone, except the prince, that there was an old feud between the Wengenholms and the Sighelms, the line to which Chancellor Duridan belonged. But it was not the nature of either house to play out the conflict in the open. Instead, both parties preferred to strike at the other silently. An especially harsh blow came from the old Baroness Erma of Sighelms-Halm when she was able to convince the prince to take on her nephew Duridan two years ago. Count Erlan had not seen the Imperial Knight in a long time, but he hated him from the first moment of their most recent encounter, just as much as he did in his boyhood when he tried to pull Duridan's dandyish hair from his head at a wake.

The chancellor, by contrast, was less candid in showing his true feelings toward the count. He continuously regarded Count Erlan with the most friendly and polite smile. Only once did his face take on the deepest expression of sympathy when he told the count that another meeting with the prince would not be possible on the following day, because a mission from Andergast would occupy His Highness for the entire day. "Therefore, if you have something to present, Your Honor, you should do so now." But the count reassured him again that he had only come to hear the tale of the prince's travels and stood up to walk around the room again, followed by the smiling eyes of the chancellor.

As the distant gongs struck five, marking the end of the princely audience, the prince had not even shared half of his travel experiences with his listeners. The count looked at the ceiling in despair. Afraid that he would soon be asked to leave, he walked up to the front of the desk and interjected during the prince's description of a truly splendid boat ride, "Because Your Highness just asked me about affairs at home, well, there is something I meant to discuss."

The prince fell quiet and looked confused. To fill the sudden silence the chancellor said, "Don't you want to hear how His Highness finally weighed the anchor? Or is the topic now politics? How fortunate that I stayed!"

Count Erlan bit his lower lip. One day he would get this dandy, this fop of a chancellor!

The prince wrinkled his brow again. "Well then, dear Count, speak up. We can conclude our story some other time. What is on your mind?"

Count Erlan forced himself to keep his voice calm. "It is in regards to those Answinite rebels, the Jergenwells."

Prince Blasius's face grew serious. "We have heard of the affair. A courier brought us the news during our travels. A terrible thing, simply terrible! Who would have suspected old Lechdan and little Selissa? An old family, nobility from Kosch with body and soul, and now this! Is the evidence watertight? Did they indeed enter a pact with our archenemy, Ravenmund?"

"There is not the slightest doubt," replied the count.

In the same breath Duridan added, "As yet there has been no judgment to confirm their guilt."

"Now, what is this clamoring?" thundered the Prince. "One at a time, gentlemen. Count, it is your turn."

Count Erlan presented the story of the Jergenwells' conspiracy at a leisurely pace. He spoke of the witnesses' accounts, documents, and incriminating signatures that could be had from the royal court's clerk at any time, and he finally came to Selissa's escape. "There could hardly be a plainer admission of guilt. Selissa was the true leader of the rebellion, and she involved her family in the mire of treason and treachery, but she proceeded so carefully as to leave no documentation behind."

"And she killed that man from Angbar," mumbled the prince, whose brow was showing even deeper wrinkles. "We do not look kindly on that. Quite a bit of trouble and correspondence will result from that and possibly even a visit from the baroness. In that case, we want to have a few appropriate words for the lady."

The count took a bow, "I can imagine. However, if I may bring an important point to your attention; in order to speak to the woman, you will first have to capture her."

"Foolish interjection that was!" mumbled the prince. "One is looking for her, correct Chancellor?"

Before Duridan could reply, Count Erlan made a dramatic gesture at the window so that the prince instinctively looked in the same direction. "That is exactly my concern, Your Highness! A murderess and traitor is on the loose out there, and, in my opinion, not enough is being done to hunt her down!"

Wildly shaking his head, the prince looked away from the window and to the chancellor. "Duridan, what do you think? Is there reason to be concerned about this matter?"

The smile on Duridan's face slipped a bit. "Certainly not," he assured. "All necessary arrangements have been made."

"Not so!" The count pounded his right fist into his left palm. "What does Your Highness say about a ridiculous price on her head of fifty gold ducats? Does that seem right? Some child molesters and arsonists are priced higher!"

Duridan shrugged his shoulders, "*And always remember, dear Chancellor, save, save, save.* Those were your last words before you left . . ."

"All in good time, Duridan. We shall raise the price to one, no, two hundred gold ducats. Are you satisfied, count, or is there more?"

"Oh yes, Your Highness, there are too few pursuers."

"We are living in troubled times, Your Highness," added the Chancellor. "One felt it was inappropriate to pull your troops back from strategic locations and send them into the forest. And it is possible that the rabble-rousers have long left Kosch by now. They probably went south toward seditious Almadan. As Your Highness knows: birds of a feather flock together."

Prince Blasius of Eberstamm raised his heavy shoulders and smiled in reconciliation at the count, "Well, my dear Count, if they have already fled . . ."

Count Erlan sat down on the chair in front of the desk again, leaned forward, and looked intensely into the Prince's eyes. "That they have fled is in no way certain, Your Highness. I have a suspicion that their route is different. However, the most important issue at hand is the lack of zeal in tracking them down. Let me give an example. Just as I learned of the rebels' escape I turned to the Lady Commander of the Ferdok Lancers and asked her to send out a posse. It seemed appropriate to me, because I am certain that His Highness is familiar with the old huntsman's saying: It takes wolves to track a wolf."

"No, we don't know this saying, but it is a good one. We will want to remember it. It takes wolves to track a wolf, a good saying indeed."

Count Erlan forced a smile to his lips. "I am flattered that Your Highness wants to make note of my choice of words, but please let me continue. The Lady Commander showed herself to be most uncooperative in her letter of reply: she would take no order from me and she would most certainly not let herself or her guardswomen be entangled in conflicts between nobility. As if that were the issue at hand! My concern is the domestic peace in Kosch, but one is accusing me of evil personal motives. The woman continued in her writings that she would only take commands directly from Angbar and from your chancellor as long as Your Highness was away. Of course, under the circumstances I immediately turned to the Imperial Knight Duridan of Sighelms-Halm. However," the count glanced over at the chancellor, "I have not seen any results!"

"There is no correspondence from the count on record regarding this matter," said the chancellor. "Perhaps it was not presented to me because its importance failed to be recognized. But I will have the matter examined first thing in the morning."

"Tomorrow!" interjected the count. "There, Your Highness, you can see for yourself my concern: no zeal. Why not send an immediate command to the Ferdok Lancers? How will this passivity and dilatoriousness reflect on the powers in Angbar and the IGI?"

"You dare call His Highness dilatory?" The chancellor leapt to his feet and raised his fist in a theatrical gesture.

Count Erlan also rose. "You know very well who was the target of my blame, my dear fellow!"

"The count was referring to you, Chancellor," explained the Prince. "And we must say you are not proving yourself to be efficient. Therefore, please see to it that all necessary steps are taken immediately! And now, my sirs, please take your seats. You know how we dislike commotion. Does this relieve your concern, Count Erlan? Please remember that our time is limited. We are expecting guests to join us for the evening meal and we will have to freshen up before then."

Count Erlan obeyed the prince's wish and took his seat, but immediately rose again and indicated his intent to leave with a bow. "It seems to me that now finally everything possible is being done to prevent trouble in Kosch. My Prince, I thank you for your attention."

Prince Blasius stood up as well and extended his right hand to the count across the table. "Safe travels, my dear Count. And when you are back in Angbar please come see us so that we can bestow the rest on you."

"The rest, Your Highness, certainly . . ." The count tried to hide his confusion.

"The rest of my travel report, of course. What were you thinking?"

Count Erlan swept his hat along the floor and took two steps back. "It would be the greatest pleasure for me, Your Highness, to hear the tales of your adventures. As soon as it is possible to do so, I will return." After taking two more steps back and waving his hat once again, the count had almost reached the chamber door. "Oh, before I forget, there is one more small thing . . ."

"Yes, dear Wengenholm?" The prince raised his hand. "Speak up!"

As the count approached the desk again, he thoughtfully removed a speck of dust from the brim of his hat.

"It truly is not important, Your Highness, it is a quick motion of the quill so to speak . . . If Your Highness could confirm my mining rights to Rotstein? You know, the dwarfs insist, otherwise they will not work."

"Certainly, that can be done," Prince Blasius said with a friendly nod. "Chancellor, perhaps you could write a few words."

Chancellor Duridan carefully readied a quill, ink, parchment, and drying sand. Humming quietly, he sharpened the quill and dipped it into the ink well. "Well, what shall we write?" he half mumbled to himself. "We cannot *confirm*—as the count prefers to express himself—the mining rights because they have been assigned since time immemorial to the Jergenwells. One would have to speak of a *transfer*. Therefore, shall I write that Your Highness transfers the rights from one house to another, my Prince?"

"Well, that is not important." Prince Blasius showed his disinterest in the minor problems of his scribe by cleaning his right ear with a white handkerchief. "Write something—you will do the right thing."

"Your Highness must excuse me," added Count Erlan, "but an exactness in the text is certainly necessary. The chancellor can write transfer as far as I'm concerned. It is most important that the narrow-minded dwarf miners are kept happy."

Duridan added with a serious look, "One must ask oneself if the dwarfs will indeed be content if we just—in an almost casual manner—commit to such a transfer. As Your Highness knows, the furnace master, from the House of Ingerimm, has always been very sensitive to issues surrounding such a transfer. I must not remind Your

Highness of how the master reacts when he feels he has been excluded."

"That is true," added the prince with a hearty nod, "if one isn't careful the master will be offended for months or even longer! We can't allow that to happen. So come up with something else, noblemen." Prince Blasius looked carefully at the white handkerchief, wrinkled his forehead, and continued to clean his ears, this time with his eyes closed.

"Do you absolutely require something in writing on this matter, dear Count?" asked the chancellor. "The mine workers may well be dwarfs, but they are also your subjects. Why don't you tan the hides of one or two of them? Then the others will obey . . ."

"Oh, you don't know of what you speak, chancellor!" Count Erlan stomped his foot on the floor. "The Angroschims of Rotstein do not listen to my words, nor yours, they only obey Furdik, their overman and ore master. But this Furdik, son of Fammerik, stubbornly takes his orders only from the Jergenwells, the prince, or the King of the Mountain. As long as there are no orders, the fellows sit on their fat asses in their tunnels and comb their beards in peace. What does it matter to them that the wooden mine props rot or the tunnels crumble? They just sit there, even though the Rotstein ore is so important to all of Kosch. Soon some of Your Highness's soldiers will be without swords and smiths will be without work if the mines deteriorate. I truly do not care if the mines belong to the Jergenwells or the Wengenholms. I'm thinking of the wealth and the strength of our country and it infuriates me to think that the work at Rotstein might come to a halt! But what can I do to prevent this from happening? Tan the hides of a few dwarfs, I am advised. How? Am I supposed to send my guards into the mountain to pull out the Angroschim? No human can find his way down there. The dwarfs have dug around in the mountain like maggots in sourdough bread and only they know the passageways, and they can start a shaft collapse at will. Should I take the rogues under siege? I have heard that it is impossible to starve out a band of thick-headed dwarfs. They'll cook a soup of pumice stone before they give up. No, no, I need a clear directive that this Furdik will understand. Otherwise there will be no work done at Rotstein."

The prince listened to Count Erlan with a smile of satisfaction and finished his ceremonial cleaning. He put the handkerchief back in his sleeve and mumbled, "Yes, yes, we know about the temper of the little bearded fellows. But we don't know what we can do for you right now, dear friend. You heard a . . ." The prince looked at the chancellor with a questioning expression. Duridan helped him find the word that escaped him and he continued, ". . . a confirmation is not possible, and we would have to call in the furnace master for a transfer. Since that won't happen any time soon, you will have to prepare yourself for a wait. Hm . . . Now I am finished with my Bosperano, as they say."

"How about a temporary transfer?" asked Duridan in the thoughtful silence. "For a relatively limited period of time, let's say ten years initially, one wouldn't have to go to the Ingerimm priests for approval. Ten years is a very short period of time for the Angroschims anyhow."

Count Erlan sat back down on his chair. "Yes, certainly, that is a possibility! And when the mining is going well and all is in order, it will not be difficult to finalize the rights to the mines."

"I am also of that opinion," confirmed the chancellor.

"Thus it shall be written!" decided the prince with a sigh of relief. "Duridan, you are certainly clever from time to time. Our respect!"

The quill scratched across the parchment. After a short time the chancellor stood up. "A transfer—even a temporary one—is only possible when all entitled parties, generally the entire house of nobility, including all heirs, are dead or have been convicted of a serious crime against the Empire. However, to the best of my knowledge Baroness Selissa of Jergenwell and her brother, Baron Ulfing of Jergenwell are not dead nor have they been sentenced. That complicates the entire matter."

"What's so complicated about it?" countered Count Erlan. "Both are despicable criminals! Without a doubt!"

"There may be no doubt, but there is also no judgment," added the Chancellor.

Count Erlan turned towards him, "What do you mean, Duridan? More difficulties? Will this never come to an end?"

The chancellor lifted a small knife a short distance above the goose quill. "Please remain calm, dear Count. Procedures must be followed. That's the way things are done. Take the youngest Jergenwell, Ulfing. No one knows the true extent of—"

"A traitor, a rebel!" shouted the count. "A subject with no conscience, by my honor!"

"By your honor?" mumbled the chancellor. He then turned to the prince. "That is a possibility, Your Highness. All complaints and accusations against the Jergenwells come together in some way at one point: Count Erlan of Wengenholm. If the count will swear the holy oath that everything indeed occurred as it stands in the letter of accusation, and that young Ulfing is also guilty of these crimes . . . If the count will make this oath then Your Highness can take the holy vow as a judgment and the transfer could take place."

"Well, if you think so, chancellor." The prince drew his eyebrows together and looked at the count gravely. "Are you prepared to take the vow, Wengenholm?"

Without hesitation, Count Erlan raised his right hand. "I swear, by my honor."

The chancellor cleared his throat. "Forgive me for interjecting again, but the holy oath is necessary for this procedure. And as highly regarded as the honor of a nobleman is, it cannot be seen as holy in this context. Your Honor, please swear by our Lord Praios, by the true light, his anger, and his judgment."

The count grew pale, opened his mouth but did not speak.

"What is it, dear Count?" asked the prince in concern.

"Nothing . . . um . . . I," small pearls of perspiration had formed on Count Erlan's forehead.

"All of my accusations against the House of Jergenwell and its members are the plain truth," prompted the chancellor with restraint in his voice.

The count wiped his forehead with his sleeve. His lips trembled. He heard what the chancellor said but he did not understand the words. There was another loud voice in his head that repeated itself over and over—caught, it said.

"Dear Count, please take a seat!" implored the prince in a concerned voice. "We will ask a servant to bring you water immediately. Or smelling salts, or a doctor, if you think it is necessary."

Count Erlan cleared his throat. Coughing, he pulled at his lace collaret. He then nodded once or twice with closed eyes and finally said, "All of my accusations against the House of Jergenwell and its members are the absolute truth . . ." The chancellor mumbled the rest of the oath, and the count repeated the words, "I swear on our Lord Praios, by the true light, his anger, and . . . his judgment."

As the count sat down in the chair breathing heavily, the Chancellor's quill quickly scratched across the page. He soon summarized the text he had written up to that point: the Jergenwell family had, as confirmed by the holy oath of Count Erlan of Wengenholm, committed unconscionable acts against the crown of the prince and His Divine Magnificence, Emperor Hall I of Angbar. For this reason, the mining rights to the ore in Rotstein are to be temporarily transferred to another party, because it was not acceptable for the wealth of a criminal to be increased by exploiting the natural resources of Holy Mother Sumu, the enemy of all crimes. The chancellor stopped and looked at the count briefly, "I just had an idea, Your Honor. If I formulate the rest of the text as we discussed, then it may seem to your dwarven miners that you made your statement and swore your oath out of self-interest. In the end the diggers still wouldn't be willing to pick up their shovels. You must consider that . . ."

"Yes, yes, I consider that!" The count angrily lifted his hand. "Please don't make this more difficult, chancellor."

"Your Honor, if I remember correctly you said earlier it is not important to you to personally profit from this arrangement. So perhaps, we should take a moment to contemplate how we could avoid giving that impression. In the end, our goal is to give the miners no excuses . . ."

"Enough!" Count Erlan's fingers dug into the brim of his hat. "I know how to disarm false impressions and the reluctance of the dwarfs is a phenomenon that need not concern you, Chancellor!"

Duridan, unmoved, continued, "There is another possibility and it may well interest Your Highness . . ."

"Well, what then?" sighed the prince. "It seems certain that we are not going to make it to supper tonight. Please, Chancellor, speak your mind."

"If one were to complete a transfer," continued Duridan, "One could assign the mines to the respectable House of Eberstamm in place of the House of Wengenholm so as to detract from the possible vested interests of Count Erlan of Wengenholm."

The count starred at the chancellor with wide open eyes, his cheek muscles twitching. Involuntarily, he extended his right hand to the chancellor, then let it fall and returned his eyes to the prince, who had sat up in his heavy chair and was now taking interest. "That is possible, Chancellor?"

"Oh yes, certainly," nodded Duridan. "And think of the ramifications: in good times the mines in Rotstein bring in more than five thousand gold ducats a year, as far as I know!"

"Impressive!" praised the prince. "I forgot about that! Yes, then you most certainly should choose that alternative. That way all are served best. Dear Chancellor, you are a treasure!"

"I must go now," said Count Erlan abruptly. His voice had a snarling tone, almost as if he were under a spell. With unsure steps he teetered to the door where it took him a moment to find the door knob, as if his sight were failing him. Finally, he turned it and stumbled from the chamber.

"The count seems to be in ill health," determined Prince Blasius shaking his head in thought. "Perhaps we should have called a doctor."

"Yes, the count did seem a bit out of sorts," added the chancellor.

"He is a bit confused, but he is such a good listener, don't you think? There are only a few of them, chancellor. You could learn something from that. And your ironic comments were not called for! Wengenholm is a terribly serious person. Did you notice how seriously he took the oath of our Lord Praios?"

The chancellor spread sand over the parchment, then said quietly without looking up, "Praios loves seriousness, but he prefers the truth. I believe firmly in Lord Praios, and I believe that his day of judgment will certainly come. What sense would there be if it didn't?"

"What are you mumbling?" asked Prince Blasius.

"Nothing important," replied the chancellor. "I will excuse myself, as it would be irresponsible for me to keep Your Highness from the evening meal any longer."

Count Erlan was halfway down the ramp that led from the palace to the city before he took in his surroundings. Now he felt the icy rain striking his face and was aware of the pitch darkness he was walking in. He reached to pull his hat down over his face, but he realized that his hat was gone. He must have lost it along the way. He accepted the loss without regret or surprise. It seemed to him as if he was a figure from one of the inexpressibly boring travel stories of the prince: "And just before Angbar, no just beyond Angbar, well, it doesn't matter, but it certainly wasn't in Perricum, we, and now pay attention, saw a man at the side of the road whose hat was swept off by the wind and he didn't notice. He must have been the greatest fool in the entire empire. The man was so stupid that when he went to get that which he had envied all his life, he lost it all again because he didn't pay attention, because he couldn't wait until the right time and because the swine of a chancellor set a trap for him. And that the man did not loose his hat once, but twice in an hour. One should kill that man because he is too stupid to live. He wants everything and when he has the chance to get it he ruins it all because he is as impatient as a stinking goblin in heat. Yes, he is scum. Brainless scum . . ."

Erlan struck himself on the thigh and cried out into the night as he strode forward in anger, "Here comes the man without a hat! See the hatless man! Hear the story of the man without a hat! You will pee in your pants when you hear this one!" He grew quiet only after he found himself surprisingly close to the first houses of the city that looked like black triangles in the rain-filled night. He passed by the small shafts of yellow light that streamed through the closed shutters. He thought bitterly of the poor, fearful citizens in their stuffy rooms, who never dared to hope for bigger things, but also never had to face failure. "Here comes your Lord," mumbled the count. "Yes, look out your windows, you pitiful masses. You will learn to fear me! You may have me where you want me for now. Or you, there in the tavern, full of beer and content, nothing in your heads but boozing and whoring, no ambitions! Venture nothing, gain nothing!"

It was dark in Angbar, but night had only recently fallen. The citizens were not yet asleep and still at work in their homes. The rattling of dishes, arguments, music, and children's laughter fell on Count Erlan's ears. There were numerous noises with which the city ridiculed him. The count looked up and down the streets like a hunted man, but he found nowhere to hide. He headed for one tavern after another, but he stopped at threshold after threshold, because he knew inside the hall apathy, cowardice, and self-satisfaction awaited him. He stood for a long time in front of an inn. He had accommodation's at the Imperial Palace and his horse was stabled there as well, but he didn't want to spend the night under the same roof as fat Eberstamm and the revolting chancellor for any price. However, he couldn't get himself to enter the inn. He imagined how the concierge would look at him with a sympathetic, knowing look and how he would drive his sword up to the hilt into the man's throat . . .

He kept a look out for shady characters of the night, for criminals who preyed on lone travelers. Let them come—he was ready. But the rain had driven everyone inside from even the darkest alleys. He was wet to the skin, cold, and ached with an odd tiredness in his bones. This aimless wandering had to come to an end. He would look for an inn and retreat into a room with a small flask of the finest schnapps. Count Erlan had almost passed a facade decorated with columns as he became aware that he was walking past the Temple of Praios. He stood still. A dark fist squeezed his heart. The House of Praios! The oath! What have I done! The anger and pain that had fermented in the count's breast suppressed his memory of the oath. He had repeatedly felt a dark something awaken in him, but he had not let it surface. It was too horrible to let it take on a concrete form. It shuddered through the count's marrow like molten lead. An agonizing sob escaped his lips. He fell to his knees. He had challenged the godly lord, given false testimony at Praios's judgment, and had nothing to show for it. What an insane act and for no reward! Where was the justice? Lord Praios, you are the god of justice, why is there no justice for me? No justice, no mercy, no escape?

The temple's facade was dark. The inside of the hall was quiet. The door was certainly closed. There was no sense in trying to go in. I also need time to think about everything before I enter Praios's house. I will go tomorrow. Tomorrow . . .

The double door opened and two citizens stepped out into the street in a flood of bright light that made the raindrops shimmer and the pavement sparkle. The count got up and climbed the temple stairs with unsure steps, followed by the embarrassed looks of the worshippers who must have asked themselves what this confused, dripping wet figure was doing in the Temple of Light, Power, and Truth.

At the same time as Count Erlan strode in through the temple's portal, a lone holy man in gold and red vestments left the hall through an altar door on the opposite wall. The temple was empty. Torches and candles on all the walls lit the room and filled it with a warm, comfortable scent. Above the altar hung a large, golden sun disk with fine, sparkling engravings. On the middle circle there was the image of the sun chariot and its driver, whose flowing hair streamed behind him while he turned to gaze at the observer with a severe look, points of light dancing like stars on his bushy brow.

Count Erlan knelt down on his right knee and crossed his arms in front of his chest. The lord of the sky, he thought, the lord that does not forgive. Lord Praios, if I have sinned, you may punish me, but please hear me out first. You will say I have given false testimony in your name, that I have tread on the truth, also in your name . . . Lord Praios, I have done so, but perhaps I also have not. Because what is the truth, Lord Praios? Is it not the truth that we are ruled by a prince who is fat and ignorant? Doesn't Prince Eberstamm blaspheme the god-willed power of his position with his gluttony and his vain chatter? So it must be the will of the gods to put an end to the undeserving idiot's reign. Lord Praios, is it not true that I would be a better prince? What do you need more than power and money to be prince? And isn't it so, that power comes with money and never the other way around? Where should I get the money if not from Rotstein? Lord Praios, you know that Wengenholm is a poor region. More than a hundred years of honesty have brought the Wengenholms nothing more than poverty and powerlessness. Yes, bitter poverty, Lord Praios, while the Jergenwells were fleecing the mines that actually have belonged to my family since time immemorial. They rolled in gold as if they were the counts and the Wengenholms their vassals. Oh, how an injustice is never righted even with time! Does not one serve the truth, Lord Praios, when one tries to right a wrong? Who will say that I have lied and blamed the Jergenwells? There are many truths in the world, lower truths mostly and one higher truth. So it may be that I breached a lower truth as I accused their house of supporting Count Answin and his rebellion. That I will admit and I will regret it. But that the Jergenwells are villains and always were villains, that is the higher truth! And so I have helped attain the higher truth by violating a lower truth. Lord Praios, the villains are punished, your will is done, the higher truth is triumphant.

Count Erlan listened to the soft crackling of the wall torches for a moment with his eyes closed, then he looked up at the figure with the flowing hair and flashing brow, at his firm fists that held the reins. It seemed to him that his eyes were less severe and that he looked over him to the temple door.

"So I am free to go?" asked the count. The old God of Light and Truth raised no objection. He was silent. The count stood up hesitantly, genuflected one more time, and walked to the temple door where he counted out eighteen of the twenty gold ducats he carried in his purse and put them in the offertory. Without looking back he walked out into the night and disappeared into the rain.

Chapter 11

ALTHOUGH THE SUN did not climb very high into the firmament during the days of Boron, it was strong enough to win the battle against the fog bank hanging over the waters of Lake Angbar. The mist dissipated into individual wisps and rose from the serene surface of the lake, climbing higher and higher until it finally disappeared into the shimmering sky. The distant, snow-capped peaks of the Kosch Mountains were a deeper blue than the sky but equally diaphanous as the heavens in the haze. A low bank of clouds surrounded the base of the mountains so that they seemed to float above the ground. Magnificent and foreboding, they loomed over the far-off foreign lands with a majestic silence, guardians of the mysterious. The image that the Kosch Mountains presented on this morning was so inspiring that Gerion pretended he knew nothing of the land on the far side of the mountains. Instead, he playfully tried to imagine an exotic empire more deserving of this substantial guardian massif. An island shrouded in fog came to life in his mind, a place where the milk-white steeds of the elves roam, where there is no pain or misery. Castles made of pure light dot the landscape, and its inhabitants never raise a hand to do anything but greet one another. They stroll through mossy valleys made of velvet and wander in forests with trees of green glass, lost in conversations about eternal things. Now and again one group greets another with a delicate gesture. Gerion raised his right hand in an attempt to copy the greeting and admitted with a smile that the customs in his fantasy world were a bit affected. He tried the gesture a second time, but it just did not suit him. Perhaps that island wasn't the haven he was looking for. He continued to gaze at the sharp cleft in the mountain chain—the Gryphon's Pass. Gerion knew it well because he had traversed it twice.

The image of the promised land was swept from his mind, replaced by the memory of the winding, rocky trail through the mountains that led to the province of Gratenfels, a poor region that wasn't particularly cherished by anyone other than the natives. There was certainly no earthly Alveran to be found there. The people of Gratenfels were a quiet folk. The innkeepers were grumpy and their home-brewed beer was awful. Gerion had noted the name of one of these establishments, the Black Boar, so as to be sure never to return there again. He had once observed an insane count there by the name of Grotho Greifax. Wearing nothing but a sash of green silk and a helmet, the man sat astride his steed, receiving the smiling peasants' greetings with an austere expression. By now the man must be long dead or taken in by the brother- and sisterhood of the Noionites—either way it was better to stay on this side of the Kosch Mountains. But even if Gerion ruled out that point of the compass, it was time that he asked himself just where he was going. A baby's cries interrupted his thoughts.

Selissa emerged from the showman's wagon. She had wrapped a brown wool blanket around her body like a Tulamidian burnous, and had secured it with a thick rope, because her clothes were still damp from that morning's washing. As she walked, the blanket slid aside to reveal a bit of Selissa's pale, slender thigh. In her arms she carried little Erborn, whose bare head turned this way and that as he cried and squirmed. He was quiet for a moment when he looked with wide eyes at Gerion, who was sitting next to the fire. Then he opened his mouth to emit another penetrating scream. "I don't know what's wrong," said Selissa. "He can't be hungry, he just ate. I hope Algunda will return from her mushroom hunt soon." She kneeled down next to Gerion and laid the infant down on her bare thighs, rubbing his stomach. The magician stroked the baby's cheek and said, "Don't take it so hard, my boy—things could be much worse."

Erborn waved his little fists and howled.

Selissa placed a piece of cloth soaked in honey between his lips, but Erborn spit it out and wailed again.

The lancer blew a strand of hair from her forehead and looked helplessly at Gerion. "He also cries when his mother holds him, but it doesn't sound as desperate."

Erborn squeezed his fists tighter and screamed. His face grew redder and redder. Selissa rocked him in her arms, which made his cry rhythmically wax and wane, but failed to silence him.

Old Gurvan grumpily lifted his gray muzzle, got up on all fours, pushed back against his hind legs, yawned, and had a good stretch. He then sniffed the air and trotted leisurely over to Selissa and the baby. He began to sniff again, closing in on Erborn. Finally, he pressed his nose against the baby's diaper-covered backside.

"Oh!" Gerion laughed. "Sir Gurvan discreetly wants to tell us that little Erborn has . . . um . . . soiled himself. Well, Selissa how are you with diapers?"

"I'll be able to do it just fine." She stood up to go into the wagon. Gurvan followed her wagging his tail, his nose barely a hand's width behind the baby's bottom.

"Get over here, you dog!" Gerion said with feigned anger. "Lay down!"

Gurvan pulled in his head and obeyed the command with all the signs of unhappiness.

A moment later Selissa returned without the baby. "He's asleep now," she announced. "You should see how content he looks!"

Gerion looked out over the lake where the last bits of fog were playing in the breeze, before turning to take in the camp fire, the neatly stacked iron pots, and the small wood pile. His eyes traveled over the tent roof that was held up by two small tree trunks, and rested on the strips of meat that Algunda had hung, with a few bundles of herbs, high on the side of the wagon to protect them from nocturnal scavengers. There was a certain coziness in all these things, Gerion thought, a certain familiarity he knew only too well from his many travels. You come into a town that receives you with unwelcoming foreign features. You ask for directions to the market square, find the way, and set up your wagon next to the tents and carts of new neighbors who do the same. Overnight a small city is built, a place of uncertain spaces and relationships, whose surprising, odd noises allow no sleep the first night. But one night is also enough to establish a certain familiarity and homeliness.

After a few days, you begin to feel at home in the short-lived city, a feeling that grows and is strongest in the moment the first neighbors strike their tents. Things are easier for Gurvan. For him, home is anywhere he has spent more than an hour sleeping. At first, he tentatively sniffs the new, foreign smells. But after he has napped for a while under the wagon he somehow magically determines that he is the absolute ruler of the campsite. Perhaps we were not made to keep moving after all, old friend, thought Gerion. Perhaps we should finally take up residence somewhere. Why not stay here with the nimble fog and the glowing mountains? He turned to Selissa, "When Algunda and Arvid return, we will have to move on. They won't be looking as intensively for us on the roads now. It was good that we laid low for a while. But on the other hand, we've been camping at the same spot for three days, and that could catch someone's attention."

Selissa walked up to Gerion and put her hand on his shoulder, "You are certainly right, but it won't be easy for me to leave. We have had a few peaceful days here. . . . After all the terrible things that have happened I would never have thought that there would be such beautiful days for me again. I'll often think of this campsite on my travels northward."

"You don't have to go to the north," said Gerion. "You're still young. You're trading a lot of life in for revenge. Why don't you leave it to the gods to punish and take revenge?"

Selissa's hand squeezed tighter around the magician's shoulder. "Oh Gerion, let it be! You know I have to go. What if the gods don't punish Wengenholm? When I think back on how I sat with him in the rose garden and promised him eternal love, and how I eagerly waited for how it would be when he . . . How pitifully stupid I was and how I besmirched myself! I'll never be able to free myself from that!"

Gerion was about to speak, but as he opened his mouth Selissa raised her hand and hurriedly continued, "What's done is done—I can't undo it! Just think: The Twelve could take a long time to determine Wengenholm's guilt. And it is also possible that the wrong that he has committed is too small to be of importance to them. But when I get my hands on that man, the gods will have to take notice and decide whose side they're on!"

Gerion shook his head. "I have my doubts if the Twelve let themselves be pulled into a matter so easily. I once had a very intelligent teacher who gave me some good advice. 'Whenever you make a plan,' he said to me, 'check it once more. And if your plan depends in any part upon the aid of the Twelve, then toss it out and come up with a new one. It may be that a god is on your side when you are making your first plan, but it is more likely that he will be on your side when you choose the second.'"

"And have you taken this advice to heart?" asked Selissa. "Have you always followed it?"

"No, of course not. One can only determine if advice

ıs wise after ignoring it. I used to count on the Twelve. I counted on the fact that I was their favorite and that they would bestow gifts on me until the end of my days. I never considered that the likes of us would awake their jealousy if we are too happy, or that they gave us hearts so they can see how easy it is to break them."

Selissa crouched down on the ground next to Gerion. "If you want, you can tell me how you came to know that. We have a lot of time until the others return."

"No, I don't like to talk about it. It's a boring story of a vain young man that climbed high and fell hard. It has been told a thousand times . . . besides, we were speaking of you, not of me."

"Well, if we are talking about me, let me ask one question: How can you advise me to trust my revenge to the gods for whom you have so little respect?"

Gerion raised his voice in surprise. "What makes you think I don't respect the gods?"

"Well, you just gave a rather blasphemous speech . . ."

"Nonsense, I did not blaspheme the Twelve at all! I respect them and I fear them, but—I admit—I don't love them, and they don't love me either. But they love you, and that's why you can trust them."

"Why should they love me?" Selissa looked questioningly at Gerion. He turned to her as well, so that their faces were very close. Gerion looked intensely into the lancer's brown eyes and said, "Because everyone can't help but love you."

Selissa blushed and looked out at the lake.

"When we say farewell tonight," said Gerion, "we may never see each other again. I will not go further north.

The winter drives me further south."

The lancer looked up from the shiny surface of the water and reached for a stick. She scratched two intersecting circles in the compacted soil next to the fire. "I will miss you," she mumbled after clearing her throat. "I'm deeply in your debt."

"One hundred ducats, I remember," said Gerion. "And that is truly no small amount to an old charlatan."

"I didn't mean the money."

"Well, that's another difference between a rich baroness and a poor traveling showman." Gerion smiled ironically. "The ducats are rather important! Have you thought about how you are going to repay me if you fall into that demon Wengenholm's hands? Have you never heard that bets are matters of honor? Come with me to the south, go anywhere, but don't go to the north. Make yourself useful somewhere, work for a while, until you can pay your debts. I must insist. I beg you . . ." As Selissa turned to look at Gerion there were tears in her eyes. He looked at her earnestly. "Don't go to Wengenholm! Think of your valiant Arvid. Don't give all that up for a villain who doesn't even deserve to be slain by your hand. Do you realize how Arvid will miss you? You will break his heart." He brushed a lock of hair from her forehead and she reached for his hand and held it tight. "Why does Arvid's heart interest you?" she asked. "Didn't you just tell me yesterday that everyone should concern themselves with their own problems?"

Gerion nodded without looking away from Selissa's eyes. "Oh yes, that is my strong conviction—it protects me from all pain. Each man should go his own way and never hang his heart on anything: not on fame, not on gold, and certainly not on another person."

"You sound like an old man!"

"I *am* an old man!"

Selissa cupped his chin and kissed him on the cheek. She intended to turn away from him, but her lips brushed across his face and dwelled on his mouth. She shuddered as if she had shocked herself, but her lips remained, as did Gerion's. Their mouths opened and pressed together even more firmly.

After a while Gerion reached for Selissa's head with both hands and carefully pushed her face back to look at her for a moment in serious silence. Her dark eyes quietly returned his gaze. Her features were motionless and her lips remained half open, just as she had been pulled from the kiss. "We should do something useful," mumbled Gerion finally. "Gather firewood or . . ." But Selissa threw both arms around his neck and covered his mouth with hers, hungrily pulling him down to the warm, solid ground next to the crackling flames . . .

As Algunda reached the path to the hidden wagon, she smiled in satisfaction at her basket full of Boron Caps. She quickly looked around to make sure she was alone before she stepped out of the bushes along the forest's edge. Then she caught sight of Arvid. The count was striding powerfully forward, his mouth opening and closing while his right hand gestured in the air. Apparently he was singing while walking.

Laughing, Algunda stepped out into the open. Surprised, Arvid hesitated a moment, then he raised his hand with a smile. "What a delight meeting you here, beautiful wood fairy! May I make three wishes?"

Algunda sighed and then struck a sovereign pose. "Just ask, good man, do not be afraid!"

"Allow me first to carry your heavy burden."

The maid handed him the mushroom-filled basket. "Your wish is granted, but, with your permission, you are being a bit careless with your wishes."

"I will take that to heart." The count furrowed his brow. After a while he said, "Now I know my second wish. Will you please allow me to offer you my arm for the walk home?" He took the basket under his left arm and extended his right arm to the maid.

Algunda blushed and hesitantly laid her hand on Arvid's arm. She cleared her throat and mumbled in an embarrassed high voice, "I'll say it again, you are wasting your wishes, dear count."

There was a moment of silence as they walked along the path, and then the count asked, "Don't you want to know my third wish, dear wood fairy?"

Algunda coughed nervously before she spoke. "Yes, indeed. What is it noble sir?"

"This time my wish is not for me," replied Arvid, "but for a good friend. I know a maid from beautiful Ferdok, and I wish that she be content forever and never have any evil done to her and that her beauty should last for one hundred years."

Algunda took her hand in shock from the count's arm. "You don't mean that seriously?" she asked.

Arvid laid his right arm around her shoulders and pulled her in tight. "Why not? I think that it is a very good and just wish. You can't deny me."

"Why are you making fun of me?"

"What? I would never make fun of a beautiful wood fairy. That would never occur to me."

Algunda threw off the count's arm. "This game is no longer any fun," she said. "I don't like that you are making fun of me, sir."

Arvid stepped in front of Algunda. She stopped. He reached for her chin and firmly lifted it up so he could see her eyes. "No more sir," he said. "Call me Arvid. And by the Twelve, I would never make fun of you. If it weren't for you, Selissa would still be rotting in the darkest dungeon and I . . . well, I certainly wouldn't be happy and healthy here in the forest and able to play silly games. No, I will never forget what you have done for us."

"Oh, it was nothing," said Algunda quietly. "Without Gerion—"

"He did his part and you did yours. You could have run off, only thinking of yourself. Most people would have. . . . That's what I'm saying: If I upset you in any way, you must forgive me."

Algunda blushed again. "It is not appropriate for a count to excuse himself to a maid," she mumbled, "that is turning the world upside down. And that bit about beauty, you shouldn't have said that."

Arvid laughed. "Why not? You are a pretty thing, very pretty indeed. Do you think that I don't see that? And why, by Rahja, should I not mention it?"

Algunda's cheeks grew more scarlet as she tried to think of a reply.

"And because you're so pretty, we're going to take you

to Geestwindsberth when this is all over as first maid or even lady stable master. It's your choice. Our neighbors will be jealous and offer lots of money for you . . . "

Algunda dropped her head again and stomped off. "Now you are making fun of me again," she chided, but her eyes sparkled in delight.

After the maid proudly presented the fruits of her labor back at camp and praised the delicious qualities of the oily, black, pointy-topped Boron Caps, Arvid reported on his reconnaissance tour. The count had left early in the morning to scout out the region and the roads. He said he ran into a small tavern five or six miles to the north of the road around the lake, but otherwise there was nothing significant. The road to the north was in pathetic condition after the rainfall of the last few days, they might possibly have to push the wagon through the muddiest parts. But at the Baltram's Beard Tavern they would finally be able to eat and sleep like civilized humans again. Plus it had a bath house. "And in the tavern," the count smiled mischievously, "I found something quite amusing. I couldn't help it. I had to pinch it so you could see it." He reached into his boot and pulled out a small flyer that he held up for Gerion.

The magician read the text aloud:

> His Highness, Prince Blasius of Eberstamm, Prince of Kosch, puts forward the reward of fifty gold ducats for the capture of the following enemies of state:
> Arvid of Geestwindsberth, who carries the title of count in his native Borland. Geestwindsberth is al-

most two strides tall and blond. He is skilled in the use of a rapier and is exceptionally insidious. He was last seen wearing gray travel clothing and a large black hat with an ostrich feather.

Selissa of Jergenwell, who carried the title of baroness until one month ago. Jergenwell is one stride and thirty-seven fingers tall and has black hair. She is very pleasant in appearance, but she can kill without guilt. Jergenwell was last seen wearing a light-colored prison shirt, but has possibly changed her clothing since her devious escape from the dungeon of Ferdok.

A deceitful rogue of unknown name, who is one stride and twenty or forty fingers tall and has either brown or blond hair and can appear in many forms. He is particularly dangerous because he is versed in dastardly black magic.

All three are guilty of treason, murder, and life-endangering black magic. His Highness wishes that these three be caught as soon as possible and will pay fifty gold ducats for their capture, dead or alive, or for information that leads to their capture.

Signed on behalf of his Highness.

Gerion looked up.

"A 'deceitful rogue'," added Arvid, "that's you, Gerion! And you are particularly dangerous!"

"What did they write about me?" asked Algunda. "You didn't read anything about me, Gerion. Look again!"

"Apparently they don't know about you," the magician replied. He turned to Selissa and Arvid. "They described you two fairly well—I don't like that. And I also don't know if it was very smart to steal this poster."

"No one saw me take it," replied Arvid. "I was careful."

"The tavern folk will start to wonder when they see the wanted poster is gone, along with the two-stride tall stranger mentioned on it. There is no way we can stay at this inn on the way north. That would be simply . . ."

"The way north?" Algunda called out in excitement. "Does that mean that you are going north with us, Gerion? But you always said the winters were too cold up there. Tonight you wanted to—"

"It seems I've changed my mind. Perhaps this winter won't be too harsh. I've never been to upper Kosch, and the region is said to be most scenic."

Selissa shot Gerion a serious look. "I can't confirm that Wengenholm or Jergenwell are particularly scenic," she said. "You will be disappointed, Gerion, but I am glad that you are coming with us."

The magician smiled. "One must learn to live with disappointments. Anyway, you know my motto: One shouldn't get one's heart caught up in anything. In the last few days I have come to the conclusion that I was getting too set on a trip south. So I am freely choosing to go north."

"With your permission," added Arvid, "your considerations seem a bit eccentric. But if that is what you want to do, I won't criticize them."

"Well," Gerion shrugged his shoulders, "How could you understand me if I hardly understand myself? And I don't understand you either: why don't you convince Selissa not to go to Wengenholm? You know very well that her desire for revenge will only end in pain."

Arvid sighed. "You know what she's made of, Gerion. Once she's got something into her head, no one can convince her otherwise, not even me. But, on the other hand, if she didn't have such a beautifully dense head, perhaps I wouldn't love her as much as I do."

Gerion didn't smile. His voice was unusually grave: "Will you stop the pleasantries and compliments for a moment and please tell me why you are not doing anything to prevent the woman you love from going to her certain death? Why you allow yourself be drug along you needn't tell me, I can guess at the reason for that."

Arvid stared in silence out at the lake for a brief time before he answered: "You have become a dear friend over the past few days, and I wouldn't want to hurt you for any price, but I have to say this. You are a showman, and we, Selissa and I, are warriors from birth. As long as we can remember we have been taught never to succumb to fear and never to accept an insult, let alone a crime. I would never say that you are not courageous, Gerion, or even a moral coward, but you simply think differently than we do. If someone insults you, you turn the other cheek, whether you can risk avenging yourself or whether your opponent is so powerful that you have no chance of victory against him. And in the case of the latter, you would swallow your revenge, clench your teeth, and move away where you would eventually forget the wrong. We can't do that. Naturally, Selissa knows that Wengenholm is one of the most powerful counts in Kosch and that he is guarded by more than a hundred armed soldiers. But these facts cannot influence her decision for a single moment. She has to do what her inner voice tells her to do. And I, her fiancé, will not leave her side, because her revenge is mine."

"Those are clear words, dear Arvid."

"That is how a warrior should speak." Arvid smiled again. "Clear and pleasing to the goddess."

Gerion shook his gray head. "Are you so sure that what you said pleased Rondra?"

Arvid nodded. "I think so."

"I have my doubts." The magician stood up and paced back and forth under the tent roof. "We should try to determine the will of the gods and then follow them, no?"

"Yes, certainly," replied the count. Selissa watched the magician with alert but cautious eyes.

"I think," continued Gerion, "that it would be godly Rondra's wish that all villains here on Ethra receive their just punishment."

"I think so, too," said the count, and Selissa nodded.

"How nice that we all agree! Then you should also agree to my next point. When you insist on carrying out this plan, you will try to see that Wengenholm receives his just punishment here on Ethra." Without giving Selissa or Arvid the chance to raise an objection, the magician continued. "Perhaps you are the only people in all of Arkania who can carry out Rondra's will against Wengenholm, and now you can't think of anything better to do than march straight into Wengenholm's dungeon! Do you really think that you are acting in accordance with Rondra's will if you run your pikes through his soldiers? That cannot be the will of the goddess: she expects no one to carry out a senseless act. It may be that Wengenholm is sitting in his castle and fears every sound at his door, he may wait in baited breath for the reports from his lookouts who are supposed to tell him when those he fears most are near. You want to free him from these feelings by laying your heads on the judgment block? He will have you hanged from the gallows like traitors! Why, in the name of the Twelve, do you not wait a few years and then sneak into Wengenholm when the count is least expecting you? Then you will be able to carry out the will of the goddess. Now you will do nothing more than make Wengenholm laugh. Go to Geestwindsberth, marry, and put this whole thing off for a few years."

"Till the fields," Selissa interrupted him with bitterness in her voice. "Serve the gods with a few children! Forget the whole thing! Oh no, that is not my choice. Every day that this villain lives with this misdeed, he mocks the goddess! If I were to wait a day longer, I would shame myself. Now is the time to act and not hide and strategize!"

"Isn't strategy one of the courses at the academy?" asked Gerion.

Selissa was taken aback. She did not know how to reply and her eyes flashed angrily at Gerion. Arvid then spoke for her, "Strategy in warfare is based on the fact that one doesn't only send true warriors into the field to fight, but rather all sorts of people—backup troops, mercenaries, peasants, elven pioneers. All of them do not feel or fight like warriors. One must take into account these uncertainties when one comes up with a strategy. In the daily life of a true warrior other things matter: Honor and obedience to the goddess!"

Selissa nodded energetically. "Well spoken, Arvid."

"Spoken like a Borish fool!" Gerion grumbled quietly as he stomped off. Gurvan trotted after him and Algunda ran to follow him as well. The magician lifted his head high, pretending to see neither the dog nor the maid. Only when he reached the path at the lake shore did he look up and down the mud puddle-riddled path. Finally he turned to Algunda, "At least you should be sensible! Don't you ever think of little Erborn?"

The maid cringed in fear. "But . . . ," she stuttered. "I always am thinking of my little one—he is my pride and joy . . ."

"Why don't you snatch up the crying bundle and get out of here? Arvid and Selissa's plan will surely end in catastrophe. And you will be in the midst of it, you and the baby! Tie him to your back and go south. No one expects you to come with us."

Algunda looked at the ground and saw her bare toes slowly sinking into the muddy path. "Did I ever fall asleep on watch?" she asked.

"No, who said that?" asked Gerion back.

"Didn't I always tend the fire?"

"Yes, you took good care of it."

"And didn't I make a good breakfast yesterday and today?"

"Yes, it tasted very good. Why, by the Twelve, are you asking me all this?"

Algunda's shoulders shook, and her toes curled in the mud. "Because I don't understand why you want to run me off! That's why!" A sob shook her body.

Gerion laid his arm around her shoulder and pulled

her head to his breast. "So, that's what you don't understand," he mumbled. "Well, why should you understand me better than Selissa does? None of you were given the gift by the Twelve to understand even the simplest things. You will have to live with that." Gerion shrugged.

Algunda pulled back and looked at him with tears in her eyes. "Does that mean I can stay? If you say that I can stay the others will agree. They listen to you occasionally."

"Since everyone only wants to hear from me that I'm sending them to their doom, I won't deny it to you either. As far as I'm concerned you can come along and die, you dumb thing."

"I don't have to leave, Gurvan!" squealed Algunda and she bent down and gave the old gray dog a big kiss on the muzzle before he could escape her grip.

Gerion turned around and began to walk back to camp. "Now let's see if we will survive your Boron's Caps, dear Algunda," he said looking over his shoulder. "We'll want to be well-fed and in the best of health when Wengenholm has us cut into little bits."

Chapter 12

A COLD WIND BLEW down the street toward Angbar, whistling between the thick trunks of the old elm trees that lined the north side of the road. It tore off brown leaves and twigs and tumbled them across the rough cobblestones, bare fields, and further over the autumn yellowness of the meadows separating the road from the north shore of Lake Angbar. On the distant slate-colored water small choppy waves crested, and along the reed-lined shore a pair of silver egrets spread their wings and took to flight.

The lancers sat silently, bending over the necks of their mounts with one hand on the reins and the other gripping their capes to keep the blue fabric from flying open. Besides the roar of the wind and the clopping of horse shoes on the pavement there was hardly a sound to be heard. Leisurely, with their heads bobbing in step with another, the heavy chargers proceeded in double file—unlike their riders they did not seem to notice the wind and cold.

A petite woman with a short blond shock of hair left the rear of the group and spurred her horse to the front, where the little red and blue pennant with the lion-headed steed snapped in the storm. She directed her mount, a slender sorrel gelding, with her thighs as she struggled to hold her cape closed in front of her chest with one hand. She carried her other arm beneath her riding coat. Grim looks followed the woman as she rode to the front, her eyes fixed straight ahead. When she reached the front of the squadron she addressed the stout soldier who rode next to the pennant, "How long do you want to continue at this pace, Sergeant Dergelstein? It seems to me that the horses have had enough time to rest."

Fiona Dergelstein patted her brown mount on the neck. Without looking to her side, she replied, "Lady Westinger . . . Your Honor, you are leading the hunt, but I am responsible for the soldiers and their horses. So please attend to your matters and I will attend to mine as I have repeatedly stated since we left Ferdok. If you are in a hurry you may be able to ride one horse after another into the ground, however we prefer to ride home on the same horse we rode out on."

The IGI officer wrinkled her brow. "Your tone is quite biting, Sergeant! You seem to be very sure of yourself— but don't overestimate my patience! Since we left Ferdok you have shown yourself on several occasions unwilling to cooperate. Don't you fear that I might mention your behavior in my report?"

Sergeant Dergelstein shrugged. "Write what you must, Your Honor. I am only doing my duty."

"So, then it is your duty to care for the well-being of

our horses at the price of our assignment?"

Sergeant Dergelstein did not reply. The baroness motioned with her chin down the road to Angbar. "In addition, I have reached the conclusion that your suggestion to follow the road to Angbar was a poor one. Why would the traitors go to Angbar of all places? Would they ask for an audience with the prince? That doesn't make sense! No, we should have followed the road along the River Ange to the north—towards Wengenholm and Castle Albumin—"

"I can only repeat what I told you this morning," interrupted the sergeant. "I think it is very unlikely that Selissa Jergenwell rode north—directly into the hands of Count Erlan. That would be absolutely crazy."

The baroness carefully examined the soldier's face, which was red from the wind. "But on the other hand it would be very courageous, wouldn't it?"

Sergeant Dergelstein stopped short. There were deep wrinkles in her brow as she looked for a reply. Finally she nodded in silence.

"The type of courage that would be appropriate for a lancer, don't you think?"

Fiona sighed deeply.

Baroness of Westinger struck the horn of her saddle so forcefully with her left hand that her chestnut mount shot forward in surprise. With a brutal jerk of the bit she brought him to a halt and waited until the pennant bearer and Sergeant Dergelstein caught up again. "Tell me, Sergeant," she hissed, "what kind of games are you playing with me? It seems to me that you were actually of the opinion all along that the rebels were headed to the north,

but you lead me and your troops to the west! All this behavior . . . are you trying to protect a traitor?"

The sergeant bit her lower lip and stared defiantly ahead.

"Oh, so you have no comment! Well, then I will tell
you what a loyal follower of the emperor would call your
behavior: treason! Yes, treason!"

Fiona's right hand flew to the grip of her saber. For a
moment the sergeant froze in the saddle and breathed
heavily through her nose. But she left her weapon in the
sheath, collected her thoughts, and asked in a calm voice,
"What should we do then, continue or turn back?"

"Turn back, this instant! And then we'll ride in a fast
gallop back to the road to Wengenholm. From now on I
am in command! So let's go, give the sign to stop and
turn around. We've lost enough time already!"

Fiona Dergelstein brought the troops to a standstill
with a motion of her hand. With the flag bearer at her
side she rode closely around to the left side of the double row of lancers until eventually each pair of riders had
turned and followed the sergeant in the other direction.

Before the IGI officer returned to her place at the rear
of the column of riders, she turned to the sergeant one
more time. "You should thank me!" she called in a shrill
voice to be heard over the drumming of the heavy hooves
on the road. "I just prevented you from becoming the
accomplice to a heinous crime!"

Fiona stared at the road. She did not reply.

As the group of riders reached the crossroads, a flock of
cawing ravens flew from the bare branches of an old oak.
The tree stood next to the road on a small earthen hill,

covered with gnarled roots. There were signs nailed to the substantial trunk that pointed in three directions: Angbar, Ferdok, and Wengenholm. Not a wagon or a traveler was to be seen in any direction. The paved roads disappeared in the distant gray haze. Even the tavern close to the crossroads seemed to be abandoned. Gaping black windows and sooty holes in the roof announced a recent fire. One at a time the ravens perched on the ridge of the house's roof. With their heads cocked they eyed the approaching lancers.

Fiona Dergelstein raised her right hand. "Halt!" she called over her shoulder. "Lancers, dismount!"

The riders pulled in the reins and brought their mounts to a stop. Heavy steam rushed out of their nostrils, and several horses' flanks were streaked with white foam.

Again Baroness of Westinger directed her gelding to the place where the sergeant stood rubbing her mount's neck with a handful of dry straw. Two men in dark riding coats followed the baroness, always staying a few horse lengths behind her.

The IGI officer's eyes flashed and a single horizontal line creased her brow. She swung her right leg over her mount's rump and strode through the high grass over to the sergeant, who was concentrating on the task at hand. "Now you have gone too far, Sergeant Dergelstein! You . . . look at me when I speak to you!"

Fiona threw the handful of grass to the ground and turned to the officer.

"Did you forget that I give the orders now? I didn't order a 'halt!' Mount up and continue!"

The sergeant shook her head. "The horses are absolutely

exhausted from the long gallop over the pavement. If we want to ride any more today, we need a break."

"Yes, well do you think I'm sitting on a horse for the first time and that you can tell wives' tales to your heart's content? My mount could easily make it for many more miles and your animals are much stronger than mine. I want to tell you what is behind your disgraceful behavior . . ."

Fiona Dergelstein's body tensed. Her angular face, which was normally slightly ruddy and seemed almost like a peasant's, grew unnaturally pale. "Well, tell me! I'm waiting."

The baroness tossed her gray cloak over her shoulder. Her broken right arm was bound tightly to her torso. Diagonally across the fabric strips hung a shoulder belt from which the baroness's dainty weapon dangled. Lightening fast her hand shot for the grip of her rapier and with a quiet scraping she pulled the narrow blade from the sheath, pointing its tip at the sergeant's face. "You are a filthy Answinite!" hissed the baroness. "A traitor against crown and emperor! Just like Jergenwell. You're helping her escape, not like I initially thought because she's one of your soldiers, but rather because your head is filled with the same rotten thoughts as that criminal's!" The baroness was breathing heavily and red blotches appeared on her cheeks. As she continued to speak she forced her voice to calm down, "As you know, your Lady Colonel explicitly ordered that I, as an imperial agent, have the right to take over the command of this mission at any time. I made use of this right earlier, but apparently you did not take heed of this change. Instead you continue to use your position to give the Answinite rogues the greatest possible lead.

Well now, Sergeant Dergelstein, I hope I can get your attention. In my capacity as commander my first action will be to take this necessary measure. Sergeant Fiona Dergelstein, I accuse you of treachery against the emperor and crown, and place you under arrest! Please surrender your weapon!"

Fiona stared at the baroness. It was not clear from her blank, pale expression if she had understood the baroness's command or not.

The officer shook her head. "What is the problem, Dergelstein? Do you mean to disobey the order?" She lowered the tip of her rapier a few fingers and added in an apparently reconciliatory tone, "You have yourself to thank for this! Perhaps there won't be an unhappy ending after all. I will write a report and there will certainly be a hearing, but if you're lucky, you may only be demoted and not have to leave the Guard. And in a few years . . ."

Sergeant Dergelstein squeezed her hands into fists. Her eyes grew moist. Indeed the stout lancer had hardly heard the baroness's last words. Only "arrested!" and "treachery against the emperor and crown!" echoed in her ears. She saw herself at the barrack yard standing helmetless before the commander, who just broke a slender rider's saber over her knee. "You did nothing wrong," whispered a voice insider her. "You can't give little Selissa to these vultures on a silver platter! What does the woman from Gareth know about friendship and loyalty? No, you cannot betray one of your fellow lancers! And now, what now?" Fiona's lips moved but no words could be heard. "Over, it's all over? Never again would she trot with her lancers on a fresh sunny morning along Ferdok's roads, listening to the pounding hooves echo off the walls and returning the friendly greeting of the citizens with a nod. Never? Never again?"

"Your weapon! This instant!" shrieked the IGI officer. "Handle first, please!"

Fiona's fists opened and closed around the saber's handle. Slowly she slid the long, barely curved blade out of the perfectly polished leather sheath. The sergeant looked up. The image before her eyes alternated in and out of focus, until things grew strangely clear. She saw the hateful, mocking, light blue eyes of a blonde woman. A flash of insecurity flickered in their depths for a moment, then they opened in horror.

The rider's saber cut through the baroness's small neck as if gliding through snow. In the same instant the IGI rapier thrust into Fiona's heart. The baroness collapsed in the grass. She lay stiffly stretched out, holding her left hand to her throat as bright red blood flooded out between her fingers.

Fiona Dergelstein stood as she had always stood before her lancers. With a straight back, her boots a half stride apart and firmly planted on the ground, she gripped the rapier that was still stuck in her chest. Tears ran down her face.

The lancers were stunned. Taking advantage of their confusion, two IGI officers who had escorted the baroness were spurring on their horses down the road to Ferdok.

Two, three lancers grabbed for their reins, and readied themselves to chase down the fleeing men.

The sergeant raised her left hand. "Stop!" she cried in

a loud and steady voice. "Let them go, lancers! Don't let yourselves be caught up in this! I want to . . . I have to . . ." The large woman fell to her knees, forming unintelligible words and then fell forward onto the rapier, which broke under her weight with a quiet snap.

An icy wind swirled past the crossing. It howled in the bare branches of the old oak and pulled at the decorations on the guardswomen's helmets. From the roof of the gutted tavern the ravens took off and flew to the south, their hollow, lost cries filling the sky.

As Gerion struck the mule with the whip and growled "Haw! Pull, you lazy monster!" Algunda took the animal by the halter and tugged with all her strength on the leather head piece. Selissa and Arvid pushed against the back of the wagon as Erborn's angry cries could be heard inside. Gurvan scurried around the wagon barking, determined to add his part to the general chaos.

They were hardly fifty strides from the little alder marsh where the wagon had been well hidden for a day and night, but it had rained during the night and the meadow had become so soft that the large spoked wheels were almost up to the hub in the soft mire. They had used Gerion's income from the fair to buy an old ox, which was now hitched behind the mule and to the wagon. Both animals strained to move the wagon, but their hooves sank so deeply into the muddy ground that they had difficulty even lifting their own feet.

Arvid sighed angrily, grabbed a spoke of the wheel and pushed it forward with all his might. With a gurgle his feet sank into the mud, but the wagon only hardly moved a finger. Gurvan barked at the count in encouragement. Arvid freed his boot from the muck and wiped the sweat from his brow with the sleeve of his jacket. "I have had it up to here! Up to here!" he said gesturing above his head. "This regal barouche has grown roots!"

Selissa leaned her back against the wagon. She was breathing heavily. "This is bad," she panted. "But your cursing isn't helping us get out, Arvid!"

"So? What *will* help us out of this mess?" replied the count.

Gerion sized up the distance from the wagon to the road, but the dark silhouettes of the trees shimmering in the fog along the road had not gotten any closer. There was neither man nor beast on the road. It was quiet. Only a small flock of ravens approached from the north and perched on one of the trees by the road. For a while the birds fought among themselves for the best spots in the tree, but they soon began to pull in their heads and fell silent.

"If we had a rope," Arvid's voice grumpily broke the silence, "A long rope, we could lead the animals up to the road and let them pull from there. Then things would be easier."

Gerion climbed off the mule's back and stomped across the ankle-deep mud that now surrounded the wagon and animals. "If we had a rope!" he grumbled. "We are not in Borland, and my wagon is not a tug boat, Your Honor . . ."

Arvid turned around angrily, but he did not reply.

"Can't you work some magic, Gerion?" Algunda suggested shyly.

Gerion stomped his foot on the ground, splattering mud in all directions. "That's a great idea! How about:

'By Duglum's stinking ear, wagon lift us out of here'?"

Algunda cringed as he mentioned the demon's name, then raised her right hand and made the sign to ward off evil and demons by extending her little index finger while her thumb pressed her middle and ring fingers into her palm. The two extended fingers pointed at Gerion whose grumpy face melted into a smile. "What are you doing pointing at me, you fearful little chicken?" he asked. "Don't you know that the Duglum and his friends always come from behind?"

Algunda turned around and held her hand toward the dripping wet alders. "That's better," praised the charlatan. "Cover our backs while we sink into the mud."

"It's no use," determined Selissa. "We can't stay here. We will have to leave the wagon behind. One could—" She stopped talking as the sounds of a heavy wagon rolled out of the fog's dull grayness from the north.

"Wait here by the wagon!" Arvid ordered Algunda. He then strode with Gerion and Selissa across the meadow and stood blocking the road, his hands on his hips. Gerion and Selissa stayed at the side of the road. Soon the contours of a tall covered wagon emerged from the fog. Four Svelt Valley horses with stout yokes were straining in the harness. White clouds of steam rose from their nostrils, and their long manes stuck to their powerful curved necks. Two men with large black coachman's hats sat on the box and a woman with broad shoulders guided the leading horse by the halter. She made no move to stop the vehicle in front of Arvid. The horses, however, suddenly came to a stop as one of them touched Arvid with its nose. The count did not flinch.

"What are you doing?" growled the woman angrily. She dropped the halter and reached for the dagger in her belt. On the box a young man with ash-blond hair and a crooked back played nervously with the reins. At the same time his black-bearded companion shook out his long whip. The narrow strip of leather hissed through the air and struck the ground next to the horse's hooves on the pavement like a striking snake. "Out of the way, stranger!" gnarled the black-bearded man. "Whatever you want from us, we can't stop to talk about it, we're late as it is!"

Arvid spread his arms and nodded politely, but he did not move. "Do not worry!" he said. "We have no evil up our sleeve. We are in a terrible spot. Our wagon is stuck over there," he shook his head in the direction of the alders, "in the swamp. You have to help us get it out."

The coachman eyed the distant cluster of trees where the wagon stood out like a large black rectangle in the fog, then he let out a malicious laugh. "Ha! You sure got off the road! Where were you going? Taking a shortcut to Albernia? And just think, we thought you were robbers. You can't be robbers, no robbers would be that stupid. Anyway, we are in a hurry. So step aside and wait for some other fool to help you get out."

Selissa approached the wagon from the side and shook her index finger. "How can you be so unfriendly, dear sir?! Is it not a commandment of the Twelve to help those in need?"

"Oh, fiddle faddle!" sighed the black-bearded man. "Are you deaf? Didn't you just hear that we don't have any time to spare? Not enough to pull you out of the Muhrsape and not enough to hear your sob story either. Hey, you idiot up front! Get out of the way immediately or I will snap off your nose with this whip."

"Dear sir, you are very coldhearted," mumbled Selissa and sunk her head in sadness. Then she grabbed the coachman's ankle with both hands and pulled him down off the wagon. The black-bearded man slid to one side on the box and fell heavily to the pavement. He rolled over, rubbing his ribs and whimpering to catch his breath. At the same time, Arvid sent the woman to the ground with a swinging punch. The driver up on the box raised his hands as Gerion's gray head popped up next to him. "Please, good people!" he begged. "Don't get excited! We will find a solution . . ."

"So you can find a little time to help us?" Gerion asked in a friendly tone.

"Certainly, certainly! If we unhitch our animals and hitch them to your wagon we will get it out. It's a cinch."

"Exactly," Gerion nodded in confirmation. "That's what we thought."

In reality, it took a good while for the train of powerful Svelt Valley horses complete with the poles, yokes, and harnesses to be led over the swamp and hitched to the showman's wagon. The ox and mule were led over to help the team, but the enormous horses bit at the strange animals as if protesting against the idea of any amateurs helping them with their task. Gurvan took a disliking to the Svelts and made a great show of snarling, growling, and nipping at the furry horse hooves, taking care that he didn't get too close to the monsters. The horses did not even seem to notice the dog as they lowered their heads and concentrated on the task at hand.

The old wagon creaked and moaned as if it were going to shatter in two as the heavy horses pulled in their harnesses. As the wagon woman's piercing voice called "haw haw" and the black-bearded man snapped his whip, the mud encrusted wheels reluctantly began to turn. Bit by bit the wagon moved forward and the hubs raised above the bog. The wide hooves of the Svelts barely sank into the meadow and once the showman's wagon was out of the mire it quickly crossed the meadow and soon rolled onto the road after swaying dramatically over the embankment.

The mule and ox stood in the tall grass looking on in wonder. Algunda clapped her hands in joy.

Gerion patted the lead horse enthusiastically on the neck. "Good job," he praised. "We were lucky to encounter such friendly coachpeople."

The black-bearded man took the horses by the halter. After he had rehitched the horses, his two companions climbed up to the box. The young man picked up the reins and slapped them against the broad backs of the horses. With a jerk the train moved on.

When there were a good thirty strides between the showman's wagon and the train, the black-bearded man turned around again. "You are trash," he yelled, "a pile of horse shit! May you roast in deepest hell. The nine-horned ones should cook and eat you! You are ogres in human form! May Basilisks nest in your beds! You brood of . . ." his voice faded as the swaying wagon disappeared into the fog.

"May Basilisks nest . . . ," mumbled Gerion, "that was well said."

Arvid and Selissa had rehitched the ox and mule and were walking around the wagon to enter the rear door, when the sound of many horses droned through the fog. The rhythmic drumming indicated they were in a trot as they approached from the north.

Gerion drove the animals on and the wagon rumbled off, swaying on the side of the road, just as the first riders appeared from the mist. They were not riding in formation, but rather alone, in pairs or three abreast. No officer or sergeant led the troops. The blue and red pennants hung limply from their lances and the guardswomen sat stonily in their saddles. They barely looked left and right and didn't seem to take interest in their environment or the showman's wagon. From the corner of his eye, Gerion took in the somber lancers, pretending to concentrate as if there were no task more difficult in the world than driving a showman's wagon.

As the last rider and a small cart covered with a tarp passed the wagon, Gerion turned around to Selissa. "You should have seen your companions! They looked as if they just lost an important battle."

Before Selissa could reply, there was a disturbance in the rhythmic pounding of the trotting horses. An irregular scraping and clatter could be heard as the riders brought their horses to a stop. Gerion leaned to one side and looked around the wagon. The lancers had indeed come to a halt and most of them were looking at the showman's wagon. At the same time a lone guardswoman broke off from the group and galloped towards Gerion. Long blond hair blew under her sparkling helmet. As the rider reached the wagon, she reigned in her horse so tightly that its hind hooves slid over the pavement.

"What is your name, old man?" asked the blonde woman.

"Alara Paligan" answered Gerion with a smile.

"I am not in the mood for jokes!" bellowed the soldier and lowered her lance so low that the point was on Gerion's chest. "Get down, but move slowly and carefully!"

"I always do that," Gerion replied as he carefully climbed down from the box and stood on the road, "even without your bidding. At my age there's not much speed or recklessness left to muster."

"What is your name?" the guardswoman repositioned the point of her lance on Gerion's breast.

"Beberot Mite."

"Oh really? I can believe that or not. You look familiar, old man!"

"It would be a pleasure to have made your acquaintance, but I cannot recall any meetings or common experiences." Gerion shrugged. He looked over at the other riders who were beginning to approach the wagon and then stopped about ten strides away. Only a narrow-shouldered redhead, apparently a Nivese, came up closer on her horse. "Let him be, Zelda," she called. "Let the old man continue! We want to go home!"

The blonde woman raised her left hand, "In a moment, Juahan!" She jabbed at Gerion with the point of her lance. He stepped back until he was against the side of the wagon. The tip of the lance cut through his shirt and bored into his skin. He shrieked in horror, "Mercy, noble soldier! Have mercy on an old man! I have done no harm."

The lancer raised her eyebrows and stared at him, "We

are looking for someone like you, old man. An old duffer, who is traveling with a few high traitors. If you cherish your life speak now and speak the truth. Who do you have hidden in your wagon?"

Gerion slowly fell to his knees. The tip of the lance followed his movement, but at least it didn't sink any further into his skin. And he would be able to duck to one side and roll under the wagon if worse came to worse. "Why would I have anyone in my wagon, noble woman?" he stuttered. "No one wants to ride with an—how did you just put it—an old duffer. Look for yourself if you like." As Gerion spoke there was a loud crash and scrape inside the wagon. "No one besides my dog!" called Gerion in a high, frightened voice. "Gurvan, bark!"

Immediately a low bark could be heard, followed by the angry cries of an infant.

"It's them!" called the blonde lancer after a few moments of complete silence interrupted only by the crying of a baby. "Surround them!"

As Gerion feverishly contemplated if he should talk, flee, or try some magic, the back door of the wagon flew open. Selissa jumped down on the road with her saber in hand.

"Are you looking for me, Guardswoman Zelda? Then come and arrest me!"

"There she is!" cried the lancer in triumph. "We got her, take her prisoner! Shackle her up!"

A few riders sat as still as statues in their saddles, others let their spooked horses shuffle side to side, but no one urged her horse forward.

Zelda Gutnot looked confused with her mouth half open.

Her eyes traveled between her comrades and Selissa, who was standing before her with her saber raised. "Lancers, what are you waiting for?" Zelda shook her head in disbelief. "No one . . . ," she mumbled. Her face grew desperate and wild hate glowed in her eyes. Suddenly she swung her lance around, aimed at Selissa's throat and lunged forward with all her might.

Selissa dodged to the side and felt the lance's shaft glance off her shoulder. She let her saber fall to the ground and then grabbed the shaft and yanked on it.

The lance was pulled from Zelda's fingers, but the leather loop handle tightened like a noose around her wrist and the guardswoman's body was pulled to the side. Her left hand desperately reached for the horse's mane to keep her from falling out of the saddle.

Before she could regain her balance, Selissa leapt up and grabbed Zelda's flowing blond hair and wrenched the guardswoman from her saddle. Zelda fell hard and her helmet rolled off with a loud clatter. Selissa raised the lance and threw it aside and slapped the horse to send it a few strides off. Then she reached for her saber and waited for Zelda to stand up, shake off her confusion, and draw her weapon.

As if in a dream Selissa took in her environment. The fog was still thick even though it was long past noon. The land all around her was hidden behind a veil of gray. Only a circle with a diameter of approximately fifty strides remained of the wide world. A length of the road and a patch of swamp on either side formed an odd stage upon which several actors had gathered in order to meet their god-given fates in front of slowly billowing curtains.

Selissa gripped the saber tightly. "One of us will not leave here, Zelda Gutnot," she said. "What a strange day to die!"

Zelda nodded, "A strange day indeed, but it may be the right one for you!" She took a step to the side, then a second, and watched carefully as her opponent eyed her. Then she feigned a third side step, but instead she lunged forward. Selissa was not surprised. She knew Zelda's fighting style from fencing classes. Whenever Zelda went to make a decisive move she always inhaled sharply through her nose first. She hisses like a snake, thought Selissa, she's so predictable. Effortlessly she parried and with a thrust she blocked her opponent's attack, forcing the blonde soldier's saber down. The blade cut a few strips of leather from Zelda's short skirt and dug deeply into her thigh. The lancer groaned and stepped back, carefully checking to see if her leg was still attached. Selissa continued her advance. The saber blade glanced off her chest armor with sparks flying. Zelda went for a powerful stroke, Selissa raised her blade, and steel clashed with steel. The warriors drew apart, taking two steps back to strike the classic stance: right side and weapon facing the opponent in order to offer the smallest possible area to attack, legs spread apart, left hand in the air to keep balanced.

Blood ran in rivulets down Zelda's leg and pooled in a puddle on the pavement. She didn't look down. There was not much time left for her to end the fight. She knew that. She feigned and then lunged hurriedly forward. Selissa parried without retreat. The women were close together and their hand guards crashed against each other. Selissa felt Zelda's hot breath in her face.

The blonde woman hissed. Selissa jumped back. Something hot tore into her ribs, ripping skin and fabric. Only then did she see the dagger in Zelda's left hand. Selissa pushed her opponent away with her left hand and her saber guard. She had to get out of the range of the menacing dagger. Zelda stepped back to regain her footing, but she slipped in the pool of blood. She stumbled, lost her footing, and then lifted her arms to catch her balance.

Selissa's blade found its way into the arm hole of her opponent's mail, cutting deep into Zelda's armpit and into her heart.

Zelda Gutnot was already dead when her knees touched the pavement. Her body lay slumped over the dust, blood, and dirt, Golgari spreading his powerful wings over her.

The guardswomen loaded Zelda's corpse onto the flat cart between the lifeless bodies of Fiona Dergelstein and Baroness of Westinger. "They got into a fight, these two guardswomen and the lady from the agency," said Juahan. "That must have been what happened. . . . Rondra be with you, Selissa!" she called after she mounted up. Nothing more was said. Selissa, Gerion, and the others stood by the wagon as some of the lancers waved good-bye. Some of the others did not turn around as they rode off slowly into the fog. Gerion cut a bandage for Selissa's wound.

A flock of ravens flew off from a nearby tree. They soared into the sky and circled. Indecisively they sought their destination. These days there were so many places for them to go.

Chapter 13

THE ROAD ALONG the Ange River rounded a tower of rock with bare steep walls then led out into the flatlands. To the north, about an hour away by foot, stood a gently sloping hill crested by a few houses with red tile roofs. It was the tiny hamlet of Wengerich that the traveling tinker had mentioned to Arvid and Algunda. An old, well-cobbled road hugged the base of the mountain, bypassing the village. Only a rutted cart path forked off to the settlement.

A bright, clear autumn sun shone on the land. The roofs of the houses and the trees bearing the last of their fall leaves stood out against the blue sky in glowing color.

Arvid stopped and pointed to the houses. "We will have to pass by the village at night. By day one could see our wagon from miles away up there . . . It's not much further to Wengenholm and who knows, perhaps the count posted spies."

Algunda looked up the hill as well. Her expression was worried. "But they won't recognize us, will they?"

Arvid pushed back the unraveling straw hat that he had plucked from a scare crow. "I can't imagine they would. You look like a traveling maid and my disguise is all but perfect."

Algunda looked dubiously at the count's expensive leather boots. "You'll have to wear straw shoes," she advised, "or go barefoot." Arvid frowned and said that he would claim to be a peasant who had inherited his valuable footwear from his rich father in the city. That was possible, and anyway he would smear his boots with dirt so that no one would take notice of them. It was hard enough for him to have left his weapon in the wagon, he said.

The count gave Algunda a friendly pat on the shoulder. "Well, come on, let's keep going. It's about time for us to buy some provisions. When your little bundle of joy wakes up he'll certainly let us know how hungry he is."

Algunda reached around and patted the scarf in which she carried sleeping Erborn on her back and hesitantly followed.

A few strides below the road a narrow river barge floated down the Ange. A broad-shouldered young man with a red handkerchief knotted around his neck lifted his barge pole in a friendly greeting. "Hey, come with me, pretty one!" he called to Algunda. "I will make you rich and happy!"

"You ne'er-do-well!" she replied laughing. "How do you plan to do that?" The blond man cupped his hand to his ear to show that he could not hear her, then the barge disappeared around the bend. Still smiling, Algunda turned to her companion, "Did you know Sir ... Arvid, that I have never gone on such a long trip? I never thought it would be so beautiful out here in the wide world. One sees so much and meets such funny people . . . it certainly must also be beautiful in Borland, and how lovely Gareth must be—"

"Gareth's charm is exaggerated," interrupted the count, "but Borland is truly beautiful. However, if any city deserves a crown of pearls, it is Festum. Festum can—" He looked down at Algunda and saw by her gazing eyes that she was not listening to him. She had not even noticed that Arvid interrupted her in mid-sentence, but now she was staring with an oddly pleased smile at the road and river that paralleled each other like two ribbons unwinding across the brown and yellow fields.

Only after a long pause did Algunda speak again. "Isn't it odd how misfortune can lead to luck? As the people from the capital arrested Selissa I thought that wretched Zelda would kill me and that I would never be happy again. It seemed that the gods had nothing but misery and suffering in store for little Erborn and me. I didn't go to the temple any more because I knew it wouldn't do any good. Only sometimes, at night, I prayed and asked Peraine and Travia and Rahja, and even Rondra once why they were doing this to me, but I got no response. I was sure that they didn't hear me because I am only a little stable maid, and that they are busy listening to the prayers of the truly important people and granting their wishes. Yes, that's what I thought. And now I am having the time of my life! There's lots to laugh about, and I have friends like no other maid ever had. Oh, if life could stay like this forever!"

Arvid looked over at Algunda with a look of astonishment. "This game of hide and seek, camping in the rain and wind, you call this the time of your life?"

Algunda nodded energetically. "Yes. And if there is a temple up there in Wengerich, I will pray there and ask the Twelve for forgiveness that I ever doubted them. They have given me such beautiful days."

The count thought of his peasants back home in Geestwindsberth and asked himself if their lives were like Algunda's. The thought had never crossed his mind that old Neesdan, or plump Jassia, or the others expected anything else from life but to till the soil, bring in the harvest, and sit in the winter by the open fire with a beer and a big slice of bacon to wait for the next spring. It may be that the people here in the Central Empire thought differently than the folks back home. Lots of things have changed here since Emperor Hal's reign and even more since young Brin took over. Some people say that things must change, and many young people were leaving farms and villages to travel the land, look for adventure, and change the world. Arvid thought of the young warrior he met at Perricum whose shield bore the motto, "For Good and against Evil" beneath a lioness's head. Gold letters for a simple solution. The man did not want to hear anything about that being the business of the gods. "Goodness is weak," he maintained, "and it will lose if man, elf, and dwarf do not help." Man, elf, and dwarf—as if they had something in common! That young man certainly had some strange ideas. Arvid shook his head, but he decided to talk with old Neesdan when he returned to Geestwindsberth and ask him if he was satisfied with his life.

"*Crying, like fire in the sun*," hummed Gerion as he tossed some more wood on the fire. The verse about the fire came from an old, dark minnesong sung to a tune from the Golden Land. Gerion sang it often as a young man but had almost completely forgotten it since it contained some verses he never fully understood as a youth. Only the flames, pale against the bright light, remained in his memory. Occasionally, he felt it to be the appropriate representation of the wretchedness of humankind and its deeds and feelings, but now he no longer cared for poetic images. Life, he felt, could only be mastered by living it, and not by putting it down in words, however atmospheric they may be. Regardless, Gerion recalled the line from this poem whenever he saw a pale flame on a bright day and the sun's rays made the hot air above the fire cast dancing shadows on the ground.

He spread out a thick gray blanket next to the campfire so that the veil of shadows now pirouetted across the woolen fabric. "Come sit by the fire," he called to Selissa. "We have to take a look at your wound."

Selissa was leaning against the wagon, her face lifted to the sinking sun. She pulled herself from her far away thoughts and walked over to the campfire. Her right hand pressed a wadded up piece of cloth against her ribs. Fresh blood had soaked through the bandages wound around her rib cage, and had also oozed through the cloth in her hand. Without cringing she sat down on the blanket.

"You're losing too much blood," determined Gerion. "I don't like that one bit."

"The wound opened up again," Selissa replied in a factual tone. "Just now, as I got out of the wagon."

Gerion remained silent. He moved aside Selissa's hand holding the bloodied cloth and began to unwrap the bandages. Selissa gritted her teeth and inhaled dramatically through her nose each time one of the sticky strips of fabric was pulled from her skin.

"Lie down flat on your back!" ordered Gerion.

"I don't know why you want to rebandage me," Selissa protested, but she sighed and complied with his request. Gerion also pulled up the bloodied cloth. Then he carefully touched the pale edges of the gash. Now that the bandages no longer held the wound tight it gaped open. It was almost twelve fingers long and there was no indication that it would close itself. At more than one point blood welled up and soaked into the wool blanket.

"Don't look so serious," said Selissa, "no lancer dies from a scratch like this."

Gerion did not reply. He laid both hands over the wound and quietly mumbled a few words. Perspiration appeared on his forehead.

Selissa flinched. "What are you doing?" she asked. "What do you have on your hands? I just felt something strange!"

Gerion held up the palms of his hands to show the lancer that they were bare. "Now stay still and relax! Imagine you are totally soft, can you do that?"

Selissa did not answer immediately. She looked pensive and then smiled. "I think I can," she finally said and stretched back out on the blanket.

Gerion placed his hands on the wound again and repeated the ancient healing words. He pressed his eyes shut, locking his face in tension and breathing heavily. Drops of perspiration fell from his forehead and rolled over Selissa's flat stomach. The lancer sighed and moved her shoulders as if she wanted to bury herself deeper in the woolen blanket. She raised her eyebrows in surprise and her lips curled into an unbelievable smile as she experienced how the searing pain left her ribs and died down to a tingling sensation. Soon the tingling subsided and a peaceful warmth spread from the area where just moments before skin and muscle lay damaged and torn. The feeling emanating from the wound was so pleasant that Selissa involuntarily thought of a potent Premian liquor after a winter's ride and of the warmth that spread through her mouth and throat as the liquid crossed her lips. The fire that she now felt was of a different sort. It streamed through her entire body, down to the tips of her toes and fingers. The lancer stretched out like a cat in front of a stove.

Gerion took his hand from Selissa's rib cage and made a line with his thumbs across her smooth, pale skin. In a few hours the line would be a bit darker than the pale skin surrounding it, but there would be no scar to remind anyone of the horrible gash.

Selissa still had her eyes closed and her hands clawed into the blanket as she slowly rolled her shoulders and hips. "Oh, your hands are so wonderful!" she whispered. "Don't take them off me."

With a gentle movement, Gerion raised Selissa's soiled green shirt. His hand wandered down again, following the smooth hard path between her gently sloping breasts. The charlatan untied the cord that held Selissa's coarse skirt in place. The lancer arched her back so that Gerion could remove it more easily. He slid it down to her ankles and Selissa casually kicked off the gray fabric. She then finished pulling the shirt over her head. Finally, she stretched again, opened her eyes, and looked at Gerion. His hand cupped Selissa's breast with fingers widespread so that the dark bud rested between them. He was pleased as the tip of her breast quickly hardened under the soft pressure of his fingers.

"Perhaps you should have lived your life in service of a different goddess, not that of the beautiful warrior, but that of the warrior for beauty . . . that is your destiny."

Selissa did not try to reply. She spread her thighs to Gerion's probing hand and tightened her grip on his neck. "I've admired your body," said the magician, "since the first moment I saw you. The uniform of a lancer is—" Selissa reached up with her right hand to close his lips, because even though the Twelve gave man a voice to speak, sometimes it was better to remain silent . . .

Arvid swung the heavy bag of provisions from his right to his left shoulder and shook the contents of the linen sack into place. Then he looked over at his companion with a serious face. "Say, what are you smirking about?"

"Oh, nothing." Algunda bit her lower lip and tried to keep a straight face.

"What kind of answer is that?" asked Arvid. "Speak up or I'll slap you!"

Algunda looked to the side in shock and instinctively reached for Erborn, who was sound asleep on her back. "No, please don't! If you slap me, Sir Count, the baby will wake up!" informed Algunda.

"Sir Count, Sir Count!" Arvid wrinkled his brow in

feigned anger. "I thought we were good friends. That's why I'm asking you, what's so funny?"

Algunda opened her mouth and then closed it again.

"Please don't be coy!"

"Should I really tell you?"

Arvid sighed and rolled his eyes.

"As you walked out of the tavern, Sir."

"Arvid!" interrupted the count.

"As you walked out of the tavern, *Arvid* and I was waiting outside and you bumped into the city guard, he said, 'Out of the way, peasant, or I'll flatten your face!' Whenever I think of that I have to laugh!" In confirmation Algunda giggled and bent forward so that Erborn bounced on her back.

"Oh, that was funny?" Arvid shook his head. "I didn't think that was funny at all, but I did take note of that lout's face and if I ever get a chance I will teach him some manners."

"But why? The man didn't do anything, that's the way guards are. He just fell for your disguise. Actually, you should be pleased. Are the guards in Borland different? Are they friendlier, even to peasants?"

"First of all, we don't have that many guards where I come from," replied the count, "and not as many peasants either. Most people are serfs and live under the protection of a feudal lord. He takes care of them and makes sure that everything runs well in the villages. Only in large cities do we have guards."

"That sounds good," said Algunda. "The people in Borland are much better off than they are here. Here the peasants work for the lord and fill his barns. If it weren't for all the country folk the noble ladies and lords would simply starve to death. How nice that everything is the other way around in Borland."

Arvid looked suspiciously at the maid, but her happy expression left him uncertain if she had said her last words out of naive seriousness or if she was joking.

"You will have to work hard when you get back home," continued Algunda, "in order to provide for all your people. Perhaps you should at least let them help you a little bit."

Arvid raised his hand and took aim at Algunda's swaying backside. She laughed and jumped out of range. The sudden jerk woke Erborn and he instantly began to scream. "You are a spirited girl," said Arvid as the maid continued walking and untied the crying baby to rock it in her arms. "I often wonder what's going on in your pretty head. You look at the world like a calf in a field of clover, keeping your thoughts to yourself, don't you? So tell me, what do you think of our little group? What do you think of Selissa, for example? Is she the right woman for me?"

"How can you ask me such a thing?" replied Algunda without looking away from her softly whimpering son. "I would never dare—"

"But I want to know what you think of us," interrupted Arvid. "Do we seem an odd couple to you? Tell me honestly, don't worry."

"Selissa is a true warrior," Algunda said with conviction, "courageous, strong, and beautiful. When I saw her for the first time I thought: She is the best of all the lancers. I don't know why I thought that, but I remember it clearly. I was very proud to be her stable maid." She cleared her throat. "She is definitely the right woman for you. You should thank the Twelve that she chose you. Oh . . ." Algunda raised her hand to her mouth in shock. "I shouldn't have said that, but it is my opinion, and you asked me for it . . ."

Arvid patted her arm to comfort her. "You didn't say anything wrong. I know how greatly indebted I am to the Twelve, and I think of Selissa as you do. Perhaps I asked the wrong question. What I really wanted to know is, do you think I am the right man for her?"

Algunda carefully dabbed at the tears that ran down her little son's face. He had already fallen back asleep so she returned the bundle to her back. "You are a good match," she said finally. "You are also big, courageous, and strong, very strong indeed! You'll make a beautiful couple standing at the altar." Since the count had initiated this strange conversation, a warm red had come to Algunda's face and it became darker with her last words. "Oh, dear Arvid, can't we talk about something else?" she asked as she brushed a stray hair back into place.

"Sure, even though I don't think that you really answered my last question . . . But tell me, what do you think of our old charlatan, clever Gerion? Do you trust him, or do you think he is a bit uncanny?"

"Yes," replied Algunda.

"What do you mean by 'yes'?"

"Yes, I trust him and yes, I think he is a bit odd. He helped us a great deal."

Arvid nodded in thought. "That is indeed true. Sometimes I ask myself why he hasn't left us yet, though. A loner like him, what does he have in common with us?

What's in it for him? He's putting his life on the line and there is nothing in it for him."

"One hundred gold ducats," mumbled Algunda smiling.

"What did you say?"

"Oh, nothing. I was just thinking out loud." She hesitated. "No, I don't know what is keeping Gerion with us."

"Did you ever think that you might be the reason?" asked Arvid suddenly.

Algunda looked over at him in surprise. "No, that never occurred to me."

Arvid touched her arm again. "But why not? You are pretty, very pretty indeed. You have a child and no husband—why wouldn't he try for you? If I were Gerion I would have you, no question! Don't think that just because his hair is gray that he no longer entertains those thoughts."

"I know that Gerion is not too old to court a girl, but I am certain that he is not interested in me," Algunda replied quietly.

"Because you are a maid?" Arvid shook his head and laughed. "Oh, Algunda don't think so poorly of yourself. Anyway, even though he sometimes speaks like a veritable king, he is Gerion, a charlatan, and certainly no better than you. And he would thank the Twelve if he had you. Believe me."

Algunda's voice grew so quiet that the count had to lean forward to hear her better. "It has nothing to do with the fact that I am a maid and he is a sir . . ."

"A sir?"

"Yes, a sir. It is because he is him and I am me and that the fair Goddess Rahja has other plans for us."

"Oh, nonsense! How do you know that?"

"I have eyes to see."

"And what do you see?"

Algunda did not reply.

"Well, what do you see? Well, fine, then I will tell you what I see. I see that you have a pretty face and a figure that would please Rahja. And Gerion sees that too. And that's why he is staying with us. That's the way it is!" Arvid laughed cheerfully.

If that were the case, thought Algunda, then why didn't Gerion ask me to join him in the wagon when he left? Why is he staying with us? Algunda looked over at Arvid. Her large eyes looked as clear and innocent as a calf's.

"You are probably right," she said. "You are so much older and wiser than I. You have traveled the world and know many people. That must be the reason that Gerion is still with us. I must say that I never would have thought of that."

Arvid hooked his thumbs in the straps of his backpack and repositioned his load. "Well," he said, "my eyes may not be as pretty as yours, but they see more."

The pair quickly covered the last few miles back to the spot where they had hidden their cart in silence.

"Tell me about Geestwindsberth," begged Selissa, pulling her shirt over her head. Her eyes were half closed as she leaned against the rough planks that formed the side of the cart. Arvid inspected the barely visible trace of the wound by the light of an oil lamp and shook his head in amazement. Outside he could hear the muted voices of Gerion and Algunda discussing the preparation of the evening meal with the fresh provisions.

"What should I tell you?" asked Arvid in surprise. "You've been there yourself."

"I know, but tell me something about it. Tell me how we will ride across the fields, how we will arrive and there will be a feast on the table prepared by your fat cook, what's his name again?"

"Lento."

"Lento will receive us with a grumpy face because we are late. Tell me about our children and the deep snow in winter. I want to hear . . ." Selissa now closed her eyes all the way and small goose bumps appeared all over her naked upper body. She shivered.

Arvid laughed deeply and grabbed Selissa by the shoulders, but kept her at arm's distance to be able to see her wondrously healed body. "It is unbelievable," he mumbled, "I would never have thought our Gerion could do something like this. How did he do it? He must have extraordinary powers . . . but that is unlikely for an everyday magician. Perhaps he has a special elixir. Did you ask him? It could be very useful for us . . ."

Selissa raised her hand in protest. "Geestwindsberth," she said pleadingly, "tell me about Geestwindsberth."

"My valiant soldier, what has gotten into you? If everything goes well we could be in Geestwindsberth by Firun. Then you will see it again for yourself. But, if it is your wish, I will try to tell you about it: Picture a few old wooden buildings surrounded by trees and everything a bit tousled from the steady sea breeze—that is what it looks like from the dunes. And when one follows the oak tree-lined road from the village . . ."

With a deep sigh, Selissa wrapped her arms around Arvid's neck and pressed him to her as hard as she could. She felt how the scratchy fabric of his hand-woven jacket scraped her nipples, and she inhaled his scent with deep breaths. He mumbled soothing words, but she closed his mouth with her lips. She darted her tongue deep into his mouth, again and again, until she felt how he returned her kiss and how his body yielded to hers as they pressed closer together. As they rolled together across the floorboards of the cart, Selissa threw herself over Arvid's muscular body and slid down his length. With flying fingers she opened his shirt, jacket, and untied his belt.

Arvid moaned loudly as her hot, moist mouth explored him. Selissa's hair brushed across his chest and stomach like a cool breeze. Her warm mouth was now at Arvid's ear, mumbling his name over and over. The count felt Selissa's slender body in passionate, flowing moments on his skin. He reached for her round shoulders and holding her tight he forced her body below him. Selissa's thighs glided apart. "Arvid!" she mumbled again and again. "Take me to Geestwindsberth soon, please . . . soon . . ."

After they separated from each other and had lain silently side by side on the wagon floor, Arvid gently stroked Selissa's stomach and whispered, "What was with you? My Rahja . . . I have never experienced you like that . . ." He let out a quiet laugh. "One could almost think that this wondrous cure was to blame." Arvid leaned on his elbows and looked at Selissa. "Say, what actually happened as Gerion healed you? What did you feel? Was it a good feeling? And above all, do you think that he has these powers himself or did he use something on you?"

Selissa opened her eyes and looked up at the dark ceiling. For a moment she saw Gerion's delicate hands before her as he showed her that they were empty. "Yes, it was very beautiful. And I think it was to blame."

Arvid reached for her hands. "But you're better now, aren't you?"

The lancer freed her hands from Arvid's gentle grasp, stood up, and got dressed. In front of a small wall mirror she arranged her hair with her fingertips then studied herself for a long time in the polished surface. "I think so," she said after a long pause.

That night Selissa and her companions silently ate the bread and barley soup Gerion prepared for them. Everyone had sunk deeply into their own thoughts. Wengenholm's lands were only about two or three days off at this pace—but a rider on a fresh horse could cover the distance in just one day. The destination of their travel had grown much closer and they should have been discussing strategies and tactics for the first meeting with Count Erlan and his thugs. It would have been wise to consider leaving the showman's distinctive wagon behind and agree on a secret meeting spot in case they should get separated.

The fire before them illuminated only an area about seven strides across where they sat sipping their soup. It excluded the world beyond with its coldness, cruelty, and eternal circle of crime and revenge. No one among the figures surrounding the fire wanted to be the first to destroy this cozy circle with talk of the outside world. So they ate, drank, and praised Gerion's culinary arts, until—

as if an unseen signal had been given—they all stood up and put their things back in the wagon. Earlier that evening Arvid had talked to a friendly peasant in the village tavern and learned that his property was a few miles north of the village. It should be possible to reach the man's farm by daybreak if they traveled through the long autumn night. There, Arvid hoped to camp for one last time before finally crossing the border to Wengenholm.

Chapter 14

WHEN COUNT ERLAN heard Ismene's quiet footsteps approaching, he gracefully spun away from the embrasure through which he had been surveying the castle's environs. He lowered his head in a brief but friendly gesture and welcomed her to the well-set breakfast table. The magicienne wore her silver-streaked hair down so that it tumbled over the golden belt of her burgundy dressing gown. With each step her elegant gown swished and a dainty golden slipper appeared. After Ismene serenely crossed the room, she took her place behind a single pewter plate on the long side of the table and quickly looked over the offerings. "Oh, you have already eaten," she determined. "It appears that I have slept longer than the custom permits here at Wengenholm. But you will certainly be so kind as to join me in conversation, dear Count."

Count Erlan requested an additional cup from the servant who had just entered the room with a steaming tea pot in one hand and an equally hot pot of milk in the other.

The count sat down on the chair across from Ismene and let his right leg hang casually over the arm rest. The magicienne broke a handful of bread from the crusty brown loaf, dipped the piece into the hot milk, and finally drizzled a thick thread of honey over the soft, steaming mass. She did not eat of it immediately, but rather she watched as the milk and honey ran over her fingers and dripped onto the plate and tabletop. After she had licked a bit of honey from her palm with the tip of her tongue she turned to the count, "Tell me, Your Honor, why are you in such high spirits this morning? You have not looked this happy since the morning after you took care of the Jergenwells."

The passing ironic mention of that deed made Count Erlan's face twitch. He turned pale and gritted his teeth, but he soon had his face under control again. "Zobot, son of Zimbodel, was my guest this morning," he announced with a pleased smile.

Ismene nibbled at her piece of bread and looked questioningly at the count, who explained, "Zobot is second face-man at the Gerdung mines in Jergenwell. That's where the collapse was a few days ago. I told you about it, didn't I?"

"Perhaps you did. But what is so important about it? Accidents happen constantly in those dank tunnels . . . besides the mines in Jergenwell don't belong to you . . ."

"That's exactly the point," interjected the count, his voice full of excitement. "All the existing mines belong to the prince now . . ."

The magicienne giggled. "I know. I vividly recall your description of your audience with him in Angbar."

Count Erlan banged his fists on the table so that the

cups leapt into the air. Milk and tea splattered everywhere. There was a deep furrow in his brow and his eyes blazed. "It is absolutely unnecessary to remind me of that!" he yelled. "As you well know I could spit every time I think of that day. So why did you have to bring it up?" He forced a calmer voice. "You enjoy poking at my wounds, don't you? Well, fine. I won't give you another chance to irk me about this matter."

Ismene broke off a second chunk of fresh bread and used it to clean her fingers, then she tossed it back on the table. "Tut, tut!" she whispered with an understanding smile. "As you know, I am interested in all extreme moods in humans and you are all too willing to give a demonstration of such extremes. Let me give you some advice, Your Honor. You will have to do a lot of work on yourself before you will be able to rule the world."

Count Erlan made a guttural sound, reached for a heavy fruit bowl, and lifted it up over his head with both hands. Golden pears flew through the air and splattered on the tiles, red-cheeked apples bounced under the table.

The magicienne raised her right hand and pointed to the count. He set the bowl back down on the table. "Spare me your magic tricks!" he fumed.

Ismene lowered her hand again. "Did you know that you just produced energies that I could actually smell and taste? If it were possible not only to sense these energies, but to absorb them and convert them into something else . . . "

Erlan sat back down and looked seriously at the table. "Don't be so sure of yourself!" he mumbled. "I have often asked myself if you are as much use to me as you are trouble. Have your fun, it will all end when I decide to break our pact!"

"You should not be so eager, Your Honor! Think, you will only have to put up with me for a few more days. The renovations at Castle Albumin are going well, and once I have moved to Jergenwell to devote myself entirely to my studies we will only see each other occasionally. Anyway, weren't you going to tell me a story about an Angroschim and a tunnel collapse? I am eagerly awaiting its conclusion."

As Count Erlan recalled the discussion with the faceman Zobot, his facial features relaxed. "Oh yes, indeed, the prosperity of Wengenholm should interest you as well." His eyes darted to Ismene as if he feared another of her ironic remarks, but she was looking at him with anticipation, so he continued, "As I just said, Prince Blasius has taken possession of all *existing* mines. Therefore, a collapse like that is welcome," Erlan smiled guiltily, "because it dries up his gold mines for a while."

Ismene shrugged. "Well, never underestimate life's little pleasures—" she began, but Erlan interrupted her. "That was a joke!" he said in a surly tone. "Do you think I am that stupid? Just listen and let me tell you the rest. Then you can jest if you like." He waited for Ismene to finish her patronizing nod, and then he continued, "Good Zobot is amazingly crafty for an Angroschim. First of all he asked me casually if I still had the Roselette. That's a bracelet," explained Erlan as he saw Ismene's confusion. "It has been in our family's possession for a long time. It is made of gold and decorated with three metal roses, each with a small ruby in its center. The three stones are of the same size and cut. It is of dwarven make and well-crafted, but it is not exactly a wonder of the world. Anyway, the Angroschim of this area know the bracelet well and like it for some reason. It may be that they expect wonders from the piece of jewelry. My father had it examined once at a shop in Punin, but they couldn't say . . .

"Well, as soon as this Zobot asked me about the bracelet, I thought to myself that he was going to offer me a deal, but I waited and let him tell me. He told me about the collapse and how difficult it would be to reopen the tunnel. The accident happened because the prince demanded the yield be increased without thinking of safety, and on and on. In the middle of his lament he said that his people would just as soon start over again than reopen the old shaft. Dig a completely new mine. A 'completely new mine' he repeated again and looked at me intensely."

"As you know," added Ismene impatiently, "I don't know much about mines and tunnels. Why did Zobot look at you so curiously?"

"Oh, I immediately knew what he meant." The count smiled triumphantly. "A completely new mine in Jergenwell would automatically belong to me. You see, the prince took over the existing mines, but he can't claim any mines that have yet to be dug in Jergenwell. No, new mines belong to the lords of the land, and because there are no more Jergenwells, they belong to the Wengenholms, as simple as that! And think, the tunnels that collapsed were the highest yielding in Jergenwell . . ."

"Then I can assume that this . . . um . . . Roselette changed hands this morning?"

To Ismene's surprise, Count Erlan threw back his head and laughed loudly. "I'm a better statesman than that! No, you should have seen Zobot's eyes. He got this typical dwarven look, that look the Little People always get when they see anything that sparkles, and then I sensed that there was more to be had. So I showed him the bracelet—I let him hold it briefly—and then I agreed to give it to him as soon as the mine in Daxhump had a collapse similar to the one in Gerdung. Zobot began to sweat, but in the end he agreed. What else would he do? As the saying goes: Once you have an Angroschim by the beard, he's yours!"

Ismene took a sip of tea and nodded as she thought. "Yes, that is indeed a fine reason to be in a good mood. Congratulations!"

Count Erlan also took a sip of tea. He placed the cup back on the table and called in his servant, "The tea is ice cold! Bring us a fresh pot, and make haste, if you will!" Then he turned back to Ismene. "It is about time that something goes my way. I take my little arrangement with the Angroschim as the first sign that my destiny is finally back on an even keel. And it won't be much longer until my people have caught that disagreeable little rascal."

"Are you speaking of Ulfing, the youngest Jergenwell? When I stopped by Albumin the people were speaking of him. It is said that he has escaped to the mountains in order to 'rally a few loyal troops and spread war across the land in revenge.'" Ismene laughed. "Apparently the boy is suffering from megalomania and has lost touch with reality. But you shouldn't take the talk too lightly, either. As long as Ulfing is running around free, the more respect you will lose with the peasants of Jergenwell. You will have to make sure order is maintained."

Count Erlan waved his hands. "I'll worry about that. As you know, I've had to manage a number of other things and I couldn't give the half-grown rebel the attention he deserves. But I have since taken the necessary measures. I have convinced Princess Irmenella of Hawkfurt to tell her Baron Nardinfield to aid in the hunt for young Jergenwell. I have learned that Ulfing has a hideout in Nardinfield. And I intend to ferret him out! And as soon as Selissa is tracked down I will have more people to send on future missions to find the boy. All in all things aren't too bad. I just need to wait it out."

"By the way, what news is there from the lancer and her accomplices?" Ismene asked. "Is it true that Selissa is on her way here?"

"That's right. The Gods must have taken away her powers of reason, but that's fine with me. If she had her senses she would be glad to be alive, and would long have disappeared to Trahelia or Yetiland, for all I care. But because she is a Jergenwell she is as dullish and stubborn as her father, and it seems that she is marching straight into my lair. She was last seen on Angen Road, headed north! My people keep me posted. As I said, I need to do nothing but wait."

The servant brought hot tea and Ismene waited for him to leave the hall before she continued. "You are lucky that you have an opponent of the old school in Selissa. Revenge makes people like her blind. Without using their heads they storm their target and are proud of their focus because they think that their stupid anger pleases the goddess. There is something revolting about that type of person. I can't stand to be around them, but I do love to be up against them. It is difficult for us to lose a battle to a warrior of her kind if you know what I mean. You can be glad that the Jergenwells have no one from my school in their ranks, for that would certainly change the game."

"I was told that Selissa is accompanied by a magician," added Count Erlan.

Ismene Fanfemur laughed out loud. "A magician! Your Honor, please! He is a charlatan, a sideshow clown! Someone like him cannot seriously be called a magician. Unfortunately, Selissa and her companions will be killed at the border, because your people want the reward . . . that's a true pity. I would have loved to stand eye-to-eye with that *magician*!"

Count Erlan shook his head and laughed. "You seem to hate that charlatan even more than you hate the warriors. I once attended a show in Angbar at a party, and I must say I found—"

Ismene cut him short. "They are a shame to the craft, every single one of them. They unscrupulously harvest the carefully preserved fruits of a thousand-year-old science and make a mockery of them. Without any sense of the astral order they carry out their ridiculous hocus-pocus and make people believe that the whole purpose of magic is to evoke pretty pictures on a curtain or make a sugar beet squeal and explode. It is amazing that the work of the great scientists is not taken seriously by the rabble, but that a charlatan's work is put on the same level! There was a time when scabs like that were burnt at the stake, just like witches. But today the merchant is worth more to the court than the magus. Money is more important than everything, even the lessons of the highest of all humanities. But they should be on guard, all those egotistical potentates, who only have eyes for gold and allow the magus to be demoted from his proper place and be ridiculed by the people. There are numerous signs that we are on the brink of a realignment of the forces of the universe. They'll be the first to know, Your Honor, mark my words!"

Count Erlan looked at the magicienne with wide eyes, his brows raised in amazement. "But, dear Ismene, I don't recognize you at all. Who would ever have thought that a harmless subject like magical entertainment would cause such passion in you?"

Ismene's cheeks had blushed slightly, but the sudden anger had left her face. She waved her hand with its claw-like fingernails. "It's fine, Your Honor. You are rightfully taken aback by my behavior. No, no, don't contradict me, it was inexcusable. Such an outburst is not appropriate for a woman of my standing—and certainly not from a scholar who has made the study of human self-control her research. Apropos research, if I may please change the topic: I could hardly ask for a better place to conduct my research than ancient Castle Albumin. Although I've only spent a few days there, I am certain of that. The Jergenwells certainly had no idea what kind of treasure they possessed. Everything is simply right. The light, the layout of the rooms. There are no disturbing traces of energies and the sheer age of the place gives it a rare sense of history. I would not be surprised if the roots of that building go back to the furthest past. The people of old knew where to build. This knowledge, as so much else, has been lost to us today. In addition," Ismene continued dreamily, "Albumin is far from large rivers or roads. Surprise visitors or curious travelers are most unlikely, an aspect that is very important for my future research. I don't know if the name Archon Megalon is familiar to you. He was an Albernian druid, who worked in the same field of study. In order to keep his research secret he had to hide, as one now knows, under the roofs of the princely palace in Havena—"

A guard stomped down the hall in clanking armor and interrupted the magicienne, "Pardon me, Your Honor. A peasant boy is here and demands to see you!"

Count Erlan raised his hand casually. "The governor can hear what the man has to say and give him a sack of last year's flour. The stuff has gone bad anyway."

"No, he wants to speak to you, Your Honor, he insists."

"That's ridiculous. Can't you see that I am presently engaged in an important conversation? So leave, before I get angry."

"Indeed, Your Honor, as you wish, Your Honor!" the guard nodded and turned to go. As he reached the door to the hall, a young boy in a blue peasant's smock squeezed under the guard's arm and threw himself on his knee before Count Erlan. "Praios be with you, Sir Count!"

A guard and another servant stormed in through the door to throw out the intruder but Ismene commanded them with a wave of the hand to let him be. "Let him speak, dear Count! I'm interested in what he has to say, and if that what he has to say proves boring you can still throw him out."

The peasant boy, who was about fifteen years old with short brown hair and bright red pimples on his nose and cheeks, looked thankfully at the magicienne and then began to tell his story: "We have them, the traitors! No, I mean we don't have them, but they are there! Father sent me! You can take them prisoner. You only have to—"

"What do you mean, 'we have them, but you don't have them'?" interrupted Count Erlan. "And which traitors are you talking about? Do you mean the woman?"

The boy nodded repeatedly. "Yes! She is at our farm with the others, the large blond man and the woman with the child! The count should send someone to take them prisoner."

Ismene stood up and poured some milk into a glass for the boy. "Here, drink! You must be thirsty. Drink, and then tell us slowly what your father sent you to say."

After he had finished the glass with one gulp the peasant boy tried to give the report in order. His words were few: His parents' farm was about half a day's ride from Wengenholm, a bit off the Angen Road. He had ridden off early in the morning to tell the count the news. The matter was very important. His father had met a wandering peasant from Borland on a visit to the hamlet of Wengerich. He was highly amused by the Borish man because he knew very little about farming and raising animals. However, the traveler was very nice and after his father had several beers with him he invited him to visit his farm, if he were ever to come that way.

"Almost two days later," the boy continued, "the man did indeed arrive at the farm. But he was not alone. He was accompanied by two women, an older man, and an infant. They were all traveling in a strange wagon that looked like it belonged to a showman. My mother was immediately suspicious because she had heard people by that description were being looked for in Wengenholm, and that there was a big reward. And my father had secretly overheard the gray-haired man address the woman as Selissa, even though she had introduced herself as Fedora . . ."

When the boy mentioned the name Selissa, Count Erlan leapt to his feet. He slapped the boy on the shoulder causing him to cower. "Indeed, it seems that you do bring us important news!" Then he took his hand off the boy and turned to the guards who were still waiting by the door. "What are you doing here? Run to the steward! Ten, no, fifteen men should arm themselves and prepare for the journey! We will leave in one hour! Today is my day, dear Ismene, I told you so! Should I have a horse readied for you? You do want to face off against the charlatan, don't you?"

The magicienne looked to the window and the bright light that spilled into the hall. "If you want to leave now, you will have to ride quickly in order not to arrive by the dark of night. Riding, and particularly fast riding, is not my specialty, but I will have a coach readied and come after you at my leisure. And if you want to make me happy, let the fellow live! I don't care what you do to the others, but I would like to meet that one."

"Good, that's what we'll do," replied the Count impatiently. "Take the boy with you in the coach—he will show you the way. The steward will be my guide, he knows every farm in the area. Now, please excuse me! I must prepare for the journey." He turned to the door, but the peasant boy stepped into his path. "Your Honor, one more word, please!"

"By the Twelve, what is it?"

"The reward, Sir Count! My father said that he would kill me if I came home without the ducats."

Count Erlan stopped and then punched the boy in the face so hard that he fell down the hall on his back. With a long stride he stepped over him and continued. "How dare he get in the way of a count regarding such a trivial matter!" He called over his shoulder. "You'll get your money, pimple face!"

As the count stormed through the hall door, Ismene intensely watched the peasant boy as he held his hand to his bleeding nose and got up, sobbing.

"I can't say why." Algunda wrinkled her brow in thought. "No, it's just a feeling, an odd feeling that I get sometimes. That's why I think it is perhaps a sign and that's what worries me."

"Oh, come on, dear Algunda," said Selissa, shaking her head. "We all get strange feelings sometimes. But we can't give up the safest camp we've had so far because of them. You know that we won't camp again after this. From here on out we will have to travel by foot and keep off the roads, cutting our way across country."

"I know that we can't ride in the wagon. Then let's go by foot—anywhere, but let's leave!"

Arvid stood next to the barn door and looked out at the rolling landscape bathed in the glowing red of the sunset. "Come here, Algunda," he said over his shoulder, "and look at this magnificent sunset. I have not seen a more peaceful place in a long time. There is not a soul to be seen, and certainly no rogues from Wengenholm. Well, come on over and look at it. It will calm you down."

Obediently, the maid got up and walked over to Arvid, who put his arm around her shoulder. "There you go," he whispered, "now you don't need to be afraid. We will leave early in the morning and Count Erlan of Wengenholm won't come tonight, you hear? It will be dark soon and cowards like him are afraid of the dark."

Gerion came back from a short walk. Gurvan was walking in front of him and rubbed his cold nose against Algunda's bare knee. Angrily she lowered her head. "What is it?" Arvid laughed. "The old dog just wants to comfort you. We all want our pretty little Algunda to relax."

Algunda did not laugh. "The oldest peasant boy, the one with pimples, he is gone," she said seriously. "Yesterday he was here, and I have not seen him since early morning."

"I also noticed that," added Gerion, "and it seemed odd to me as well. So I asked the farmer where his son was. He told me that he rode to Wengerich to get a new plow from the blacksmith. He showed me the old plow and it was cracked."

"It is further to Wengerich than it is to Wengenholm," said Algunda stubbornly. "Why didn't they go to a blacksmith in Wengenholm?"

"Now, come on!" Gerion shook his head. "Would you prefer that the farmer told us that his son rode to Wengenholm?"

Arvid and Gerion brought the blankets out of the wagon and laid them on the straw-covered floor at the far end of the barn. "Tonight I will finally get a good night's sleep," said Arvid. "I will have enough room to stretch out, without having to sleep outside. You must admit, Gerion, that the ducat I gave the peasant was truly well spent. Dinner tasted wonderful and his wife promised me that breakfast will be equally good. After a meal like that I'm not afraid of Wengenholm, even if he arrives with a dozen pale guards!"

From where she was standing and watching the ember-colored sun Algunda said, "He is too friendly, the peasant. He is a free peasant and a rich one. He has six cows in his barn. That type is never friendly to people like us, I mean, to the people he thinks we are . . . you know what I want to say."

Before any of her three companions could reply, Erborn began to scream. Algunda picked him up and carried him outside to enjoy the last light of the day. She leaned back on the open gate and felt the sun's warmth radiate from the wooden planks at her back. She rocked her son and quietly sang him the song about the little horses.

As the count and his riders saw the farm belonging to free peasant Hensel, the hills and buildings were glowing in the warm red of the setting sun. The valley through which they traveled was already deep in the shadows. A cool evening was upon them and the horses' nostrils were already steaming.

With his right hand raised, Count Erlan gave the sign

to halt. "This is where we will split up," he said. "Steward, take six men and ride to the hill over there. Hide in the bushes at the top, wait and keep the farm in sight. As soon as you see anyone trying to escape, go after them. If we are going to take these traitors back to Wengenholm then they should be as still and quiet as stones. The others will follow me. We are going to continue down this valley, and come back from the other side. We are eight, and I don't think that we will need your help." The count pointed at a narrow-shouldered man with black hair dressed in green clothing and carrying a powerful long bow. "Hunter Emeran, will give you a signal. When he blows three times into his horn it will mean that we have the villains and that you can leave your post. If he only blows once, something has gone wrong. Then spur your steeds on and come to our aid! Any questions?" The man with a gray beard and a large broad sword at his side nodded in silence. "Well, then!" called the count. "With Rondra and Praios on our side we will succeed!"

With a gentle squeeze of the thighs he directed his horse deeper into the shadowy valley. His men followed him. In a silent walk they rounded a grass-covered hill that was crowded with trees and bushes, as were most of the hills in the area. Count Erlan again gave the signal to stop. "Let's dismount and lead the horses up to those bushes. We will have a good view of the farm from up there. Once I have seen what awaits us I will decide if we should proceed on horse or foot."

When they reached the top of the hill, Erlan and his men left the horses with a guard and carefully proceeded to the edge of the bushes. There were only fifty or sixty strides of bare, tilled soil between them and Hensel's farmhouse. The building closest to the observers was a large barn. Its huge doors were open and swung against the barn's side. In the dark opening one could vaguely see the shape of a wagon. A young, dark-haired woman was leaning against one of the doors with a bundle in her arms.

"Indeed, it's them!" whispered Count Erlan. "I see the wagon, and that slut there, holding her brat to her breast, that must be the maid from Ferdok."

Silently, like a feather falling to the ground, the hunter had drawn his bow and nocked an arrow. "I would be able to get her, Your Honor," he whispered. "Allow me to shoot. There would be one less traitor."

Count Erlan quickly looked over at him and then shrugged. "Fine, my good man. Why not? One ducat for you if she doesn't scream."

Algunda's high, clear voice wafted in through the open barn door. *"Close your eyes, little baby, fall asleep! When the morn' comes it's yours to keep . . ."* Her song went so well with the peaceful evening, as if it came straight from the glowing red sky. Everyone in the barn stopped working and just listened. *"All the pretty little colts and fillies, brown and white, roan and chestnut, all the pretty . . ."* A dry, hard impact rang out, followed by a quiet sigh. Selissa and Arvid immediately recognized the sound and rushed outside.

Algunda stood leaning against the door, holding her child. Her dark eyes were wide open. There was deep surprise in her face, but she didn't look at her companions, but rather at the endless row of hills as if she saw something terrible there. Her lips moved and formed unintelligible words.

Selissa reached for the child, but the blanket it was wrapped in was stuck on something. A brown arrow's shaft had pinned the blanket to Algunda's upper body, about a span below her left shoulder.

In order to take the child she had to unwrap him.

Algunda swayed and Arvid took her in his arms so that she would not fall. There was a soft snap and the arrow, whose point was in the barn door, broke under Algunda's weight. She fell forward and was caught by Arvid's strong hands. The count let out a painful sigh as he felt how her warm body collapsed into him. That was not the limpness of unconsciousness, but the limpness of a body that had given up life. He carefully lowered her to the ground and looked hopelessly all around. It was difficult for him to focus his eyes, but he blinked away the tears and looked at Gerion and Selissa, who had drawn her saber. They were standing side by side in front of the barn, and then he saw six or seven armed men and women approaching across the field. They were about fifty strides off and closing in fast. Then he noticed a man, almost hidden, behind the others. He was dressed in green and holding a low bow.

Arvid did not look at his friends, not at the approaching flashing swords. He only saw the man with the bow. He stood up, pulled his saber from the sheath, and ran.

"A masterly shot," praised Count Erlan, as nothing more than a barely noticeable flinch from the woman at the barn door announced that the arrow had found its target. "You are a good man, Emeran."

Three small figures rushed out of the barn and looked around. They crowded around the woman in front of the door. "There they all are!" called the count in excitement. "I recognize Selissa. And that beanpole with the ridiculous hat must be the twit from Borland! By the Twelve, we've got them! Who would have thought that it would be so easy!" He jumped up. "Let's go people! Get them! And don't forget: I want them dead!"

Followed by his soldiers, Count Erlan stormed out into the field. They stumbled as they ran, then the small group by the barn broke up. A tall man, saber in his hand and an unraveling straw hat on his head, rushed toward them. "Great, we'll get the scarecrow first," grinned a woman at Count Erlan's side.

Arvid had only his eyes for the man with the bow, who had just nocked another arrow to his bow and aimed. An arrow skimmed over Arvid's shoulder, tearing the skin. The count didn't feel it. "Do you know what you have done?" he called across the field to the distant marksman. "Do you know how good she was, and how beautiful? Do you know that she was worth more than the entire lot of you. I will kill you like a dog!"

Selissa stood by the barn and watched Arvid run blindly into the fray. Should she rush after him and take part in his madness? She then caught sight of the Count of Wengenholm. Oh no. She couldn't make it that easy for the bastard. She could not run straight into a massacre—

that was not what the goddess wanted. So should she run away? As long as there was time? Selissa glanced over at Gerion with a look of despair. He was crouched by Algunda's lifeless body, stroking her hair and moaning.

Selissa threw back her head and looked at the sky. "Oh Rondra, what shall I do?"

Several figures appeared before Arvid, blocking his view of the bowman. "Out of the way," he bellowed, but they only sneered and refused to obey.

A wiry young man in a bright red quilted jacket leapt forward, brandishing a long sword. Arvid raised his saber and the man mirrored the move. Then Arvid kicked him with all his might in the stomach. With a dull gurgle the man sank to the ground. Arvid stomped on his throat.

The next opponent approached—a strawberry blonde woman. Uncertain after what she had just witnessed, she raised her saber. She turned into her attack, but it came a second too late. Arvid had already raised his left fist into her saber arm and thrust his blade deep into her body at the same time. He braced his foot against her stomach, pulled out his weapon, and readied himself to parry with the sword that suddenly appeared next to him. With a high-pitched clang Arvid's saber blade broke into numerous pieces.

"Get out of my way! Are you deaf?" yelled Arvid as he thrust his right fist, still clutching the hand guard of his shattered blade into the face of a bearded man. Moaning, the soldier raised his hands to his bloodied face and sank to his knees. Arvid picked up the man's sword, weighed it in his hand, then looked around and spotted the bowman. He was retreating with his mouth wide open. From

Arvid's right two figures approached—a woman and a man with silken hair and dressed in expensive blue velvet. The man was half a step ahead. He held his sword above his head, too high, like a coward protecting his face. His body was unprotected. Arvid decided for a quick attack. The man leapt back, turned, and ran. The woman hesitated and then followed the man in blue. Arvid looked for the archer. He had also fled, leaving behind his long bow.

Everything happened very quickly and Count Erlan no longer looked at the screaming mad man with amusement. The first of Count Erlan's people, the young Guardsman Resmin, fell to the ground as if he had been struck by lightening. Blonde Eldina of Eichberg, she-warrior at the count's court, was tossed to the side, where she lay still and covered in blood. And barely two strides in front of Count Erlan the giant-like catapulter Ernfried crashed to his knees, dark blood seeping between the fingers of the hands he held to his face. Now nothing separated the count from the angry man from Borland, who suddenly wielded a long sword.

Count Erlan raised his blade and quickly inspected his opponent's face and size. With disgust he determined the giant's blue eyes were hardly looking at him, but were focused instead on a point behind him, somewhere further off. There was cold anger in his face, not a sign of concern, care, or even fear. The stranger did not even show a trace of interest in his new opponent. The man doesn't see me—I'm already dead in his eyes, he thought as the man with the ridiculous straw hat approached. The count turned and ran, his heart pounding and his lungs desperately pumping. Behind him he heard heavy foot-falls of the eerie stranger and of his own troops. Count Erlan did not look back.

The dandy in blue velvet had suddenly turned tail and ran, followed by two other rogues. They went to the right. Arvid didn't care. Fifteen or twenty strides remained be-tween him and the archer, who was running like a hunted animal towards the shadowy bushes that covered the hill in front of him.

Arvid ran as fast as he could, but the distance between him and his victim did not decrease. He would reach the safety of the bushes before Arvid caught up with him.

Then the man tripped. At first it looked as if he would be able to regain his balance, but then he fell belly first into the furrows. With a wail he tried to get back up, but he fell again, and crawled on all fours until Arvid caught up with him and kicked his legs. Now he fell forward in-to the dirt, whimpering like a child. Arvid put his boot on the man's back and pressed him into the ground. The man grew quiet. "She never did an unkind deed!" pant-ed Arvid. "She was a good girl . . ."

The man whimpered a few words that Arvid could not understand, and his hands clawed at the soil.

"She never had much in life," Arvid forced each word out, "A few days ago she said these were the best days of her life. And you? You just killed her!"

Arvid grasped his sword with both hands, raised it above his head, and struck down Emeran the archer like a squirming pig.

Chapter 15

THE RED SUNSET in the western sky had given way to darkness. The heavens sparkled with stars over the nightscape and black shadows were all that marked the trees and buildings on the horizon.

Kurek, the steward of Castle Wengenholm, still awaited the blasts of the horn. "I don't like this," he mumbled over and over without looking away from the farm on the next ridge. "We should go see what happened." However, he knew from bitter past experiences that the count insisted his orders be followed to the letter. So he did not leave his post and reminded his people to be on their guard.

"Someone's coming!" reported the archeress Freda quietly. "But not from the farm, from down in the valley."

The steward looked in the direction Freda indicated and saw a single man struggling up the hill. Freda and the second archer prepared to shoot, but Kurek told them to wait, sensing something familiar about the figure. Yet it was eagle-eyed Freda who recognized the man first. "By the Twelve!" she mumbled. "It's the count!"

As Count Erlan reached the riders at the top of the hill he was breathing so hard he could hardly speak. He gripped a bloody sword in his hand. "There was a battle!" he wheezed. "The traitors had help. There were eight or ten attackers! I killed two of them, none of the others survived!" He gave his sword to a guard. "Here, clean this!"

"They are all . . . all dead?" stuttered Kurek.

A few unclear images swam through Count Erlan's mind. He vaguely recalled the moment he had thrust his blade into the backs of the two witnesses to his disgrace. "All of them," he said. "But we left Jorn with the horses. He could still be alive." He told himself that he couldn't have seen anything.

"What are we going to do?" asked Kurek. "Shall we attack? Your Honor, give the order!" The riders from Wengenholm swung into the saddle. A guard returned the count his sword.

Count Erlan could barely close his hand around its grip. He felt nothing but an overwhelming dullness in his limbs. He wanted to sleep, to hide somewhere he would not be found. But his people wanted to fight, they wanted to take revenge against the traitors who killed their friends. It would be best to attack without further delay, every squandered moment would only be of advantage to the enemies. He needed to give the order to attack. But . . . but over there by the dark house the blond giant awaited them. Boron looked out through that man's eyes. Count Erlan's neck prickled with goosebumps. "Attack, Wengenholmers!" is what he should have said, but he could not get his mouth to move.

Suddenly, the highest roof on the Hensel farm burst into flames. There was a sound like a distant clap of thunder.

"It's on fire!"—"The farm is on fire!"—"The traitors have set it aflame!" voices called all around Count Erlan in confusion. The horses picked up on the excitement and began to dance and whinny. The group could hardly be held back.

"Attack!" said Erlan in a dull voice. The riders stormed off. Only the archeress Freda remained behind. She jumped out of her saddle and held her reins out to the count. "If Your Honor would like to take my mount? I can catch up on foot!"

The count scrambled into the saddle and spurred his horse toward the distant flames.

When they reached the farm, the riders landed in the middle of a chaotic scene with crackling flames, acrid clouds of smoke, bellowing animals, and panicked people all around. The peasants, maids, and farm laborers were releasing the animals from the barns, drawing water from the well, or running with full buckets to the blazing barn. The Wengenholmers maneuvered their balking horses through the tangle, adding to the confusion.

It was all but impossible to stop any of the peasants as they rushed by. The warriors needed to know where the strangers were hiding. The hasty reply would have been the same from any of them: No, I don't know where the rogues are. Their wagon was still in the barn and already in flames. Everyone had heard the battle on the field behind the barn, but no one had seen anything.

As Count Erlan wandered aimlessly through the mayhem on his horse, Kurek had his people dismount and look for tracks. But the Wengenholmers could only determine that the farm animals had long destroyed any useful evidence. The steward found the catapulter Ernfried over by the burning barn. He was moaning in pain and pressing a blood-soaked rag to his face, but had not seen where the traitors went either. Kurek ran to the count, who had somehow ended up in the farm's vegetable garden. His hands on the saddle horn, he was calmly watching the flames consume the farm.

"Your Honor!" called the steward, but the count did not look away from the flames. "Your Honor, one should . . ." The count did not seem to hear him. Kurek shrugged and turned away. "What are you doing standing around?" he commanded his people who had gathered in a semicircle around the vegetable patch. "Tie up your horses down by the entrance and help put out the flames!"

"Gerion, what is with you? Are you well?"

It took a while for Gerion to understand the question and find an answer. A deafening roar in his head drowned out all other sounds and made it difficult for him to think. The nightscape before his eyes was speckled with red dots. "I'm fine," he said finally.

"Selissa, we had better take a break," he heard Arvid say, "otherwise Gerion is going to fall off his horse." The Borish count took Gerion's reins and brought both their horses to a stop. The magician felt strong arms around his waist as they helped him from the saddle. The same arms laid him down on the cold, damp grass. Gerion locked his hands behind his head and looked up at the stars. The ugly red spots were gone.

Gurvan shoved his muzzle into Gerion's armpit. The magician didn't scratch him on the head as usual, so the dog carefully placed a paw on his arm.

"This is as good a spot as any to wait for morning," suggested Selissa. "If they have not caught up with us by now they must have lost the trail. My horse is slow because of the double burden. Hold onto Algunda when you help her down. She is not unconscious, but she's not really awake yet either."

Selissa let go off Algunda's waist and helped Arvid to carefully lift the maid from the horse. While Arvid held Algunda upright, Selissa unrolled a blanket on the ground. Arvid gently stroked her cheek. "I can see that she is alive," he said, "and I can feel it, but by the Twelve, I still can't believe it." He looked over at Gerion who was lying motionlessly on his back and looking up at the stars. "What he did," he whispered to Selissa, "can only be done by the true greats. Who is this man?"

During the night Arvid did not have a chance to ask Gerion that question. He recalled that the sleeping magician did not even wake as Arvid and Selissa carried him to the small fire they built to keep Algunda, Gerion, and little Erborn from freezing.

The next morning there was also no opportunity to ask, because there were more pressing matters to attend to. "We will have to find a place for her," said Gerion, looking at Algunda. "I was able to steal her back from greedy Golgari, but she is not completely healed. She needs a bed in which she can rest, good food, and care. And we will have to find it nearby, because she won't survive another ride like the last one." Gerion made a painful face, "And Boron's servants don't ever let themselves be outwitted twice."

"And you need rest too, Gerion," stated Arvid. "Your face looks as white as a sheet and look at your hands!"

Gerion reached for his shaking left hand with his right and pressed both hands into his lap. "That's nothing," he reassured them with a wry smile. "I'm fine." To change the topic he gestured with his head towards the horses that were a few dozen strides off. Tied together, they were leisurely enjoying the yellow autumn grass. "Five horses, and they all have such elegant blue saddle cloths. I do believe we are rich. Which one did I ride and how did you get them? I think that my memory of last night's events is rather sketchy."

"Do you know who they belong to?" Arvid asked grinning.

"That carrion-eating peasant?"

"No, Wengenholm himself! Selissa found them as she chased after the fleeing rogue. She couldn't catch up with him, but she did find his horses. They were standing in the brush on the hill, completely alone. You rode on the fashionable chestnut, by the way. I ponied two by their reins and the little bundle of joy was on my back. Believe me, it wasn't easy keeping everything straight."

"Did you also remember to bring my bundle?" Gerion asked suddenly.

Arvid pointed to a roll that was about half a stride long

near the horses. "Don't worry. There it is. What's in there, anyway?"

"I'll show you sometime," Gerion replied. "Now—"

"Now Arvid and I will continue," interrupted Selissa, "and go look for some good people who will take care of Algunda."

Without wasting another word Arvid leapt up. As the two rode off, they led a third horse by the reins, first removing its bright blue saddle blanket.

Gerion slid several glowing logs closer to Algunda. Then he took softly crying Erborn in his lap and looked for the last crumbs of bread in the almost empty bag of provisions. He chewed them and then put the soft gruel into the baby's mouth. Erborn smacked and swallowed but as soon as the food was gone he began to cry again.

"Sing him the song about the little horses," murmured Algunda without turning her head towards Gerion. "He likes it."

Gerion slid closer to Algunda with the baby in his arms. "Oh, you are awake," he said, and after a pause he continued, "I should really sing that?"

"Why not? I will sing it whenever I can, and each time I will be happy that I can still sing." She closed her eyes and rested silently while Gerion hummed the lullaby. Erborn's little head sank to one side and then he began to breathe rhythmically. The magician carefully laid the child in the grass. "He preferred to fall asleep rather than listen to my droning," he determined. "Now I know what lullabies are all about."

Algunda laughed softly. "Dear Gerion," she mumbled, and then she fell asleep.

Clouds closed in and it began to rain. Gerion fashioned a tent out of a horse blanket and two branches for Algunda and her baby. He stoked the fire and thought about last night. He recalled the wrenching of his stomach that pressed up to his throat the moment he realized Algunda was truly dead. He thought of the hot flash of lightening that snapped through his bones as a deep inner voice told him he was the only one who could save her. Then and there Gerion realized that whenever he had tried to recall the thesis of the greatest of all magic healing spells, his old friend and teacher, the great Elcarna of Hohenstein, appeared before his eyes. Elcarna had not only taught Gerion the ancient ways of healing, he also had warned him of the consequences if he were ever forced to use this particular magic healing spell. "You will only be able to work this magic once in your life," Elcarna had told him, "only once, my friend. Regardless whether it works or not, you will always carry its memory within you. The spell will haunt you, it will become a part of you and if you try to analyze it, revulsion will well up in your soul and envelope the spell. It is not our business to try our hand against the gods and that's why we work our magic only in the area Hesinde has prepared for us. Only the crazy or the utterly fearless dare knock on Boron's door. Once you perform this great act of healing you will feel who you are up against. You won't be able to see Him, but he'll notice you and for a very brief moment, he'll let you feel his attention. Some of the greatest men in our art have lost their minds at that moment, others died of heart failure. Neither scholarly knowledge nor experience in magic will help you then. Only two things will matter:

your utter will and your honor! If you have the slightest hint of fear, abandon the experiment before it is too late! And always remember: even if the magic works it may be the will of mighty Boron to take you in the place of the victim you stole from him!"

It was the horrible warning in Elcarna's last words that helped Gerion to overcome his fear of the step into the unknown. "We will trade places, if that be Boron's will," he said to himself, "and a good trade it is indeed. The few years that remain for me in the place of Algunda's entire life. Whenever I looked at her I thought I saw life itself in her red cheeks, in her laughing and her crying. How horrible that death should choose her over me, an old magician who doesn't know what to do with his last days. Yes, I want Algunda to live and I want it at any price. I want it!"

And then Gerion fell into a deep darkness. Twirling and spinning through the pitch black, no wind pulling at his clothes or hair. Deeper, deeper. Yes, there was an up and a down, he felt that throughout his fall, happiness and pain, hope and fear, desire and suffering—and nothing at the bottom. It was the Sea of the Netherworld, not Boron, and not Alveran. His fall would lead into space, because it was endless. Nothing would remain for him, except to wish for it to end . . .

Then something entirely amazing happened: A being glanced at Gerion. The being had no form that Gerion could discern. All he could see was a gesture, a free movement. The gesture was so familiar to him that he recognized it immediately. This realization occurred to him with such surprise that it took away his breath and brought him hot, blazing hope that all was not lost. Gerion recognized the gesture from the academic days of his youth. Quite a few scholars had looked over their shoulder like that if they wanted to rebuke an undesired disturbance that distracted them from their studies.

The next thing Gerion could remember was Selissa's hand patting his cheek and her anxious cries, "Gerion, Gerion, wake up! Oh, what have you done? What have you done?" And he answered, "Who would have thought that Boron's anger and his mercy are the same . . ." But Selissa had already jumped to her feet and was tearing across the field.

By the time Arvid and Selissa returned, Gerion was also asleep under the blanket and the fire had burned down low. They gently woke him and Algunda and helped them into the saddle. Then Erborn was put on Arvid's back and the equipment was secured to the remaining horse's back. After a short ride through the sparse autumnal foliage, they came to a narrow path that led to the northwest.

Gerion steered his chestnut horse next to Selissa's sorrel mount. "So what if those charcoal makers are from Jergenwell? What makes you so sure that Algunda will be safe with them? Jergenwell certainly has its share of greedy and fearful people, too."

Selissa looked at him seriously. "I know that, but Traviane Krafindal and her people are of a different sort. She hasn't always been a charcoal maker. She used to serve my father as a huntswoman and then went to serve at Castle Wengenholm at Erlan's father's request. Traviane must have been very skilled because after a few years of service she was appointed his personal huntswoman. But one time she blocked his spear as the count wanted to kill a white wolf. Traviane's ancestors come from Nivese where the wolf is considered sacred, but Hakan cast her out and cut off her right hand, the hand with which she diverted his spear. You need not worry: She would never help a Wengenholm. I almost believe it to be a gift of the gods to have run across her cabin as we were looking for a place for Algunda."

Gerion nodded thoughtfully and then fell back to the rear.

Soon the narrow forest path ended in a circular clearing with a few charcoal kilns and a low, grass-covered log cabin. Pale blue smoke rose in a slowly twisting wisp. When the riders reached the cabin, the entire family, including three blond children, were already waiting outside. The children hid in fear of the strangers behind their mother's skirt as their parents greeted the riders with modest bows, pressing them to come inside to the warm fire.

The couple's neatly made bed of straw stood in a corner of the cabin. There was also a small low bed for the three children, a chest, a few stools, some chairs, and a large stone fireplace over which hung an iron pot that was full of good-smelling barley soup with lots of bacon.

After Algunda sighed and fell asleep on the soft bed, the others turned their attention to the hot soup. The family looked on proudly as the honored guests enjoyed the meal prepared for them.

After they had eaten, the guests were asked to tell stories about the wide world beyond. The children listened intently as Arvid told how he had stood eye-to-eye with a woodland gnome, or when Gerion pressed his lips together to imitate all sorts of Tobrien military horn signals.

That afternoon Arvid helped at the kilns. The cover, made of brushwood and earth, had to be removed and the charcoal had to be put into jute sacks once it had cooled. He watched in amazement as the woman used her artificial right hand, which was made of leather and iron.

Before dinner the guests tried to give the family something in return for their hospitality and Algunda's care. Arvid thought they should have one of Wengenholm's horses, but they declined, not because it was stolen, but because they had no use for the animal and would not be able to sell it in Wengenholm. Traviane did not want to slaughter the animal either, because "it would be a sin against the Twelve to kill an animal so young and strong." They would not take even one of the few silver crowns that Arvid still had, because, in their eyes, hospitality is not something that a Jergenweller sells.

After the meal the family would have liked to hear more stories of faraway lands, but their exhausted guests were too tired to speak. They spread some more straw in front of the fireplace and soon Selissa and her companions were sound asleep. Only the children continued to whisper until late that night.

After breakfast the next morning, Selissa, Gerion, and Arvid said good-bye to Algunda. Her face had regained some color overnight, and it was difficult to convince her to stay in bed. "But you need someone to tend the fire and cook for you," she pleaded.

"There won't be much more cooking to do," replied Selissa, harsher than she intended.

Algunda turned to Gerion, "I can come. You promised."

As the magician searched for words to answer her, Arvid bent over Algunda and gave her a kiss on the cheek. "Stop pleading with him," he mumbled. "He used all of his strength to save you, and I think he even jeopardized his own life in the process. If you come with us, it could all be for naught. Be good and stay with these kind people and get well. That is the best thing you can do for us."

Erborn, who was laying quietly at Algunda's side, woke up and began to cry loudly, drowning out Algunda's reply, but everyone saw the big tears roll down her cheeks.

"We'll be back," promised Arvid in a confident voice. "In ten days we will have returned to your bedside, all of us, if the Twelve are just."

Each one of them gave Algunda one last hug before leaving the cabin. The family was standing by their horses. They shook hands and wished the riders luck. Then the trio mounted up and left. The children ran alongside with Gurvan barking and chasing them, but they soon fell behind as the riders charged off in a gallop.

At dusk they carefully looked for a good place to camp. Gerion had made it clear that he needed to gather his strength and that he needed some deep, undisturbed sleep. Selissa had no objections. They wouldn't reach Jergenwell until the next day, and a few hours either way were not critical. The three had agreed to Gerion's wish not to continue toward Wengenholm, where Count Erlan and his thugs would be waiting for them like a dragon in his lair. Instead, they planned to hide out for a while in Jergenwell. Selissa knew her way around the country and she was familiar with numerous hideouts. They could also search for her brother Ulfing, who was, according to Traviane's family, still hiding in Jergenwell.

As they sat somberly around the fire, Arvid spelled out what they were all thinking, "We miss Algunda, don't we? She is the kind of person that one gets used to quickly. It seems to me as if I have known her for years and I keep thinking that she is going to come back with an armload of firewood and start chatting . . ." He laughed nostalgically. "You two can't replace her. Somehow you lack her humor, no, how should I put it, her special liveliness . . . hm, yes, you don't have that."

"I'm not in the mood for jokes," replied Selissa dryly. "And we can't replace Algunda with a few jokes."

Arvid was busily cleaning the blade of the long sword that he had taken from the Wengenholmers. He raised his hand. "That's fine. I was just trying to have some fun. We have enough gloomy days ahead of us, I think."

Selissa smiled in apology. "Tomorrow I will take you to a truly gloomy place: Borrestock. When I was a girl I called it a ghost town, even though there are no ghosts anywhere near."

"What's the story behind the town?" asked Gerion.

"It was abandoned a hundred years ago or more. Many people fell ill in Borrestock, so the inhabitants came to believe that their town was cursed and they left one by one. Towards the end there was only a miller left. He had built an impressive new windmill only a few years before. Without grain to mill there is not much work for a miller, so he set the mill, his pride and joy, on fire one night. Some people say that he and his entire family burned up in the mill, but nobody knows for certain. In any case, the millers were never seen again. Today the mill looks like a gigantic black, hollow tree stump. When the wind blows across it you can hear sounds that give even the bravest man goosebumps. As a child I visited the place with my younger brother a few times, and once he spent the night there as a test of courage. Borrestock is in the middle of a dense forest now. The old fields and meadows are long grown over. No one goes there anymore, and most Jergenwellers don't even know about it or think it is the setting of a made-up ghost story. I have not been there for at least six years, but I don't think it has changed much. We will be safe there."

"A windmill in the middle of a forest clearing?" Gerion remarked somberly. "Why didn't they build a water mill?"

Selissa shrugged. "I don't know. Maybe the miller was new to the area, maybe the stream didn't have enough water . . . My story certainly does not seem to have impressed you."

"Oh, indeed, I'm just very interested in windmills. My family has one . . ."

"A windmill . . . ?" Arvid looked at Gerion with his eyes wide open. "If that is supposed to be a joke, I don't get it . . . But I have been meaning to ask you to tell us about yourself. Perhaps you can start with the windmill?"

Gerion rubbed his nose in embarrassment. "I haven't told anyone about myself in ages. It is not a topic I enjoy, and you probably won't either."

"Let us decide," replied Selissa. "Don't you think we

have a right to know who you are?"

"Who I am . . . ," Gerion repeated softly. "I would lik to know that myself . . . But if you insist, I'll try. We can start with the windmill. My father's mill was in a coastal village in Tobrien, not far from Ilsur. I had five brothers and sisters. Thalia, the oldest, was supposed to take over the mill. I was the second child and no one was really sure what would happen to me. Everyone in my family thought I was strange. Sometimes I would project images of things I desired very much, but neither I nor anyone else was able to predict when it would happen. I could even manipulate people. I created my first illusion when I was five years old. My drunk mother was once again beating up on my father. Suddenly there was another set of my parents in the room, but instead of fighting they were holding each other and smiling." Gerion looked at his companions. They looked at him in suspense. But they didn't ask any questions, so he continued.

"As you can imagine, they were stunned and stopped fighting. I never was able to repeat that illusion again, but later I made more. I let the sun shine in the window on a rainy day, put a candy dish on the table, and things like that. But my family never valued my art. They found it eerie. At least one day my father took me to Mendena to introduce me at the small academy there.

"Although I was not able to make a carrot or house fly appear that day, the gray-bearded man who sat across from my father and me didn't doubt my magical skills. I was grateful from the bottom of my heart to the old man. His name was Rakaton the Elder and he took me on as his personal student. Rakaton was a friendly man, but he was scatterbrained and filled with restlessness. He was seldom in Mendena. He was always on the road and spent much time in Northmark and Ysila, which used to be a beautiful city before the ogres attacked it. Once he even went to Borland. In order not to fall victim to his own absentmindedness, Rakaton had to introduce me early on to the deepest of his magical secrets. He needed me to maintain his books and paraphernalia. So I became a very good student, without really trying. Quite a few years later, when Rakaton could no longer travel, he returned to the academy in Mendena. He taught for a few more years and then he died. I took his position on the faculty. That same summer I met a beautiful woman from Borland. Her name was Winja. I have no idea how it happened but she fell in love with me and loved me just as much as I loved her. No, that's not right, she loved me even more . . ."

Gerion's voice grew hoarse as he said those last sentences. He cleared his throat and continued. "She died, and I left Mendena." He paused and looked silently at the flames. Finally he raised his head. "Well, I did leave out some parts, but now I will tell you how it was. I worked very hard at the little academy. My research was going well. I was lucky in most things and I was liked by my colleagues, both young and old. I was elected dean and felt very honored and dove even deeper into my research. I wanted to make that little academy in Mendena a famous institute and there were many signs that was happening. In the meantime, I had found a smart, beautiful wife, who gave me two beautiful, smart twin girls, but I didn't have much time to spend with them. Often they were asleep when I got home from yet another scholarly debate at work. It wasn't as if I didn't know to treasure my family, on the contrary, I saw them as my greatest prize and I treated them as a rich man probably treats his dearest treasure. I was happy about it while saving it for later. Yes, that is what I did. For example, when I found my family asleep I went from bed to bed with candle in hand and watched them, thinking to myself that three of the dearest people are waiting for me and that someday soon I would be able to devote myself to them entirely and then the most beautiful time of my life would begin.

"Just after the twins turned six, they sailed with my Winja to Festum. The ship went down in a storm and only one man survived. The Twelve had taken my treasure that I had clearly not valued enough. It was their wish that through the loss I would learn how highly I was favored by the Twelve and how blind I had been. I learned my lesson.

"A few months later, Lady Master Finda said to me with the best intentions, 'You have suffered a terrible loss, but now you can devote yourself entirely to your valuable research.' On that day I left the academy and never looked back. My work had become revolting to me and it had gotten worse day by day. The high art was never my treasure and now it could not replace my loss. The art had made me blind so that I did not see where true, warm life flourished while I was enthralled with my research . . . I gave my house to the servants and my books to my colleagues and took off to see the world. That was eighteen years ago. I have not found the ideal life, but I think I'm more a part of things now than I was at my desk in Mendena. The academy no longer exists, no great loss . . ." Gerion tossed a log into the fire and sparks flew out in all directions. "Well, there you have it. Go on, say something! For example, we knew that you were crazy all along, but we never thought it was that bad . . ."

Selissa grabbed Gerion by the shoulders. "Stop it, Magician!" she said quietly. "Why do you want to hurt yourself, or us? Your story was sad enough. You don't need to belittle yourself. If everything went as you said it did, then you were never mad. No one can guess the plans of the Twelve. They grant and revoke their favor at will. And the ideal life is not something that one can go find. It is always there and always close by, only the close-minded and the embittered don't see it."

"Then I would say that I belong to the latter," said Gerion.

"I would say you are more like the first," replied Selissa with a friendly smile. "You are fooling yourself if you think that you are not taking part in life, that you are really nothing more than an observer. That might have been the case at one time, but now the events are too close to you. You have to get involved in the chaos around you, you can't help it. And I thank the Twelve that you are as you are."

Gerion smiled. "You are probably right. On that evening Algunda sat crying in my wagon and told me what had happened to you, I felt that something had changed and that everything would be different if I got involved in your story. I want to tell you one thing. Of course I was afraid when we freed you that night in Ferdok. Something could have easily gone wrong, and then . . . But at the same time the whole scheme was fun for me. I felt more alive than I have in years." He stood up. "It seems that the days of the charlatan are over for the time being; my wagon is burned out anyway. That must be a sign." Gerion walked over to the horses, where the three travelers' luggage was piled up. He pulled his long bundle out from underneath the other packs, threw the roll over his shoulder, and disappeared into the darkness.

Arvid and Selissa watched him walk off. "What's he up to?" asked the count. "I like him a lot, but he is an odd fellow. On the other hand, I've never understood any magician I ever met. They live in a different world, I think."

"All magicians seemed odd to me before," mumbled Selissa, "odd and a bit eerie, but Gerion is the first one that I understand and I understand him all too well . . ."

She spoke her last words so quietly that Arvid did not hear them, but he did not have a chance to ask what she had said because Gerion appeared out of the darkness and stepped into the light of the fire. He was wearing a black, peaked hat with a wide brim and a long coat of the finest silver gray taffeta. The coat's midnight-black silk lining was visible at the collar and along the front lapels. There were numerous symbols embroidered in gold on the silk. In his right hand Gerion held a staff of dark, polished wood. It was almost one and a half strides long and at the top there was an artfully carved raven's claw holding a milky-white glass ball the size of an apple.

"Tomorrow we will enter Jergenwell," said Gerion smiling politely, "I brought my best clothes for the occasion."

During the night Firun's breath set a harsh frost on the land. When Arvid, Gerion, and Selissa awoke the next morning, every bright fall leaf, every bare twig, and every yellow blade of grass was covered with a thick coat of hoar-frost. A perfectly blue sky spread itself out over the land. When the sun came over the eastern hills, the light was as bright as could be and the white-dusted landscape began to sparkle as if it were made of silver.

A lone falcon was hunting from high in the sky. Selissa greeted it with a smile.

Chapter 16

OUNT ERLAN INTERRUPTED his hasty march across the Great Hall at Castle Wengenholm and stabbed his right finger toward the window at the lands beyond. "They can't have dissolved into thin air, Warden! You people are either incompetent or blind! They should have found them by now."

Warden Kurek kneaded the black-feathered hat he held before his stomach with both hands. "A troop of eight or nine people can never get by unseen. But, with your pardon, what makes you so certain that the traitors will come here? They would have to be crazy—"

The count cut him off in midsentence. "Perhaps there were fewer than eight or nine. Perhaps they have split up, but they are coming, I can feel it! They have been creeping here since they fled Ferdok. Of course, it may seem insane that they are on their way to Wengenholm, but perhaps they have a secret plan. Perhaps there is a traitor here who will let them into the castle." His eyes involuntarily scoured the hall that was brightly lit by the midday sun.

Warden Kurek raised his left hand in opposition. "A traitor—never! I would—"

He stopped short, interrupted by an extremely extraordinary sight. A falcon shot into the room through one of the windows to the courtyard as if hurled by a catapult. In the middle of the Great Hall it opened its broad wings and decreased its speed, landing near the long table on the wooden floor. Then it stood up straight and cocked its head in order to inspect the men with its yellow eyes.

The warden's reflex was to draw his sword, but Count Erlan motioned for him to put it away and he slowly slid it back into its sheath. "Not so fast!" warned the count. "The bird does not seem to be dangerous. Perhaps it brings us a message. Let's take a closer look at him."

As the two men took their first steps toward the falcon, it began to shake violently. The dark feathers on its head and back bristled and the light, speckled breast feathers ruffled up as well. Count Erlan and the warden stopped. The falcon opened its beak wide and closed it with a loud click.

"That is no normal animal!" mumbled the count as the air began to shimmer above the bird's bristled plumage. The light around the bird trembled like a distant mirage on a hot summer's day, yet it was far more intense. Soon the falcon was barely visible in the shimmering veil of light, while its silhouette appeared to grow in size.

Quietly, the two men stole backwards. Warden Kurek carefully drew his sword anew. This time Count Erlan didn't hold him back, but drew his weapon as well.

The flickering form on the other side of the room was

now the size of a swan, and it continued to grow larger and brighter. Torn between the desire to flee and speechless fascination, Count Erlan and Kurek watched as the object took on the color of very pale human skin and assumed a completely new form. It was dead quiet in the hall as the shimmering veil diminished and one could recognize the body of a naked woman crouched on the ground. Slowly the incredible being turned its face toward the men.

"Ismene!" stuttered the count.

The magicienne stood up in one fluid motion and stretched her arms above her head as if she had just gotten out of bed. She presented her unprotected, pale, slender body with its small, firm breasts to the bewildered men. As Ismene strode silently across the room on her bare feet she made no attempt to cover herself. She stopped in front of the count and looked over at the warden at his side. "Do I look so dangerous, Your Honor, that you have to threaten me with naked steel? And do you think it is a good idea for Kurek to hear what we have to say? I don't care, but . . ."

Count Erlan was struggling to regain his composure. It took him a moment to get his sword back in its sheath, dismiss the warden, and call a servant to bring the magicienne a dressing gown. Ismene put on the garment and told him briefly how she had left her quarters at Castle Albumin in the form of a bird to reconnoiter after her lookouts had failed to find Selissa and her companions. "And now I know exactly where they are!" she announced triumphantly. "There is no doubt. There are three of them and five horses. I didn't find a trace of the other rascals that you recently mentioned, Your Honor."

"They must have split up," Count Erlan added.

"Possibly, but these are the three that matter. I saw the baroness and the giant from Borland. The third man must be the showman, but the shameless moron is wearing the clothes of a magus. I was disturbed when I first saw him, but then I realized what he must be up to. He wants to impress your soldiers with his costume. I am very anxious to face off against that charlatan. I will punish him—I owe that to the high art."

"I would not want to be in that rogue's shoes then!" complemented Count Erlan. "I am still impressed by the demonstration of your amazing abilities."

"Thank you, dear Count. But let's not tarry. It would be very disappointing if we lost track of those vermin again."

The count was about to respond, but she soothed, "It's fine, really. We will get them, I assure you of that, because I know where they are going to hide. I clearly saw the place from the air, even though those limited to the land think it is secret and secure."

Less than one hour later Count Erlan's henchmen were on the march. There were twenty people on foot and fifteen on horseback, no more could be summoned on such short notice. A light two-horse carriage was readied for the count and the magicienne. Countess Ilma, Erlan's stepmother and old Hakan's widow, was left to lead a few hundred armed troops into Jergenwell in case there was any unrest after the announcement of Baroness Selissa's death.

Fanfare echoed through the clear, frosty air. The platoon set out.

Selissa led her companions through a thick forest and out onto a wide road that was rutted by wagon wheels. After a few miles she gave the signal to stop. She jumped off her horse. "Here it is!" she announced. "Look at the old stone!" She kicked aside a few thorny vines so her friends could see the coarsely chiseled boulder in the middle of the forest. It had sunk into the earth, but there was clearly an arrow carved into its side that pointed deeper into the forest. Above it were some depressions grown over by moss. Selissa rubbed off the green fur. "Just as I thought. 'Borrestock, under Peraine's protection, 6 miles.' I always used to scratch off the moss when I came by. It seems that no one has done that for a long time." Her fingers scratched down to bare stone so that the simple inscription could be read by everyone. "Now, that's better," she said and looked up. "You should dismount as well. This is where the road to Borrestock was, even though you can't see it anymore. If we go dead west we will find the ghost town with no trouble. But you can't go through the forest on horseback. So we will have to lead the horses by the reins."

After Gerion had reluctantly taken off his flowing gown and stowed it along with his hat on a horse's back, the group set off through a gap in the brush. Selissa wove around shrubs and thorn bushes, brushing aside the tall fronds of ferns and leading the two horses around fallen trees. But she stayed on course, delving further into the heart of the forest.

"It used to be easier to see the path," she said over her shoulder. "The trees here weren't as tall as those all around. But the last part of the road to the village is cobbled, so the going will be easier there."

Almost an hour later they reached the paved road. The cobble stones were covered in moss and dirt, but the path was treeless. After another half hour the path opened up into a round area where the trees were younger and the trunks more slender than the rest of the forest. On the far side of the old clearing there was a low hill topped by a black tower. Selissa stopped. She didn't point to the tower but to a bramble of birches and elderberries and said, "Borrestock must have been very well to do. In any case, there were a few large farms here."

Only then did Gerion and Arvid see the eight-span-tall wall of weathered stone that was hidden among the birch boughs. Trees and bushes grew inside and outside the walled-off area, and the stones were overgrown with blackberry vines. But if one looked closely, it was clear that part of the wall was the remnant of an old house. After Arvid and Gerion had picked out that odd sight, they then discovered numerous similar structures all around them. There were other things to see as well. Here and there rusty fences stuck out of the knee-high, yellow grass. A few house walls were taller, a few slender alders grew through the black remnants of a roof's timbers. The broad, overgrown road was the former main road through the godforsaken village of Borrestock. They continued on to the far hill, where the stump of the ravaged mill stood. Selissa led her friends up to the grass-covered hill. They unsaddled the horses and hobbled their front legs so that the animals could not run away, while still being able to graze on the fall grass along the hillside. They then climbed over a crumbling wall that blocked the narrow entrance to the stout tower and entered the building. The round room was about seven strides across. The entrance faced the village and the opposite wall had a small window, through which one could see the forest. All the upper floors in the mill were destroyed by the fire so that if one looked up through the gloomy tower one could see a circle of blue sky. The stone floor of the mill was partially covered in rubble. A lone vine of ivy climbed up the inside wall. Selissa pointed to a circle of stones on the floor. "Look, that's the fire pit that I made here years ago. No one has been here in a long time."

As the evening approached, the group built a cheerful, crackling fire in the pit. Gerion held a small copper kettle on a stick over the flames to boil some water for tea. Gurvan was curled up at Gerion's side and snoring noisily. Arvid nocked an arrow to the long bow he had taken from the Wengenholmer hunter and tied off the string to make the weapon ready to fire in the night. Selissa lay on her elbows with her head in her hands and watched the sparks fly up the tower as they were tossed by the tongues of the flame. "It's too bad that it's such a still night," she said dreamily. "You should hear how the wind makes the tower sing. Sometimes a strong wind makes it sound very eerie, but sometimes it's also very beautiful."

"Are you certain that there are no ghosts here?" asked Arvid, as he checked the tension of his bow.

"What do you mean by 'certain'?" Selissa replied with a smile. "My brother and I have never seen a ghost so we don't really know if we should be pleased by that or not."

Neither ghost nor human appeared that night to interrupt their sleep. Like the day before, the morning broke with a clear sky and sunshine. The companions decided to stay at the tower for a few days. Only after the hubbub surrounding the battle at Hensel's farm had died down and the count's spies had gotten careless did they want to plan their next moves. So Arvid and Gerion happily busied themselves building a shelter inside the tower out of pine boughs to protect them from rain and snow. Selissa took to the hunt with the long bow and came back with a buck over her shoulder less than two hours later.

Dinner that night was accompanied by all sorts of jokes about Selissa's bag. Gerion believed that the buck had freely thrown itself onto Selissa's arrow out of bitterness at the frailty of old age after a long hard life. Arvid was of the opinion that the buck had never been alive in the first place, but had been a robust toy animal for a troll child, sewn by a sweet troll mother out of leather and stuffed with buffalo hide. Only Gurvan had no complaints. He stuffed himself with the pieces of meat that were too tough for human teeth until his stomach was as round and taught as a drum.

From then on the dog lay motionless on his side, too lazy to budge even a paw. His stomach rumbled, and he repeatedly opened his mouth to let out a solid burp. As Gerion awoke in the night to the grumbling from Gurvan's direction, he initially thought they were the sounds of his dog's indigestion. "You're a disgusting glutton," he scorned quietly. "And you have the manners of a coachman." Then he noticed that the dog had raised his head, lowered his ears, and growled softly toward the door.

Gerion got up silently just as a dark shadow appeared in the opening. Instantly the magician cast out a bright flash of lightening toward the intruder. The figure screamed and struck blindly into the dark with his sword. Gerion thrust the dull end of his staff with all his force into the doorway. The glass ball at the end of the staff dug into the intruder's stomach. The stranger bent over and rolled moaning down the hill. At the foot of the hill Gerion saw two more figures, their helmets and drawn blades shimmering in the moonlight. The pair helped their fallen comrade to his feet and carried him off.

Arvid was at Gerion's side and sent an arrow flying after them. There was a loud scream, followed by numerous malicious curses to announce that the shot had found its mark, but that it probably had not inflicted a very serious wound.

"There are some more of them over in the forest," announced Selissa from the back window. "Four or five! All are wearing helmets—they're not robbers."

"Our horses are gone!" determined Arvid. "They must have led them off quietly!"

"The Wengenholmers?" mumbled Gerion.

"Who else?" hissed Selissa.

They stole between the door and the window and looked out into the darkness. Eventually they counted twenty opponents. Most of them were standing on the old village road, but some were also in the forest. Arvid shot an arrow into the largest group. It wasn't clear if he hit anyone, but they did move further back.

A moment later two arrows whizzed in through the door, struck the opposite wall and clattered to the floor. Arvid rolled a few rocks over the rest of the fire to make sure it was completely dark, even though the embers were almost burnt out. Bright starlight shone on the tower, no one could see inside the ruin. Gerion pointed to a spot out of the line of fire and told Gurvan to stay. Then he turned his gown inside out so that the arcane symbols could be seen and he pulled it back on. He put his hat on his head and crouched over by Gurvan. He held his staff across his knees. "Well, this is it," he said. "Sooner than we expected. Now all we can do is wait. They won't attack during the night, but we can't leave the mill either. We will have to see what the new day brings."

Another arrow flew through the room, this time lodging in a crack in the wall. Arvid pulled it out, inspected its head, and put it in his quiver. "You can't be serious," he said to Gerion. "We can't just sit here and wait for those thugs to finish us off. We have to do something!"

Gerion shrugged. "Suggest something."

For a long time no one said anything. The silence outside was broken by the occasional clanking of metal or murmur of voices.

"If we were to storm out," proposed Arvid, "down the hill and into the forest, it might be possible to lose them in the darkness."

"We can't storm out," replied Gerion matter-of-factly. "We each have to squeeze through the narrow opening and as soon as the first head is out the door, they will sound the alarm."

Selissa leapt up and strode decisively to the door. Thinking fast, Arvid dove for her legs and pulled her to the ground. At the same moment an arrow struck the wall. "What are you doing?" bellowed the count as he covered Selissa's body with his. "Are you insane?"

"I didn't want to do anything crazy," wheezed Selissa, trying to free herself from Arvid's grip. "Wengenholm wants me, not you. And I was the one who got us into this mess by suggesting this brilliant hideout. So let me go! There's no choice!"

Arvid held the baroness in an iron lock. "Explain things to her, Gerion!" he panted.

The magician shook his head. "Oh Selissa," he sighed, "what makes you believe that nonsense? Wengenholm would never let a witness, or a traitor, live. If you go now you're dead and so are we, by morning at the latest. Wengenholm's thugs would have it easier then because we'd have one less warrior. So stop struggling and conserve your energy."

Selissa stopped struggling. "You can let me go," she said to Arvid. "I won't go out there. I promise." She turned angrily to Gerion, "Then tell me how we are going to get out of this, Magician Smart-Aleck! What's your clever plan?"

"I don't have a plan. As long as we don't go out and they don't come in, we will live—that much is certain. We'll have to wait and see about the rest. The night is still young."

"How about some magic?" Selissa's voice rang with desperate bitterness. "Let's see some of that high art!"

Gerion looked at her with a serious face. "My powers aren't at their strongest. I might have enough for a single act of magic. But right now I don't know if I would use it to save you or to kill Wengenholm. Both are impossible. And do you think that we would still be sitting here if I could conjure up a trick to free us?"

"I'm sorry," mumbled Selissa. "I've forgotten my manners, and I'm behaving like a child. Promise me one thing, magician, if you really must make that choice—kill Wengenholm! That is my greatest wish."

"You will have to let me decide," replied Gerion, his voice strong. "I'm not good at killing, I have little practice with it." He was silent for a moment and then he turned to Gurvan and scratched his head. "What's going to happen to you, old friend? Are you smart enough to run away?" Gurvan licked his fingers. "No, you aren't, I know," added Gerion quietly. "You never had much brains."

"Don't talk like that," grumbled Arvid, "Wet blankets never helped anyone."

Gerion lifted his knees and let his staff roll into his lap, then he repeated the movement.

"You don't know what you want, magician!" continued Arvid. "Just a moment ago you spoke to give us hope, and now you are complaining to your dog . . ."

"What do you expect from me, Sir Count?" Gerion's voice was bitter. "That I show the same face, no matter the predicament? I'm used to speaking the truth with Gurvan. And the truth is that it doesn't look good for him . . . and possibly for us, too, but Gurvan isn't here by choice. He is here because I brought him here. We, on the other hand, made the free choice to take up this fight against Wengenholm, and now it looks as if our destiny is upon us. I don't feel sorry for us, but I do for Gurvan."

It grew silent again in the mill. At some point Arvid spoke, "What do you think, Gerion? How much longer before daybreak?"

Gerion's observation post was close to the door. "About three hours," he said without turning around.

"So the night has three more hours to bestow us with our salvation," grumbled Arvid. "If we . . ." He stopped short. Soft scraping sounds were coming from the pile of rocks beneath the mill's window. Two rocks on the top of the pile clattered to the ground. Gurvan looked up and stared at the rubble.

"Rats?" suggested Gerion.

There was another rumble and another hunk of stone rolled to the ground. Arvid picked up a rock from the ground and threw it into the pile. The noise continued. "Those aren't rats," determined Arvid, "they would have run off."

Somewhere from deep in the pile there came a knock. Three times, at regular intervals. Gerion, Arvid, and Selissa looked at each other in dismay. Arvid gave voice to their thoughts, "If the Wengenholmers had tunneled underneath us, they would certainly not signal us by knocking!" He was quickly over at the pile tossing the rocks aside with both hands. Selissa helped him, while Gerion kept watch. As soon as they discovered a smooth, flat stone, it cracked open like a hatch. "Who's there?" asked a voice through the dark, narrow gap. "Wengenholmer or honest folk?"

"Honest folk, who else?" exclaimed Arvid as he reached to lift up the slab.

"Hands off," growled the voice from the darkness, "or I'll cut them off!"

Arvid pulled back.

"If you want to open this doorway, you must first answer my question—then we will see: Where does Baron Lechdan keep his small collection of erotic woodcuts?"

"In his library next to the book about the Greifenfurt Medical Almanac," said Selissa anxiously, "but why . . . ?"

With a push the slab popped up, revealing a rectangular shaft. In the tunnel one could barely make out the nodding gray-haired head of a dwarf. "Drogosch, son of Dhurn," said the voice, "It is an honor, Lady Baroness."

"Drogosch," stuttered Selissa. "I know you . . ."

"Certainly you know me, Your Honor," replied the dwarf, lifting himself out of the hole and taking a deep bow. "I had the honor to call your father my friend. Your brother has sent me here. If you," he waved his hand in a gesture of welcome, "and your friends would please follow me." As a matter of course he began packing up the group's cooking utensils and other odd belongings in a bag.

Gerion was the first one to regain his composure. He picked up his staff and said, "I'm ready."

"Ulfing, my little Ulfing!" mumbled Selissa, "Where is he?"

"He's waiting outside for you," replied the dwarf. "He's fine. Let's go now, please."

Gerion stepped up to the shaft and saw the wooden ladder. A faint light flickered from below, but he could not see the bottom. "How far down is it?"

"Not very," replied the dwarf, "perhaps five strides . . ."

Gerion wrapped his arm around his dog and helped him get settled on his shoulder. Then he tossed his staff down the hole and stepped onto the ladder.

The dwarf waited for everyone to climb down, then he closed the stone slab again and secured it from below with a stout stick he ran through two iron rings. After he had climbed down the ladder, he led the group around a bend in the tunnel. Around the corner there was a lit torch on the wall. He picked it up and pointed the flickering end toward the darkness ahead. The tunnel was about a stride wide, hewn into stone, and shored up with boards that were now half rotted away. "I built it myself," explained Drogosch matter-of-factly. "In my youth. It was for a miller who was a bit crazy. It was an escape tunnel, because the peasants were apparently out to get him . . . He's long dead. But as your brother told me of your childhood games of hide and seek in the old mill, and believed the baroness could have hidden there, I remembered the tunnel. There is nothing better than a good memory, I always say."

Led by Drogosch's torch, the group walked through the gently climbing tunnel that took soft turns around eerie rock formations, but otherwise proceeded dead straight ahead. "Sir Ulfing would have liked to come along, Lady Baroness," explained the dwarf, "but we were not sure what would await us at the mill, so I talked him out of it." Suddenly the dwarf let out a soft, melodic whistle. Then he turned around. "Careful, these stairs are slippery!"

The group carefully climbed the smooth stairs, and suddenly they were outside in a narrow ravine with a small, splashing brook at its bottom. Drogosch put out the torch. When their eyes had readjusted to the darkness, the group saw a circle of shadowy figures about twenty strides away in a small meadow. One person broke from the group and hastened across the rocky brook. Selissa ran towards him. They flew into each other's arms, fell to one side, and rolled on the ground near the rushing water.

They released each other, stood up, and brushed the dirt from their knees as Arvid and Gerion approached. "This is my brother Ulfing," said Selissa, catching her breath, "We haven't seen each other in a long time."

Ulfing still had his left arm around Selissa's shoulder as he extended his right hand to both men.

He was a bit shorter than his sister, and finely built, but he had the same wild, black curls. "You must be Arvid?" he said. "And this is Gerion, the magician!" added Selissa.

Ulfing led Selissa and her friends over to his companions. The baroness held back a cry of joy and threw herself into a stout, gray-haired woman's arms. "Guscha, dear Guscha! My nurse and fencing teacher, Guseline Klaborn," she told her companions in a hoarse voice. Tears ran down her cheeks. "And this is Jero, our stable master." She hugged the short, well-fed man and kissed him on the forehead. "Thorn and Rovena! You won't find better warriors anywhere!" Selissa ran from one person to the next, hugging and kissing foreheads and cheeks as she went.

Ulfing introduced a group of seven Angroschim who were standing slightly to one side silently watching the reunion. "Parbosh, Son of Hurfing, Gurbuin, Son of Gorosch, Furesch, Son of Fagol, Ture, Son of Torremuin, Drugol, Son of Adrosch, Hammok, Son of Atamok, Kuruin, Son of Kibosch. And you already know Drogosch." Each dwarf took a deep bow as his name was pronounced. They all wore helmets and softly shining shirts of mail. Double-sided axes or short broad swords hung from their belts. Four of them had large crossbows on their shoulders.

"They have come from the mines," explained Ulfing, approaching the Angroschim. "They won't dig for the prince or the count, they say. They caught up with us just yesterday. They—" He interrupted himself to add quickly. "The stone! How good that you scratched the moss from it, Selissa! When I heard that you could be nearby, I thought that you might go to the ghost village, but when I saw the moss was scratched off the marker, as you used to do, I was certain. And then when Drogosch here told us of the old tunnel . . . Oh, Selissa, I am so happy!"

"Not as happy as I am, little brother! An hour ago I thought my life was over . . . Not even clever Gerion knew what to do! And now . . . Now we can retreat. We have to find a secure camp. We will have to drum up more warriors, and then we can go to Wengenholm . . ." She stopped and looked her brother in the face. "Dear brother, what is it?"

Ulfing spoke in a soft voice, "I have already found the warriors. These people are very good, every last one of them. Of that I am certain. That's why I thought that as soon as you joined us . . ."

Selissa raised her hand to her mouth so forcefully that there was a clapping sound. "By the Twelve! Ulfing, you are right! Was that really me who just spoke? Oh, Rondra forgive me! Ulfing, let me tell you, once you have begun to run then you don't even see when the tide has turned! Oh, gods, how I am ashamed!"

Arvid stepped to her side and slapped her on the shoulder. "Well, enough talk! Let's go get Wengenholm!"

In the first light of morning Count Erlan summoned together his people. Only a few archers remained in front of the mill to keep an eye on its entrance. He drew his sword and waved it in a dramatic gesture toward the sky. "Now is the time!" he cried. "Now we'll show the traitors how the Wengenholmers reward treachery!"

Without waiting for the order, many people drew their weapons and waved them in the air while cheering.

"But you will have to remain calm for a moment longer!" warned the count. "An attack in blind anger will only bring us bloodied noses, so I expect everyone to obey orders." Count Erlan nodded to Warden Kurek to divide his henchmen into groups. Most of them were to approach as close as possible to the mill tower, the others were to light fires of dry grass and pine boughs to push into the mill. "They will give themselves up, whether they want to or not! Then they will get to taste Wengenholmer steel!" He ordered a man to go wake magicienne Ismene. "She certainly won't want to miss this memorable morning, and perhaps she will be useful." Then he turned to his people, "Let's go, Wengenholmers! May the Twelve be with you!"

The Jergenwellers had circled around the ghost village and were now approaching the ruins of Borrestock from the road. Before they reached their destination they made one last stop. Weapons were drawn and inspected. The squeak of crossbows tightening could be heard as the Angroschim prepared their heavy bows. There was not much to say. Their simple strategy had been discussed during the approach. Selissa gave the signal to spread out and nodded. The group did as ordered, so that there was about three strides between them as they continued.

Gerion was on the far flank with his staff in both hands

to push aside the odd bush that hung in his way. The red-bearded dwarf Drugol strode next to him with his loaded crossbow. He smiled grimly over at Gerion. Gurvan was sniffing at the ground close by the magician's heels.

There was a square dark form behind some under-growth. Drugol pointed towards it with a nod of his head. Crouching down, Gerion and the Angroschim approached it. They saw it was a small tent of dark fabric. Just then a man in a blue tunic entered the tent, cleared his throat, and said in voice loud enough for Gerion to hear him clearly, "You will want to get up, Lady Magicienne. The count requests your company. We are about to storm the mill."

"Fine," said a voice in the tent. "Dismissed. I will be there."

The man turned away. Drugol loosened the string of his crossbow. The bolt pierced the Wengenholmer's ribs and brought him to the ground where he remained motionless. Gerion and the Angroschim stormed out from their cover.

A woman with black and silver hair dressed in a flowing garment slipped out of the tent and took a quick look at the fallen man. She then glanced up and saw the two enemies approaching. In a flash she raised her right fist and cast a spell in the direction of the Angroschim. Drugol's crossbow clattered to the ground as the dwarf raised his hand to grab his painful chest. Moaning, he fell to the ground, rolled over, and curled up. Gurvan rushed past his master—there was something to attack up there! A blazing flash of light brought him to a stop and tossed him onto his side. Howling, he bit at the grass while his hind legs scratched the earth. Then he stretched out and lay still . . .

Gerion stopped. There were only a few strides between him and the strange magicienne. She curled her lips into a derisive smile. "This is just what I wanted, old fellow! There he is, the charlatan, wetting his pants and wishing he was a thousand miles from here . . . Right, you bungler? Now you wish you had a least one real trick . . ." Gerion smoothed a wrinkle in his gown, which glistened with a particular brilliance in the early light. "Yes, go ahead and fumble with the gown you don't deserve to wear, you fraud! Before you die, I will rip it from your body with the riding whip! But first I want to teach you about real magic. Come closer!"

Gerion raised his head and took a step towards her. Ismene raised her hand. "That's enough! Look at me!" Gerion looked up. The magicienne peered deeply into her opponent's light eyes. Her face grew taught, the skin on her forehead and cheeks tightened. Then she nodded in satisfaction. "Now go and kill Baroness Jergenwell, I command you!"

"Not now!" replied Gerion with a friendly smile, "I have more important things to do!"

Ismene flinched. "What is that?" she muttered. "Why won't you obey me? If you had overcome my magic I would have felt it!" She was silent. "He must be under another spell. Fine, we'll see. Come here, come close!" she commanded. He calmly obliged and she put both hands on his temples and repeated the spell. This time beads of sweat appeared on her pale forehead as she said the words that were supposed to put the charlatan under her spell.

"Now go kill the baroness!" Ismene's trembling hand pointed in the direction of the village.

"Your plans do not coincide with mine," Gerion responded with an understanding smile, "and I cannot comply with your moral standards."

Ismene raised her hand to her open mouth and took a few insecure steps backward. "Who are you?" she mumbled in despair, then she raised her hands, and threw forward her fists to dispatch another bolt of lightening, like the one that had knocked down the dwarf. But the bolt came too late. In the brief moment of Ismene's confusion, Gerion had swung his staff in a circle above his head to weave a magical field of protection. There was a barely audible crackle as magic crashed against magic.

The eerie sound came after Ismene had turned to run. Gerion followed her. The magicienne threw off her coat and ran naked through the brush. For her last trick she needed no clothes. Although twigs and vines scratched across her skin, Ismene was gaining ground. Gerion also threw off his gown, and the magicienne had increased her lead even more. In a small clearing she quickly crouched down, and her naked body covered with red scratches began to shimmer.

"Hesinde, give me strength," moaned Gerion but he knew that he would not reach the magicienne before her transformation was complete. Behind him he heard Gurvan's hunting bark. The dog had already rushed past him, shoving his master out of the way with a rough toss of the head. His nose showed him the way. What did he care if what he was chasing shimmered or transformed itself, if it was a master of magic or a magical animal? It mattered what it smelled like, and if it was large or small and if it had long fangs to defend itself.

Gurvan saw the creature that he and his master were chasing on the other side of the small patch of grass. It was much smaller than he remembered—but that was all the better—and its scent had changed, now it was a feathered creature! With three strides Gurvan flew across the clearing and dug his fangs into the strange bird. His victim did not defend itself, it didn't even struggle. It screamed, with two voices, one as shrill as a bird of prey and the other in human despair. Gurvan attacked again and clamped down. Something snapped, once and again, and the cries ended.

When Gerion reached the place where Ismene died and saw the bloodied form that was made of human skin and brown feathers, his throat grew tight. He grabbed Gurvan by the nape of the neck and pulled him off his prize. Then they ran together toward the mill tower.

Arvid proceeded to Selissa's right, and Drogosch was on her left. When they reached the first ruins of buildings, they stopped to search for Wengenholm's lookouts, but the crumbling walls lay silently in the morning light. Apparently no guards were left behind. Count Erlan's voice drifted over from the old mill. He was ordering those covering inside to surrender. Selissa stood up and gave her people among the bushes and ruins the hand sign to proceed faster. Finally, the mill hill rose up before them. From the safety of cover they watched Wengenholm's thugs who had gathered at the foot of the hill. A thick gray column of smoke rose from a fire surrounding the tower.

"Fine, then I will smoke you out!" Count Erlan called in a shrill voice. "As you wish! I'm not surprised that you prefer a coward's death to an honorable fight."

"You are wrong on that account, Wengenholm!" Selissa's voice echoed through the cold, clear air. "That's one mistake too many!" As Selissa spoke the dwarves loosened their crossbows and Arvid shot an arrow from his bow. Three Wengenholmer thugs fell screaming to the ground. The others scattered in panic, their eyes searching for their invisible attackers. The battle cries of the Angroschim suddenly came from everywhere. Broad axes clashed against iron shields, hoarse voices cried, "For Ingerimm! For Jergenwell!"

Count Erlan desperately tried to bring order to his troops, but no one seemed to heed his commands. As Selissa's small army emerged from the brambles, almost half of the Wengenholmers fled in fright. Warden Kurek yelled hoarsely at the deserters, but no one returned. Now it was the Jergenwells' turn. The sound of steel on steel and the dull crack of an ax biting through a shield rang out.

Arvid and Selissa fought side by side.

The Borlander fenced with extreme concentration. His long sword whistled through the air and crashed into iron and wood. He jabbed and parried, and seemed to be everywhere at once, because Arvid not only had to cover himself, he had to protect Selissa, who seemed to have forgotten all the rules of battle. The baroness used her saber half heartedly, and she barely saw the thugs that got in her path. She took on her opponents as if she were facing off against drunken ruffians, not as if she were up against warriors with deadly weapons. When one of them fell, she climbed over him without even looking at him. She was looking for the Count of Wengenholm, the murderer of her father and her brother, her nocturnal companion in the musty forest, her first lover . . .

When she stood across from him, a strange anger ripped through her heart and soul—an ice-cold fire known as Rondra's breath. It burns away despair and gives thoughts and movements deadly speed and accuracy.

That fire was not burning in Count Erlan's eyes. They shone with fear and anguish. He wanted to find a way out of this embarrassment and hopelessness more than he wanted victory in the battle. And so the runes had already been cast in the decision over Count Erlan's life. He knew it as soon as he looked at his opponent, and she knew it, too. Selissa defended herself almost casually from Count Erlan's desperate attack and waited her turn. Then her saber came down twice in quick succession. The first stroke bit deep into the count's shoulder and the second cut into his neck as the screaming man fell towards her. He crumpled to the ground and tensed as blood boiled over his head and back.

The fighters now retreated. It grew quiet at the Borrestock mill. The only sound to be heard was the distant cawing of a few ravens.

Epilogue

THE EVENING AFTER the Battle of Borrestock, Selissa and her friends marched triumphantly to Castle Albumin. It marked the beginning of a period of celebration. The old walls had never rung with so much laughter and singing in all their days. On the fourth day after the battle, just as it had been decided to send a coach to fetch Algunda, the maid came running into the hall. She was laughing and held little Erborn in her arms. The joy of the reunion was immense and the feast that evening was sumptuous.

On the fifth day, however, bad tidings arrived from Wengenholm. Countess Ilma of Wengenholm had readied more than one hundred and fifty armed troops and was nearly prepared to march on Jergenwell. She was only waiting on a contingent from Angbar. Duridan of Sighelms-Halm, the Chancellor of Kosch, and a squadron of armored knights had officially agreed to assist the countess in putting "an end to the usurpation and restore Law and Order in Jergenwell," as the official proclamation from

Angbar announced.

The entire day at Albumin was spent in battle deliberations. It was clear that it would be impossible to right the wrong committed before the prince and emperor against the Jergenwells. The dastardly letters with Baron Lechdan's signatures still existed, but all the witnesses who could prove them to be false were dead. There was no choice but to fight.

The Angroschim who had gathered around Drogosch were able to muster up ten more warriors, including younger family members. That would mean ten more skilled hands at Castle Albumin. Word also had it that quite a number of peasants and servants would rush to the baroness's aid with clubs and picks in hand. They would form a veritable army, but they would still be dramatically outnumbered by the countess's troops.

"It's going to be a bloodbath," determined Selissa. "Our side will never win."

"We don't have a choice!" Ulfing yelled in a rage. "Do you want to run?"

Selissa was silent for a long time. The entire hall grew quiet. The baroness's firm voice cut through the silence, "Yes, I think we should flee."

Ulfing leapt to his feet. "Get serious, Sister!"

"I have never been more serious," replied Selissa.

Ulfing reached for his goblet and hurled it against the wall. "Shame on you! If that is your choice, I no longer know you! And Rondra will not be pleased!"

Selissa now rose as well, pushing back her chair. Her face was as pale as a ghost's and her dark eyes flashed. "Hold your tongue, Brother!" Her voice shook as she attempted to remain calm, "And leave the goddess out of this! We have taken revenge for our father's and brother's deaths, which should please Rondra! The matter now at hand is to undo the consequences of Father's innocence or stupidity. And for that I cannot jeopardize the lives of all these good people. I know in my heart of hearts that the goddess would be against such a senseless sacrifice. Many lives have been lost recently, and most of them died for a cause that was not theirs. The dying must come to an end! Castle Albumin is dear to me, perhaps it is my favorite place on earth, but I will not sacrifice a single Jergenweller for stone, wood, and fond memories!"

"Is that your final decision?" Ulfing asked, his face flushed.

Selissa nodded in silence.

"Then this is our last good-bye. I will go with Drogosch and the Angroschim, where to, I don't know. But I will return someday, with an army behind me. Then I will take back Albumin, even if I have to torch all of Kosch!" Without making eye contact he stormed out of the hall. Drogosch and the other Angroschim stood up and bowed their heads in a parting gesture and silently followed Ulfing.

The next morning Selissa went to her chamber to collect a few things she wanted to take with her. Gerion sat on her bed and watched as she walked back and forth across the room, picking things up and looking at them, putting some back and placing others into a large trunk, only to take them out again and wrap them in soft cloth.

Finally she fell with a sigh into a chair which stood

across from Gerion. "Ridiculous, I know I'm being ridiculous. I really don't need any of these things. And I don't know if they will help me remember Castle Albumin ..." She reached for a large doll with a rosy wooden face marked with deep horizontal cracks and pulled a few hairs from its dusty gray head. "Do I even want to remember Albumin? I'm revolted by the thought that that woman lived here and slept in this bed. I get chills when I think of last night's events, of my break with Ulfing, of his words, of his face ... Why should I try to preserve an image of this place? Oh, Gerion, my life is in tatters!"

The magician smiled wistfully. "Your life, Selissa, has only just begun. Everything will be fine once you've spent a few years as countess in Geestwindsberth. Come, tell me about the place. They say it's a very beautiful."

Selissa looked at him questioningly. "You want to distract me, don't you? You are not truly interested in Geestwindsberth."

"Of course I'm interested in it. I need to know what kind of setting awaits my jewel."

The lancer smiled. "You can be so charming ... Well, if you must know, Geestwindsberth is fabulous. From our bedroom windows you can see both the village with its tiny Temple of Peraine and the Sea of Pearls. There is a paddock full of horses, and even some white shadifs. Arvid's people are all very friendly to me, and it will be nice to see them again ... and Arvid, of course ... he's so at home in that building, from the hall with its cozy fire and its sturdy rafters, to the easygoing people. I don't know if you understand what I am trying to say."

"Oh, yes, I think so. You will be well taken care of,

safe and warm."

"Safe and warm," Selissa repeated thoughtfully. "It will be good for me, won't it?"

Gerion nodded.

"Why don't you want to come with us? You prefer things to be dangerous and cold?"

The magician laughed. "That's the way it is." Then he grew serious. "Don't press me. You know why I can't come with you."

Selissa didn't reply, lowering her head and fingering the dusty hair of her old doll. Finally she looked up, "Where are you going to go? Are you ever going to settle down?"

"By the Twelve, I don't know what I'm going to do. I'll go south and see what happens. Gurvan likes it there and I can't think of anything better to do!"

"But that's no way to live . . ." Selissa shook her head.

"I'll be fine and see a lot of new things."

"You are dense and think only of yourself. That may well suit you, but you can't expect anyone else to play along. But if you were to find someone, a woman . . . she wouldn't want to move from town to town like a wandering tinker and not have anywhere to call home."

Gerion stood up. Gurvan, who was asleep at the magician's feet, lifted himself up, too. "You're certainly right," said the magician, "I will never find a woman like that, but," he patted Gurvan on the head, "we aren't looking for a woman, we're looking for fame and eternal youth . . ."

Then he left the room to finish his packing.

Shortly after the noon hour Algunda, Erborn, Selissa, Arvid, and Gerion set off. Algunda drove the small two-horse, flat-bed wagon covered with a tarp. Her load consisted of the bassinet with Erborn and Selissa's few souvenirs of Albumin. The others were mounted on large Jergenwell horses. Gerion also led a mule by the reins. Because he and Selissa were very quiet, Algunda and Arvid made it their business to keep up the conversation. Algunda's curiousity about Geestwindsberth was insatiable, and the count was more than willing to tell her about it until Algunda's cheeks glowed in anticipation of the lovely days awaiting her in Borland.

Gerion stopped his horse at a crossroads from which one could see the low hill with Albumin's formidable tower in the far, hazy distance. The others also stopped. The magician was wearing a large green cape that had belonged to Baron Lechdan, and his wild gray hair was uncovered. The long bundle with his hat, gown, and staff was tied to the mule along with a few other possessions. He pointed at the road that led to the south. "Almadan must be along there somewhere, and they have an excellent wine." He cast down his eyes and forced himself to smile. "And on the other side of Almadan is the Lovely Field. I've never been there."

"I have to tell you one more time," said Arvid, "how happy I would be if you were to join us. We have plenty of room for a good friend. It may get cold during the Borish winter, but never at our hearth. . . . Come with us, good friend!"

Algunda nodded energetically. She could not speak. When she opened her lips all she could do was sob. Tears ran down her cheeks and dripped from her chin.

Selissa sat stiff in the saddle. Her eyes were moist. She

cleared her throat several times before she spoke. "You will be happy in the south. You know what you are doing and why you are going there . . ." She stopped short.

"Very happy," said Gerion with a hoarse voice. "I will see the canals of Grangor and the hundred towers of Vinsalt. Perhaps I will attend the Rahja celebration in Belhanka, who knows? I will miss you, lancer!" he added softly.

"Take care!" pleaded Selissa as she sharply turned her horse and galloped past Algunda's wagon. The wagon horses were startled and also started to move, suddenly leaving Arvid and Gerion alone. Arvid shrugged his broad shoulders, "Well?"

"Well," said Gerion and turned his horse down the road to the south.

After he had ridden at a leisurely pace for about half an hour, he heard fast hooffalls behind him. He looked over his shoulder. A woman on a horse was coming around the bend behind him. She galloped towards him with her dark curls bouncing. Gurvan leapt up and wagged his tail.

Just in front of the magician Selissa brought her horse to a sudden stop that caused its hooves to slide. "I still owe you one hundred gold ducats," she said breathlessly.

"That's right," Gerion replied stiffly. He could not get his tongue to move.

Selissa dropped her reins and held her empty palms to Gerion. "I don't have the gold."

The magician stared at Selissa's hands and then looked at her face. He searched for the right thing to say, but for once he could not find the words.

"So I thought if I could go with you I would work it off . . ."

Gerion remained silent, so Selissa continued, "Is the wine in Almadan really that great?"

Finally, a smile crept across Gerion's face. He had found his tongue, "The best, they say. A present from the gods to spoil us, because the gods are good-hearted. Sometimes they even give an old fool like me a second chance for absolutely no reason at all . . ."

A Glossary of Arkanian Lore

Deities and Months

1. **Praios** – Sun God and God of Justice; corresponds to July
2. **Rondra** – Goddess of War and Storms; corresponds to August
3. **Efferd** – God of Water and Wind and Lord of Seafaring; corresponds to September
4. **Travia** – Goddess of the Hearth, Hospitality, and Marital Love; corresponds to October
5. **Boron** – Lord of Death and God of Sleep; corresponds to November
6. **Hesinde** – Goddess of Wisdom and the Arts and Mistress of Magic; corresponds to December
7. **Firun** – Lord of Winter and God of Hunting; corrsponds to January
8. **Tsa** – Goddess of Life and Ressurection; corresponds to February
9. **Phex** – God of Thieves and Merchants; corresponds to March
10. **Peraine** – Goddess of Fertility and Mistress of the Healing Arts; corresponds to April
11. **Ingerimm** – God of Fire and Lord of the Trades; corresponds to May
12. **Rahja** – Goddess of Wine, Drunkenness, and Love; corresponds to June

The Twelve – the totality of the deities
The Nameless One – the adversary of the Twelve

The Four Points of the Compass

Rahja = East
Efferd = West
Praios = South
Firun = North

Measures, Weights, and Currency

1 mile = 1,000 strides
1 stride = 5 spans
1 span = 10 fingers

1 block = 1,000 stones
1 stone = 40 ounces
1 gold ducat = 10 silver crowns
1 silver crown = 10 copper bits

Characters, Places, and Terms

Al'Anfian jungle – a tropical rain forest region south of the city state of Al'Anfa, also known as "Green Hell"

Albernia – western coastal province of the Central Empire

Alveran – home of the gods

Angbar – the capital of the province of Kosch

Angroschim – the Arkanian term for dwarf

Answin of Ravenmund – an Arkanian count and rebel leader who pulled off a coup d'état, usurped the throne of the Central Empire, and wrongfully ruled for several months

Answinites – supporters of Count Answin, the usurper

Beilunker Riders – Arkanian couriers

Blasius of Eberstamm – prince of the Central Empire; his residence is near the city of Angbar

Borbarad Mosquitoes – a species of mosquitoes kept by the late Borbarad, once Arkania's mightiest magician

Borland – a region in northeast Arkania

Bosperano – an ancient tongue

Central Empire – Arkania's largest state

Darpatia – a province in the Central Empire

Difar – an exceptionally nimble Arkanian demon

Duglum – an exceptionally foul-smelling Arkanian demon

Ethra – a primitive world which most Arkanians believe

to be flat Ferdok – a city in the province of Kosch

Festum – the capital of Borland, also known to be one of the most gorgeous and pleasuring harbor towns in all Arkania

Gareth – the imperial capital of the Central Empire

Geestwindsberth – a city in Borland

Golgari – Lord Boron's messenger, who appears in the form of a giant black raven. He bears the souls of the dead across the Sea of the Netherworld

IGI – Imperial Garethian Intelligence, the Central Empire's secret police

Karen – Antilope-like animal at home in the northern regions

Khom – desert in south Arkania

Kosch – a province in the Central Empire located on the east side of the Kosch Mountains

Medena – harbor town in east Arkania

Meskinnes – honey liqueur

Moha – a dark-skinned tribe that inhabits the damp woods near the Rain Mountains in southern Arkania

Muhrsape – a swamp near the western port city of Havena

Nivesians – a nomadic tribe in northern Arkania; the Nivesians have almond-shaped eyes and are mostly red-haired

Noiona – an Arkanian patron saint and protectress of the mentally ill

Noionites – an order of the Church of Boron, with both sisters and brothers; their main cloister is in Selem

Orcland – a highland in northwest Arkania, populated by blood-thirsty, dark-furred hordes of Orcs

Perricum – a port city in east Arkania

Praiosdisc – Arkanian term for sun

Premian fire liqueur – the only true fire available in Arkania, distilled according to an ancient recipe from Prem; its authenticity is discerned by looking for a red flame when the noble liquid is burned

Prince Brin – son of Emperor Hal and his wife, Alara

Paligan, and ruler of the Central Empire; Prince Brin had to defend the his claim to the throne against the usurper, Count Answin of Ravenmouth

Satinav – a large, bright star in eastern sky; in astrology the Satinav represents time

Selem – a city in southern Arkania

Shadif – a Tulamidian breed of horses

Svelt Valley Horses – a hearty breed of horses from the area around Lowangen, used in battle as well as in the harness

Tobrien – coastal province in east Arkania

Tulamidians – a proud race of desert nomads

Twelve – short for the twelve gods

Vinsalt – the capital of the rich and fertile land of Lovely Fields in southwest Arkania

Yaquir Valley – a wine-growing region near Vinsalt, famous for its sweet wines

Ulrich Kiesow is the spiritual father of the Realms of Arkania, Germany's largest and most popular RPG whose featured fantasy world has enchanted gamers and readers since 1984.

Amy Katherine Kile is a writer and translator who divides her time between Munich, Germany, and San Luis Obispo, California, and the founder of German Akzent, an international communications firm.

**In the Realms of Arkania,
even a heroine as brave as a lioness
can find herself overwhelmed by misfortune!**

THE LIONESS

**A Novel
by Ina Kramer
Translated by Amy Katherine Kile**

SYNOPSIS: Thalionmel—the greatest warrior's name is pronounced with reverence in the temples and around campfires throughout Arkania. The bravest among the followers of Goddess Rondra, Thalionmel distinguished herself fighting against the hordes of the heathen Novadi in one of the bloodiest battles in the history of her native Lovely Field. *The Lioness* delves into the early years of this Arkanian warrior and noblewoman who led a cheerful, sheltered life until a tragic event wrenched her from this idyll forever.

Ina Kramer is deeply involved in the ongoing German obsession with Arkania, contributing to a companion volume lexicon of terms as well as other books on Arkania and the world of Ethra. She lives in Germany.

Her translator, ***Amy Katherine Kile***, lives in San Luis Obisbo, California. Ms. Kile has also translated *Realms of Arkania: The Charlatan—A Novel* (ISBN 0-7615-0233-5).

ISBN: 0-7615-0477-X PRICE: $5.99 U.S./$6.99 Can./£4.99 U.K.

COMING IN APRIL 1996

Masterminds
of Falkenstein

A Castle Falkenstein Novel
by John DeChancie

SYNOPSIS: When Jules Verne and hero Tom Olam infiltrate a secret meeting of the infamous World Crime League, trouble would just have to ensue. And when the beautiful Countess Marianne Theresa Desiree joins them, masquerading as mathematician Ada Lovelace . . . well, things don't get any simpler. Fortunately Marianne can hold her own in a brawl. Meanwhile, Verne disappears and, while trying to find him, Tom must help Mr. Griffin decide: Is he the Invisible Friend or Invisible Foe? And then things get complicated.

John DeChancie is the author of over twenty science fiction and fantasy novels, including the *Castle Perilous* (ISBN 0-441-09418-X) series from Ace Books, *MagicNet* (ISBN 0-380-77394-5) from AvaNova, *Castle For Rent* (ISBN 0-441-09406-6), and *Living With Aliens* (ISBN 0-441-00204-8). He wrote *From Prussia With Love* (ISBN 1-55958-772-5), the first Castle Falkenstein novel. He lives outside Philadelphia, Pennsylvania.

John DeChancie's work is "a welcome sigh of relief . . . shamelessly droll, literate, and thoroughly entertaining."
—*Booklist*

ISBN: 0-7615-0484-2   PRICE: $5.99 U.S./$6.99 Can./£4.99 U.K.

COMING IN APRIL 1996

**Are they thieves from the future,
or valient rescuers of irreplaceable artifacts?**

OBELISK

A Novel by Judith Jones

SYNOPSIS: In the present Egyptologist Virginia Alexander is assigned to investigate the mysterious disappearance of artifacts from Egyptology collections around the world.

In the future archaeologist and historian John Howard is stymied in his work by the huge amount of historial material that was lost in the Cataclysm of 2479. When an alien technology makes time travel possible, Howard becomes obsessed with retrieving an unimaginable hoard of artifacts: the treasure trove of humanity's history.

The gates by which the time travelers reach our time to struggle through a collapsing time matrix to rescue Roma, restore the gates . . . and permit the continued pillaging of the tools of her trade. Is it worth the risk?

Judith Jones is a professional Egyptologist and the author of Obelisk, the computer game. She lives in Fremont, California.

ISBN: 0-7615-0419-2   PRICE: $5.99 U.S./$6.99 Can./£4.99 U.K.

COMING IN APRIL 1996

One of science fiction's greatest masters and one of its rising stars—
teamed to create an unforgettable universe!

CHRONOMASTER

A Novel by Jane Lindskold

SYNOPSIS: At least two pocket universes are in mysterious states: no one can get in or out. All trade is stalled, and no one knows what happened, or what to do about it.

No one doubts Rene Korda is the best man for the job, except Rene Korda. He's retired. He likes sitting back on his ship and listening to the rain. He doesn't want to go traipsing around pocket universes where the laws of physics work in different ways, saving the world for mega-business.

But his ship's computer is an impudent personality Korda names Jester, and she won't leave him alone until he at least talks to the recruiter. And he wouldn't be the best man for the job if he couldn't be intrigued by a problem, But this time, even Korda may have bitten off more than he can chew.

Jane Kindskold is the author of *Brother to Dragons, Companion to Owls* (ISBN 0380-77527-1), *Marks of Our Brothers* (ISBN 0380-77847-5), *Nine Princes in Amber* (ISBN 0380-01430-0), *Trumps of Doom* (ISBN 0380-89635-4), and two other novels from AvoNova Books. Before he died, Roger Zelany described her as "terrific . . . one of the brightest new writers to come along in years."

Roger Zelany, whose name will appear on the cover, is a household word in science fiction and fantasy. He is the award-winning and best-selling author of the *Amber* series, and *A Night in the Lonesome* October (ISBN 0380-77847-5).

ISBN: 0-7615-0422-2 PRICE: $5.99 U.S./$6.99 Can./£4.99 U.K.

COMING IN MAY 1996

QUANTUMGATE

A Novel by Jane E. Hawkins

SYNOPSIS: Drew Griffin, astronaut, is charged with defying the threat to the planet Earth. To reach this goal, he must go to distant planet AJ3905, and obtain the rare iridium oxide, humanity's only chance of reversing the coming environmental Armageddon. But the denizens of AJ3905 don't necessarily care about Earth, and they're not there to make Griffin's task a simple one!

Jane E. Hawkins is a mathematician and computer programmer who lives in Seattle, Washington.

> **"Better than any since Blade Runner...
> a future shock film on par with Aliens."
> —Computer Gaming World on Hyperbole's
> Quantum Gate**

ISBN: 0-7615-0198-3   PRICE: $5.99 U.S./$6.99 Can./£4.99 U.K.

COMING IN APRIL 1996

Other Proteus Books Now Available from Prima!

Hardcover

In The 1ist Degree: A Novel *Dominic Stone*	$19.95
The 7th Guset: A Novel *Matthew J. costello and Craig Gardner*	$21.95

Paperback

From Prussia with Love: A Castle Falkenstein Novel *John DeChancie*	$5.99
Hell: A Cyberpunk Thriller—A Novel *Chet Williamson*	$5.99
The Pandora Directive: A Tex Murphy Novel *Aaron Conners*	$5.99
Star Crusader: A Novel *Bruce Balfour*	$5.99
Wizardry: The League of the Crimson Crescent—A Novel *James Reagan*	$5.99
X-COM UFO Defense: A Novel *Diane Duane*	$5.99

FILL IN AND MAIL TODAY

PRIMA PUBLISHING
P.O. BOX 1260BK
ROCKLIN, CA 95677

USE YOUR VISA/MC AND ORDER BY PHONE:
(916) 632-4400 (M-F 9:00-4:00 PST)

Please send me the following titles:

Quantity	Title	Amount
_____	_____	_____
_____	_____	_____
_____	_____	_____
_____	_____	_____
_____	_____	

Subtotal $_____

Postage & Handling
(*$4.00 for the first book*
plus $1.00 each additional book) $ _____

Sales Tax
7.25% Sales Tax (California only)
8.25% Sales Tax (Tennessee only)
5.00% Sales Tax (Maryland only)
7.00% General Service Tax (Canada) $_____

TOTAL *(U.S. funds only)* $_____

☐Check enclosed for $_____(payable to Prima Publishing)
Charge my   ☐Master Card   ☐Visa

Account No. _____Exp. Date _____

Signature _____

Your Name _____

Address _____

City/State/Zip _____

Daytime Telephone _____

Satisfaction is guaranteed— or your money back!
Please allow three to four weeks for delivery.
THANK YOU FOR YOUR ORDER